THROTTLED

LAUREN ASHER

DIRTY AIR SERIES BOOK ONE

THROTTLED

Editing: Erica Russikoff

Proofreading: Sarah, All Encompassing Books

Cover Designer: Books and Moods

Interior Formatting: Books and Moods

Mom,
Thank you for everything,
including the holy water
you'll bathe me in after you read this book.

PLAYLIST

THROTTLED - LAUREN ASHER

God's Plan – Drake	3:19
High Horse – Kacey Musgraves	3:34
HUMBLE. – Kendrick Lamar	2:57
I Think He Knows – Taylor Swift	2:53
Antisocial – Ed Sheeran and Travis Scott	2:42
Mixed Emotions – Emily Weisband	2:40
Animals – Maroon 5	3:51
Bailando – Enrique Iglesias	4:04
Torn – Ava Max	3:18
Sorry (Latino Remix) – Justin Bieber ft. J. Balvin	3:40
Never Be the Same – Camila Cabello	3:47
Dusk Till Dawn – Zayn ft. Sia	3:59
Locked Out of Heaven – Bruno Mars	3:53
Proud – Marshmello	3:11
Anywhere – Rita Ora	3:36
Die a Happy Man – Thomas Rhett	3:47

PROLOGUE

Noah

I inhale deeply, welcoming the smell of rubber and engine exhaust before I pull down the visor on my helmet. Gloved hands grip the steering wheel of my Bandini Formula 1 race car, my fingers trembling from the engine's vibrations while the metal hood rattles. The Abu Dhabi Grand Prix crowd bursts with excitement as the crew pulls off my tire warmers. Yesterday's successful qualifier sets me up in a first-place grid spot, and as long as I don't fuck it up, the World Championship title will be mine for the taking.

One by one, red lights illuminate above me, shining off the hood's glossy red paint. Fans silently wait. Lights shut off to signal the start of the Grand Prix. I press against the throttle, and my car rushes down the straight road before I pull up to the first turn. Tires skid across the pavement, squeals sounding off behind me from other drivers. But I suffer from tunnel vision on the track. It's just me and the road.

"Noah, I want to let you know Liam Zander's behind you, followed by Jax Kingston and Santiago Alatorre. Keep up the pace and mind your turns." The team principal's voice carries over the radio in my helmet.

I stay defensive of my position, making it difficult for anyone to overtake my car at the turns. The hum of the engine fills me with exhilaration as I speed down another straight at over two hundred miles per hour. Fans scream as I pass them. My foot presses on the brake seconds before I make another turn, soft tires screeching against the asphalt. Music to my ears.

The first few laps of the race go without a hitch. Adrenaline flows through my body as Liam's car comes up next to mine at one of the curves, the recognizable steel-gray paint glistening under the desert sun. His engine roars. I pull a risky move, pushing on the brake a few seconds later than recommended for a curb. Metal trembles as the right tires lift off the ground before slamming back down. Liam pulls back, unable to pass me, as my car surges forward.

A mechanic talks into the radio. "That was a dangerous turn. Relax out there, you still have fifty-two more laps to go. No reason to drive cocky."

I chuckle at the advice. After a grueling season fighting off Liam, Santiago, and Jax, I have one last Grand Prix between me and the World Championship win.

"Santiago cut in front of Liam at the last turn. Don't underestimate him, he wants the win." More chatter echoes through the radio.

Speak of the devil, Santiago's royal blue car shows up in my side mirror. I shake my head as my car hugs another turn. He acts like a young shit who tries to show off a little too much, attempting to make a name for himself with his team and the F1 circuit. His skills are decent for a new guy, but one too many close calls during this race season make me hesitant to let him get close.

The fucker races right up to my rear wing, closing the gap between our cars—unwise for the narrow set of twists coming up. My heart pumps rapidly. Hands clench around the steering wheel as I take a few deep breaths. Inhale, exhale—yoga shit. I don't fold on my first-place spot, having no interest in letting Santiago overtake my car. Gray pavement blurs past me. On the next straight road, Santiago pulls up to my side, our wheels nearly touching. Just a few inches apart.

Both engines rev as the accelerators hit their maximum. I push into first place again at the next turn, my front wing creeping ahead of his.

Fuck me.

Instead of Santiago jerking back, he speeds up. *Motherfucking idiot.*

The whole situation happens in slow motion, like a movie, playing frame by frame. Me, a useless bystander. Bandini's team principal yells in my ear about pulling back, but the sound of crunching metal tells me I'm too late.

Santiago's car makes contact with mine at about one hundred and ninety miles per hour, a catastrophic hit I won't recover from. I curse as the wheels of my car lift off the ground and I end up airborne. Fucking flying before making contact with the road.

My race car flips over twice and drags across the pavement,

sparks flying around my head, cement within touching distance. Thank fuck for the protective halo. The shrill sound of scraping steel hurts my ears until my car stops moving. Ragged breaths leave my lungs, pushing through my tight throat.

"Noah, are you okay? Any possible injuries? The safety team is on their way."

"Negative on any injuries. That piece of shit fucking hit me, knocked me out like a fucking bumper car." Anger courses through me at Santiago's carelessness. I plan on punching him the moment he enters the Cool Down room after the Prix. Knock that pretty boy smile right off his face.

"Oh, shit! Noah, brace yourself!"

A chill runs down my spine. Unable to move with my body trapped, I sit while Jax's car swerves before ramming into mine, the turn from earlier making me vulnerable to another hit. *Holy shit.* My body shudders and my head painfully bounces against the headrest while our cars spin out of control. The hit jerks me, my body aching in ways I didn't think possible.

I can kiss my Championship win goodbye. All thanks to Santiago and his stupidity, pulling a move he shouldn't have to get seconds ahead. Fucking reckless of him. My head clouds as adrenaline wears off and my body gives in to the pain.

"Fuck you, Santiago. Enjoy your Championship win because it'll be your last." I don't give a shit about everyone hearing my team radio. Let fans and him know I hate his guts. Santiago can act like hot shit now, but I'll come back for him. Asshole started a fight he won't win.

Black spots fog my vision, the combination of being upside down and being hit twice is too much for my body to handle. I'm fucking helpless as the safety crew works to situate my car right-side up. I stew in my toxic mood and smack my hands against the steering wheel to the hammering of my heart.

I grunt at paramedics who check for any injuries. My body gets an all-clear with nothing to report except for a bruised ego and blood pressure through the roof. The safety team drops me off back at the Bandini suites, and I surge past the pit crew, not interested in pleasantries or fake claps on the back telling me how everything will be okay. I don't want to hear people say how I'll win the Championship next year.

I take the steps up to my suite two at a time, ready for who waits behind the doors. My lungs burn from taking a deep breath. Fuck, more like ten breaths, in and out, the rhythm finally calming me.

I open the door to find two people I'd rather not see anytime soon. Preferably not within the next ten years, give or take. My dad paces the small suite, his broad shoulders commanding the space, chest heaving in and out to the tempo of his feet. His dark hair looks disheveled for once, and his deep blue eyes narrow at me. Mother dearest parks herself on a gray couch. Her icy eyes don't meet mine as she stares at her nails. Blonde hair perfectly coifed, her body is posed against the cushions like the has-been model she is. Lucky for her, she sunk her claws into my dad and snagged the ultimate prize of a child with a famous F1 racer. She hit the DNA jackpot with a son who rivals the man she married.

Quite the family, right? A broken, mangled history of missed birthdays, uncelebrated holidays, and empty bleachers at most Formula races. The only reason they both attended this Prix was because Dad wanted to reminisce while Mom showed off to her friends how grand life is for someone who birthed a racing all-star. Neither one came for me.

"What the fuck was that?" My dad's voice grates across my skin like a knife. His pointed eyes cut into mine, assessing for any signs of weakness. He suffers from resting dick face with wrinkles marring the sensitive skin near his eyes. Unfortunately for me, I look like him. Dark hair with a wave, blue eyes that challenge the Caribbean ocean, and a tall frame that stands toe to toe against him.

I place a palm against my race suit. "Well, shit. Someone told me I was driving for a top F1 team, but maybe I shouldn't have believed them."

"Someone told me you were supposed to be a World Champion this year, but maybe I shouldn't have believed them." My dad's voice snaps back.

Ah, there's the viper we all know and hate. See, my dad may be a legend to everyone in the F1 community, but to me, he's a snake straight from the pits of hell. One sent from the Devil himself. A venomous man who does nothing but scold me, funding my career with the lovely bonus of tearing me down whenever he has the chance. But in front of everyone else, he acts like a doting dad who supports my racing career, both financially and emotionally. He could win an Oscar for Best Supporting Jackass.

"Scared of me contesting your three-title standing? Thought you'd be happy with me staying in your shadow, forever trying to catch up to the *legendary* Nicholas Slade." Distaste colors my voice.

He closes the gap between us and grabs me like the good old

days. His fists tighten around my race suit, eyes barely concealing the rage that bubbles within. I can tell he battles between hitting me and verbally sparring with me.

I roll my eyes, feigning indifference despite my heart rapidly beating in my chest. "Your predictability bores me. What are you going to do? Slap me around to remember how much of a dick you are?" My voice stays firm.

My dad and I have a tumultuous history at best. The first three years of my life were fun, but ever since I began karting, it was game over. Ironic how the best years of my life became the worst. Gone was the dad who took me to the park to ride my bike or throw a football around. Every year he got worse when all I wanted to do was please him, pushing myself to become one of the best drivers in karts. Then it became Formula phases, forever seeking his love and approval at the expense of my childhood. Desperate for anything to stop his private rituals. Fans don't know the real me, the shit I dealt with to impress my dad, the weekly beatings I received if I placed anything below first. My ass never met a belt I liked.

Slaps became punches that upgraded into verbal lashings once I reached his height. My dad stripped away my childhood at the expense of my humanity. Because to survive the worst of them, you eventually become them.

I stare into my dad's eyes and look at the monster who made me. He got his wish. To please him and protect myself, I became everything he is, minus smacking people around. I'm an asshole with walls higher than the Grand fucking Canyon.

He leers at me, his words a snarl against his clenched teeth.

"I lost thousands because of your shitty-ass display out there. Congratulations on being runner-up. Wonder how it feels to kiss a whole year of your life away. You can't live in my shadow when you don't deserve to breathe the same air as me."

His anger doesn't faze my mother, who sits there and watches us, eyes cold and dead, just like her personality. A useless waste of space who plays the role of a mother whenever convenient. She chooses to turn a blind eye every damn time he gets this way, indifference evident in her blank gaze. I'd honestly forget she talks except for when she calls me to ask for exclusive tickets and backstage passes.

"Then you should step away. Don't want to get near me because I hear being a loser is contagious." I grip his hands and push him the fuck off me. He doesn't back down, keeping eye to eye with me as he sneers.

"You're such a fuck-up, ever since you were born. The only reason you got this far was because of me and my investments since no other person would have sponsored your sorry ass. A pompous brat who acted out, pretending to be tough when you really cried into your pillow at night about a mommy who didn't love you and a daddy who beat your ass weekly."

I shrug, hoping to come off careless. Inside, my blood burns hot, edginess creeping up my spine in the hopes of a fight—an unlucky genetic inheritance from this man.

"Darn, Dad, sorry. Would you like to wipe your eyes with a couple of hundred-dollar bills? What a disappointment to raise someone who has three World Championship titles already."

"The disappointment wasn't raising you. It's seeing the

pathetic excuse of a man you've become. Enjoy your second-place parade. I know it's been a while for me, but I heard the first-place view on the podium is best." He sends me an evil smile before stepping away.

Check-fucking-mate.

CHAPTER ONE

MAYA

"**M**aya Alatorre, Bachelor of Arts in Communications."
The announcer states my degree in both English
and Spanish. My parents and Santi beam at me
from their seats off to the side of the stage, waving signs amongst
other parents of graduates from the Universitat de Barcelona. I
clutch the most expensive piece of paper in my hands, the rough
texture pressing against my fingertips, reminding me of my
efforts to graduate today.

I sit myself back in the sea of students cloaked in cheap
polyester gowns. After a few speeches, we move our tassels to
the side, signifying the end of our university days. Five grueling
years and two major changes later, I can happily say I graduated.
Turns out I wasn't cut out for a biology degree; I fainted during
a dissection lab when my partner cut into a baby pig's stomach.
And pre-law didn't exactly work out for me; I threw up in a nearby
trash can during my first debate, forfeiting before the questions
began. People would count these restarts as failures, but I think

they built character. That and resilience for messing up.

It took me two internships to discover my interest in film and production. I add myself to the unemployed post-grad statistic because finding jobs in film is a lot harder than I thought.

My family meets me outside, the views of Barcelona greeting us while the cool December air brushes against my skin, which is poorly protected by the cheap grad outfit. We all pull in for a group hug before they take pictures of me. I get a boatload of congratulations and kisses, along with a slip of an envelope from my brother, Santiago.

"For the graduate. Took you long enough." He sends me a smile before smacking the top of my cap. We look similar yet different, thank God. Dark, thick hair matches our light brown eyes, long lashes, and olive skin. Our similarities end there. Santi inherited a tall gene from a distant relative while I stopped growing by eighth grade. He rocks week-old stubble and a goofy smile while I prefer a more mischievous grin that matches the glint in my eyes. He works out seven days a week while I count climbing up stairs to get to class as my daily workout.

Santi's phone rings and he steps away to answer it.

My mother poses me and takes more pictures. She and I look alike, all honey eyes, short stature, and hair with enough wave and volume to look good when I wake up.

"We're extremely proud of you. Both of our babies are out doing good things in the world," my mom says as she snaps a picture of me rolling my eyes. Her accent has a lull to it, a product of learning English from hotel guests at her job.

I groan when she smacks a big kiss on my cheek, leaving behind a smudge of her lipstick.

My dad mumbles about her needing to treat me like a grown woman. Look at me, now called a mature adult, all at the toss of a graduation cap. His smile reaches his brown eyes, wrinkles creasing at the corners as he looks down at me. He has thick hair that competes with Santi's, a short beard, and a lean frame. Santi looks like a younger, more muscular version of our dad.

"Who wants to grab dinner?" my dad says while rubbing his belly.

Santi steps back toward us, looking paler than usual. He comes up to my side and whispers into my ear, "Sorry about this. But they'll get pissed if they find out from someone who isn't me."

I look up at him, confused why he needs to say sorry.

Santi takes a deep breath before he breaks out a smile. "My agent just told me Bandini offered me a contract for next season."

Well, shit.

Santi doesn't need to steal my thunder when he robs the whole damn storm.

I place Santi's green smoothie on the table next to his workout bench. Four measly ounces of juice mock me, the goopy evidence supporting how I belong nowhere near a kitchen for the unforeseeable future. Especially since green liquid still drips from the kitchen ceiling. What a mess. It's all fun and games until I forget to put the cap on the blender, making contents splatter everywhere, including my hair and clothes.

"I don't need you waiting on me hand and foot. You should

be out having fun because we won't be back home for a while." He grunts as he lifts a weight above his chest.

"I want to make myself useful and not feel like I'm taking advantage of you for a free place to stay." I fidget with my hands while he counts his lifts, his deep exhales filling the silence.

Sleek equipment gleams under the overhead lights, a testament to his commitment to Formula 1. His new home is a far cry from the bedroom we shared while growing up. This new one has six bedrooms, a personal gym, a mini movie theater, and an Olympic-sized pool. A whopping six thousand square feet.

He sighs. "Money isn't a worry anymore."

"I know, I know. But I want to make a name for myself because I can't live in your shadow forever." My hand itches to twirl a piece of my hair, but I resist the nervous tick.

I don't think I'll ever forget how his bank account has a ridiculous number of zeros. The first paycheck from F1 paid for my college in full. No questions asked. Santi didn't blink when he signed the check like he expects to provide for our whole family now that he's made it big, which can't be further from the truth. We appreciate everything Santi does. Him wanting to help in whatever way he can comes from a meaningful place rather than a sense of obligation.

When we were younger, our parents worked two jobs to save up every penny for Santi's racing career. My dad repaired karts as a side gig while my mom cleaned houses on weekends. Unlike most wealthy "trust fund" kids in F1, my parents are middle-class on a good payday. Santi made a name for himself without the financial backing or a famous pedigree. He finally has sponsors who believe in him and his skills, making life easier and racing a hell of a lot more fun.

"I want you to come to my races this season. You can take the year to figure out what you want to do next. Plus it'll be fun because this is our chance to finally travel together." He sends me a goofy smile from behind his barbell.

Santi gets to live out his fantasy of being a top F1 racer with Bandini—the top team in the sport. Driving for them is my brother's dream come true. I didn't hesitate to say yes when he asked me to join him because my big brother is basically a superstar. His bombshell of a revelation at my graduation a couple weeks ago stung, but I pushed past it because he had a valid reason of not wanting us to find out from paparazzi. Unlike other siblings, I don't mind sharing the limelight.

"That's the plan. Your assistant sent me all the travel info and bookings."

It feels odd to say he has an assistant in the first place. She runs all his gigs, like checking in on his hotel accommodations, making sure he has weekly groceries, and booking sponsorships.

"Did you get the camera I picked out for you?"

I have no idea how to pay back his generosity, especially with such expensive gifts. He still buys me things even though he pays for everything. Lately, I struggle between feelings of guilt and gratitude.

"Yes, thanks again. I have it all set up, and I'm pumped to vlog. I already bought a hand-held tripod to film F1 stuff." I smile down at him.

He doesn't miss a beat, lifting the weight over his chest as he continues to chat. "Can't wait to watch the videos once you start. And you have all your stuff packed up?"

"Yes, Dad, I got everything ready two days ago like you asked." I roll my eyes.

He chuckles as his almond-shaped eyes look into mine. "I hope I won't have to put up with this attitude all season long. I can't keep up with your teenage hormones."

"You're a year older than me. Relax with throwing the *teenager* word around. Any hormone issues are a thing of the past. I'm twenty-three, not fifteen."

His body shudders. *Good. That's what he gets for not thinking through his words.* He needs to watch what he says since film crews will follow him around all the time.

He gets up and wipes down his gym equipment because that's the kind of guy he is: put-together, organized, and responsible. Respectable people clean their workout equipment, making sure to put everything back where it belongs, while people like me never enter the gym to begin with.

Where Santi's dependable and secure, I tend to have good intentions with poor execution. I respect my brother's life decisions, but I'm in a transitional phase at the moment. So I get to travel the world, learn about myself, and grow up. Our family knows I have to pull it together eventually. And I most definitely will. But like a fine wine, I'm taking my time.

My *time* includes sipping drinks by the pool while Santi competes across the globe in twenty-one different races. No, I'm kidding. Like any other decent European, I love F1, which means I'll cheer him on every step of the way, or wheel rotation. But you get what I mean.

My brother and I did everything together while growing up. His kart races were what we all did as a family activity, and no one was shocked when he became an F1 racer—all at a world-record-breaking age of twenty-one years old. I can't imagine the gratification Santi experiences knowing that Bandini realizes his potential and wants to capitalize on it. His new contract reinforces his lifetime efforts in the racing community, representing a new chapter in his driving career.

Basically, my big bro has the talent and drive. Pun intended.

It's in Santi's weight room that I make a promise to him.

"I solemnly swear I'll be up to good."

His eyebrows draw together. "Did you quote *Harry Potter* to me?"

"Not really. I changed it up so it's all me."

He snickers at me. "You're a piece of work."

Oh, sweet brother of mine, don't we both know it.

Our parents show up an hour later for Sunday dinner. Mom's homecooked paella invades my nose while sangria coats my tongue. They beam when Santi and I tell them how I plan to join him for the race season, pride and happiness flowing off them.

"All your hard work has paid off, including those long days on the dirt tracks before you moved up to the big leagues with the Formula divisions. We appreciate all the sacrifices you made, including school." My dad tips his glass before taking a sip of his drink.

Our parents like to share their appreciation for everything Santi has done since he gained his massive contract with Bandini, including paying off the rest of their mortgage, setting up a savings account for them, and sending them on a vacation. More selfless acts from him. An uncontrollable pang of jealousy runs through me at his ability to care for our family. The uncertainty of never living up to anything he does intimidates me. His success makes me happy—don't get me wrong—but I'm nervous about not accomplishing anything close to his greatness.

"We can't wait to visit Bandini when you compete in Barcelona for your home race." My mom claps her hands, a gesture I tend to copy. Her eyes shine under the chandelier in Santi's dining room while her brown hair flows around her.

Santi smiles at our parents. "I can't wait to be back and competing in Spain. Home races are the biggest races for drivers."

We all clink our glasses to Santi's words.

"It's great that you'll follow him around and keep him company. I'm sure it's lonely on the road. Plus, you'll have your vlog," Mom says between bites of her food.

I love her for including me in the conversation. She supports my whole process, sending me different articles and videos about marketing myself while building an audience.

I don't intend on following him around from country to country because that's lame. My ideas mean something to me, but vlogs can't compare to driving around in the fastest and most expensive cars in the world.

"I can film everything because Santi bought me a camera. Hopefully I meet people along the way and make connections because I want to keep active while he's busy." I hold my chin up high, exuding confidence I don't entirely feel at the moment.

"We're happy you are going with him. Your mom and I worry about you and hope you find your way. Use that communications degree to its fullest potential." My dad runs a hand through his gray hair. He means well, and since my previous track history isn't the greatest, I can't judge him for it. Doubt seeps into my bones at his comment, but I push it away.

"Santi's lucky his life panned out like he wanted. He's an all-star at twenty-four years old. I'm only twenty-three, which means I have the world ahead of me." I shoot my parents a smile, ignoring the sense of panic running through me at disappointing them.

"I went over a few ground rules with Maya, you know, to keep her out of trouble. God forbid I find her drunk and crying on a bathroom floor to a Jonas Brothers song."

I throw my cloth napkin at Santi. "That happened one time! It was my birthday and they had just announced they were getting back together. I was super emotional, okay? Feelings hit me all at once, right there while I was washing my hands."

Everyone chuckles at the table.

"And I told her not to hand her camera over to random strangers because of the last incident." Santi's eyes shine with humor.

I withhold the urge to roll my eyes. "How was I supposed to expect that a random guy would run off with my phone when we asked for a picture? Who even does that? It goes against every code of ethics ever written." To be fair, some situations are a consequence of me being in the wrong place at the wrong time, while trusting a shady person.

"People without morals, that's who. You should be careful with those types when you're gone. People need to go to church more." My mom does a sign of the cross for good measure.

Leave it to my mom to think religion will solve everything. *Bless her heart.*

I enjoy the rest of dinner with my family, grateful when the conversation sways away from me. No one gets how tough it is to live up to everything my brother does. Not that I want to, but still, Santi leaves behind colossal shoes my whole body can't fill. But I want to push negativity aside and enjoy the trips we have planned.

Because you know what's worse than complaining about your big brother?

Complaining about a big brother who is so damn perfect all the time.

CHAPTER TWO

Noah

I toss a pillow over my head to block out any light streaming through the window. Sheets rustle next to me and a warm hand finds my dick under the covers.

"Okay, this is the time you grab your stuff and go." I point to the door while my other arm holds the pillow on my face. *Please don't be confrontational.*

"You're kicking me out of bed while my hand is on your cock? We had sex three hours ago." She fails to hide her disbelief.

She's smart and good with time.

"Yup, last night was fun and all but I have to get up for practice. I enjoyed it. Thanks."

She snatches the pillow off my face, revealing a feisty woman with blonde hair that's a ruffled mess and her makeup smeared. I smirk at a job well done.

Her eyes shoot daggers at me, matching the sneer on her face. "You're as unbelievable as they say. Are you always such a dick to people?"

I blink a couple of times, not in the mood for her attitude. Talk about a complete one-eighty from last night. *Go figure.*

"I'm glad my reputation precedes me. You overstayed your welcome; be sure to be gone by the time I'm out of the shower." No use staying in bed. I get up with my dick hanging out and my ass on display. Her lips gape apart as I close the door on her face, ending our conversation. They always leave by the time I get out anyway.

I make it a long shower to avoid seeing the blonde chick again. Amber-Aly-whatever her name is—shit if I know since they eventually blur together, becoming one mindless fuck after another. Now with the season starting again, I won't be drinking like I did last night. I have to stay sharp and keep the sponsors happy. Getting drunk isn't a habit for me anyway because I have to keep myself in top physical form.

I'm one of Formula 1's best, after all, which means I have an image to keep up.

See, to answer the chick's question, I'm a dick. But I don't exactly hide it. People like her don't sleep with people like me in hopes that I'll cuddle and say sweet nothings after a good screw. I find it hard to see where women like her come from, getting all flustered after a good lay, calling me all types of curse words. Can't help being the "fuck them and chuck them" type. But ladies know the score, lining up at nightclubs to salivate all over my Gucci loafers for a chance to go home with me. They use me as much as I use them. A quick, meaningless fuck to let off steam.

And I have a lot of steam to let out.

A couple weeks ago, Bandini hired Santiago Alatorre as a second racer. My rival is now my teammate. A scrappy little shit who likes to go balls to the wall, consequences be damned.

I can respect the fact that he drives well, but he has a lot to learn about the sport. A shit ton of lessons I'll happily teach. Like when to back the fuck off, or how to apologize for a nearly fatal crash. Crap like that.

Unbelievable how Bandini hired him despite our rocky history.

So I did what any reasonable person would do to pass time during winter break. I got shit-faced last night, where one drink turned into five and here I am, being called a dick by another chick. Some consider me nice. I make sure she comes multiple times before I do because my nanny raised a gentleman after all, no thanks to my parents.

But I can't blame my terrible mood on a blonde chick with a sour attitude. My anger is all due to Bandini's new contract with Santiago. Now I have to share my team with a guy I don't even like, our rivalry burning strong since he hit me during the Abu Dhabi Grand Prix. What a wreck, my car unrecognizable after that crash, retired and bent out of shape. My loss was Santiago's gain. He won a World Championship thanks to my collision. Doubt he loses sleep over it.

Santiago comes across as deceptively careless. Even in those tense situations, he calculatingly thinks about the moves he makes on the course, doing anything to end up on the podium. Ballsy motherfucker.

I have little respect for him since our collision, but I don't blame him like people say I do. At the time I did. But after lots of thinking, I came to the conclusion that he didn't cost me the World Championship. That was all me. The real reason I can't stand him is because his rashness almost landed me in the hospital, a memory not easily forgotten.

I plan on playing civil with him since we have to act like teammates. We don't need to compare dick sizes to see who's the best when my driving does the talking. He gets to come onto my team and into my house and show his skills. Meaning I can sit back and relax while he proves himself worthy of the money they paid him this year. It will be intriguing to see where it goes and who performs better. No more excuses, because an even playing field means the better driver will win. And we all know who that is.

My phone rings on my dresser. *Father.*

I battle between picking up the phone and letting it go to voicemail. Deciding on the latter, I step away before the phone rings again. Clever man knows I avoid any contact with him. Not wanting to prolong the inevitable, I take the call.

"Dad. How are you?" I shuffle the phone between my shoulder and ear while I grab my workout bag.

"I read the news. Bandini added that child to the team. What are they thinking? He's barely proven himself." His gruff voice reverberates through the small speaker, skipping over pleasantries.

"Nice to hear from you too." My words pack their usual bite because asshole genes run in the family.

"Cut the shit, Noah. This is serious, especially after he screwed you over before. You've got to stay sharp this season and not let him get the upper hand."

"We can let the crash go since it was forever ago. I'm not worried about a racer who got lucky once." I double-check that the chick from earlier left, not wanting another encounter with her. *All clear.* I grab my keys and lock up my Monaco apartment.

"I didn't invest a ton of money into that company for them to mess around with your career. If they think a kid is going to get the best resources without showing his worth... What a sad mistake."

I rub my eyes. "We can see how he does before you pop off on some Bandini rep. I doubt he can beat me like that again since it was a fluke. A lucky hit where I lost control."

"Damn straight he won't. Don't fuck it up again; you don't want to crumble under pressure when you're at the height of your career."

Thanks for the love, Dad.

"Yup, sounds like me. Talk to you later. Bye." I don't wait for his reply before I hang up.

My dad can't help being an asshole, but the public likes him, so he saves all his pent-up issues for me. He gets his way no matter what. His solutions to problems include money, threats, and throwing his weight around. Me moving across the Atlantic Ocean hasn't put enough distance between us. Even with an insane time change between Europe and America, he finds a way to contact me.

Whatever races he graces with his presence end up being a shitshow. Fans call me F1 royalty, an American Prince because of my dad, the *amazing* Nicholas Slade. Who is still called one of the greatest racers in F1 history. Lucky me to have him breathing down my neck about everything I do wrong or where I can improve. Yes, he kick-started my career. I appreciate every investment he's made to help me along the way, but I race cars every weekend, proving to him and everyone else that I'll be a legend too. The driving world has changed a lot since he raced twenty years ago. Cars I drive today shit on whatever hunk of metal he drove, making the sport into what fans love today. A sport with drama, high speeds, and intense risks.

My phone pings from a new message.

> **Dad (12/24 10:29 a.m.)**: Booked my flight to Barcelona.

Merry fucking Christmas to you too, Dad.

CHAPTER THREE

MAYA

hree months have passed since Santiago signed his new deal with Bandini Racing. I am living with him while he gets ready for the new season, making sure to keep myself busy by starting my vlog. I want to share all my travels while I follow Santi around the world. My computer is jam-packed with research on different things to do in each city while he preps for races. Pride surges through me at my foresight to plan.

I inhale the exotic smell of Melbourne, Australia. All right, the scent lacks the exoticness I had hoped for. A mix of car exhaust and airport fuel wafts through the air since the Outback is a far reach away. Best I'll get for now. But it seems foreign enough, and I relish in my first experience of visiting a different continent.

Professionals call Santi's first Prix a "flyaway race." I made sure to catch up on all the F1 terms because I don't want fans to think of me as ill-prepared.

I say "G'day mate!" to one of the flight attendants as I exit the plane. A poorly executed slip of the tongue. She doesn't look amused in the slightest at my poor attempt to crack a joke, so I delete the saying off my phone once I step inside the airport.

I keep a translated list of popular phrases from each country we visit to prevent making myself look like a fool, at least not more than usual. *Note to self: double-check what phrases sound stupid.*

I stretch my sore legs after a twenty-hour flight from Madrid, my muscles thanking me for the special attention. Santi grabs my luggage off the carousel while I find the Bandini town car.

We get dropped off at the hotel where the team stays. I look around the elegant lobby, distracting myself with a funky art piece while Santi talks to the front desk. He texts his assistant to check each accommodation for two-room suites because he tends to be a needy man-child.

Our suite looks modern and fresh, with a minimalist color palette and a balcony overlooking the track. I throw myself on the living room couch. Comfortable cushions practically swallow me whole like a welcoming hug after a long day.

"I have to go to a couple sponsor meetings before working out kinks in the new car. You'll be good without me?" His brown eyes gaze down at me as he places a Bandini baseball cap over his head.

"Sure. I have plans for the day anyway. Don't worry about me." I shoot him a toothy grin.

"I'll always worry about you. You are a handful."

I send him a mock-offended look. "No need to throw around charged words."

He waves at me over his shoulder before exiting the suite. I throw a pillow at the door as it closes, missing my opportunity by a few seconds.

I take in my surroundings. The suite can't compare to Santi's previous digs, our upgrade having a television the size of my bed back home, a dining table fit for eight people, and a large sectional that surrounds me.

After changing into my bathing suit and grabbing my camera, I check out the hotel. My stomach grumbles during my tour, encouraging me to grab a quick bite to eat before I head to the pool. I relax and doze off on a lounge chair, heat from the sun enveloping me like a warm blanket, tanning my skin. An afternoon nap tempts me, my body giving into jet lag despite the regret I'll feel later about my decision.

"I have a press conference today and I want you to come." Santi walks into my room and plops himself on my bed. His post-practice round makes him a sweaty, sticky mess, with dirty skin contrasting against the white comforter.

"Oh, please come lie on my bed in your sweaty clothes. Make yourself at home." My voice drips with sarcasm.

He ignores me as he grabs one of the pillows. I continue to put on my makeup, keeping it fresh and light, my go-to look. My skin glows in the mirror after my long tanning-session-turned-nap yesterday.

He lets out a grunt. "Noah's an ass and you keep me in check. I won't be an idiot if you're there. *Please* come." His words distract me, and I stab myself in the eyeball with my mascara wand. *Shit. Is there a greater pain than mascara on your eye?*

My heart accelerates at the thought of Noah Slade. He's hot, in a devilishly handsome kind of way. Messy hair so dark it looks black, sharp cheekbones that can shave ice, and lips every woman can envy. I see pictures of him everywhere—ads, commercials, gossip mags. You name it, he's been on it. Not to mention how my brother has stood at the podium with him multiple times. I may have watched one or twenty times on my TV at home. Hard to resist seeing Noah get showered with champagne on a Prix podium while he beams down at the trophy in his hand.

I let out a sigh. Noah's the type of guy you don't bring home to mom; he's the one you screw around with before you find the guy you finally take home to mom, ensuring her you've moved on from your wild ways. His list of past partners happens to be longer than my grocery list and to-do list combined. Gross yet oddly fascinating how women like that.

"You do understand you're an adult, right? How on earth do I keep you in check?"

"Because I won't say anything too nasty for my sister's ears." He bats his long, dark lashes at me in a ridiculous gesture that softens my heart. Damn him and his goofiness. I fall for it every single time, a victim to Santi's boyish ways.

"Your innocent ploy is nothing short of terrible. Is that how you get laid?"

He throws a pillow straight at my face, smudging my mascara even more.

"Ugh, you're messing up my makeup! Fine, I'll go. But get off my bed. *Now.*"

He hops off my bed triumphantly because I fell for his plan. Hook, line, and sinker.

"See you later. I'll send up someone to grab you when it's time." He taps away at his phone.

"The things I do for you. I'll try not to fall asleep on the side of the panel, but no promises."

He lets out a deep laugh. "F1 panels are juicy. You'll enjoy it, I know it." He leaves with a smile plastered on his face. I can't tell if he means to be serious when he rubs his hands together like an evil genius. Shady side eye included.

I wrap up getting ready. An attendant shows me the way to the press conference area where my brother waves at me from the panel table. My grin mirrors his own. Warmth fills my heart at seeing him up there living his dream, wearing signature scarlet Bandini gear—everything he's wanted since he was a kid.

I snap a quick picture for my Instagram story. Hate to break it to the thirsty females out there, but I'm his number-one fan. After fiddling with my phone, I glance up at the panel, my eyes meeting Noah's blue ones—a strikingly beautiful color framed by dark lashes and brows. His plump lips turn down as he checks me out. My body heats at his appraisal, aware of the beautiful human in front of me because I'm dumb not blind. I find it impossible to calm my racing heart, thumping against my rib cage, as I take him in. *Fuck me.* I don't think I've ever thought of a guy as gorgeous until now.

He rakes a hand through his thick, unruly strands. His hair looks like he continuously runs his fingers through the locks all day. Corded arms lay on the table, revealing tan skin and large hands, taking my mind to dirty places. Noah's lean kind of muscular is ideal for racing. Shit, the kind of muscular perfect for fucking against a door, in a shower, or on a counter. Vivid images fly through my head of Noah in compromising positions. My body hums with excitement at the sight of Noah smirking at me, my lower half clearly not understanding the difference between danger and lust. Turns out press conferences offer more eye candy than I thought.

I lick my lips at the sight of his arms. Nothing makes a girl swoon quite like a guy dedicated to his gym regimen, but this guy is more likely to commit to his gym than to another girl. He notices my reaction and winks at me. My cheeks flush at his attention, an embarrassing display that makes my attraction noticeable. *Can I be any more obvious?*

Frustration rushes through me, washing away thoughts of his lips against mine and his hands in my hair. How on earth will I survive a season around someone who looks like him?

God plays cruel jokes on me. Just when I promised to be good, he wants me to fall right into the arms of the devil. Men like Noah are only built for wickedness.

I force my eyes away and try to find something interesting in the room. *Oh look, a middle-aged man setting up his microphone. Riveting stuff.* The same man glares at me before he grumbles something about hot chicks not being allowed in the press room.

Noah's deep rumbling laugh sends a shiver up my spine. *Since when do laughs sound sexy?* My body finds it difficult to ignore him, my eyes wanting to pull back to him like a magnet. I refrain because I don't want to lead him on. But he makes my body stand to attention, my posture never looking better.

My interest in the reporter appears short-lived once questions come from all different directions. Each journalist reeks of desperation to add their tidbit, enthusiastically raising their hands every time a round of questions wraps up.

One question makes me pause my Instagram scrolling.

"What have you two been doing to prevent another Abu Dhabi situation?"

Ugh, this again? Aren't there juicier stories to bring up? Noah seems to share my same sentiment, his low groan permeating through the crowd and gaining my attention.

"Are we seriously bringing up a race from two years ago? That's below you, Harold. Find fresher drama to bring up because your questions bore me."

Turns out Harold is the same reporter I was staring at earlier. My mouth drops open, shocked Noah Slade knows these reporters by name. He has no shame calling them out.

But Harold refuses to let Noah off easily, especially after a tongue-lashing.

"One would assume the competition is back in full force. How does it feel to be working closely with someone you publicly announced as a rival on the track?" Harold licks his lips at his own line of questioning. *Must be proud.*

Noah's jaw ticks, accentuating razor-sharp cheekbones. His icy gaze makes my blood run cold. "Seeing as we're teammates now, his performance is contingent on my own, and vice versa. I wish Santi the best of luck; this year will be competitive between everyone."

My brother opens his big mouth, piggybacking off Noah's last words. "We discussed team strategies and what situations can be prevented. I highly doubt Slade will make that mistake again."

Santi, so sharp in racing, so unaware of real life. Noah turns his head slowly toward my brother. I rub a palm across my face like it can rid the image of Noah's death glare and clenched jaw from my memory. *Abort, Santi.* Uncertain of who will say what next, the media room remains silent as reporters anxiously wait for a reply.

Noah faces the camera crews again. "We all learn from mistakes here. The sport is about growth and personal development on the course. Accidents happen. It's all about what you do after that matters."

One point for Noah Slade. He handles the situation like a pro who was well-trained by a publicist. The rest of the press meeting remains mundane after the spur of drama, not as juicy as my brother promised. A blessing in disguise for him since he's already messed up.

Relief floods through me when an F1 member announces the end of the media conference. He reminds everyone about the gala being hosted tonight in honor of the Bandini racers, plus information about a few other press sessions taking place after practice rounds and qualifiers. Excuses of how to get out of those pop up in my head. Thankfully for Santi, he can do most of them alone, minus Noah and myself.

Noah approaches us outside of the press building. My skin prickles at our closeness, his body hulking over my five-foot-two frame, making me feel smaller than usual.

"I don't know how your last team worked but let me handle the big-boy questions. You should re-watch the tapes from Abu Dhabi if you think it was a mistake on my end because it sure as fuck wasn't. That should be your first order of business around here. Well, that and staying the hell out of my way." His fists clench together and his jaw ticks under pressure.

"I didn't mean for it to come out that way. I'm sorry. I wasn't thinking," my brother says with earnest.

"Clearly. You're new to the team and we have a system here. One that doesn't include stupid answers. You should ask around if you're not sure how things work."

"There's no need to be rude to him. He said sorry," I snap, my eyes meeting Noah's cold glare. I can only take so much of his attitude when my brother's already said sorry. Santi acts tough, but issues affect him more than most, his emotions swirling inside of him like a slow-moving tornado.

Noah's sapphire eyes trail down my body. He licks his bottom lip, drawing my attention toward them, noticing how the bottom is fuller than the top. They look soft and plump. Perfectly kissable.

Skin heats wherever his eyes roam. I feel betrayed by the way my body acts around him, like I can't control the draw I have toward him.

He opens his mouth. "Side pieces don't come to these types of things either so she can stay away. Maybe you'll be less of a dumbass."

My head snaps up, waves of attraction replaced by anger. All at the flip of a switch. He did not insinuate what I thought he did.

Before Santi or I can get a word out, he continues. His blue eyes gaze into mine, dancing with delight. "If you ever get bored of being with him, I'm always free. With age comes more experience." He shoots me a ridiculously smug smile, and I can't wait to knock it off his face.

I start toward him, wanting to get uncomfortably close because death stares look better from inches away. Santi grabs my hand, halting my attempt to get up in Noah's space, but he can't stop my mouth. *Oh, no.* My mouth has a mind of its own because words flow without a second thought.

"He's my older brother, asshole. Can't you see the family resemblance? Or is the cloud of superiority around you so thick that you didn't notice?"

I imagine the wheels turning in Noah's head as he makes the connection. His eyes dart between Santi and me, looking at our dark hair, olive skin, and same honey-brown eyes. My head tilts to the side and I shoot him a smirk.

His jaw drops open and his cheeks tinge a light pink color. I gloat at his embarrassment, mentally dancing around at my sassiness. Everyone knows what they say about people who assume.

"I'm sorry, I clearly shouldn't have spoken to either of you like that." His voice has a hint of regret. I shrug, ignoring the tug on my heart at his remorse because I get petty when mad. Assholes don't do it for me, no matter how pretty their faces are.

My brother offers a handshake because he acts like a real man. I try my best to disregard how good Noah's ass looks as he walks away, but I take a peek because a woman can only have so much restraint. He gives me one last look over his shoulder before he disappears around the corner of the building.

I sigh softly, my heart slowing down for the first time in an hour. Santi gives me a quizzical glance before we take off in the opposite direction. Looks like tonight's gala just got a lot more interesting.

CHAPTER FOUR

Noah

I mull over the conversation with Santiago and his sister while I eat lunch in the Bandini area. Santi has a sibling I had no clue existed. *Where was she throughout his racing debut?* I feel like I would've recognized her. Instead, I made myself look like an asshole on the first day. An image of her brown eyes boring into mine like she wants to skin me alive has singed itself into my brain. She's a stunning woman even when mad with flared nostrils, flushed cheeks, and waving hands.

I need to come up with a plan for the Bandini gala. It was never my intention to get off on the wrong foot with Santiago already, or his sister for that matter. Looking like a dick before the season begins doesn't make me happy. Santiago and I will spend countless hours together doing press tours and going to sponsor meetings, which means his sister will be around just as much.

I snapped when he blamed me for something that wasn't my fault. Let this be a lesson for him to not open his mouth without

thinking, a prime example of what can go wrong in the public eye, shitty consequences included. But it's not right how I took my anger out on his sister.

During our earlier walk-through of the course, I apologized to him again because I was ashamed of what I'd said. I'm not above cornering people to get what I want. He begrudgingly accepted my apology, his jaw tight as his fist squeezed my extended hand.

I spend the rest of the day sitting through more press sessions, the less desirable side of F1.

I make it back to my hotel room with enough time to get dressed for the event. Santiago and his sister plan on attending the gala, my thoughts confirmed when I discreetly asked around. No need to draw attention to myself.

The poorly lit lobby bar welcomes me as I order a Scotch from the bartender. Out of the corner of my eye, I see a woman sitting in a booth, twirling a straw in her drink. She looks vaguely like Santiago's sister. I head on over to her, confirming she is, in fact, the Alatorre I need to speak to. *Perfect timing*. Getting an apology out now sounds like the best idea because I don't dance around problems to avoid confrontation.

Some people scurry at trouble. Me on the other hand? I drive my car straight into problems at two hundred miles per hour. Fuck the consequences.

"Do you mind if I sit here?"

Her body tenses at the sound of my voice. I'm not off to a great start by the looks of her grimace, rigid body posture, and stilled hand holding her straw. But I can work with it. I shoot her a dazzling smile that makes women drop to their knees. *Tested and verified.*

I remain motionless as her almond eyes look up at me. My heart rate speeds up as I gaze upon her, taking in her smoky eyes that cloud at my perusal, lush lips that purse, and high cheekbones I want to run my knuckles across. Her dark hair piles on top of her head, begging to be let down. A few soft curls escape and trail down her thin neck. Her dress dips low, accentuating tan skin and a fully displayed back. My fingers itch to stroke her skin and test how soft it is.

She pulls me out of my thoughts. "And if I do mind?"

Shit. Forgot I asked her a question. "I would probably sit here anyway then." I give her a wide smile, enjoying her quick tongue.

"Fine, go ahead." She lets out a soft sigh and waves toward the empty booth in front of her.

Don't need to be told twice. I settle myself into the seat, adjusting my pants because my semi hard-on is pressing against the zipper. My throat welcomes the burn from a swig of Scotch. A little bit of liquid courage to make it through this conversation without flirting with her.

"I wanted to apologize about earlier because I shouldn't have insinuated something like that. I'm not proud of myself for what I said."

Brown eyes linger on my face as she gauges my sincerity. I take another look at her because shock still courses through me at how she disarms me. Her bone structure adds to her allure, along with full red-painted lips, long lashes, and straight, white teeth. She has a strikingly exotic look—a Spanish heritage evident by her dark hair, tan skin, and hint of an accent.

My head takes off. I imagine her red lips wrapped around my cock as she sucks me off, her lipstick marking me while my hands tug on her hair. Can't help my sexual appetite when I fuck like I race—wild, risky, and often. Blame the adrenaline rush or feeling like a god behind the wheel.

"It's fine." Her flat voice tells me differently. *Fine* is a woman's equivalent to a land mine because you have absolutely no idea when or where that shit will explode.

"It isn't, and I don't want to annoy you anymore. Honestly. I want to put it behind us and say I'm sorry for insinuating you slept with your brother." I withhold the urge to cringe at my own stupidity.

"Consider it dealt with. Apology accepted." She fiddles with the straw of her drink.

"What are you doing here with your brother?" I take another sip of Scotch, the cold liquid sliding against my tongue.

"I'm actually following him around this whole year." She tilts her head at me.

Great. She'll be spending ten months with us, and I already fucked up.

"You'll be attending a lot of races then. Are you a fan?"

A small smile tugs at her lips. "My weekends growing up included following my brother everywhere. Kart races, real races, all the Formula phases. He has the talent." She looks down at her hands. "Of course, I'm excited to join him because I'm proud of how far he has come. New car, team, and everything." She glances at me, her eyes gleaming in the low light of the bar while her lips fight a smile.

I smirk at her. "He'll be in good hands with the equipment and engineers. Bandini cars are the best. There's a reason they're the most sought-after team, so it'll give him an advantage. But he still has to deal with me."

The sound of her soft laugh stirs something up inside of me.

"How do you keep your ego in check?"

"I don't." My grin expands.

She rolls her eyes, and fuck if it doesn't turn me on. Her delicate features entice me, tempting me to scoot in closer to check her out and catch a peek at her chest. But I stop myself because I have a cap of one sleazy move per day. *I can't believe I insinuated she slept with her brother. I'm losing my touch.*

"You need someone to rein you in." Her cheeks turn a pretty shade of pink before she shakes her head. "I mean, not me, but it's always good to be grounded." She puts a stray curl behind her ear.

"Being grounded is dull. I don't drive cars at two hundred miles an hour to stay boring."

Her lips purse and her brows pinch together. "Being grounded isn't boring. It's realizing that, when all of this—" she waves her arms around us—"is over, you still have people there for you in the end. Good people who are humble because no one wants to hang around an asshole."

I'm going to guess I'm the asshole here. I sit with her words and consider my situation. But I know good people—who is she to judge me when she's young and naïve?

Her phone rings. "I better get going. My ride is here."

"I'll walk you out."

Her face flashes with surprise before she recovers. Mine probably matches hers because I can't remember the last time I walked a girl out of anywhere except a club.

I get up from the booth and offer my hand, acting the part of a gentleman. She looks at it for a moment before placing her palm in mine. My skin buzzes at the physical contact. She shivers when my thumb runs across her palm, her soft skin smooth under

my calloused digit.

Hmm. Her body reacts to mine in the same way.

I remove my hand from hers and place it on her exposed back as I lead us toward the entrance of the hotel. Our physical connection is an exciting development, one worth exploring further at another time. She sucks in a breath when I stroke my hand down the ridges of her spine. I tend to be a cheeky bastard. Her skin feels warm and soft beneath my palm, her shallow breaths matching the rhythm of our feet.

Maybe I'll enjoy having Santiago around after all because it seems like her hanging with us will stimulate me. I want to see what other responses she has to me. Or under me. Or on top of me.

I need to get myself under control.

We exit the hotel to find her brother leaning against a town car near the entrance.

"Maya, let's go! The driver's been waiting." Santiago's voice booms off the walls.

Maya. I like the name.

She jumps a foot away from me, breaking our contact. Her eyes glare at me before she says a rushed goodbye and walks away. I shake my head, trying to rid my naughty thoughts, a gesture worth chuckling at. Her perky ass stands out, the tight black material of her dress hugging her curves. *Damn. I definitely will like seeing her around.*

Her brother helps her into the car before he turns back toward me. His stare speaks a silent warning I choose to ignore, instead deciding to shoot him a cocky grin and a chin tip. He disregards me and enters the car.

CHAPTER FIVE

MAYA

The air in the car is thick with tension, and not the good kind. Bright lights reflect off the car's window as we pass through the city. Santiago hired a driver to take us to the gala, reminding me how I'm in over my head. A poser surrounded by the rich and famous.

"Why were you walking out of the hotel with *him*?" Santi seethes.

"He actually came to apologize for what he said at the press event. We chatted and then I came outside. It's not a big deal, no need to get annoyed."

Placating Santi has been my job for years. He tends to be a situational hothead, much like other F1 racers. High-stress situations usually call for it.

"You should stay away from him. Hell, stay away from most of the F1 drivers. They're not here for happily-ever-afters, white picket fences, a dog, and two kids. They fuck around. *A lot.*" His hands clench in front of him.

"You are aware I lost my virginity like four years ago, right? No need to protect me anymore when my virtue is no longer intact."

If looks could kill, Santi would have murdered me twice already in this car alone. Wrong joke at the wrong time. *Message received.*

"I don't want to be aware. No. Keep that shit to yourself. These guys are different from boys you dated in college. They're the ultimate fuckboys. Liquor, ladies, maybe even drugs. Who the hell knows. I haven't hung around them much since I kept to myself with Kulikov."

"I'll be careful. But Noah is part of your team now. We're all stuck around one another and I don't want things to be awkward with us. At least not more than they have to be."

No use denying my physical attraction toward Noah, but I can sure do my best for Santi. I owe him that much.

I give him a sweet smile while I pat his hand, hoping to calm him. His lips tip down. He must be concerned because none of my usual tactics are working on him.

"You're my little sister so it's my job to protect you. Be careful, okay? I can't keep an eye on you all the time. Especially with someone like Noah. His bedroom has a revolving door and a waiting list."

My body tenses. *Thanks for the reminder.* Nothing like a classic manwhore, one so stuck in his ways he can't see straight. Good thing those types of relationships aren't on my radar.

"You don't need to worry about me. I'm up to only good, remember?" I shoot him a goofy smile.

He grins at my cute stupidity and tugs me in for a hug,

constricting my air supply.

"I love you. You know that, right?" His chest vibrates while he speaks.

I return his hug with a squeeze. "Of course. I love you too. Now let's go party!"

The swanky event, in fact, surpasses my original idea of a sponsor party. I picture old men rubbing elbows and chatting about their stocks. But it's all so much more. We walk into a ballroom decorated to the nines with crystals and flowers hanging from the ceiling, waiters walking around with food, and dripping champagne towers on several tables. I grab a couple of fancy-looking appetizers while I walk around the room.

Lots of bigwigs visit to shake hands with the elite of racing. But the scene includes unlimited alcohol, a decent DJ, and silk dancers spiraling from the ceiling. It resembles more of an overdone wedding than a gala for race car drivers. F1 is pretty hip, not going to lie.

Santiago reluctantly leaves me to my own devices after being called over by his agent. He gives me a warning look before walking away, but I brush off his worries with a flick of my hand. I follow his rule of not talking to the other drivers. But he can't fault me when others talk to me because I can't control everyone else. Loopholes make life interesting.

I occupy a seat at the bar when He Who Is Definitely Up to No Good shows up and sits next to me. His intoxicating cologne short-circuits my brain cells. Somehow his hair already looks like a disheveled mess and his bow tie lays crooked against his pressed shirt. His unruliness brings a smile to my face. Sturdy hands that caressed my spine an hour ago hold another glass of Scotch. I regret looking Noah straight in the eye, caught off guard by a penetrating gaze, his deep blue eyes framed by thick, long lashes.

A simple smile he sends my way tugs at my lower half. I can't control my body's response to him, especially when he looks at me like he wants to kiss me.

"What's a pretty girl like you doing all alone at an event like this?" Noah's voice has a rough sound to it like he spent the night partying and drinking—sensual and gravelly all at once.

"Aw, you think I'm pretty. How charming. Santi left me alone because he's busy kissing ass." I point a pink-nailed finger toward my brother who is chatting with a group of sponsors.

"More than that." Noah's megawatt smile makes my heart clench. *Well, don't you have a way with words.* "Ah, a day in the life of a celebrity. A tough cross to bear."

I chuckle. "I doubt I'll ever get used to hearing that. Can't imagine my brother as a celebrity. So weird."

"It takes time. Wait until he's followed around by paparazzi to the point where he can't even eat or shit in peace. This place corrupts the best of us, surrounded by endless money, booze, women—you name it. A playground for the privileged."

I turn toward him and glance down at his outfit. He pulls off a tuxedo, looking roguishly handsome with smooth material clinging to his body. My fingers twitch at the temptation to run through his tousled hair that hints at his rowdiness.

But I don't because it'll ruin my efforts to be good.

"Did this place change you?" I try to keep my voice neutral, not giving away any feelings. He's the last person Santi would want me to hang around with.

His eyes harden. "I was born into it. Son of a legend and all." He flashes me an eye roll. "So technically, no, since it's all I've ever known. Can't be corrupted by something that made you."

I scrunch my nose. "We aren't like that. We were raised in a small home by modest parents. Santi didn't even go to college, so he could race to make money. Gave up a lot to pursue a dream. He paid my parents back everything they've ever invested in him because it means the world to him to provide for them."

"Humble beginnings make the best success stories. Your brother signed a twenty-million-dollar contract though, and that's a lot of money, so with it comes responsibility." His eyes stare intensely into mine.

I sigh, aware of Santi's most recent financial gain. He may surround himself with pompous people, but he isn't like most of these greedy and egotistical guys.

Noah takes a big sip of his drink. I copy him, chugging my champagne—a dose of liquid confidence to dull my nerves.

"What was it like being a kid around here?" I look across the room, imagining a young Noah hanging out with these people.

"While growing up, I thought it was the coolest thing ever. And I still do. But my dad isn't exactly father of the year. Nannies took care of me while my mom was off yachting the world. But woe is me, the hard life of someone who has it all." The sadness in his voice betrays his attempted nonchalance.

"Do your parents come to see your races?"

"Every now and then. Dad's coming to the Barcelona one. My mom's another story, occasionally popping in when it's most convenient for her and her friends." He tips his glass and clinks it against mine before we both drink to that notion.

I sense parent issues with this one.

He looks at me with bright eyes. "What about you? What brings you to the crazy life of F1 racing?"

"Do I need a reason besides my brother competing?" I smile at him.

"Well, I assumed you were here for me, but now that you mention it, that sounds plausible." He hits me with a playful grin that sparks something inside of me.

I shake my head at him. "I just graduated, and I wanted to travel the world." I hold back on mentioning my vlog because I don't want to be judged by someone like him—a man who thrives and succeeds.

"Well you picked the right year to join. You get to see exotic locations with a bonus of me kicking your brother's ass. You can't Pinterest that shit."

I throw my head back and laugh. His cockiness has no bounds, but I like the way he teases, uncaring with a glint of mischief in his eye.

"How do you fit your head in your helmet? I'm worried it must expand the more people stroke your ego," I say with fake concern.

"I have one custom made to avoid that issue."

We continue our banter until someone calls him away. He looks unenthusiastic at the interruption, his feet remaining planted to the ground.

"Duty calls." I tilt my empty glass to him.

He sends me a smirk and mock salute as a goodbye.

I explore Melbourne on Friday since Santi has a busy day with practice and press events. As interesting as his plan sounds, I decline his invitation to join him.

I spend the day taking photos and discovering the city. A local street-art tour gains my interest, and I enjoy the ability to fade into the group while surrounding myself with fellow tourists. When I hang with Santi, it feels like I'm on display. The attention he receives stifles me. People always take pictures, ask questions, or request autographs. And I hate feeling watched. He tells me everyone eventually gets used to it and I won't notice them after a while.

That type of complacency scares me.

The rest of the day goes by quickly. Newfound privacy comforts me so much that I eat lunch alone, at a table for two no less. My solo day seems short-lived when an old man sits in the chair across from me. He eventually gains the courage to strike up a conversation after fifteen minutes. I politely engage in the discussion of his arthritis, nodding along like I understand the struggles of chronic pain. He even shows me about one hundred photos of his grandkids.

What can I say? I'm a sucker for never saying no, because how can I look that poor older man in the face and decline seeing photos of his little tater tot? His words, not mine. I can't. So I end up spending an hour entertaining a man named Steve, even offering him a signed Bandini baseball cap as a parting gift along with a promise to text him a picture of the Prix track on race day. I don't know the risk of giving a grandpa my cellphone number. But he seems sweet, so I give in.

My mom calls me while I'm walking down a side street.

"*Cómo estás?*" My mom follows my vlog religiously, commenting on all my posts with encouraging messages and quotes. She's cute like that. I even get texts with gifs as a way for her to express her feelings.

"I've been having fun so far. Santi's pretty busy with the business side of things. I don't know how he finds the energy."

We stayed out late and he got up at the crack of dawn to go drive on the track. Meanwhile, I hit the snooze button about five times before I finally got up.

"He lives for the sport, so he puts up with the social side of things. Keep an eye on him because he works too hard." There goes my mom, always the worrier.

"I'll try my best. I can't do what he does, schmoozing and boozing. People here are snooty and full of themselves."

"I've been reading gossip about those different drivers. Men like Liam Zander and Noah Slade pop up all the time, and you should see what women say about them. Don't get me started on Jax, that man has trouble following him like a bad smell." Her voice fails to hide her disdain. I don't ask for more information because gross details don't interest me.

"Be careful what you read. They can start spinning stories about Santi one day. Reporters are aggressive. And they love an interesting story, whether it's true or not."

"Have you met his teammate?" She can't conceal her curiosity about Noah, and I can't blame her.

"Yeah, he's not as terrible as stories claim. But he's still the ass who thought I was Santi's girlfriend."

"*Que bruto*. Someone should've raised him better, given him extra love and attention. That must've been embarrassing for him."

"I think that's his problem. It must be such a lonely life for him, screwing around with whomever and having no one to celebrate wins with. His own family barely comes to the races. Like his dad visits a few times a year, his mom even less. Makes me wonder if there is more to this show he puts on. I doubt he even realizes it though, especially when people like him always think they're happy until they aren't anymore. But who knows, I'm speculating, and it's not fair to judge." Unfiltered words rush out of my mouth.

"*Cuídate*. Behind the glitz and glam, people live with lies and unhappiness."

I change the topic, not wanting to talk about Noah anymore. It feels wrong to expose the small truth he shared with me last night about his parents. My mom and I catch up on plans for the weekend, and not soon after, I hang up the phone and go back to the hotel.

CHAPTER SIX

Noah

Qualifying on Saturday is the second-best part of racing because a successful Saturday is essential to winning on Sunday. A position for Sunday's race depends on the qualifier. Getting a sucky start on Saturday means you're fucked on Sunday, unless you put in extra work to get on top.

Pole positions are my and everyone else's favorite. I can bounce back from a second-or third-place starting point though, not needing to pressure myself to over-perform. Back of the grid tends to be the worst. I haven't placed there since the start of my career, always preferring spots between P1 and P3.

Squeals of the tires hitting the road bounce off the pit walls as I walk toward Bandini's area. Each team has their own garage on the pit lane where the team preps before the race, including small rooms above the workstation where Santi and I get ready. I gear up in my suite for my two practice sessions.

I complete two successful practice rounds like I wanted. My qualifier went even better, landing me the pole position for the

Australian Grand Prix. Best spot on the grid. Santiago isn't far behind, qualifying third, right behind Liam Zander. Not bad for the new guy.

For the sake of the team I want him to succeed, since we also compete together during individual races. I'm not totally selfish. He needs to do well for us to win a separate Championship, the Constructors', which happens at the same time as the World Championship. A total of twenty-one races and two coinciding Championships.

Santi can settle for winning the Constructors with me because I want to be the World Champion this year. My teammate can keep his shiny consolation prize.

Santiago, Liam, and I attend a press conference meant for the top three qualifiers. I sit between the two of them as reporters hit us with questions.

"Liam, can you tell us about your strategy with McCoy this year?"

"Besides fucking through the McCoy family?" I whisper under my breath, the microphone attached to my cheek not picking up on my voice.

Liam chuckles and shakes his head. We fuck around with one another, keeping the conferences interesting while breaking up our routine.

"Team strategies are the best kept secret. Can't have Bandini here catching onto all of my tricks, particularly the hothead over there." Liam points to Santiago over my shoulder. "But we have big plans for the upcoming races, including new specs on our cars. Going to give Bandini a run for their money."

"What he means to say is the view sure looks nice behind

P1." My gruff voice makes reporters laugh.

"P2 allows me to screw Noah's car from behind, hitting him at the right angle. Oh, wait. That's Santiago's job, my bad."

I smack Liam's backward ballcap off his head.

Thankfully, Santiago refrains from any stupid comments this time around. He looks at Liam and me oddly. I let Liam's comments slide because he's actually one of my good friends and greatest opponent, at least before Santiago came around. Our verbal sparring makes it on YouTube every time.

Liam's a German guy who drives with McCoy, another top team. Blonde-haired, blue-eyed man with a god complex. I like him a lot since we became friends during our young karting days. Raced together in the Formula phases and we even competed on the same team when he started, both rising up together.

He acts like a total douche to women, and that says a lot coming from someone like me. I may be an ass, but Liam can be worse. His preppy looks deceive the best of them. A fuck-ton of pressure rests on him this year because his contract with McCoy will expire, and he slept around with the owner's niece.

Unlike my preference for one-and-done situations, Liam actually keeps girls around for longer than one time. I can't fault him when women willingly agree. But his F1 seasons include one or two girls on rotation who eventually get their hearts broken, spilling their story to the gossip rags. A yearly cycle. But now he needs to keep himself locked up like a good boy after pissing off Peter McCoy.

I occasionally watch the trashy gossip videos of us on YouTube, shameful to admit they entertain me. McCoy can't be happy with Liam. Recent videos have focused on Liam's lack of foresight, calling him out for fucking around during an important year. Sleeping with your boss's niece tends to stir up lots of emotions.

Maya hangs out in the corner of the press room, trying to blend into the wall. Fat chance that's possible. She looks beautiful in ripped jeans and a T-shirt that clings to her chest. Her wavy hair is up in a ponytail that bobs while she leisurely scrolls through her phone.

It annoys me how she only tunes in to Santi's answers, staring up from her phone every now and then to watch him. It's like Liam and I don't exist. If she doesn't care then she shouldn't come, plenty of reporters would kill for a spot in here. *Why does she find her brother fascinating?* It blows my mind how she looks at him like he hangs the moon for her, her eyes all proud and shit when he talks.

Is this usual sibling stuff? I glance over at Santi while he speaks, curious to see what gains her interest.

"Santiago, how do you feel about your new contract with your rival's team? Any stress that comes with driving against one of the greats?"

I school my features like a well-trained PR puppet. Inside my irritation grows, an eye roll barely contained. When will these guys let go of the contract deal? They lack original questions, the same type asked each conference, forgoing the hype of the first race of the season.

"Uh, it's not about contracts, but rather how well we drive. I don't think about dollar signs or Noah when I'm out there. I think about the next turn and the finish line, with a possible podium ending."

Okay, not bad. The team publicist must be helping him after yesterday's disaster.

"Noah, who do you consider to be your biggest threat this season?"

A cocky smile breaks out across my face. *Show time.*

"I like to consider myself as my biggest threat. When I race, it's me versus my instincts. Everything around me disappears. I test myself, seeing how long I can wait before pressing the brake, or how to overtake another person. I don't think about the other drivers out there more than I have to. That's where others screw up."

Camera bulbs flash in front of me and capture my confident smile. Maya shakes her head, apparently not a fan of my response. The idea displeases me. My eyebrows pinch together, and my lips turn down into a frown. Appearances represent everything in this line of work because fans buy into this shit and love it. They even make videos about our bizarre press conferences every race like bromance videos and rival compilations. You name it, there's a video on it.

A reporter moves on to Liam, asking another pointed question. "Liam, what game plan do you have to clear your name in the media?"

"Why don't you ask me in a few months? I want to keep my plan to myself, in case it goes wrong." Liam shrugs.

I nudge him with an elbow. "That tends to happen with him."

Liam turns toward me and brushes his eyebrow with his middle finger. My head drops back and I laugh. I lift my head, catching Liam shooting Maya a grin that she returns, no longer inattentive. My fists tighten under the table as I stare straight ahead.

Liam can be considered a good-looking guy. A six-foot tall German jock who needs a short beard to hide his baby face. Basically, a glorified tool. Women dig his positive vibes and carefree attitude, along with his preference for multiple repeats. Everything about him screams good parents who gave him sugar, spice, and everything nice. Unlike me who reeks of broodiness and bad memories, driving away from my demons week after week.

We finish up answering questions and I leave the stage. I don't want to be there for another minute more. I'm mentally done with today.

Nothing tops the buzz of a race day. Everyone deals with their pressure differently, tensions escalating as we approach Prix time. Anticipation of events keeps everyone up and running. Sundays are my favorite day of the week because who needs a church when I have a front-row seat to heaven.

Every racer does quick rounds to appease fans and sponsors, including meet-and-greets, parades, and interviews—the usual crowd-pleasing and ass-kissing. Following that, I do my typical engine checks and attend a pre-race stage event with an end goal of alone time in my Bandini suite.

This sport exhausts the best of us. I love it, but it wears a person down through the years.

The small Bandini suites can't compare to the motorhomes the team builds during the European leg of the tour. The plain room gets us by, with enough essentials to appease the racers, including a couch and a mini fridge stocked with waters.

Music is my preferred method of easing nerves before races. I have a playlist and everything for each day of racing since I tend to be a creature of habit who prefers solitude. Unlike other drivers, I leave the celebrating for after a race when I actually win. No one likes a guy who parties prematurely and doesn't even end up on the podium. We leave that for the sucky teams.

Maya's laugh seeps through the thin walls. Santiago acts differently from other Bandini guys, not minding Maya hanging around with him while he preps for the race. Small quarters don't allow for much privacy around here. I try my best to not listen, but I find the task difficult with our shared wall, telling myself whatever I overhear isn't my fault.

Maya's voice carries into my room. "Remember when you had your first kart race? You almost threw up inside your helmet, your nerves shot after that kid nearly crashed into you."

I like the sound of Maya's soft laugh.

"It was intense. Never underestimate an adrenaline rush because they're no joke. I think it took an hour for my heart to slow down and the nausea to go away. How do you even remember that? You were like six at most."

"Mom showed me a video of that race. They were reminiscing the day you signed the Bandini contract, including showing me tons of videos of you in your kart. They're so proud of you." Maya's voice sounds sentimental.

My parents never filmed my races, let alone watched them with a wave of nostalgia.

"You know they're proud of you, too, right? With starting up your own vlog and supporting me."

Maya sighs. "Yeah, but you're the success story, and they sacrificed everything for you. The vlog is starting out, and things like that take time. Let's see what happens because I don't want to disappoint myself or anyone else. It's hard to get a decent following."

"I'll share something you post to help you gain followers. Plus, you're around a bunch of famous people—word will get out eventually. Just watch."

Curiosity pushes me to see what she vlogs about. I pick up my phone and google her, quickly finding and bookmarking her channel for later when I have time to check it out.

I also go ahead and request to follow her on Instagram since she set her account to private. *Fuck it, why not. I'm curious, nothing more.*

Their voices drop too low for me to catch the rest of their conversation. I find it difficult to imagine a childhood like Maya's since I'm an only child with no competition for my parents' limited attention. Hit the parent jackpot. They never married, avoiding a financial train wreck, messy divorce, and custody agreement neither of them wanted.

I put my headphones on and tune out the rest of their conversation. Eavesdropping distracted me enough, pulling me away from my usual mental clearing before races.

Not soon after, Santiago and I prepare for our cars. We zip up our matching race suits and grab our helmets. I touch the scarlet red paint, my hand running across the signature glossy coat of Bandini cars, the warm engine running beneath my fingertips. Ready to go. Even after all these years with the team, I still do this same pre-race ritual. My favorite lullaby is the rumbling sound of the car.

I lie down in my seat and strap myself into the cockpit, the clicking of the belt further securing me. One of the techs hands me my gloves and steering wheel as I take a few deep breaths to ease my nerves.

The crew and I roll up to the front of the group, situating me in the P1 spot while testing my radio connection. I grin to myself beneath my helmet. Pole position will always be the most ideal spot in the whole Prix, and pride fills me that I claimed it. Have to start the year with a boom.

My heart pounds in my chest, the rhythm similar to the shaking of the engine. The team slips off my tire warmers before they rush off the pavement.

One. Two. Three. Four. Five.

Five red lights shut off. My foot pushes on the accelerator and my car speeds down the runway, hitting a neck-breaking pace as tires rub against the pavement. Commotion buzzes through my earpiece. Team members speak to me, telling me how Liam stays behind me, with Jax overtaking Santiago at the front.

Fuck, I love this feeling. Nerves fire off in my body as adrenaline seeps into my blood, the sound of tires screeching across the pavement competing with the whooshing in my ears. Bodily sensations breathe new life into me. The engine hums as I push the car to its max capacity, testing the limits of the new race car model. My lungs tighten in my chest as I approach the first turn. I tap into my reflexes, becoming one with the car.

The beautifully executed turn happens in a blink. I tune out most of the radio chatter that sounds off through my helmet, concentrating on breathing in and out to relax my heart rate.

I continue to hold down my position as the race leader while we twist and turn down the track. If the team didn't keep me updated, I'd lose count of the laps. My car rips through the road like nothing. Liam tries to overtake me at one of the turns but fails, his car falling back behind mine, sucking up the dirty air. The team principal shares who else may threaten my lead.

The race is touch and go between Liam and me for a while. A similar season start—both of us vying for the top-place spot. We have a competitive relationship on the track, knowing each other's moves since we were kids in karts. Both of our teams strategize with us for ways to beat each other.

Santiago isn't even a blip on my radar, seeing as the team hasn't spoken a single word about him.

I take a quick pit stop halfway through the race to get new tires. My car stops in the pit lane, allowing the mechanics to take over with their drills and machines. Process takes one point eight seconds. I thank the team via radio for their quick turnover time. A speedy pit crew are the unsung heroes of F1, the ones who make the magic happen once I box in the garage area.

I talk back and forth with a race engineer during my drive, communicating competitors' positions and specs. He wants to check in on how the car feels for the first race. The team shares strategies and I follow along for the most part, but some calls I make on my own because they don't pay me millions to follow every command. They trust me behind the wheel.

I continue to hold the front-runner position for most of the fifty-seven laps. Liam overtakes me a couple times, but I beat him back into second place with ballsy turns. He flips me off after I threaten to hit him during one curve. With one lap left, Liam will come out in second place, and Santiago will end up in fourth.

The sweet sound of engines roaring fills my ears. My hands grip the steering wheel tightly as I make the last turn toward the finish line. I push down on the peddle a few seconds early, allowing me to surge past the waving checkered flag before Liam. Fans scream as they announce I won the Prix.

"Fuck yes, guys, what a big win! Thank you, everyone. Amazing first race. Let's fucking go!" My foot lifts off the throttle.

The radio buzzes with cheers.

I throw my fist in the air, proud of a race well done. *Suck it, Santiago.*

CHAPTER SEVEN

MAYA

My heart speeds up as Noah passes the finish line. Santi follows soon after, his car a red blur as he completes a cool-down lap. His performance on the track will frustrate him despite driving well. He still gets points for the Constructors' Championship, but in the end, against these other guys, it's not good enough. That's the life of high stakes and large salaries. Plus, the pressure of a big racing team and a pricey contract are on my brother's mind.

I meet Santi near the pit area. He smiles at the team when he gets out of the car, shaking hands and thanking the pit crew—an image of good sportsmanship. His jaw twitches while he signs fans' gear at a crowd barrier. Not wanting to get in the way, I decide to meet him in his suite instead of waiting outside. Better for him to relax first.

By the time he makes his way back to his room, he looks calm. I get up from the small couch and give him a hug. His sweaty body plasters to mine as my lungs get a deep inhale of oil, sweat, and rubber. Kind of gross. I pretend to gag as I wrap my arms around him, my head barely reaching his shoulders.

"You tried hard. Fourth place is good, and you'll be on the podium next time."

He returns my hug. "I'm disappointed I didn't try to cut around more. I played it too safe because I was scared of messing up the car."

"You can't race with a fearful mindset. You never have before, and you shouldn't start now, not when you're racing against the best. Think of it as another car with plenty of parts to fix anything."

Despite today's cautious performance, Santi has a rep of being ruthless on the track.

"You're right, I'll bring my best next time. Screw it." He pulls away from me.

Santi beats himself up whenever he doesn't place on the podium. I believe he can succeed next time out on the course, especially with plenty of races for him to improve his standing for the World Championship.

"I'm going to have to show up at the after-party to congratulate Noah. It's what sponsors would want, and I don't want to look like a sore loser." He sticks his tongue out at me. "Top five isn't that bad for the first one. I'll bounce back." A telling smile crosses his face. Santi cares about losing, but he won't let it get in the way of his professionalism. What an adult.

Yay for team spirit.

"Then we better get going. Let's go wish Noah a job well done." I give him a mischievous grin.

Noah may put on a whole arrogant show, but he backs it up with his racing. His performance makes it obvious why fans love him.

I sense the excitement from the rowdy crowd once Santi and I walk up to the podium event. Groups of them gather around, bouncing along to the music streaming from the speakers on the stage, waving around face poster cutouts of Liam and Noah. I can't imagine being so famous that people actually pay for big blown-up pictures of your face. Watching my own face staring back at me would make me die of embarrassment, right there on the stage floor.

Santi and I hang out in a VIP area off to the side, enjoying the show from a less sweaty and chaotic distance. My preferable choice. We have a full visual of the winners' podium, including the perfect view of Noah spraying his champagne on Liam. I sigh at the display. Santi looks over at me and raises his brow. I cover up my laugh with a cough, embarrassment tinging my cheeks.

In F1, champagne is the messier equivalent of confetti launchers at other sporting events. Drivers shake bottles and splatter the contents everywhere. The crowd roars as champagne splashes on them, opening their mouths to capture droplets. Who needs Girls Gone Wild when you have F1 podiums?

Santi drops his disappointed mood, replacing his frown with a smile as all of them celebrate on stage. He even cheers when they announce all of the winners.

We find Noah, Liam, and the other winner outside of the press building after a post-race conference to say congratulations to them. I choose to give a thumbs up while saying hi, barely suppressing a groan at how awkward I look. *Smooth, Maya. Killing it.*

Noah lets out a gruff snicker at my attempt, along with Liam barking out a laugh, adding to my embarrassment. Can't fault myself when I have no idea how to greet them.

I stand around awkwardly. Santi offers Noah and Liam a typical guy handshake and slap on the back move. Noah's eyes heat up at the sight of me, swirling with deeper shades of blue than usual as they trail down my body. He flatters me. Either he sucks at subtlety, or he doesn't care if I notice.

My breath hitches when I check him out in his red race suit. Tight material presses up against firm muscles, highlighting a strict workout schedule. His hair looks sweaty and unruly, with a few pieces sticking up in different directions, and his wicked smile shines. He makes wild look sexy. I glance away before he catches me staring at him like a weirdo.

Being around all these hot guys throws me off. I need to stop having these intrusive thoughts about Noah, especially since he's my brother's teammate. How do other women keep up with these men? My brain bombards itself with images of puppies and grandmas to avoid checking him out again.

Liam's eyes gaze up and down my body. These guys boost my self-esteem by the second because they don't give a damn about hiding their attraction. He gives me a lazy grin when he notices my lifted brow and crossed arms. But I feel disappointed when my body doesn't have the same reaction to Liam that it does with Noah, my insides not heating up from a glance. Not even a flare of attraction. No racing heartbeat or warmth pooling inside of me at his perusal, only a basic acknowledgment of his good looks.

"I'm Liam. We haven't had a chance to meet yet, but I saw you in the press conference and had no clue you're Santi's sister. You were a sight for sore eyes in a sea of old male reporters." He takes my hand and gives it a kiss like a prince from the olden days. *Oh, this one is full of pick-up lines.* Hanging around him will be a good time.

I chuckle, snapping back into the conversation. "I'm making it my mission to attend as few of those events as I can. It's surprising how they let you get away with taking shots at one another, and at the reporters too."

Nothing short of a comedy roast each week with Liam and Noah teasing each other, their candidness pleasing reporters and fans.

Liam beams at me. "You haven't seen anything yet. Wait for the dirty race moves, crashes, and losing streaks. That's when it all gets exciting." Liam cups a hand to his face, like he shares a secret, except his voice keeps the same volume level. "Noah here is a sassy one when he gets mad."

Noah looks at Liam with a glare that gives me chills, a feeling running from the base of my neck to the bottom of my spine. His narrowed eyes are ones I'd hate to be on the receiving end of. *No thank you.* He can be intimidating as hell, but Liam seems unphased as he laughs and nudges Noah in the arm.

"Told you." Liam winks at me. His blue eyes twinkle as he beams at me. He has this lightness about him that automatically brings a smile to my face.

Santi shifts his weight from foot to foot. A signal that he wants to get going, since we need to pack and get ready to travel to the next stop in the Prix. Blame the busy schedule and long flights.

"We'll see you in Bahrain. Maya and I head out tomorrow morning on an early flight. We better get going because we need to pack and everything." Santi runs a fidgety hand through his hair. He loves to pack three days before his flight ever leaves, so it must eat him alive to have put it off this long.

"Man, you'll have to come on my private jet next time. Maybe we can shift around a few flights so you both can join." Liam's eyes sparkle as he pulls the slick move. He has this *Devil Disguised as an Angel* kind of look, with blonde hair, baby blues, and beaming white teeth. Although his exterior screams innocent, his eyes say everything but.

I give him a small smile in return, highly doubting that his invitation to fly in his jet has much to do with my brother. Probably has a lot more to do with me. Santi doesn't notice Liam's flirting, shocking since he bothered me all weekend about how these guys are after two things only: trophies and ladies. And preferably in that order.

"That'll be cool. We'll definitely take you up on the offer," my brother says.

Noah gives Liam a side glance and crosses his arms. *Did he just roll his eyes?*

I don't have a chance to analyze the situation further because Santi pulls me away.

My vlog picks up more followers after Santi put it on blast for a week while we were in Sakhir for the Bahrain Grand Prix—growing from a few hundred followers to a solid thousand. The idea hits me of posting YouTube videos of vlogs from each stop on our list. Last week, I filmed during our time in Bahrain, including a video from the practice sessions and interviews with the fans around the racetrack.

I edit and share a video of Santi placing fourth again in the Bahrain Grand Prix. Another loss for him, which makes for an unhappy brother. He says he's worked out the kinks of his new car. We move along, ready to hit the next race, time passing quickly with all the traveling from city to city.

Followers comment on how they love seeing behind-the-scenes footage of F1 racing. Turns out a lot of subscribers enjoy that part of my vlog, asking for more webisodes. After all the positive feedback, I dedicate a portion of videos to F1 racing and related activities. Not exactly my original plan. But hey, give the fans what they want. The change helps my numbers increase within a short amount of time. Thousands tune in weekly for the new videos.

New follower requests flood my Instagram, including Noah, Liam, and a few other racers. I accept them and decide to keep my profile private from fans because I want to separate my vlog from my personal life.

Liam and Noah give my channel a shout-out on their own social-media platforms when I tag them in racing clips. My numbers skyrocket, blowing my mind. Amazing what two pretty boys can do. By the time we fly to the third race of the season, I already have over ten thousand followers. *Ten points for Maya growing up! Look, Ma, I made it!*

We land in Shanghai for the Chinese Grand Prix. Santi takes off soon after we get set up in our hotel room since he scheduled tons of meetings. I hang around the suite and relax after a long flight because my body aches from sitting upright for hours. Another race, another basic hotel suite. White sheets and understated color palettes have become a staple of my life.

I eventually head over to the Bandini motorhome, located right next to the Shanghai racetrack. Easy access allows the crew to take breaks during busy days. It runs like a mini headquarters, with suites for the racers to hang around, along with meeting rooms for pre- and post-race consultations.

While grabbing a snack to eat, I run into someone. My eyes meet a pair of green ones that belong to a woman about my same height. She looks about my age with her blonde hair wrapped up in a top knot, golden pieces escaping the haphazard hairdo. Dressed casual, she rocks a white slogan T-shirt, jeans with more holes than fabric, and white Adidas. She gives off a California beachy vibe from American television shows.

"Oh, sorry about that. I'm such a clumsy person." Her neck and chest turn a shade of pink that contrasts against her tan skin.

"It's no problem. I run into things all the time too. I haven't seen you around here before." *That sounded weirder out loud.*

"I'm Sophie. You probably haven't because I just got here." She offers her hand and I take it.

"Maya. I haven't seen anyone my age except my brother. Glad I ran into you—literally."

She laughs. "It's my first time joining the race. I wrapped up my classes early for the year to spend time with my dad while he tours. Can't say no to a free vacation."

"I graduated in December! And who's your dad? I guess he's with Bandini then?" I wave around the lobby of the motorhome that bustles with activity.

She fidgets with her gold star necklace. "My dad is the team principal. He's the one who runs the show around here."

"Oh, wow. And you're going to be here for the rest of the season?" I try not to sound too excited because I don't want to scare her off yet. But the idea of a new friend sounds nice.

"I'm going to try to convince my dad to let me take my fall classes online so I can stick around for the whole Prix schedule. It's my first time around since I was younger, so I have to take advantage." Her smile makes the dimples in her cheeks pop out.

"Nice, we can hang out since I'm going to be here for the whole season. It'll be awesome to have someone my age keeping me young." I smile at her.

"What's the deal with everyone around here? Spill the deets." She abandons her previous nervousness. *Does she get tense when people bring up her dad and his job?* He keeps Bandini up and running because team principals are bosses without owning the company.

We both pull out a chair at one of the nearby tables, ready to chat and eat.

"If you're not yet aware, my brother is Santiago Alatorre."

Her eyes bulge out of her head. "No way. I can totally see it now that you mention it though. He's got that young Spanish hottie vibe going for him."

I hold back a groan. Can't say I think of my brother in that way, nor will I ever.

"Yeah, we both have the typical dark hair, brown eyes thing going for us, even though I'm the better-looking sibling. But don't tell him that. These racers and their egos, fragile little things." I give her a cheeky grin.

"He's the new guy around here. Must be a lot of pressure

to keep up with some of the best. How's he getting along with Noah?"

"Uh, it's been all right so far. They haven't crashed in the past two races. Go team." I do a cheerleader arm pump.

Sophie lets out a snort. "My dad was stressed to sign your brother on. He worried about how Noah would take it since he's been with Bandini for years. An original Bandini boy. The team doesn't take on young drivers, it's like their standard, but your brother's a World Champion now, which makes him a hot commodity in this industry." She lifts one brow on command.

I lift a shoulder. "Yeah, he's grateful to be a part of the best team. I still think it's crazy he's one of the youngest members to ever join Bandini. But Noah has handled the transition okay, seeing as he hasn't chewed out my brother yet. Well, besides after the first press conference."

She waves her hand at my words. "Those meetings are fifty percent serious and fifty percent drama. Fans love to watch, sitting on the edge of their couches—" she looks at me pointedly before continuing—"Be careful with Noah though. I hear all kinds of stories from my dad and other people."

"Like what?" I lean in, not wanting to miss a word of Sophie's insider info.

"He's cocky, self-assured, and kind of a jerk. Plus, he sleeps with lots of groupies. Yuck, yuck, and yuck. He's the guy your dad threatens to bury in a cement block. Well at least my dad would, said so himself before I joined the tour." Her nose scrunches. Seems like her dad may be slightly overprotective. "But Noah has a right to be confident, being a three-time World Championship winner and all at such a young age. He can race for years to come if he wants."

"Lovely. Nothing like a good playboy story to start the year off strong." Sarcasm weighs my words down.

"My dad has dealt with one too many phone calls from sponsors who were concerned with his behavior. But what can my dad do? Noah remains a professional out on the track and he has proven to be one of the best racers out there. He could just chill with the confidence sometimes."

"You know, Sophie, I think you and I are going to get along fine."

She returns my smile. We clink our water bottles together, cheering to our new friendship.

CHAPTER EIGHT

MAYA

Turns out Sophie and I mesh well together. We both love listening to the Jonas Brothers, eating the same Ben and Jerry's ice cream flavor, and shopping at Zara instead of Fendi. Fundamental pillars of friendship.

I like having a new partner to attend sponsor events, press meetings, and any other snore-worthy activities. Especially one as quick and witty as Sophie. She comes off sassier than I'm used to, but I like how she doesn't take shit from anyone.

I tell Santi that I'll meet him at the sponsored event since Sophie and I will take a car together. He fails to hide his curiosity when he asks to meet the new friend I made, claiming he wants to make sure I'm not out corrupting a poor soul. His overprotection has hit new levels ever since we joined the F1 tour.

"Okay, break down the guys for me. I haven't been around these people for like three years." Sophie doesn't miss a beat, wanting a rundown before we've seen any of them inside the ballroom. Not that I blame her. I wish I had been half as prepared because these men ooze confidence and sensuality.

"You know my brother and Noah, obviously. I met Liam at the other Prix, and he's a total flirt. No promises that he may or may not eye-fuck you. Just a warning."

Sophie's eyes narrow. "I haven't seen him since before my freshman year of college. But I've read stories of him in the tabloids. Lately he's been popping up everywhere after he slept with his boss's niece." Her lips tip down in a frown.

I cringe at the information about Liam because what a low blow for his standing with McCoy. Bad timing with his contract renewal.

"Yeah, I don't know how wrong the gossip columns are about these guys, so I barely pay attention to them. But that's all I can share because I haven't met any of the other racers yet."

"This sponsor event is for the entire Prix so I'm sure you'll see them in all of their hotness, at least from far away. Sometimes I question if it's a requirement for F1 racers to be ridiculously attractive. Sex sure sells." She lifts one brow.

I shake my head at her comment. Her assumption can't be far off, at least from the press videos and interviews I've seen on YouTube over the years.

We enter the ballroom. There are ginormous chandeliers hanging from the ceiling, dimly illuminating the room as classical music fills the air, while waiters offer appetizers and small plates of food. I love attending these events to see what party planners come up with. The venue looks beautiful and extravagant, bright lights glistening off my sequin dress.

Sophie and I make our way toward the bar, linking our arms together to make it through the crowd, sliding past a series of suits. Alcohol is a must at these types of events. I quickly learned that lesson after one too many boring conversations about race cars and bank accounts.

Sophie pulls us into an empty spot at the bar. Liam conveniently occupies the area next to her, not holding back as his eyes roam over her.

"Sophie, I haven't seen you in years." His baby blues smolder. I try to not feel offended that he shares an interest in her after flirting with me. But I guess I should expect it since all these guys have the sex drives of teenagers.

"Liam." She nods her head politely. Strange way to greet someone you haven't seen in a while.

"What can I get you two fine ladies?" He waggles his brows.

"Isn't it an open bar?" Sophie's wit shines through and I love it. She may become my favorite person during this whole Championship business.

"Doesn't mean I can't order it for you. Make a man feel useful." He places a hand on his chest and pouts his lip.

"Because you, of all people, need your ego stroked more than usual. Yeah right… But I'll take a Moscow Mule." Sophie flashes a smirk, making a dimple pop out.

He grins at her before he looks at me expectantly.

"I'll have the same."

Liam politely covers the tip for the bartender, making himself needed after all.

"Why do you two want to spend your night hanging with stuffy men? They're such a bore." He clinks his beer bottle to our glasses, along with a quick *cheers* before he takes a swig. Sophie's eyes stay planted on Liam as his lips tug on the bottle.

"I'm on the hunt for my future husband. Was thinking of someone between the ages of forty and fifty. Old enough to pay for everything I want, young enough to not have a wrinkly dick."

I choke on my drink. Sophie shrugs at me while Liam's eyes linger on her chest for a second too long.

Pull it together, man.

"Sixty and older means you'll only have to rinse your mouth with bleach for ten years instead of twenty." Liam weighs the invisible options in his hands, beer bottle bobbing along with him.

"Unlike Sophie who wants to become a mail-order bride, I came because my brother drags me everywhere."

"How's your brother transitioning with our broody prince?" Liam turns toward me before his eyes drift back to his new interest. His eyes narrow at her lips wrapping around a straw, eye-fucking her as she sucks on her drink.

I shoot him a look that tells him he can't bang my new friend because I actually want her to join me at events. Hopefully, my eyes say, "hands off." Nights like these tend to be lonely and dull with Santi always being busy.

He catches it and subtly nods with understanding. *Good.*

"Sophie's dad handles them, giving them enough love and attention to not make them jealous."

"He's a hard chief, running his team in tip-top shape while expecting the most from them. I wonder what it's like growing up in his home. Care to share?" Liam looks eagerly at Sophie while flashing her a bright smile.

"Wouldn't you like to know. Can't reveal our secrets to the enemy." Sophie pretends to seal her lips.

"I drive for a different team. Not quite enemies, don't be dramatic."

"Oh, that's rich coming from you. Drama seems to follow you wherever you go." Sophie says the words with a smile on her face.

Liam's smile becomes a full-blown grin. "Keeping tabs on me?"

Sophie's cheeks flush at Liam's raised brow before she takes a drawn-out suck from her straw.

I break it up. "*All right.* Oh look, it's Noah."

I grab onto Noah's arm and drag him into the conversation, no longer wishing to be the third wheel.

Noah looks down at my arm like it offends him. *This is going swell.*

"Noah, this is Sophie. Sophie, Noah." I speak without thinking.

"We know each other. I've been on her dad's team for five years." He gives me a puzzled look that is immediately replaced with one of hunger as his eyes take me in, raking down my red dress. *Thank you, Sophie, for the outfit idea.*

My stomach dips as I check out his tux, a new weakness of mine. *Resist the bow tie, Maya.* This weekly situation tortures me. *What have I done to deserve this type of punishment?*

No matter how many times I tell my brain Noah isn't worth the trouble, my body won't agree. Out of nowhere, his index finger drags across my knuckles, an electric connection sparking at his touch. My drink sloshes when I pull my hand away in a jerky motion. Cool liquid trickles down my skin.

Noah's thumb picks up the droplets before he brings the pad

to his mouth, his eyes remaining on mine. *Oh my God.*

I inhale deeply, filling my lungs with air. He shoots me a telling wink.

I let out a breath of relief as Noah talks, placing his hand in his pocket.

He smiles at Sophie in a caring way. "Nice to see you though, Sophie. Your dad sure sounds happy to have you visiting us. He talked all about it at lunch the other day, not shutting up about you finishing up your degree. Says you should manage my funds."

Sophie gives a shake of her head. "And he told me lots about his dream team and how smitten he is with all the new changes. Are you playing nice with this one's brother?" She points at me and smiles.

Thank you for bringing up his rival, Sophie. Is it too late to cancel our friendship?

Noah chuckles. "Don't insult me, I thought I was his dream racer. But yes. I share all my toys with Santiago, making sure to play nice together at recess."

I roll my eyes at his smug smile, questioning why I thought bringing Noah here was a good idea. Just when I think he can be normal he turns into an arrogant jerk.

Our exchange is saved yet again by a random guy. Based on his looks alone, I peg him as an F1 racer.

His British accent breaks up the current conversation. "Hey guys. What an event, am I right?"

Sophie and I both swoon at the Englishman in front of us, his accent packing a punch. The Brit greets us with dark eyes, bronzed skin, and roguish curly hair that no brush can tame. His unbuttoned black shirt displays neck tattoos trailing down the small reveal of his chest. He nails the quintessential bad boy look. A tattooed hand grips a glass tumbler, showing off inked knuckles and fingers.

Liam and Noah greet the stranger and introduce him as Jax, Liam's teammate. No wonder barely any women have jobs in the F1 industry. I doubt I'd be productive working around this hotness day in, day out.

"Who are these lush young ladies? You two have been holding out on me, I see." He gives Liam and Noah a wild smile and tips his glass up to them.

Sophie blushes, not immune to his charm. F1 hires the lookers of the group. Honestly, I doubt I'm any better off at the moment, with my cheeks matching the color of my dress.

"I'm Maya Alatorre and this is Sophie Mitchell." *Go me for getting the words out.*

"Quite a duo you two have here." He shakes his head at Liam and Noah.

"We wanted to keep them away from your ugly face. Don't want to scare the girls away before they get to spend more time with us." Liam tips his beer in Jax's direction before taking a swig.

Noah suppresses a groan, barely audible over my laugh.

"Who knows, maybe we can have them root for McCoy over Bandini one day. Women tend to be suckers for our accents." Jax lays the British accent on real thick this time.

"I'd rather *die* than cheer for your team." Sophie looks mock-disgusted with a wrinkled nose and wide eyes.

"Don't go saying things you don't mean. One day in my pit garage and you'll be wishing you never have to leave." Liam suggestively smiles at Sophie. She smacks him on the arm before messing around with her drink again.

"Catch you all later." Jax tips his glass toward us before he steps away from the conversation. Sophie practically drools on her dress, unprepared for the hotness that seeps out of F1 racers. I tried to warn her earlier.

"Nice chatting with you both. We're going to be on our way now. Thanks for the drinks, Liam." I shoot him a grin while grabbing Sophie's hand and tugging her away.

"The drinks are free. Seriously, Liam, you're strapped for cash? McCoy not paying you enough?" Noah's voice carries over the music.

Liam lets out a deep laugh while I run away from Noah because bow ties are my kryptonite.

Not Noah. Nope.

CHAPTER NINE

MAYA

The crowd stirs with enthusiasm as pit mechanics prepare for the Chinese Grand Prix. Team members huddle around the cars, conducting engine checks and ensuring everything looks good to go. It's chaotic yet organized all at once. Hundreds of people help run the operation, from feeding drivers to running electrical tests on Bandini cars.

Noah goes through his solitary pre-race ritual. I don't blame him for his preference, with the immense amount of pressure during every race. Plus, how draining fans and crowds can be. Santi and I hang out while he signs hats and gear for fans. He likes how I keep him company, telling me it eases his pre-race jitters. Whatever works for him.

I enter the suite area, silence welcoming me since most of the crew work in the garage, making sure the cars are in top condition for the race.

On my way to the bathroom, I slam into a firm body, confirming how running into people is becoming my specialty.

A hand grabs my arm and steadies me. My eyes land on Noah's face, his deep blue eyes piercing mine. His hand remains on my arm while goosebumps break out across my skin.

I sigh at the contact, not liking these uncontrollable physiological responses. "I'm so sorry, I should watch where I am going." First Sophie, now him.

He pulls down his headphones. "No problem. These halls are pretty tight." His voice rumbles. Why can't he have a nasally voice that throws me off, something to take away part of his sex appeal? I doubt it's too much to ask.

My eyes have a mind of their own, taking a quick peek at his body because I lack self-control. His race suit fits snugly against him, emphasizing his muscular form, the vibrant red color flattering his tan skin. My eyes close in a useless effort to try to rid the image of him. I wish Santi had an unattractive teammate because I'd describe this experience as the worst kind of punishment.

"Have to get used to how busy it is around here on race days. What are you up to in there? You always seem quiet." I point my head in the direction of his door.

He taps his headphones. "I listen to music and get in the mental state for racing. Give myself a pep talk and work out."

"*You* need a pep talk? I can't believe it. I thought the fantastic Noah Slade could do no wrong, with no feat too scary." I look up at the ceiling wistfully as I place a hand on my heart.

His smirk falls, but he recovers quickly. "Even the best need to get motivated. We drive cars at super speeds, so it can still be intimidating as fuck."

His arm grabs mine again and pulls me toward the wall. An

attendant runs by, hands full of car parts and bags.

"Gotta be careful around here. You're small enough to be run over by a cart or something."

I look up into Noah's eyes and immediately regret it. His shade of blue easily becomes my favorite, reminding me of Barcelona's coastal waters.

"Good to know. I'll leave you to it then." My hand taps on his headphones before I turn toward Santi's room. I need distance from him, anything to break his arm away from mine.

"Wait." A calloused hand strokes my arm again, heating my skin where his touch lingers. Noah's lack of personal space frustrates me. His touchiness overwhelms me and overrides my brain, making me crave him. My body refuses to follow my brain's memo about Noah being bad news.

"Uh…" I can't form logical sentences while his hand lingers on my arm.

Not sure where this is going, a feeling of uneasiness flows through me.

Noah speaks up. "Why do you spend time with your brother before races? It's distracting."

I blink once, twice. And one more time for good measure. *Okay then, who died and made you king?*

His fingers trace patterns on my skin like he didn't say something rude. I doubt he grasps how his words come across to others. Why would he when he always gets what he wants anyway, and is never told the words *no* or *please*. Entitled prick.

Dislike rolls through me at the response my body has toward him, the way my heartbeat picks up at his touch, and how it ignites something inside of me. I stare at his hands and will them away. He has strong hands that look large enough to dominate. Ones I want to feel on me, touching and squeezing.

My physical restraint around him is commendable. I deserve my own trophy and champagne shower, especially when his intoxicating clean scent confuses me. He makes it challenging to think about anything but him.

"It's not disturbing to my brother and that's who matters to me. No offense." My breathy voice doesn't pack the punch I intend. I blame Noah's stupid hands for disrupting my brain cells, making me unable to form coherent sentences.

"I can hear you through the walls sometimes, your laughs included. Must be fun in there."

My body tenses at his admission. He sounds sincere. Maybe even wistful? I can't tell if I am imagining things, guessing emotions that could be wrong.

"I'll be sure to keep my voice down and not laugh too much. Don't want to disturb the Champ and all." Sarcasm packs a blow this time around. *High five to myself.*

I confidently gaze into Noah's eyes again as he lets out a deep sigh. "I'm sorry. I didn't mean to offend you."

A little too late for that.

My gaze remains on his face, silently encouraging him to continue. I can wait for apologies.

"I'm not used to you or Santi being here. It's usually quiet on race days. My old teammate was like me; he typically listened to music and worked out. He took naps too. I don't mean to make you feel bad about it so please don't take it the wrong way." He shifts his weight from one foot to the other.

He comes across genuine at least. His hand runs through his hair, making the dark strands stick up everywhere. A typical look for him. I smile at his state of disarray, aware I've found Noah's nervous tick. Who would have guessed the hotshot had one?

"It's okay. I don't want to be distracting for anyone either. I'll keep it down." I offer a sincere smile.

"All right, thanks." He turns toward his door.

"Noah," His name rolls off my tongue, prompting him to look over his shoulder. "Good luck today."

"Thank you."

Part of my heart melts at the sight of him winking before he closes the door.

I lean against a wall and wait for my heart to stop racing. Once I finally relax, I enter Santi's room again.

Liam leads the group today with pole position. Finally, a change of pace from Noah's usual P1 spot, with my brother as runner-up, and Noah in P3. A third-place qualifier for Mr. Slade. What a tragedy. Bandini and McCoy outperform other racers every time, which seems unfair since money makes all the difference in a sport like this. Top teams hire the best engineers and crew. A couple others follow close behind, working toward upper grid positions and better cars.

Racers take off down the course once the lights fade from above the grid. The smell of fuel fills the air, strangely calming me. My hands clap as cars drive by. I love standing near the track's safety fence, feeling the vibrations of the engines as the cars rip past the lane, metal rings trembling underneath my fingers as I clutch the barrier.

On TV, cars may look like they hit normal speeds. But in person, F1 race cars rush past in a blur of colors and a burst of air, the roar of engines rivaling the crowd's cheers. My dark waves blow in the wind as Bandini's red cars fly by. The fast pace makes it difficult to tell which car Noah drives versus Santi, making me tune in to the speakers for race standings. Sparks fly as cars brush up against the pavement. Others cruise by, a mix of colors ranging from gray to pink. Race car models vary from sleek to clunky. I film the event from the sidelines today, wanting to stand at a popular turn overlooking the finish line.

No significant hiccups occur within the first twenty minutes. During the twelfth lap, a driver runs into a barrier, his car hitting protective blockades. Water splashes against the road from exploding plastic jugs. The driver unbuckles himself and yells expletives before throwing his helmet. He ends up kneeling next to his wrecked car, his body tense and shaking. Fans underestimate how emotional racers get when they crash. A failure to complete a Prix. After all the hard work and sacrifices from the team, they retire with no points for the Championship.

I turn my camera back toward the racetrack, getting fantastic shots of McCoy and Bandini cars rushing by, metal frames nearly touching as they try to pass each other. The howl of the engines brings a smile to my lips.

Liam and Noah fight it out for first and second place throughout the forty laps. Excitement has yet to wear off after the first hour of watching them compete against each other, the crowd's still yelling chants and cheers. My legs cramp at standing for an hour and a half. In hindsight, I should have packed a chair and snacks.

By lap fifty, my brother tails Noah's race car. Santi's defensiveness keeps me on edge. I grip the fence as they careen down the track, Noah holding his lead. Santi's car hangs uncomfortably close to Noah's. *Too freaking close.* During a straight stretch, my brother speeds up before he swerves while trying to get around Noah.

I gasp as the front wing of my brother's car hits the back of Noah's race car. Santi spirals out behind him, both cars trembling as they drag across the pavement. My brother has crashed into Noah at about one hundred and eighty miles per hour. The Bandini cars spin around like two red yo-yos across the track, the drivers unable to do anything about the loss of control. My stomach lurches. The crowd quiets and listens to the grating sound of metal, a path of sparks and smoke trailing behind the Bandini cars. Their cars finally stop near a side barrier. Smoke plumes from both engines and billows up into the blue sky.

Shit. Noah and Santi climb out of their cars. The safety team ensures that the drivers remain uninjured while a tractor picks up the messed-up Bandini cars with a crane. Noah flails his arms around at my brother. He throws his helmet off to the side while he grabs my brother by the race suit and pushes him. My brother catches his footing before he falls over.

I take in a deep breath, relief rushing through me that they both are safe. The risk of crashing always hangs over the heads of drivers in this sport. Some have died during crashes like today. But most racers get out of their cars unharmed because of all the safety precautions like fireproof race suits, helmets, and the bar above the car that protects the driver from barrel rolls. This crash proves why F1 has safety protocols in the first place.

The broadcaster announces how Noah and Santi will retire for the Prix, the worst news for the Bandini team. A major loss since neither racer will receive points for the Constructors' Championship. Plus, it's a strike against my brother's confidence.

I wait for them in the pit suites, in the same hallway where I ran into Noah earlier. Noah and Santi make their presence known the moment they enter.

"What the fuck were you thinking? What type of reckless, amateur shit are you trying to pull here? That crappy move cost us everything today."

My body stiffens at the way Noah talks to my brother. I peek around the hall's corner, wanting to get a look of the scene. Noah's back faces me while my brother looks furious, a rare happening for him. He has flushed cheeks, narrowed eyes, and pinched brows.

My brother's eyes flare. "I already said I'm sorry twice, Slade. Do you want to kiss and make up?"

Last-name dropping and the sarcasm dripping from Santi's voice is never a good sign.

"If you want to prove your worth, try to do it without crashing a million-dollar car. It'll serve you better in the long run. But if you wanted to ride my cock, all you had to do was ask nicely." Noah's hard voice carries through the halls.

"Fuck you. You act like your God's gift to Earth. Newsflash, I'll beat you one day and so will everyone else. Get over yourself."

My eyes strain and I press a hand against my mouth. Noah doesn't respond. He turns toward my hiding place in the hallway and practically runs me over on his way to his room. His hands grab onto me, stabilizing my body before I topple over.

Dull eyes and rosy cheeks greet me.

"Sorry," he mumbles before shutting the door to his room.

My heart squeezes at how unhappy he looks. I don't want to feel bad for him because he acts like a dick to my brother, but I can't help pitying him. It sucks how my brother made a stupid move that has severe repercussions for the team. Points aside, morale between these two can't be lower.

I enter Santi's suite to sit on the couch when Noah's phone rings next door. He rarely gets phone calls, so I can't fight my curiosity. I try my best not to listen in on what happens in his suite. And by trying my best, I mean I currently have a cup held up against the wall to try to amplify the noise. All I get are muffled words. A pretty unsuccessful spy mission if I do say so myself, my ears only catching a few words like *father* and *crash*.

Santi comes into the room while I google how people use glasses to eavesdrop. He eyes the empty cup in my hand curiously but doesn't mention anything about it, choosing to ignore my playful smile.

Santi plops himself on the couch next to me and lets out a sigh, the defeated look on his face pulling at my heartstrings. His fingers fumble with unzipping his race suit while his feet toe off his sneakers. He puts his head in his hands. The room fills with the sound of his deep breaths in and out.

I give him a few moments before I probe. "How did the talk with the chief engineer and Noah go?"

I learn from my mistakes, making sure to keep my voice low enough for Noah to not overhear us.

"Noah's pissed to say the least. And I get it because I fucked up bad. But I apologized to him the moment we got out of the cars and when we got back here. I hadn't even seen the footage yet, but I knew it was my fault."

"He shouldn't have yelled at you like that in front of everyone, making a scene. It's wrong and embarrassing for both of you. And not mature when you already said sorry."

Okay, the volume of my voice has increased a bit. Noah may or may not be listening in on our conversation at this moment, no thanks to me.

"I screwed him out of a good amount of points. It's going to take time to recover from that loss. I would be angry too if it were me." His hands pull at his hair while his face stares at the floor.

"You both are teammates trying to figure each other out. The two of you have different styles of racing, and you need to find your groove and work together." I root for both of them. For the sake of Bandini and the Constructors, they need to put aside this rivalry between them.

"F1 Corp will make us do a post-race conference together to represent Bandini." He looks up at me finally. His red-rimmed eyes lack their usual shine, and his sadness makes my heart hurt for him.

I take a deep breath, knowing what I have to do. "I'll join you. What's the worst that could happen? It's not like you can crash again."

Famous last words.

The press meeting is not the same as watching Santi and Noah crash in real life. On the racetrack, you can't see or feel the tension between the drivers. Except for the team radio, but not many people listen in unless the videos end up on YouTube.

See, in a press meeting, all the emotions hang around like unwanted female groupies. Reporters salivate at the idea of these two guys sitting on a duo panel. Tension fills the room like a dense cloud, my brother shifting in his seat while Noah's gaze focuses on the bright lights in front of him. I cringe at the awkwardness between them. The guys have many cameras on them, making it hard to hide anything.

I take back my previous comments about press conferences being yawn-worthy. I'd take snooze fests over train wrecks any day of the week.

Noah's jaw ticks when the reporter asks Santi a question.

"It shouldn't have happened today. Our team lost a lot of points because of it."

The reporter doesn't let Santi off easily because good answers don't sell magazine covers.

"Is it true that the team engineer told you to brake the car and pull off of Noah's tail, but you didn't listen?"

My brother moves around in his seat. "I don't want to discuss it. The team already lost today. It's bad for us. Do we need to harp on the logistics of how I messed up?"

Noah subtly shakes his head before his sharp eyes look straight ahead. He replaced his tight race suit with a sponsor polo shirt, his hair pressing smoothly against his scalp with not a single dark strand out of place yet. I prefer his charming wickedness over this sad state any day of the week. His arms cross against his chest, bringing my attention toward the ridges of muscle etched into them, tan skin gleaming under bright lights.

I check out reporters around the room, searching for any distractions, but my eyes drift back to the press table and roam over Noah again. *Ugh. Why does he have to be my brother's racing rival?*

I shift on my feet, my sneakers scuffing against the slick tile. My attention snaps back to my brother, choosing to ignore my attraction toward Noah because I don't want to accept those feelings. Instead, I list off all the reasons Noah's bad news in my head.

It's way too soon.

I barely know him.

He's my brother's teammate. Rival even.

He's a manwhore with more hookups than all the Bachelor *seasons combined.*

He looks like he'll screw with my head as well as he'll screw me in bed.

Working out all of the reasons why Noah Slade is a bad idea is a useful distraction, keeping me away from the drama ensuing in front of me.

I tune in again when the reporters decide to move their attention to Noah.

"Noah, tell us your thoughts on the situation."

These reporters decide today is the day for such open-ended inquiries.

"It's a shitty situation that should have never happened. Santi's apologized and we are sorry. Our racing team has to fix our mistake and we're appreciative of their efforts to get our cars up and running for the next race. We love this sport, bad accidents aside. We're not in it to retire early from the race and go home empty-handed. This is the worst-case example of teamwork, but we'll work on it."

He handles questions like a professional. *Not bad.*

My brother visibly relaxes in his seat, relief evident in his eyes.

My expectations for today didn't include Noah acting like such a pro. He pushes aside his earlier bad mood in front of the cameras, presenting himself as the ultimate teammate. I can see why Bandini keeps him around besides his talent behind the wheel. His appearance makes it obvious why women gravitate toward him, with him being such a smooth talker, willing to put on a show.

The rest of the conference is dull. I sneak glances at Noah because what is a girl to do during the rest of a boring meeting. He catches me staring at him, making my cheeks flush.

And that wicked smile he sends me when the cameras stop rolling? The one promising more? Yup. I see it.

Oh man, I'm in trouble.

CHAPTER TEN

Noah

Maya totally tries to hide how she checks me out. I no longer think its mild curiosity, chalking up her initial reactions as her way of sizing up her brother's new teammate. But we've danced around each other for a month—ever since the season started, glancing at each other and avoiding physical contact. She fills me with a different excitement—because of her and the reactions she thinks go unnoticed.

My new relationship with Santi is already off to a bad start. No need to fuck it up more with a quick hookup, no matter how hot his sister is. And I mean she is a drop-dead gorgeous woman. Thoughts plague me about ways I would defile her like wrapping her ponytail around my arm while her lush lips wrap around my cock, pump after pump until I finish. I'm a dirty bastard, but I can't do that to my teammate—no matter how much I want to. So I lock up my fantasies for another time with another girl.

I don't shit where I sleep. Period. End of story.

My dick retaliates against my brain though because I peek

glances at her across the Bandini garage. I could lie to myself and say its sheer curiosity. Based on the way my cock hardens around her, it's more than that, and frustration runs through me at denying myself.

I'm ashamed to admit I jerk off in the bathroom sometimes after seeing Maya. No use denying my terrible habit. It happens mainly after races, with all the pent-up adrenaline begging for release. But she always hangs around, so lately I've been taking a lot of cold showers, trying to rid the images of her from my head. She wears these tight shorts that show off her tan legs, plus she looks fucking fantastic in Bandini shirts. It brings out a possessive side of me, happy to see her in my team's colors, bobbing around the pit garage with her camera.

Can I ask the chief to ban attire like hers altogether from Bandini's motorhome? May solve half of my problems.

She bends over the cockpit of Santi's car, checking out the inside with one of the engine mechanics.

The mechanic darts his eyes everywhere except on Maya's jean-clad ass hanging in the air. Thank God she didn't wear her scrappy shorts that look shredded and two washes away from breaking apart. I can only take so much. She doesn't even notice how the pit barely buzzes with noise as she busies herself with filming the inside of Santi's car for her vlog.

I shift my jeans because my aching cock is pulsing uncomfortably against my zipper. My eyes glance around the rest of the room, catching how the pit crew steals glances at her perky ass. And I don't like it one bit. Where the fuck is Santiago when you need him?

Santiago, please come collect your sister. She fucks up everyone's work schedule.

Thank God Maya finally pops her head out. Her hair lacks her usual ponytail with wavy brown strands flowing down her back and framing her face. I'd consider her angelic-looking, except her body is meant for sin—to fuck hard and long. My type of damnation. I suppress a laugh at the comical display of many heads snapping back to their jobs. A hum of drills and the beeps of computers start back up again, heads no longer facing in Maya's direction.

Her smile beams at me once I catch her attention, filling my chest with a kind of warmth I don't recognize often. I return her smile with one of my own because I'm not a total asshole. My eyes snap toward the small black camera and tripod she grips in her tiny hand, the lens taunting me as she inches toward me.

Ah, explains the warm smile. I shake my head at her cleverness, a smirk replacing my grin.

"And here we have Bandini's finest, but not to me because I still think my brother is the best. It's Noah Slade. Say hi to everyone." She points the thing directly up at me, not asking for approval. I like how she's the type to ask for forgiveness instead of permission. Reminds me of myself.

I don't like interviews that aren't mandatory. But fuck it, if it helps her get new followers, I can go along with it.

A megawatt smile breaks out across my face. I lie and tell myself I do it for the fans, but my dick and I both know what's up.

"A real vlogger shouldn't be biased," I grumble.

Her soft and breathy laugh makes the tripod shake, and damn if it isn't the best sound I'll hear all day. What other noises can I get her to do between the two of us?

Get your head out of the pit lane, Noah.

"More on that later, everyone. So, Noah." My stiff cock stands to attention at the way my name rolls off her tongue, sultry and lulling on the vowels. I shift my feet subtly to ease the ache.

I would love to hear her repeat my name under different circumstances. Behind closed doors, where no one can hear us, preferably without clothes on.

What a sick joke on me where I crave attention from the one girl I want but can't have. And even worse, she remains oblivious. I want to spend more time around her and suck up her happiness like the goddamn black hole I am.

Maya resumes, unaware of my inner conflict. "Would you want to give the fans a tour of your own car?" She bats her eyelashes, laying the charm on real thick. Her brown eyes gleam up at me. Damn, who the fuck could resist looks like that?

"Sure, fuck it. Why not."

Nice, Noah. Cursing on camera.

Her head bobs with excitement at my agreement. Knowing her, she's resisting clapping her hands because of the camera.

We walk over to my car. Engineers take the cover off to give me easy cockpit access. My hand drags across the front of the car, giving the hood extra attention. Maya's eyes darken as she focuses on my hands. Further evidence that she is affected by me too, proving our attraction is not one-sided. My brain logs this information for another time.

If she wasn't Santi's sister, I would invite her back to my hotel room and show her a good time, help her give into temptation. But since she is, I have to be respectful. Not typically my status quo.

I do it for the good of the team of course.

"Care to share with viewers what it's like behind the wheel?" Her lips tip upward.

I nudge a pit crew attendant. "Hey, can you grab my steering wheel? Please." He hurries away at my request.

"While we wait, I'll give fans a tour. New watchers of the sport don't know how we F1 drivers are practically lying down inside the car. Sometimes it's even hard to see over our steering wheels. Makes turns more difficult if you can imagine." I casually lean against the car.

Maya's bright smile encourages me to keep going.

"Depending on the type of damage we sustain during the race, the pit crew may have the spare part needed to fix it. Here's the wheel now." Maya steps into me, angling the camera to get a good shot. I inhale the fresh floral scent of her perfume, a recognizably addicting smell.

I explain the mechanism and buttons on the wheel. Bandini likes to keep tight-lipped about our technology, so I withhold spilling any trade secrets. Maya nods along while paying attention to everything I say. Her head bobs, and small smiles make my heart clench—a new sensation that spreads through my chest, unlike any feeling from winning a race.

I wrap up my explanations. She flips the camera screen up and turns the tripod toward the two of us. Her body presses against my side as she tries to get us both in the frame, distracting me with the contact of her skin.

I shake my head at her attempt to film us together with her short arms. The camera cuts off part of my head, prompting me to grab the tripod and fix the angle to fit us in the frame. Her intoxicating scent washes over me again. The smell of her turns me on, like fucked-up pheromones drawing me in, showing how screwed I am.

"And that's what it's like behind a driver's steering wheel. Next week I'll be meeting up with the pit crew as they tackle the Russian Grand Prix."

I smile down at her. Her enthusiasm about her vlogging rubs off on me, uncharacteristically agreeing to this segment despite my usual distaste for these kinds of things. Not to mention how I check out her Instagram daily since she approved my request. My dirty little secret.

I lie to myself about how I don't want to miss out on her vlogs when I appear in them. But I have a hard time convincing myself when I check out her travel videos too, curious about what she does during her free time away from the racetrack.

"Any last words you want to share with Bandini fans?" She nudges me with her elbow.

"Tune in next week to see me kick Santiago's ass." I smile at the camera.

She laughs and elbows me harder this time, the tiny bone barely making a dent.

"Spoken like the conceited athlete we all know. See you next time." She waves goodbye to the camera and shuts it off. I take in one last breath of her addicting smell before she pulls away, the heat of her body gone.

Yup. I'm a sick motherfucker.

"Thanks for doing that. I wasn't sure if you would, to be honest." She tucks a loose lock of hair behind her ear.

Her nervousness comes back in full force, guilt tugging at the few heartstrings I have left. I can't help being an asshole.

"No problem. Can't have you only showing Santiago's side

of things. It's good PR for the company anyway." *Right*. I have trouble believing my own lie despite how easily it flows off my tongue.

"Yeah sure…" Her voice tells me she doesn't buy my brand of bullshit. "Maybe you can join another time again. I better get going since I have to edit all of this before the race tomorrow. Congrats on your pole position." She sends me one last smile over her shoulder.

"Thank you."

She walks away before the last word leaves my lips.

CHAPTER ELEVEN

MAYA

I upload the video I filmed in the garage where Noah made his cameo appearance. The comments section floods with positivity and excitement. People share how they're happy to see Noah in a more relaxed setting, away from the press circuit and racetrack. Hard to miss the barrage of horny women asking to be Noah's baby mama.

With every day I spend around Noah, I learn more about who he is once the cameras stop rolling. Before qualifiers, he likes to drink two espresso shots, which can result in him bouncing off the walls for a solid hour. Turns out he loves to chat while espresso runs through his veins. He also enjoys a session of yoga early in the morning before race days, a tradition he invited me to join during the last Prix. Safe to say yoga is not my workout of choice. *Namaste in bed, thank you very much.*

Noah even tugs on my ponytail now whenever he passes by me. At some point, lines blurred as we accepted a new level of comfortability with one another.

I learn details about him that chip away at my resolve, making it hard to resist him. He no longer is just a conceited guy who makes my eyes roll into the back of my head. Don't get me wrong, he still acts smug as hell—that has not changed. But I like it. The more time I spend around him, the more he draws me in.

Imagine my surprise when my usual mantras won't work anymore.

Not even I'm only up to good.

Because I want to be really bad.

Hooking up with Noah is the same as picking up two BOGO pints of Ben and Jerry's. It sounds and tastes like a great idea at first. But you overestimate your self-control, and next thing you know, the whole thing is gone and you have a stomachache.

Basically, Noah is a heartache disguised in pretty packaging. He has the same allure as a pint of Chocolate Fudge Brownie ice cream.

And no sex on Earth is worth his kind of trouble.

See, Mom, I told you I would try to be more responsible! Look at me go.

The current standings of the F1 World Championship include Noah in first place, Liam in second, and Santi in third. My brother bounces back up the ranks after his second-place performance in Sochi.

Noah is a force to be reckoned with. His confidence is well-deserved because the guy is a badass behind the wheel with spot-on instincts and fast reflexes. My brother could learn a lot from him if they put aside their dislike for each other. Things have been tense since the Shanghai fender bender, their dynamic not entirely back to normal despite how two weeks have passed.

The best thing about this next Grand Prix is that we get to go back home to Spain. I can practically taste the sangria and paella, along with the shores of Barcelona, calling my name. Our parents will visit us and watch Santi race. We look forward to returning to our home country after being gone for two months because time flies by while on the road.

Hence why my resolve slips around Noah. We've played around each other for months, with me putting in extra effort to resist his sex appeal. Hard stuff when he wears his race suit.

Our driver drops us off at the F1 paddock area. My eyes widen with surprise as I take in all the different style buildings made out of motorhomes. A distinct setup compared to previous races.

No words pass my lips as we walk down the row of uniquely colored buildings. Each team has their own motorhome with dining halls, meeting rooms, and larger suites. The building allows for a place of relaxation during the hustle and bustle of the busy race week. We still have our hotel rooms to sleep in, but this is where Santi and Noah spend a lot of their downtime.

We stop next to Bandini's motorhome. Red paint gleams under the sun, looking sleek and modern while still carrying the classic feel of the brand.

The motorhome has a luxurious feel when compared to pit suites from the flyaway races. People hang by the bar and restaurant on the bottom floor. Santi shows me the upper levels, including private suites and an outdoor patio where I see myself setting up my laptop to edit videos and content.

Bandini's motorhome shows how much funding the brand has from sponsors, including Noah's dad, who invests heavily in the team. Supposedly it looks good to have a previous race legend backing a brand.

I get tugged to the side before I can enter the suite.

"I need your help," Sophie whispers despite us standing in an empty hall. Her wide green eyes and heavy breathing make me hesitant.

"With what? And why are you whispering?"

"I was invited on a date." She chews on her cheek.

"That's great! Do you need help picking out an outfit?" Her glare makes me stop clapping my hands together. "Or not?"

"Not. This is the worst thing. Liam bet if he placed on the podium in Russia, we would have to go on a date. I stupidly agreed because I was buzzed at a sponsor event. Plus, his previous track history in Sochi was awful so I didn't think he would actually make it."

My eyes widen. "Oh, you didn't." Bets never ever end well.

"Tragic, I know. So I'm going to go because I don't rescind bets. But…he never specified the type of date." Her smug grin sets off a few alarms.

"Am I missing out on different types?" Not exactly connecting the dots here.

"I'm going on a double date. And you're coming with me." Her small hands grip my arms.

"What! No way," I sputter.

She's crazy. The last thing I want to do is go on a double date with them. Talk about awkward. Sophie and Liam have enough sexual tension between the two of them to make me sweat. And I highly doubt Liam wants a double date to start with, seeing as he salivates when Sophie gets close.

"It'll be us, Liam, and Jax. You remember him, right? British, hot, looks like he wants you to call him daddy in bed. It's a win-win for us." She gives me a sickly-sweet smile.

I burst out laughing. "Where do you even come up with this stuff?"

"I'm full of ideas. Will you do it for me? Your only friend here?" Sophie clasps her hands together and rocks back and forth on her feet. She plays the innocent card well. I grimace at how it works on me, a sucker for helping others no matter how bad the idea sounds.

"I'm game. But I'm only doing this for you. When is it?"

"Tonight! Before they get busy with the pre-racing stuff." Sophie rubs her necklace. She throws this on me in the same day, how thoughtful.

Lovely. I'm bursting with excitement here.

"My brother is going to kill me," I mutter.

"Oh, nonsense. He hooks up with a few ladies on the side anyway. He gets it."

Who the hell says things like that? She should count herself lucky that I like her and she's one of my only friends here.

"Ugh, come on. Get a filter. Gross." I stick my tongue out at her. That's absolutely the last thing I want to hear about, like ever. Right up there with hearing how my parents still have sex together.

"We better go pick out our outfits. We should look our best." She grips my hand in hers, demonstrating a shocking amount of strength for a tiny person.

The whole thing may be a terrible idea, but at least I can look good while doing it.

We end up going shopping together around the streets of Barcelona. I don't mind because I love feeling surrounded by my type of people for the first time in months. Hearing others speak Spanish and smelling fresh food from different restaurants makes me feel at home.

Sophie and I grab lunch together at one of the local spots. We chat while stuffing our faces with tapas, draining the contents of our sangria glasses. *Home sweet home.*

Sophie's cheeks flush, alcohol getting to her head, as she admits a fascinating tidbit of information to me.

"One of the reasons I'm stuck going on this date isn't only because of the bet." She lets out a deep breath.

My eyebrows draw up. I keep quiet, not wanting to interrupt and make her lose her nerve. Call me curious to get more information about her and Liam.

Sophie rattles on. "I created a Fuck It list for my time traveling with Bandini. Basically, it's a mix of different things I googled, from normal bucket list stuff to sexy items."

I choke on my drink. "Did sweet Sophie come up with a naughty bucket list? How bold of you." I waggle my brows at her. She snorts, not holding back.

"I was tired of living the perfect life my dad wanted. So I decided to create a list before I came here." She pulls out a small laminated square from her purse, unfolding the page so it becomes the size of a standard piece of paper. I have no clue how she did that.

I check out the different items, my eyebrows rising at a few of them.

"Then what's the connection to Liam?"

"Well…remember the time we sang karaoke in Shanghai?"

I nod my head.

She swallows a gulp of sangria before continuing. "The list fell out of my bag and Liam grabbed it. He knows about it and added, 'Go on a date with a bad boy.' See?"

Black scrawl mars the bottom of the page, messing up her perfectly color-coded list of items. Dots connect in my head.

"Oh my God, he offered to help with these?"

Red flush crawls from Sophie's neck to her cheeks.

"I only agreed to this one date. That's it, no others because I don't want his help. No matter how hard he tries. But I wanted to tell you because we're friends and all, which means we share everything together." Her honesty fills me with happiness because our friendship has reached a new level of trust.

My brother did, in fact, disagree with the date. Not a shocker.

He paces the floor of my room while I finish getting ready, his feet dragging across the carpet while he mumbles to himself. I snicker as he runs a hand down his face for the fourth time today.

"You're going to give yourself wrinkles by thirty if you keep that up." I point to his face with my mascara wand. He crosses his arms against his chest and scowls at me.

"Why Jax and Liam? Seriously, it couldn't be anyone besides them?"

I give him a pointed look. *Yeah, right. Imagine if I had said Noah asked me on a date.*

"What about the nice guy you talked to at the press conference last week? Nerdy, has a combover, but can ask a decent question?"

If the combover isn't enough to ward me away, the suspenders are a hard no.

I shake my head at him and exhale. "It's a favor for Sophie. She begged me to join her because she didn't want to go alone with Liam. So here I am. No need to freak out about it."

He should congratulate me for sacrificing myself for the greater good and my friendship.

"Do you need to wear *that?*"

I look down at my short red dress and shrug. "Eh, it's cute. I don't want to be underdressed since we're going to a nice restaurant."

A growl of frustration leaves his lips. His overprotection may be sweet, but the charm wears off pretty quickly when I deal with it weekly.

"Don't worry, big bro. I'm not even interested in Jax. I would rather be in the hotel room in my pajamas than going out right now." I find minimal appeal in attending a fancy dinner, unlike my brother who lives for this life, with crowds of people feeding his energy. He loves the glam and glitz of the F1 community. But me? I prefer a cozy life of snuggling up with a good book or a new TV show.

I shudder at the thought of him hooking up with other girls. *Damn, Sophie, why did you have to tell me about that?*

"Fine, but try to be back here before midnight. I won't be able to fall asleep thinking you're out there with them." He doesn't have to tell me twice because I like midnight bedtimes.

The last thing my brother hears is my laugh as I exit the hotel room, the door thudding behind my back. My eyes meet Noah's as he exits his room.

Seriously, he stays on our same floor?

These run-ins are becoming way too common with us. It concerns me since I feel like he's wearing me down, little by little.

His gaze explores my body before he closes his eyes, his lips moving like he's saying a silent prayer. His reaction tells me I get a gold star for the red dress choice.

I giggle at the sight of him being rattled, which is so unlike his usual calm and collected self.

"Going somewhere?" His blue eyes reflect two dark pools. My breaths shallow as his eyes rake down my body again. He follows me to the hotel's elevator bank, meeting my strides, step for step.

I take a deep breath before I respond to him. But I realize a little too late how much of a terrible idea it is as his smell engulfs me and makes my brain foggy.

Clean, fresh, bone-jumping worthy.

Another deep inhale before I speak. "Yeah, I'm going to dinner since we have a free night and all."

Wednesdays are relaxation days for crew and people like me who don't have to do too much.

He presses the elevator button and turns toward me. "Few and far between with such a busy race schedule. Who are you going to dinner with?"

All right, back to asking about the date.

"Sophie, and uh, Liam…and Jax." My execution is anything but smooth.

He remains silent as he checks out my outfit again, lingering on my legs before his eyes meet mine. I send a prayer for someone to get me out of here ASAP. The elevator takes forever, the lit-up button taunting me as I will it to come quicker.

"Hmm, I didn't get an invite." He pulls his phone out of his pocket and scrolls through it, searching for an invite that never happened. I use the opportunity to check him out. Powerful forearms taunt me, on full display because of his rolled-up button-down shirt, along with jeans that hug his tight ass and muscular legs. His dark hair is slicked back, not yet disturbed by his fingers. My teeth bite down on my bottom lip to suppress a groan.

His lips turn down as he locks his phone, making me feel both satisfied and sad for him. *Is it possible to have such a mix?* Noah screws up everything inside of me, including my common sense.

I shrug at his response, playing it off even though my heart races in my chest. "Maybe they thought you were busy. We'll be sure to invite you next time."

We won't because there can't be a next time.

The doors open. *Thank the Lord.* We both enter at the same time, brushing against each other. My body responds to the physical contact, desperately wanting more, but my brain makes a wise decision to situate myself in the opposite corner of the elevator.

"Yeah, maybe. Where are you having dinner then?" He runs a hand through his hair, now messing it up like I knew he would. I smirk at his signature style.

"I think it's called Bouquet. An expensive place I assume based on the outfits Sophie picked out." I bring his attention back to me. *Crap.*

He coughs. "Hmm." One word that has a heavy weight to it, stifling us in this stuffy box.

He remains silent for the rest of the descent. Air charges as movie scenes of couples hooking up in elevators flash through my mind. My body presses up against the side of the cart, my hands gripping onto the cool handlebar as I rid the dirty thoughts from my head. Our closeness and the delicious fumes of his cologne wreak havoc on my body.

He glances over at me one more time before the doors open up to the lobby and I dart out. I peek over my shoulder and give him a quick wave, my spine tingling at his devilish smile, feeling his eyes on me as I power-walk to the group. The glint in his eye and the smile on his face promise more.

That's a problem for future me.

Damn, I coined my new mantra.

We're two drinks into the night. And dare I say, the date is turning out to be a fun time.

Liam whispers a few sweet nothings into Sophie's ear. Every time he says something to her, she takes a chug of wine like a messed-up drinking game between the two of them.

Jax comes across as a nice guy. A bit withdrawn, but funny and edgy. Sophie's daddy comment pops up in my head because I mean, come on, the guy is sexy. But honestly, does she think he does that? She wouldn't say something that ridiculous if there wasn't a little bit of truth in it.

Jax has curly hair he inherited from a combination of his

"mum" and dad, who is one of the best black boxers from the United Kingdom. He gets his hazel eyes, sharp cheekbones, and pouty lips from his Swedish side. A total knockout with muscles and brains to match. I ask him about his family, but he closes himself off, switching the subject back to me.

Jax can check off most people's hot-guy boxes, but I can't figure out what doesn't work for me. *Maybe I don't like tattoos?* He tells me they cover his body, black ink peeking out from the collar of his button-down shirt. Intricate designs cover his knuckles and right hand. I ask about a couple of them, but there are too many to get into.

When he grabs my hand across the table, my body doesn't respond to it; it's the equivalent of holding a stranger's hand. I frown at the lack of flutters in my stomach or racing heartbeat. By the time we order our entrees, I've come to the conclusion that I don't feel a sexual connection, which is fine because it puts less pressure on me. Friendship sounds like a good idea.

"Oh, hi, guys. I heard you were out here tonight. I think my invite got lost in the mail."

My stomach flips at the sound of Noah's voice. I suppress the temptation to rub my eyes as though he'd disappear from my vision.

Heat rushes up my chest and neck. Liam and Jax look confused, and a surge of guilt rushes through me. Sophie kicks me under the table and I kick her back. I have no words to explain what is happening now, despite the questionable look she sends me.

Liam and Jax greet him reluctantly. Sophie and I get up from the table to give him quick hugs, except Noah holds on to me a second longer than necessary, a clear fuck-you to Jax. I choose to ignore him as I struggle to process everything.

What the hell. Why is he even here?

"So what gives? It's unlike both of you to not invite me somewhere."

My mouth falls open at Noah's boldness. I fight the urge to bolt from the table and make a run for it, deciding to deal with the consequences of my big mouth. How responsible of me.

Noah's hand rests on my chair, distracting me from the table, instead choosing to concentrate on how warmth radiates from his body. He pretends I didn't tell him about this double date. I feel like this is an episode of *The Twilight Zone*, the strange occurrences just part of the show.

"We're on a double date." Liam blushes while rubbing the back of his neck.

"Oh, a double date? Mind if I crash it for a second?" Noah doesn't mean to ask for permission, seeing as he commandeers the situation. He pulls up an empty seat next to Jax and me. I have a feeling he wants to stay for longer than a moment when he grabs my menu from my hands. My throat bobs as his fingers brush against mine.

I pull away from his touch and rub my temple with my hand, attempting to prevent a tension headache. Could be a good excuse to get out of this situation.

"Seeing as you already are sitting, does it even matter?" Liam fails to hide his annoyance.

My head snaps up and catches his stormy blue eyes. Sophie covers up her laugh with her hand, the muffled sound carrying past her fingers. At least one of us finds this amusing.

"Is Team McCoy trying to snag information from our Bandini ladies?" Noah rests his elbows on the table and places his chin on top of his knuckles. He doesn't pull off the innocent look well with his wicked gleam and smirk.

I speak up. "Because everything goes back to racing for you. It's not because they're interested in hanging out with us outside of a track, right? God forbid that were to happen." My statement silences the table as everyone stares at me.

Noah's lips gape before he clears his throat. "I didn't mean that. I was only joking around…" And there goes another hand through his hair. I gloat at his embarrassment because he deserves it after crashing our date and making dumb assumptions.

"I thought you would be busy since you usually are on Wednesdays. Jax was free and agreed to join. It's nothing personal." Liam returns to his usual pacifist self.

Everyone in the racing world is well aware of Noah's Wednesday ritual. Those days usually include models, fine dining, and an exclusive tour of his bedroom. Every tabloid knows it, and hell, I know it, no matter how much I want to ignore it.

"I would've canceled any plans to come. They're not that important anyway."

Wow. Way to make any of the girls you sleep with feel special. His wicked Wednesday ritual leaves a bad taste in my mouth.

Noah cocks his head to the side when he catches me scrunching my nose.

Jax and Liam offer him blank looks. They don't hide how much they want him to leave, but Noah steamrolls along, his presence authoritative.

"Maya, you're from Spain, right? Do you live near Barcelona?"

He acts like we are the only ones at the table, going as far as to turn his back on Jax.

"No, I live in Asturias. It's up north." I respond to the whole group, my eyes pleading with Sophie's, looking for an out. I'd wave my white napkin up in surrender if it meant escaping this situation.

"How is your English so good then?" Sophie finally chimes in. *That's my girl.*

I bark out a laugh. "I barely have an accent anymore because I went to an American school."

"You have a little accent. But it's cute," Noah says.

My cheeks warm at his comment. *Cute?* Since when has that word ever left Noah Slade's lips before? Sophie's wide eyes meet mine.

Jax and Liam stare at Noah. Even Noah looks surprised at what came out of his mouth while another hand runs through his hair. Someone should tell him about his noticeable tick because it gives him away.

We continue the conversation like Noah didn't act extremely out of character. I choose to overlook what he said, preferring my usual ignoring techniques with anything related to Noah. If it makes my heart race and my thighs clench, I pretend it never happened. Works like a charm. At least so far during our time at different Prix stops, except we never find ourselves this close together.

A muscular thigh brushes against mine under the table, his existence made known as a hum of energy courses up my leg. His proximity muddles my brain. I push my thighs together, half to avoid him, half to ease any aches that happen whenever he gets near me.

Every day I convince myself that I don't need someone like him in my life—a guy who breaks hearts as a side gig. I prefer to keep things simple and avoid problems. Label it a sixth sense, or an in-depth Google search. I still regret that one because nothing good ever comes from checking out famous people online.

We carry on with our dinner. Noah orders something to eat when our appetizers come out. Jax and Liam give up on the double-date idea at this point, filling me with relief.

Liam covers the check at the end of the night. I can only imagine how expensive this place is, even though I ordered something cheap on the menu. Hanging around guys who make more money in a year than I expect to make in a lifetime makes me uncomfortable.

Noah unexpectedly wraps his arm around my waist while we wait for the driver to pick us up at the valet area. My body jolts at the contact of our bodies pressing together. What has gotten into him today? The moment I think I have him all figured out, he does something like this, switching up the game on me.

"Maya and I can ride back together since we're staying at the same hotel." His hand possessively splays across my stomach, holding me hostage. I like it as much as I hate it. My body tries to wiggle away from him, but I stop once my ass rubs against his front.

I choose to ignore the bulge I feel pressing against me.

Nope. Not today, Satan. Stop tempting me.

"What a great idea. Can I tag along? I'm staying there too." Sophie shimmies on over to us, her green eyes humorously gazing at me.

Noah's arms squeeze me before he lets go. Sophie winks at me, and I'd give her a hug if it didn't draw attention to us.

Liam chuckles. "Trying to run away from me? This doesn't count as a date, thanks to Noah and his love for messing shit up. A bet's a bet. Unless…you want to back out? What did we say was the price for whoever quits? I can't remember. Maybe we can check your list."

Uh-oh. Liam doesn't seem like he will let Sophie off easily. Jax and Noah look confused at the mention of a list, but Sophie's nostrils flare as she glosses over the information.

"Mm hmm, I don't need money to keep me honest. I'm no quitter." She says a quick goodbye before walking toward the street.

"Thanks for dinner. We will have to do this another time." I give Liam and Jax quick hugs.

"Un-fucking-likely," Noah says the word low enough for only me to hear. I shake my head and walk away to join Sophie in the car.

This night did not go exactly how I thought it would.

CHAPTER TWELVE

Noah

I spend time relaxing on Bandini's deck after a successful qualifier. Barcelona's afternoon sun warms my skin as I lounge on a couch overlooking the ocean, blue waves rolling against the sandy coast while birds fly above.

It's purely coincidental when the Alatorre family shows up on the deck. I take the opportunity to watch Maya and Santiago hang out with their parents, curious to see what their dynamic is like with the people who raised them. Something heavy presses against my lungs at the idea of not having a family supporting me at a race. Must be nice to share the weekend with people you love.

I never had that. My dad usually shows up for the Sunday race and ditches after I place on the podium. He doesn't care to join me at different events, forgoing a post-race dinner unless he wants something. Manipulative motherfucker. My mother equally disappoints, recently contacting me to hook her up with tickets for her and her friends to see a Prix. The usual shit from them both.

Maya's mom looks like an older version of her daughter,

making it easy to see where Maya gets her good looks from. Her dad rocks Bandini's gear and a permanent smile while his gray hair peeks out from underneath a scarlet cap. Their parents seem to be loving the F1 experience.

I find it difficult to ignore the pang of jealousy swirling around in my chest, mixing in with sadness and wistfulness— an unwelcome feeling I want to push away. Maya's family seems simple yet extremely happy, making it hard to overlook how I grew up with a crappy dad and an absentee mom. And it annoys me because I never wanted for anything except attention, something fundamental yet robbed from me. The Alatorres' ordinariness and my shitty thoughts put me in a negative mental space.

My scowl lifts to a smile at the sight of Maya coming up to me. Her brown hair bobs in the usual ponytail I love to pull, held up with a scrunchie, along with ripped overalls and a white top. I don't miss the hint of cleavage. The outfit would look ridiculous on anyone, except Maya's sensual enough to pull it off. A fucked-up nineties girl grinning at me.

"Hey, want to come and meet my parents? They've asked about you a few times, wanting to know who Santi has to compete against every week." She focuses on her feet, absentmindedly pushing around invisible dirt with her sneaker.

If it puts a smile on your face…sure, why not.

I get up and introduce myself. Her mother pulls me in for a surprise hug, showing me how touchy Spanish people are.

"Maya shares such nice things about you. It was kind of you to help her with her videos."

Not what I expected to come out of her mouth. *Maya says good things?* I look over at the girl I can't get out of my head lately.

Her face turns red as she stares at her sneakers again, making my small smile break out into a full-blown grin.

"It's no problem. I had fun helping her out."

"She's lucky to have you around. Especially since she's all alone when Santi is busy. We tell him he works too hard."

I doubt her mother would have the same opinions about me if she knew half the thoughts I have about her daughter.

Her dad glares at me like he wants to assess me from the inside out. He acts like he can read the expression on my face, his scrutiny and deep brown eyes making me shift uncomfortably.

"Take care of my little girl." Hidden meaning fills his statement. I don't try to get into his daughter's pants, I just think about it a lot. But I've been respectful compared to the way I act with girls I want to fuck. He should be grateful.

Call me an entitled prick. Fuck if I care.

"Santi's not the one who needs help because he always was our good kid. Maya, on the other hand—" her mother brushes a stray lock of hair out of Maya's face—"trouble. But the good kind with such a big heart. She's a little rebellious like her dad." Maya's mom smiles up at her husband with love and affection.

I chuckle. "What is the good kind of trouble? I'm curious how I can sell that one to my PR team when I mess up again."

"She always has good intentions, but they sometimes miss their mark. Overall she's the best daughter anyone could ask for." Maya's mom gazes at me with the warmth only a mother can have.

"Mom," Maya groans. "Stop talking like I'm not right here." Her honey-brown eyes look at me for the first time in a while. "Ignore her. She loves telling ridiculous stories."

"Do you know she used to steal Santi's kart and ride it around the neighborhood? She was only five years old. Santi exploded when she put a couple of unicorn stickers on the steering wheel."

I barely contain a laugh as Maya rubs her face, hiding behind small hands.

"Ugh, not a good moment. Santi was mad at me for weeks." Maya's lips turn down.

"You liked karting?" I pull on her ponytail to get her attention.

Santi's eyes narrow in on my hand while her dad scowls at me. *Message received.*

"I did it a few times on the side, but it was more Santi's thing. I liked to do whatever he did, including beating boys his age." She smiles up at me. Damn my chest tightens at her smile, proof of how much of a sucker I am for them lately.

"How about the time she tried to forge her middle-school report card?" Santi fails to control his amusement.

Maya's cheeks turn into two bright red blobs.

"Maya Alatorre, did you live a life hardened by crime?" I scoff.

"Oh, I remember this one since her mother made me punish her after. Always got stuck disciplining. She actually took her report card out of the mailbox and tried to white-out her bad conduct grade. She sealed the envelope with a steamer before putting it back. If we hadn't been so angry, we would have been impressed. She cried when I took away her cell phone for a week." Her dad joins in on the fun.

Maya looks everywhere but at me.

"You guys are literally the worst. Santi, if you keep it up, I'll tell Mom and Dad about the time you drove their car at fourteen because you wanted to go do donuts outside."

Oh, shit. The looks on her parents' faces tell me they don't know about this story. Maya's statement shuts up Santiago quicker than I ever could.

He puts his hands up in a mock surrender.

"Truce. No need to fight so dirty."

The idea of Maya fighting dirty entices me.

Fuck.

I banish those thoughts, choosing to focus on having a normal conversation with my teammate's parents. We all end up having a good time together until my dad shows up on the deck, sneaky like a snake with enough venom to match. I am surprised he showed up earlier than race day, a rarity that makes me regret skillfully avoiding his phone calls for two days.

The time we spend apart never seems long enough. Cold eyes land on me, two blue orbs as inviting as skinny-dipping in the Arctic Ocean. He keeps his dark hair slicked back and his suit perfectly pressed with not a wrinkle in sight. To others he comes off as welcoming, but his deceptiveness covers up all the darkness simmering beneath his skin.

Maya eyes him curiously. My dad ignores her family, passing by them without a glance. He comes to greet me, giving me a pat on the back, acting happy to see me. Nicholas Slade couldn't give less of a shit if he tried. But since he cares about a show and his image, my life acts as a side project to keep him busy from decaying during retirement.

He watches Maya's family suspiciously, paying attention to them for the first time by assessing each of them. Competitors getting along is his worst nightmare. And for a moment I forgot Santiago and I are just that, talking with his family like we don't have a rivalry.

It felt nice. To be the three of us hanging out with their parents, the Prix on the backburner while they got to know me. Parents who actually seemed curious to ask me questions and learn about the man outside of a Bandini car.

"Son, a second of your time?" The tick in my dad's jaw tells me everything words won't.

"I'll see you all later at the event." I throw the statement over my shoulder as I follow my dad toward the suites.

"You ignored my calls. I fly all the way out here for you and this is how you treat me? I expect better from my son."

Right, we both know why he comes out to these events.

I bite back a snarky comment. "I've been busy qualifying and getting ready for tomorrow. It's good that you found me between events." *Lies.* But I've learned from the biggest fraud of them all.

"Yeah. We need to come up with a plan for tomorrow."

We enter my private room. My dad settles into one of the couches, a dark cloud against the white walls of the room as he sucks the energy from me. He grabs one of the red pillows and props himself up against it.

"How are you going to go about winning the race?" He jumps into it.

I haven't seen him in almost a year, and he doesn't even ask how I am, unsurprising, but still grating on my nerves.

"By racing the best I can?" I meet with strategists and engineers for hours each week to prepare for a Prix. Don't need his shitty two cents.

"It's Santiago's home race. That means it's a big one for him. You should have seen his parade today. Thousands showed up."

"That's awesome for him. A home Prix is usually the best for those racers. I can't wait for the Austin one, to go back to the States and eat Southern food." My mouth waters at the idea of barbecue food.

"Well, you obviously need to wipe the floor with him tomorrow. There's nothing worse than losing in your hometown," my dad sneers.

I struggle to hide my irritation. Racing fuels a passion of mine while easing the edginess inside of me. Yeah, it's a job, but it's much more because I enjoy it and compete against the best. My dad sucks the fun and excitement out of anything, making everything a rivalry. No wonder he had no friends back in his day.

"Sure, Dad. I'll try my best."

"You better. I'm here and the press will eat that shit up. They love a good father-son moment." He treats me like a shiny accessory.

"I need to get going. It's a busy night before the race tomorrow." I throw him a wave before taking off.

Race day in Barcelona. The crowds bounce around in the stands, charged up with excitement. Machines buzz, drills hum, and computers beep in the pit. Sophie's dad tests out the team radio in my ear to ensure we have an open line of communication.

I zip up my racing suit and put on my flame-retardant headgear. I look down at my helmet, savoring the moment of representing Bandini's brand and appeasing my fans. This life is all I know, and it brings me comfort to put on my helmet. *Honey,*

I'm home.

Crew members push my car toward my grid location. Liam has pole position, while I'm second, and Santiago's third.

Before a race, I spend hours studying the track, making sure I've memorized all of the turns. A total of sixty-six laps made up of sixteen turns stand between me and the Spanish Grand Prix's podium.

The race kicks off with a bang. An American team driver crashes his car into the barrier on the first turn, taking down two other drivers with him. What a shitshow as metal flies around and cars run into one another.

Liam holds first place for the first few laps. We play a game between the two of us, me trying to pull up to his side and him being aggressive on the turns. Sweat trickles down my neck as my skin warms from the heat of the engine. I take a couple sips of my drink to stay hydrated because nothing is worse than getting woozy as I drive around at top speeds.

I narrowly avoid clipping Liam's tire at one of the sharper turns. He pulls away from the curve, flashing me a glove-clad middle finger. His rattled state makes me chuckle. The car continues hauling ass down the racetrack as I hit a main straight. An opportunity for overtaking presents itself when Liam lets down his defenses for a split second. I pass him at one of the turns. My foot presses on the accelerator, allowing my car to pick up speed and race down the straights, leaving Liam in my rearview mirror. *Too bad, so sad.*

Fans wave their Spanish flags and big face cutouts of Santiago in the air. They blur past me as I continue down the track.

Negative thoughts fill my head about the crap my dad said

yesterday. I don't want to be a teammate who steps on others, trying to one-up them every time, acting like my father. No one likes a piece of shit. The type who takes everything, not caring how it affects the other person. Santi's had a rough go starting out this season. His rashness fucks me up, but he wants to win as much as anyone else.

Losing in Austin would suck. How disappointing—all those fans showing up, hoping you represent them well but falling short.

Fuck me, I hate thinking while racing.

After a pit stop, I make my way back up the race ranks from fourth to first again. I hold onto my first-place spot for another twenty-six laps.

"Noah, Santiago's gaining speed behind you. He's in second now. For the love of God, don't crash into each other at a turn." My radio relays the team principal's message.

"Copy. What happened to Liam?" I growl at his words because I'm not crashing into anyone today.

"Don't worry about that now. Santiago is behind you by about five seconds. Be careful not to let him overtake you."

"Got it, thanks."

My defensive position at the head of the pack takes minimal effort to keep. Blurring crowds welcome me as I pass the starting point again, a wave of red and gold colors flying by me, matching the Spanish flag the Alatorres had earlier. Their cheers get louder as Santiago passes them while he closes the gap behind me. A few seconds away from me now. If I were Santiago, I would do anything to win this race.

He tails me the whole time, waiting for me to slip up.

The image of Maya and her family coming all this way to see him succeed flies through my mind. *Shit.* I try to push away the thoughts, but the invasive images don't let up, accompanied by sounds of Maya's laughs and cheers. My hands grip the steering wheel as I think about the sacrifices his parents made for his career. Sacrifices Maya made living in his shadow. Never being one to steal the spotlight, preferring to dance around in the dark while her brother gets all the attention. Unfortunately for her, people like me thrive in the shadows.

Fuck. I never think this much during a race, like ever, because thinking makes me stupid. Thinking leads me to come up with my rash, selfless plan in the first place.

A fucking anomaly.

On the sixtieth lap, I let down my defenses more. I do it slowly, making sloppier turns, allowing more space for anyone to overtake me, while I still stay in control of my car. Messing up too quickly would draw negative attention to myself.

"Noah, is everything all right? Santiago's gaining speed. He wants to overtake you. Make your turns tighter."

"Copy. I think something's off with the car, but I can't figure it out. Do you see anything on the screens?" I sure as shit know there is nothing wrong, but I have to milk it to the point where I believe my own words. Fans can tune into my team radio via live television.

"Nothing over here. Can you describe what's happening? We can figure it out for you." My engineer sounds hopeful.

"Not really. I think there's something wrong with the steering wheel. It feels loose." The lie leaves my lips easily as I make another bad turn.

"Got it. Just keep going and we'll figure it out later." They all buy it, my authentic display working on the team. I still want to land on the podium anyway.

By lap sixty-four, I make worse turns that leave myself open for an overtaking. To no one's surprise, Santiago passes me at one of the corners, rattling my car as he zooms by.

My lips lift at the corners.

The crowd goes wild, releasing deafening roars when Santiago crosses the finish line first, red smoke billowing up into the air from canisters. I solidify my second place on the podium when I get the next checkered flag.

Better luck next time.

Santiago's family celebrates behind the barrier next to the podiums as they watch us on the stage. His parents light up the entire stage with their smiles alone. Maya has decked herself out in Bandini gear, with a Spanish flag wrapped around her as she dances around to the music streaming from the stage speakers. Watching her happy makes my heart clench like a chick.

Usually, when I meet a woman, the first thing that attracts me is a set of perky tits, a tight ass, and seductive lips. But for the first time in my life, I'm interested in someone for a different reason. With Maya, the most beautiful thing about her is how her eyes light up with happiness when she grins, an infectious smile that makes my lips turn up every time. Her beam is hands down one of my favorite things. A bubble of positive energy, dancing in circles without a care in the world.

Does she have a great body? Sure.

But at this moment, her smile draws me to her. I want to keep them all to myself and bottle them up for the bad days. Don't get me started on her laughs. I feel them all the way down to my cock, every single time.

Champagne sprays all around me, but I barely pay attention, too enamored by her.

And fuck, it scares me.

I smirk one last time at the sight of her before turning back to the rest of the crowd. They chant my name, and although it feels great to hear them, nothing beats the smile on Maya's face as she watches us.

My dad paces the motorhome's lobby after the winners' ceremony. He follows me to the private suite area, his agitation evident in his jerky steps. The sounds of our shoes against the smooth floor distract me. I pull him away from others because we don't need an audience for his explosion. He enters the suite first, and before I have a chance to close the door, he shoves me toward the center of the room. His dirty move catches me off guard. My feet trip on the slick tile, but I right myself before hitting a couch.

So this is how today is going to go.

"What the fuck, Noah? You call that racing?" His voice echoes off the walls. *Someone's cranky about my second-place win.*

"Last time I checked we called it racing. But maybe the concepts have changed since you last drove. It's been a while."

My dad's chest heaves up and down as his eyes dart around, wild and uncontrolled. It's the same look he gave me every time I failed to land on a shitty kart podium or crashed my F2 car. A glare he saved for our alone time in his office before he smacked my ass into the next day. Lucky for us bruises aren't visible when you wear race suits daily. Not a single scar was left on my skin except for the mangled remains of my heart, a mistrusting organ ruined by the man before me. A cliché of the worst kind.

"I don't sponsor this team to see a shitty performance like that from my own son. I don't buy your crap with the steering wheel. All the tests came back fine; nothing seemed loose." His voice gets louder as his agitation grows. My face remains flat because I don't feed into his anger. The fallout from his rage is a lesson I don't wish to revisit anytime soon, at least not in this lifetime.

I look over his shoulder and catch the suite door ajar, a shocked Maya staring back at me through the crack with a hand covering her mouth. Acting like Spanish Nancy Drew piecing together what I did.

Just a bad day in racing. Steering wheel problems happen all the time.

"There was something off. Hopefully they find out what happens before the next race, that way I can get first place next time."

"Bullshit! Don't try to pull something over on me, acting all coy. You know I basically fund your career here. People would kill for your seat. I could replace you like that." He snaps his fingers.

"Go ahead. I'm sure McCoy would offer me a seat in a heartbeat. That team probably pays more than Bandini does anyway. Wouldn't you like that?"

A resounding crack fills the small room as my head snaps to the side. My dad fucking backhanded me. I try my hardest not to start something with him, my breaths becoming labored as my self-control teeters. Maya's gasp and the whooshing sound in my ears make it difficult to make out any other noises.

I wipe away blood trickling down my mouth. It feels like I'm ten years old again, getting third place in a kart race, my dad pissed and taking his anger out on me. *Looks like old tricks never die.*

"Oh Father, I thought we were past this. You should put more meaning behind a hit like that; maybe age is getting to you."

"I thought we were moving on from your shitty attitude, but I guess I was wrong. Fix yourself up. You look like a fucking mess."

Thank fuck Maya has the foresight to disappear because my dad barrels through, ending our crappy conversation. I take a deep breath before looking into the hall, surprised yet relieved to find it empty, a nosy Maya long gone.

CHAPTER THIRTEEN

MAYA

Holy shit.

Holy fucking shit.

I can't get the image out of my head of Noah's dad hitting him because how does someone hit their thirty-year-old child?

My brain runs a million miles an hour, unable to keep up with the surplus of information. The steering wheel problems, the race, his dad freaking hitting him across the face. The way Noah's eyes looked into mine, sad and so damn lost. It gutted me to see him like that. Stripped down to nothing more than a man with weaknesses and a fractured past. Nothing like the cocky man I see daily, unaffected and disinterested in the people around him.

My family shows up in Santi's suite five minutes after the Slades' fight. No one notices my silence or how my leg bounces up and down while I mull over what I saw: a family dynamic no one knows about. I took an Intro to Psych course, and I know the stats about parents hitting their kids. This is not a one-time thing, a fluke because of a messed-up steering wheel or a lost race.

Noah's dad is a messed-up man who lives through his son.

I spend time with my family before excusing myself. Santi looks at me weirdly before returning his attention to my parents, their wide smiles bright after his success today.

I go to the kitchen and grab an ice pack, the cold plastic numbing my hand as I walk up to Noah's suite. My stomach rolls from nerves because I don't want to overstep after his bad day. Another deep breath expands my lungs. I wait for a moment, unsure if I should knock on his door.

I dig deep and lightly rap my knuckles.

The door opens a crack. A moody Noah looks down at me, blue eyes shadowed by a Bandini hat situated low on his face, a poor attempt at hiding his reddened skin.

"Hey, I come bearing gifts." I jiggle the ice pack. No point in hiding what I saw earlier.

Noah pushes his door open wide, and I pass through. His suite has the same layout as Santi's with plain white walls and red accents with Bandini's logo covering one wall. He takes a seat on one of the white couches, grabbing the extended ice pack while I take up a spot on the opposite side.

"Come to admit you suck at eavesdropping?"

My cheeks flush at his tactlessness. "Well, sorry." Might as well apologize even though they left the door open.

"And sorry you saw that. I should have closed the door, but he surprised me for the first time in a while." Noah's words tug at me.

His statement is a lot to unpack, and I don't understand why he apologizes. My head pounds as I wrap my mind around Noah's toxic history with his dad.

"You don't need to be sorry. He's a total ass. You warned me a while ago, but I guess I didn't think it was that bad."

Noah winces as he presses the ice pack against his face. "No one knows." He lets out a deep and shaky sigh. My stomach dips with unease at his lowered defenses, a rare sighting for someone as confident and self-assured as him.

"I'm going to go out on a limb here and assume this isn't the first time he's hit you."

Noah's blank gaze reveals enough.

"How long has he been doing this? That's not right. It's not how parents should be, especially at your age. You could kick his ass into next week."

"A while, but I'd rather no one finds out, so let's keep it between us."

My heart cracks at his admission. I can't imagine growing up with someone rude, condescending, and disgustingly competitive. Hard to picture what Noah's life was like. He puts on an image for others, but is this what he deals with once the Prix lights shut off?

Santi and I don't share his same problems because our parents have always treated us with respect and love. Growing up without wealth could be a better option. I live a happy life, and no one holds money over my head. Not Santi, who pays for a lot of things. Even though I make money from YouTube ads and sponsorships, the funds don't have the same weight as an F1 contract.

"I won't tell anyone. But I don't understand why you cover up for him." A wave of nausea hits me as I consider how people act around his dad, idolizing him as a racing legend. Fans call Noah the American Prince. One stuck wearing a crown heavy from deceit and expectations. No matter how much Noah dislikes his dad, he lives in his legacy.

"Who would believe me? He's a racing icon and a big sponsor for this team. People see what they want to see anyway." His head faces up to the ceiling. Liquid from the ice pack drips onto his race suit, running down the red fabric like tears. *How symbolic.*

"I don't know. Anyone. There's always someone filming something. Cameras catch everything nowadays."

I recognize how I saw Noah how I wanted, believing the show he puts on for everyone. Smug, overconfident, rebellious. My chest tightens at my quick judgment.

"Please leave it alone." His voice has a sense of finality to it. I drop that part of the conversation because I don't want to push him too far when he opens up to me.

I choose to address the second issue because I can't help myself. "Is it true what he said? About your steering wheel?"

He lets out another deep sigh. "Don't trust everything you hear. My dad gets pissy when I don't place first. My steering wheel was loose, no matter what people say." Words leave through gritted teeth.

"But you were in the lead for like forty laps. Defensiveness is your thing."

"Maya." His gravelly voice captures my attention, making me look up into his intense blue eyes. My name rolls off his tongue, hitting me in the heart and below the belt at once. "Drop it. Forget what he said. Your brother won the Spanish Grand Prix fair and square. You should be happy for him instead of thinking up conspiracy theories."

His eyes dart to the side as he avoids my gaze for a second too long.

Holy shit. Noah totally threw the race. Why would he lose?

We sit together in silence. I attempt to work through these new revelations, getting lost in my own world, not noticing how he gets up and sits next to me.

He clasps my hand in his, ice pack long forgotten. My pulse quickens at the contact. I tell myself it must be because his hand is freezing from the ice, the cool touch jolting my body. It has nothing to do with our connection. *Right?*

I try to pull my hand away, but he holds on, his calloused fingers brushing against mine. My skin tingles where his thumb lazily rubs against my hand.

"Listen. Let's forget what my dad said. No need to give attention to a piece of shit who gets mad when I don't place first. He's irrelevant and barely shows up anymore, that is unless it's convenient for him and his bank account."

"Uh, yeah. Sure." I barely pay attention to what he says. My eyes stay pinned on his tan hand engulfing my small one, his thick thumb brushing against my bony knuckle in a mindless pattern.

The room warms as tension thickens, choking me as it wraps around my head and my heart. His silent confession about the race feels like too much between us. I don't want to share secrets together, opening myself up even more to him, a point we can't turn back from.

But he doesn't need to admit anything to me. He threw his chance at winning today, from a quick gaze and a bob of his Adam's apple. Label it a sixth sense for bullshit.

Relief fills me when his hand stops caressing mine. I finally breathe easier, gaining the mental clarity to tug my hand away.

"I better get going. I'm going to dinner with my family before the after-party. Maybe we will see you there."

I lean over him and give him a kiss on his non-red cheek. His breath catches at the touch while my lips tingle at the contact, lingering a second too long.

I bounce out of my seat and reach for the door handle before he can react.

He remains sitting on the couch, unphased, except for a tiny lift at the corner of his mouth. If I didn't know him then I would have missed it. But we've spent two months together, and I've been learning his ticks, the tells he gives when no one watches him.

"See you later. Thanks...for coming over. And the ice pack." He repeats the same jiggle I did earlier. I laugh at his ridiculousness, blue eyes lighting up when they land on me.

"No problem." I don't bother looking over my shoulder as I softly shut the door.

Noah doesn't show up to the main after-party. I hate to admit it feels off without him there, missing how he entertains me while Santi and Sophie are busy.

During the party, it hits me how much trouble I'm in. A cardinal sin has been broken.

I think I *like* Noah Slade.

CHAPTER FOURTEEN

MAYA

Monaco. The ultimate racing Prix to attend. Bandini's week is packed with events before the world-famous Monaco Grand Prix, known as one of the oldest races in F1 history, fueled by wealth and luxury. Celebrities from all over the world come to attend. Yachts litter the sea, glittering under the bright sun as I observe from our hotel room.

The Bandini team schedules a week packed with boat trips, interviews, galas—you name it, they have it. Which means I get to go, too. My supportive sister role has no bounds, and although I usually try to avoid these types of events, I don't complain about this race week.

Because not even I can resist a party with one of the Kardashians.

Monte Carlo is the coolest place ever. Pictures don't do it justice; they're unable to capture the picturesque shoreline and old-world feel. I can't believe Santi wants to buy an apartment here. We picked one out earlier in the week before he got busy, a modern two-bedroom overlooking the Mediterranean Sea.

I can tell the stress is getting to him. He seems edgier than usual, getting heated at smaller things, like when I left my makeup all over the bathroom counter. Monaco's race is a big deal and he feels pressure from Bandini to perform well. It doesn't help that this Prix happens to be one of Noah's best, a place where his racing skills shine.

What exactly am I doing on a Tuesday in Monaco?

I'm on a boat.

Bragging isn't something I usually do. But come on. This is Monaco... By boat, I mean one that is at least a hundred feet long, the white fiberglass gleaming under the hot summer day. But I don't ask the owner about footage because that's rude and not high class.

And I want to be posh and proper this week.

My body lies on a lounge chair on the front deck of the McFloating Mansion. I already toured the four different floors, drank a cocktail on the back deck, and did a vlog interview with my brother while breathing in the crisp ocean breeze. Talk about living my best life this week.

I grab a sunscreen bottle out of my bag because my skin is warming under the intense sun. Noah, a man with impeccable timing, decides to plant himself in a lounge chair next to me.

"Avoiding the sun?" He taps at the pink bottle in my hand. Dark sunglasses make it difficult to see and read the emotions swirling within his blue irises. To be honest, his whole look unsettles me. His preppy bathing suit looks shorter than regular swim trunks, accentuating muscular thighs and calves. Plus, he's lost his shirt somewhere between the cocktail hour and now. My eyes flick across his tan, sculpted body before focusing on the deck.

"No tan is worth aging when I'm already naturally golden." My heart quickens when he leans in closer.

His hand brushes against mine, causing an intense buzz of energy, one that never goes away no matter how many times his skin touches mine. He grabs the sunscreen bottle right out of my hand.

"Uh. I can handle that!" I sound breathy. *Can he tell?*

His cocky grin tells me that yes, he can. I grab my sunglasses from the top of my head and pull them down onto my face, creating a barrier because two can play this game. An immature move I have no problem with.

"Turn around. I'll help you."

Is it possible to die of a heart attack at twenty-three? What are the stats?

I pull out my cellphone, desperate to check.

"What on earth are you so interested in now? Every time I'm around you, you're always doing something fidgety."

I want to disappear in the lounge cushions or melt away into the sea. He's onto me.

He plucks my phone straight out of my hands.

"Excuse me! Hand it back. Now." I use my best mom voice, but it lacks the desired effect I want, making Noah chuckle instead. *Going to suck at punishing my kids one day.*

He ignores me, choosing to swat away my grabby hands.

"*What are the chances of dying of a heart attack at twenty-three?* Seriously, you're googling this? I didn't know I had such an effect on you. You flatter me."

I shoot him my best scowl, but he just laughs. A full throw-your-head-back laugh, and if I weren't peeved, I'd find it extremely attractive. *Who am I kidding?* I do. Annoyed or not, this man is fine. Handsome and absolutely fuckable.

I take advantage of his moment of weakness and snatch my phone back.

He rotates his finger in a motion to get things moving here, his previous task no longer put off. I reluctantly turn and lie down stomach first on the reclined lounge chair. Noah sits by my side, the cushion dipping under his weight as his thigh presses against my body.

He toys with my red bikini strap before squirting the sunscreen bottle. "You look good in red."

Does his voice sound huskier? Is it just me? I can't see his face since I'm looking out at the Mediterranean Sea.

My body jerks when the cold liquid hits my back. I lie to myself, chalking up my goosebumps to the cold sunscreen. Not because of Noah rubbing sunscreen all over my back. *Nope.*

I tell myself so many lies about Noah that I convince myself to go to the local confessional. A priest will have a field day with this type of stuff, offering sage advice before sending me off with at least five Hail Marys. I can't blame myself. Noah has the sex appeal of about one hundred men combined, making this whole process hard.

My arms grow heavy as he continues to rub lotion into my back; I'm enjoying the feeling of being cared for while Noah's hands caress me. His strokes leave a path of warmth behind them. I let out an embarrassing moan that I try to cover up with a cough.

His laugh—all throaty and deep—makes my body sing. He acts like this is natural, just the two of us hanging out on our private yacht, enjoying a casual day on the water. We might as well be because not one person passes by to save me.

He can't see my face, thankfully, because my cheeks sear at his unrelenting touch.

And that's not the only thing heating up.

My core pulses at the attention from him. How long has it been since I've slept with a guy? Maybe my junior year of college? My brain draws up a blank, which I don't find to be a good sign. I decide this must be my issue with him. Not because he knocks off every attractive thing on my checklist.

Sure.

His hands move to the dip in my lower back and I groan as they knead my skin.

I'm so very fucked.

My body hums with excitement at Noah's touch, not understanding why this is all so very, very wrong.

He pulls me out of my thoughts.

"Did I tell you that you look beautiful today?"

Nope, you didn't. But I'll take it now, with my head pressed against the comfy lounge chair as his hands rub my back. I don't think he has a drop of sunscreen left on his fingers.

"Hmm. Not sure."

Okay, good job. That didn't sound half as desperate as your moan.

"You look stunning today." He ramps up his charm.

He shocks me by doing the unthinkable. I suck in a breath as his lips press against the curve of my neck. *Swoon.* It takes everything in me to not bolt from the chair. My fingernails claw into the seat fabric to hold still, leaving indentations to match the ones Noah burns into my brain.

My body feels on fire and my most intimate places are worse off. How is it possible to get turned on by sunscreen application? There should be a warning label on the back of the bottle for this. Screw damaging rays, this shit with Noah burns me up worse than any SPF below fifty.

He lets out another chuckle that prompts me to turn around and face him.

He looks unaffected, and it ticks me off. I check for signs. His eyes remain hidden, and his face looks neutral. My eyes surpass his golden chest and abs because I have absolutely no time or restraint for that.

I smirk at the bulge in his bathing suit. His cheeky grin makes me want to kiss it off his face, replacing the humor in his eyes with lust.

Our attraction threatens our semblance of normalcy with one another. Not sure what to make of this. I need time to process, concoct an avoidance plan, set up defenses against the ultimate playboy. This will take effort. I may even need Sophie's help with reinforcements because plans are her thing; she's been successfully avoiding her attraction to Liam like a plague.

Thou shall not bang your brother's teammate rings in my ears, a new mantra for me by now. Yes, my mantra list continues to grow, but you haven't met Noah Slade. You don't understand how sensuality seeps from his pores. Never underestimate the power of pheromones and wicked smiles.

He even makes sunscreen application into some kind of foreplay.

Guilt rushes through me because I don't want to be attracted to Noah. Although he does nice things for me, he stills acts like a dick to Santi. I'm a walking contradiction at the moment, battling the pros and cons, weighing catastrophic situations if Noah and I got together.

Noah gets up from my chair, placing the offensive sunscreen bottle next to me. A wave of uncertainty passes through me. Part of me wants to make him stay while the other part of me wants him to go. My brain needs to digest this information. His boner distracts me enough, drawing my attention to it, the bulge looking much larger as he stands. I need it removed from my vicinity ASAP.

He tugs on my ponytail. I smile up at him because somehow it's become our thing.

How can he be so hot yet so cute at the same time? Troubling.

"Don't think too hard. You'll be stuck battling the 'what if you dos' and the 'what if you don'ts' instead of living in the moment. Call me if you need my help again. I'll be around." He gives me one last cocky smile before disappearing below the deck.

I let out a deep sigh.

I'm so royally screwed, by the F1's American Prince no less.

I can lie and pretend I'm a mature woman. I can say I've kept it cool in front of Noah and my brother. But I haven't. Why bother lying when I suck at it anyway?

My butt plants itself on the bench inside of a local priest's confessional. My mother loves how I've found time to go to church while in Monaco. The priest wishes me lots of luck with my life and tells me to go to Mass more. It feels good to let it all out, even to a man of the cloth, like my own therapist on the road. I'd describe the experience as cathartic. No shame as I spill my guts to him, letting it all out in a confessional booth.

Surprisingly, he sends me off with three Hail Marys, two Our Fathers, and a bottle of holy water to cleanse myself whenever I have impure thoughts. *Confessions come with goody bags—who knew?*

I start a new Avoiding Noah campaign. It goes strong for two days, thanks to Sophie's obsession with lists and plans.

Two long days. If anyone understood the amount of effort it takes to avoid him, they would be impressed. He and my brother have to do everything together in Monaco since a united team looks great to the public.

I spend a lot of me-time in our Monaco hotel avoiding parties and cocktail hours. To pass the time, I book myself a massage. It doesn't yield the same physical reaction as Noah's back rub, but I attribute it to having a woman massage therapist. She doesn't physically do it for me. Santi covers the cost, but unbeknownst to him, he basically rewards me for my good efforts of avoiding Noah. I take one for the team here.

I would count my evading techniques as successful, at least until my brother asks if I can attend a fashion show that apparently is a big deal. An A-list event I should be grateful to have an invite to.

Santi makes me watch him practice his runway walk to make sure he looks good. He loves the limelight, but not this kind— with the expectation to model. And I do not blame him at all. If I did a show like this, I would definitely fall flat on my face before rolling into the pool.

"Do you really need me there?" *Please say no.* I can only execute so much control around Noah. And once you add a tux element into the mix, it's a recipe for disaster.

I feel like my brother sets me up for failure here.

"I never thought I'd have to convince you to go to this. Everyone wants a ticket." He pouts at me, a bit extra for his standards. It impresses me yet flusters me all the same because he uses my own strategies to get me to agree.

I can't get out of this when his words sound absolute. So I engage in the next step of a desperate woman's plan.

I bargain.

"Can Sophie come—if she doesn't have an invite already—because I don't want to be alone during it." *I don't trust myself,* I mentally add before putting my two hands together in a silent plea.

He texts away on his phone, searching for the answer to my question, unable to resist my charm.

"All right, I got her a ticket too. But you both have to behave because I won't be out there protecting you from the old men."

"But I've always wanted a sugar daddy!" I whine while throwing my hands up in the air.

He throws a pillow at my face. Santi may have won this battle, but I'll win the war.

CHAPTER FIFTEEN

MAYA

"I can't believe you scored us tickets for the fashion show. It's one of the biggest events of the year." Sophie bounces up and down in a chair. We went on a shopping spree earlier to buy dresses for the event because she claimed what we had wasn't enough.

"Oh, believe it. We better finish getting ready. The car's coming in twenty." I don't feel guilty about using Sophie as a cockblocker because her enjoyment rubs off on me.

Two birds, please meet my one stone.

I run a hand down the silky material of my blue dress. Looking at it now, I realize the blue matches the color of Noah's eyes.

Fuck me. A fashion equivalent of a Freudian slip.

I grab my heels and book it out of the hotel room, wanting to get this night over with.

Sophie can't stop chattering the whole car ride to the oceanfront destination. "Did you know all the guys will be modeling tonight?"

Can't say I did.

"Are you excited for anyone in particular?" I want to pull any information about her thing with Liam. Sophie hides her attraction well, but I catch the briefest glances she gives him. She tells me they're "just friends" ever since she pulled that card on him after our fail of a double date.

"Mm, no. Such an odd question. Are you?" She stares at me. *Point taken.*

We arrive at the fashion show location soon after. A cross-shaped stage floats in the center of a pool, lit from within and emitting a purplish glow. We make out different yachts anchored out in the ocean. The event bustles with enjoyment from the attendees while waiters walk around with food and drinks. Music streams from speakers around us.

"Let's get a drink. Time to get this party started." Sophie pulls me toward the bar area.

She handles ordering. "Can we have four shots of your finest tequila?"

My eyebrows rise. *Two shots already?* "I don't want to end up a blubbering drunk mess tonight. Tequila makes me embarrassing." Hard to forget how I cried in a bathroom. I blame the Jonas Brothers and their fourth band member, José.

"Relax." She pats my arm for good measure. "We can get buzzed now so we can enjoy the show. We won't have more until the alcohol wears off."

She slides the two glasses toward me and we knock back the shots.

Sophie was right. This fashion show is way better with a buzz. Guys strut their stuff down the stage, each looking handsome in their different evening wear. I even whistle when Noah comes out. Not my fault he looks beyond fuckable in his tux, which calls out to me.

Whoops. This is the alcohol talking. A slip of the tongue. I do not want to fuck Noah Slade. I nudge Sophie when Liam comes out, his body pressed against the tailor-made suit and his blonde hair slicked back in his usual style. He even points her out of the crowd and sends her a wink. That one is a flirt, and honestly, I have no idea how Sophie resists him because her eyes light up whenever she sees him.

Once the show finishes, Sophie and I get the party started. Sophie bribes the DJ to let us behind his setup. She spins the turntables while I pick out songs from a playlist. We get a few people to bounce up and down, creating a small mosh pit at the center of the dance floor. I don't think I've laughed any harder than I have with her.

A Bandini rep eventually pulls us away from the DJ area after we play our third reggaeton song. Apparently, it's not well-suited for the elite crowd.

Two older guys ask us to dance and we agree. Not exactly my type but the haze of alcohol says yes for me as they pull us toward the dance floor. Sophie and I aren't drunk. Only a little on the tipsy side, still managing to stay put together.

A crowd of dancing couples engulfs us. I dance around with a middle-aged man who has gelled-back hair and smells strongly of alcohol. My eyes search for Sophie between songs, but I can't find her. The man's hand creeps its way toward my ass at the same moment I conveniently step on his toes. Hard. He lets out a yelp while I fake an apology.

Music shifts to a classic salsa song DJs play at our clubs back home. A shadow looms over my dance partner. By now, I can recognize the reason for the tingle in my spine anywhere. Two months of resisting him does that. Strobe lights basking him in an ominous glow, my naughty knight in a shining tux sizes up my pervy dance partner.

"Mind if I cut in?" Noah's irritated voice carries over the music. *Or am I hearing things?* Alcohol confuses my brain.

The man sputters out a reply as he lets me go. Noah grabs my hand while placing another at the dip in my back right above my ass. It feels way less invasive than my previous dance partner, like his hand should be there. Plus, Noah doesn't smell like whiskey and old money. He needs to bottle up his scent and sell it on the mass market. I would buy a few bottles and spray it on my pillows at night, not creepily of course.

I smile at the idea. *Real mature, Maya.*

He shakes his head like he can't believe the sorry state I'm in at the moment. He and I both.

I place a hand on his shoulder. His tux feels smooth under my fingertips, the strained material pressing against his muscles.

"I thought you were avoiding me because I haven't seen you at any of the events this week."

I think out my reply carefully. Well, as carefully as alcohol allows me to.

"Where did you learn to dance salsa?" *Suave change of subject if I do say so myself.*

His deep laugh makes me feel all warm inside.

"I lived in Europe long enough to pick up on it." He sways us to the music.

A kernel of jealousy blossoms at the idea of Noah dancing with other girls.

"Hmm. Cool." I feign indifference, but I can't tell if I succeeded.

Noah turns me, pulling my back to his front. My ass presses against his crotch as his hand runs down my arm.

"Uh, we learned two different types of salsa. They didn't teach me this in class."

The rumble of his chest is the only response I get.

I look around, curious if anyone else sees this. My body molds into his. A crowd of people dances to the music, oblivious of Noah's advances as his stiff cock presses against my ass cheeks. I press into him, unintentionally of course.

Sign me up for the next confession slot.

Turns out Noah seems into this back and forth, or lack thereof. He moves us along to the music. One of his hands presses on my hip, holding me flushed against him while his other hand pushes my hair away from my neck.

"Did you wear that color dress for me?" His husky voice makes my head swim. *How can he tell what color my dress is when it's dark outside?*

"It's navy. What do you mean?" Okay, it isn't. But boys suck at knowing anything beyond basic colors.

"Hmm, weird. On your Insta story it looked like the same color as my eyes. But maybe I'm wrong, just seeing things."

"That's often a sign of narcissism. You should get yourself checked out when you have a chance. I don't do everything to appease you." Unfiltered words flow from my mouth.

He shuts me up by pushing his rigid length into me. I groan at the feeling, my body heating up at his boldness.

"Tell me you're not affected by this connection between us." His husky whisper sends a shiver down my spine. He trails a finger down the length of my throat to my collarbone, stopping right above my cleavage.

No way I will admit anything to him.

"Not sure what you're talking about. Do you try this with all your floozies?" Who the hell says *floozies* anymore? Alcohol makes me stupid. So, so stupid.

"I think you know." His hands grip me possessively as our hips move to the music. I withhold a moan as my head rolls back into his chest, his dick pressing into my ass, a hint at the size of him.

He blows hot air into the shell of my ear, causing my core to pulse with need. My body burns wherever he touches, his fingers skimming down the smooth material of my dress. A delicate layer protecting my body from his touch.

"You drive me crazy. I keep thinking about fucking you, wondering how you sound when you explode in ecstasy. The moans you'll make while you greedily take my cock. Is it breathy? Loud?"

My stomach flutters at the sensation of his teeth grazing my ear lobe. I tilt my head to the side, giving him better access to my neck, his lips trailing kisses down the curve of it. His touch makes me pant. My resolve slips, begging me to give into him.

Take me home, I want to say. But I don't, letting my body say the words my mouth can't get out.

It's a problem for future me.

What's one night with him? We're adults who can keep a secret.

Noah senses my submission. His lips press against the hollow of my throat, his tongue darting out to taste me, making my body shudder as he sucks on the sensitive skin.

Someone grabs my hand and tugs me away, cold air hitting my skin in Noah's absence. He growls at the intrusion.

"Maya, just the girl I've been looking for. Your brother is searching for you. You remember him, right? Noah's *teammate.*" Sophie emphasizes her words. How did she even find us in this crowd, a cluster of bodies dancing together?

I shake away the lust-induced cloud. Music thumping in the background washes over me, reminding me of where we are. Dance lights illuminate my shoes. If I click them together, can I go home?

"I better get going. Sister duties and all. Thanks for the dance," my voice rasps.

Whatever we did is nothing like any dance I've experienced in my life. My eyes meet Noah's intense ones, a swirl of lust and frustration evident even in the dark.

"This isn't over." His husky voice hints at a promise.

"It is for now, Romeo. Let's go, Juliet." Sophie pulls me away, proving herself to be the best cockblocker.

She keeps her cool until we find an empty corner.

"Uh, where's my brother?"

"Who the heck knows. I needed an excuse to get you out of there before you and Noah screwed each other on the dance floor. What happened to you staying away from him? I was practically fanning myself while watching the two of you." She demonstrates with her hands.

My lips tip up in a smile. "I didn't peg you for a voyeur."

"You're not using your shitty evasion techniques on me. I see through them a mile away; don't insult my talents. Are you trying to get with him or avoid him? You need to decide." She taps her sneaker on the ground and crosses her arms. A ridiculous look only Sophie can pull off, her fluffy dress and white sneakers shining in the dark.

"I don't really know." I shrug because I genuinely don't know what to make of this thing between Noah and me. An out-of-control magnetism I can't describe.

"You guys were a modern-day *Dirty Dancing* scene. I don't buy it. What are you going to do about this thing between you both?"

"Uh, 'thing' is a bit of a stretch. That's the closest we've ever gotten to each other. Attraction, yes. Thing, no." I shake my head from side to side.

Her elevated eyebrow fails to reassure me. "You're into your brother's teammate. And rival I might add."

"No," I stutter. My weight shifts from foot to foot. "I'm sexually attracted to him. Not like into him as a person because I barely know him."

"*Right.*" She draws the word out. "We'll have to keep you away from him."

"We?" My turn to be confused.

"Liam and I. Duh. That's what friends do."

Never have I been so thankful for a friend. Sophie and I stumble out of the party hand in hand, leaving behind sucky decisions and bad boys.

CHAPTER SIXTEEN

Noah

'm into Maya. Like *really* into her. She scrolls through her phone, unaware of her surroundings, or of me checking her out.

I want to hash it out, test the physical connection to its maximum. See how explosive the sex is. Fuck her against every hard surface in my apartment and show her a good time. The idea of exclusive fuck buddies for the rest of the Championship can be on the table if our sex proves to be as good as I imagine. Never had a permanent fuck buddy before, but I think we can be that great together.

Liam jerks me out of my daydream. He nudges my side and looks toward the cameras and reporters in front of us.

"I wasn't paying attention to the question. Can you repeat it?" I offer a sly grin.

The group of reporters snickers at my honesty. Maya glances at me with lit-up eyes as her chest shakes from withheld laughter.

"What strategies have you taken to defend your undefeated

Monaco Prix title?" The reporter stammers out his question again.

"Uh, well I usually get in the car and practice. Try to go my fastest. You know, the basics." I play the jokester today. Stifled laughs carry through the crowd while a couple cameras click, taking photos and videos.

Everyone knows I hate questions like these. This reporter is probably new and unaware of my preference. Viewers eat this up, loving the way I act and how I present myself. They're fans of mine for a reason.

Reporters drone on. Not wanting to make myself look like a total idiot before a race, I make sure to pay attention to them this time. Sponsors may assume I partied too hard in Monaco. I even listen when they ask Santi how he feels about his second-place qualifier.

"Pretty good. It's nice when my hard work pays off. Last year I retired early from Monaco after an engine failure so I'm excited to get back out there and compete against people I've looked up to for years."

I nod, impressed with his answer. It seems like he's been working on his PR skills.

Once the press conference ends, I stroll off the stage and head straight to Maya. "Funny, I never saw you again after the fashion show. Where did you disappear to?" Both my dick and I are curious where she and Sophie ran off to.

She keeps scrolling through her phone. I push one finger down on it, revealing the screen. *She's ignoring me for Instagram?*

I press the auto-lock button on the side of her phone. The dark screen taunts her to look up at me, and she plays right into my hand.

I don't like how her brown eyes intensely stare into mine, guarded and unexpressive.

"I spent time with my brother and Sophie before calling it an early night." Her eyes dart to the side while answering.

"Funny thing because I ran into your brother five minutes after you left. He was surprised when I asked if he was able to get in contact with you. He tried to call you, but you didn't pick up. We ended up spending the rest of the night talking with sponsors." I shrug, trying to come off unfazed. In reality, it ticks me off how Sophie dragged Maya away. How messed up. Sadly, I had to whack off in the bathroom after Maya left to relieve the raging hard-on I had. Embarrassing as fuck. Sophie's the worst cockblocker ever, taking Maya away right when she gave in to me.

The pink shade of her cheeks deepens, revealing enough to me.

"Would you look at the two of you, all cozy and shit. What secrets are you discussing? How to beat me tomorrow?"

I roll my eyes at Liam's interruption before I run a hand down my face. Can Maya and I not get a second alone?

"I'm spying for my brother. My loyalty is always to him." Maya taps her Bandini hat. The brim shows an embroidered seven on it. What would it be like if she wore my number twenty-eight? I envision her in a shirt with my name on it instead of Santiago's.

She screws me all up inside, making me want ridiculous things.

"I better get going anyway because Santi and I have a lunch to go to. Good luck tomorrow, Liam. See you later, Noah." She scurries away.

"Bro, you don't want to tap that. She's your teammate's sister.

Not worth it."

Liam telling me to not hook up with someone is unheard of, the equivalent of him telling me to throw a race. It just isn't done.

"Seeing as you tap anything with two legs and fake boobs, why are you giving me advice right now?" I struggle to cover up my annoyance. That came out rough, even for my standards.

Liam puts both palms in the air. "Woah, no need to take it out on me. Or make it personal for that matter. If you need to fuck someone, pick a girl up at one of the events. They're easy ass."

Therein lies the problem. I have no interest in hooking up with a random chick, and I haven't for a while. When was the last time I slept with someone casually like that?

Liam mistakes my silence for acceptance. "Listen, bro. A word of advice—even though you're being a dick right now. People like Maya don't casually hook up with people like us. She's the type to get feelings and end up wanting more." Liam shudders dramatically.

"What's wrong with feelings?"

He looks at me like I've grown two heads. Granted, I guess I usually don't care for women's feelings.

"They develop into more. Then it becomes proposals, sacrifices, babies crying. The works. One day you wake up and wonder where time went. You'll be forty years old, your wife will barely fuck you anymore, and next thing you know, you're masturbating to porn every day to get by."

I still jack off now. Not exactly a trade-off.

Liam comes off uncharacteristically bitter, which I find weird because his parents have a perfect marriage. I mean, I'm already thirty. Not like I want to be alone for the rest of my life, only while I compete in racing and live on the road.

"Not sure how hooking up with Maya turned into a ten-year life plan. But thanks for your concern." I pat him on the shoulder while rolling my eyes.

"I want to warn you. She's one of those girls that'll bring you to your knees. I'm telling you. You'll be turning in your man card and wondering where you went wrong. Swapping out new girls for the same chick. Same pussy for the rest of your life."

His vision of marriage is kind of dark, unlike his usually optimistic self. Don't know what crawled up his ass today. I leave him behind, my mood tainted by his words.

The day of the Monaco race, I search around for Maya because I don't see or hear from her. I end up in the Bandini bar area in a last-ditch effort to find her. Sophie sips espresso at one of the tables, casually flipping through a magazine, not a care in the world.

"Have you seen Maya?" I keep my voice low as I plant my butt in the chair across from her.

She sips her drink. "Like recently?"

Why is she playing dumb? "Yes. Within the last few hours?" It takes effort to keep my teeth from grinding. My dentist won't be happy with me next time he sees me.

She finds my reaction funny, her eyes betraying her amusement. "Why do you want to know?"

"Answer the damn question. Not that hard," I blurt out.

Her eyes roll at my rough tone. I've visited her house during the holidays, so we've known each other casually for years. She reminds me of an annoying third cousin because we're not close enough to be considered siblings.

"No need to get your race suit in a twist. She decided to watch like a normal bystander today, wanting to film the experience for her vlog."

Doesn't Maya know that's not a good idea? People will recognize her; drunks will try to grope her. I don't like the thought of her being out there by herself.

"Why aren't you out there with her?" *AKA why are you sitting here drinking coffee while your friend is out by herself in a crazy crowd?*

"I was going to hang out in the pit with my dad. This is one of the biggest races of the year, so I'm sure it'll be crazy down there."

I pull out my phone before she finishes her sentence. She watches as I tap around on the screen.

I break the silence after a few minutes. "What's your number?"

"Seriously, you try to hit on me after you ask where my friend is? You were dry-humping her the other day."

My jaw clenches. "No. You're skipping out on the pit today. Your dad sent me a ticket, beyond enthused that you want to see the race like a true fan."

I smirk at her wide eyes while she tells me her number. She doesn't speak another word, thank God. Maya can avoid me all she wants, but it doesn't mean she has to do it alone. I'll get my way eventually. These types of games don't phase me because I have enough stamina to outdo her.

My lips twitch as I think up a plan to get her alone after the race. She can evade me all she wants, but it doesn't mean I need to. *Two can play this game.*

CHAPTER SEVENTEEN

MAYA

I hear Sophie before I see her. She yells at a guy to stop accosting her in the stands. Her vocab choices are something else, a testament to reading one too many classic novels.

She makes her way toward the seat next to mine and settles down. We look the same, twinning in Bandini polos and ear protection gear.

"What are you doing here? I thought you wanted to spend time in the pit."

Nearby fans give us weird looks. I tug my hat lower on my face and pull down my sound-reducing earmuffs to hear her better.

She shrugs, picking up that trick from me. I nudge her in the ribs.

"Ouch. Fine. No need to get physical. Noah cornered me earlier asking where you were." She rubs her rib.

Did I hear her right? "And you ended up here how?"

"Noah forced me to, I guess so you're not alone."

It shocks me that he even cares.

"Did he say anything else?" I fiddle with the settings on my camera.

"He said, and I quote—" her voice drops lower to imitate Noah's—"I didn't know she was a fan of hiding. Let her know when I find her, she won't like it. I was the champ at hide-and-seek growing up."

"*What*? Seriously?" My voice screeches.

"No! That's a terrible pick-up line. He's better than that. I'm messing with you." Her laugh fills the silence. She's giving me a severe case of emotional whiplash today. "But there was some observable tension. I may conclude that he likes when you hang out on race days?"

"I didn't think he cared if I was around on Sundays."

Her eyes shine. "Hmm. I don't know about that. Noah seemed agitated that you weren't around earlier. At least enough to ask me about it."

Announcers cut off our conversation, letting the crowd know the race will begin momentarily.

The crowd quiets down as red lights flash above the grid. Everyone holds their breath for the start of the race, electric energy charging the stands as race car engines rev. My heart beats along with the flashing signals above the grid. The moment the lights change, cars take off down the track toward the first turn. The Monaco Prix circuit can be unforgiving, especially if a driver makes an error, like under- or overestimating a speed during a curve.

Noah keeps his lead around the first bend, with my brother not far behind. Santiago's car zooms past one of the straightaways before turning another tight corner. Liam and Jax compete against each other for the third position.

Monaco's track seems unlike any other in the Prix schedule. Constricted roads keep cars compacted, not allowing much room for mistakes. Jax and Liam avoid a disastrous collision with each other at one of the turns. Pieces of metal fly as the cars graze one another, the sound of clanging metal against the ground ringing across the Prix. The crowd gasps as Jax's car careens toward the side. He uses his momentum to get back on the track, narrowly avoiding a catastrophic crash.

Hums of the cars zipping across the pavement fill me with excitement as Noah and Santi pass us, completing their first lap. The crowd feels alive and energetic, chanting out the names of their favorite drivers while waving flags and signs in the air. My own body pulses with exhilaration as Sophie and I get up to cheer. Fans hang out on nearby balconies, overlooking the race from hotel rooms.

The smell of burning rubber fills my nose, a scent I've come to love during my time here.

Noah continues to fight for the lead with my brother. He remains defensive of his position, which makes it hard for Santi and others to get ahead of him. My brother tries to overtake him multiple times but can't since the Monaco course makes it tough to rise up the ranks. Often, the position you start with is the one you end with as long as you don't crash.

At one of the sharper turns, my brother tries to overtake Noah again. He does it sloppily, brushing Noah's front wing, causing Noah's car to fall behind. My brother secures the first-place position. Noah must be pissed because he detests when cars have contact with one another. The whole race turns out to be a messy one with shrapnel flying and cars colliding.

The crowd grows silent as Liam crashes into one of the barriers. His front tire flies off, and the severe damage makes him retire from the race early. He splays his hands against his helmet as the cameras pan over him. Sophie's eyes cloud and her teeth chew on her bottom lip.

During one of the final laps, my brother lets down his defensive position enough for Noah to sneak up next to him. Their front wings drive side by side, almost touching, as they race down a straight together. They approach a narrow corner. I hold my breath, unable to look away as Noah accelerates while turning. His side tires lift from the ground, losing important contact and traction to turn. A dangerous move that pays off as his car surges past Santi's, securing first place again. The crowd goes wild at the move Noah pulled, and I'm finding it hard to hide my bounce of excitement.

Noah ends up passing the finish line first. A checkered flag waves in the air, rustling against the wind. The fans eagerly cheer when they announce Noah as the winner of the Monaco Grand Prix. Sophie and I bounce up and down when my brother zooms past the finish line as the runner-up.

Bandini had a great racing day. They prove time and time again to be one of the strongest teams with Noah and Santi at the wheel, another race closer to winning the Constructors' Championship.

Sophie and I wait with the masses while the drivers complete their victory lap. We end up leaving the stadium area once the guys start their usual press circuit.

We meet up with the Bandini team at the winners' podium. Noah stands in the middle, with Santi and Jax at his sides. It fills me with happiness to see both of the Bandini boys getting along with one another, laughing at something going on between the three racers.

Santi and Jax pour champagne all over Noah. The crowd screams as champagne sprays all over them, the sticky alcohol making the air smell like a classy frat party. The podium area is a mosh pit of alcohol and cheering fans.

Noah notices me from my spot behind the blockades, shooting me a panty-melting grin. He tips his big champagne bottle to me before he chugs. I smile back at him and give him a thumbs up, incredibly proud of him. The sight of his lips wrapped around the bottle brings naughty thoughts to the forefront of my mind.

Sophie joins her dad in the celebrations with the pit team while I head back toward the suites to chill while Santi does his other interviews.

I wait in the suite, surprised when the door opens earlier than I thought.

"Hey, you're back earlier—" I stop mid-sentence when Noah smiles at me.

He recently took a shower. His hair is slicked back, no evidence of his hands raking through the strands yet. A new Bandini shirt presses against the tight muscles of his chest. I lick my lips as my eyes roam over the rest of him, taking in expensive looking jeans that cling to his legs.

"What are you doing here? Your suite is next door." I don't like the mischievous grin plastered on his face at the moment.

Not one bit.

He closes the distance, shushing me by pressing his finger up against my lips.

"I came to collect my post-race winnings." He drags a calloused finger from my lips to my throat.

"Uh, I'm pretty sure they already gave you the trophy," I whisper huskily.

Noah's grin widens as his blue eyes pierce mine. The air in the small room feels heavy, like all the oxygen was sucked out of it. He's a hurricane catching me in the eye of the storm, giving me a false sense of security before the winds pick up again. A catastrophic and relentless disaster in the making.

He steps away from me. The click of the lock sounds loud, sending a shiver up my back.

"This isn't funny, Noah. Go to your own suite." I take a step back while he takes a few steps forward, eliminating the gap.

"I'm not trying to be funny. You've been avoiding me."

Uh, yes, I have. After the fashion show I've made myself scarce around here. I don't trust my urges around him, but I don't say anything because his ego gets fed enough.

"Not sure what you're talking about. I've been busy." I'd probably sound ten times more convincing if my voice wasn't rasping. My body betrays me, unable to keep up with Noah's persistence.

"I follow you on Instagram. I've seen your stories."

Oh. This is the second time he's mentioned watching them. I didn't even think he had the time to see them, but he must have checked out my movie and spa day posts.

"Sometimes you need a day off."

"You took two." The back of his hand strokes my face. *When did he get so close? And why does that feel amazing?*

I shut my eyes at the incredible contact.

The same hand wraps around the back of my head and pulls me forward. My eyes snap open. His clean scent surrounds me and muddles my thoughts. He doesn't give me another second to think before his mouth is on mine, soft lips pressing against my own.

At first, the kiss is soft and sweet—innocent and unexpected from a man like him. He plays, leaving behind gentle pecks.

His teeth graze my bottom lip, rough with a bite of pain. I gasp at the sensation. His tongue takes the opportunity to invade my mouth and stroke against mine, a relentless exploration demanding everything from me. He tastes like mint and champagne, a shockingly wonderful combination. Kissing him is a mind-numbing experience. His hands roam over my body, pulling me into him as his mouth stifles my moan. An impressive erection pushes against my jeans. One of his hands runs through my hair while the other grips my face, making it impossible for me to get away. Not like I want to. Oh, no, when I commit to being bad, I'm all in.

My heart hammers in my chest. I wrap my arms around Noah's neck, pulling him in closer, giving in to our attraction. His hair feels soft and smooth beneath my fingers as I run them through his strands. Knees threaten to buckle. I try to make sense of all the sensations happening inside me, experiencing the best kiss of my life—both intoxicating and exhilarating. My body feels like putty in his hands, begging to be touched.

"Why is my door locked? Hello, Maya, are you in there?

Open up." My brother's voice hits me like an ice-cold shower. Pounding fists against the door beat alongside my heart.

I break apart from Noah's mouth and take a few steps back, nearly stumbling over the couch. A disheveled mess of hair makes me smile. His eyes stare at me, wild-looking and hazy, and his pants have a prominent swell. I can't deny the pride that surges through me about doing that to him.

Go me.

He holds up a finger to his mouth. One side of his mouth tips up, and his eyes shine, swirling shades of blue I've come to like. How is he always so unaffected? It seems unfair. I look back down at his pants to double-check.

Nope, he's affected.

The doorknob rattles, guilt replacing the pride I felt seconds ago. Santi would kill me if he found me in here with Noah.

"*Carajo*. How is my room locked? Who has the key?" My brother's voice fades away with the sound of his footsteps.

"You need to go *now*. I'll make sure he left." I push past him.

He grabs my elbow and pulls me back toward him. A quick peck silences me. My brain hasn't caught up to my body yet, leaning back into him like we can continue what happened.

"Relax. He doesn't have to know." His wicked eyes graze over me one more time before he exits the room.

I plop myself down on the couch, running a hand down my face. *What the hell did I do? I can't do this to Santi. Can I?*

Why did one kiss feel like it opened me up for anything?

Two weeks have passed since The Kiss. I needed to take a temporary leave of absence from the race schedule, which meant I skipped out on the Canadian Grand Prix. Santi begged me to come, but I made up an excuse about wanting to go home. Lying to him made me feel worse, my stomach in endless knots as I packed my bags and purchased a ticket to Spain. I told him the traveling exhausts me. Which isn't far from the truth; I can't help how the man we travel with tires me emotionally and physically. Life's all about semantics.

Sophie pled with me too, but my mind was made up. I needed to clear my head.

Jax took home the trophy for the race with Liam being runner-up, and my brother placing third. For the first time this season, Noah didn't make it to the podium.

Sophie must have given Noah my number because he sent me multiple texts last week. I made an incognito contact name for him, just in case Santi gets a hold of my phone. Blame reading *Harry Potter* during my race hiatus for the contact name.

> **He Who Shall Not Be Fucked (06/10 5:00 p.m.):** Are you flying in late? Santiago is here but you aren't.
>
> **He Who Shall Not Be Fucked (06/11 2:37 p.m.):** Found out from your brother that you're not coming. Isn't he superstitious? You've been to every race so far.
>
> **He Who Shall Not Be Fucked (06/13 4:56 p.m.):** Didn't place on the podium. Maybe I'm the superstitious one.

My stomach dipped at the last one. I didn't want Noah to

do poorly since he is my brother's teammate, but he didn't lose because I wasn't there.

I pulled up a YouTube interview of Noah after the race, telling myself I did it to ease my curiosity.

Noah looked good in his red race suit with his sweaty hair plastered to his head. He rocked the messy look.

The reporter jammed the foam microphone in Noah's face.

"What happened today out there on the track?"

"Just an off day. It happens. I'm happy for my teammate and my friends who did place." His tight smile begged to differ.

"Have anything different planned for the next Prix?"

Noah glanced at the camera. His deep blue eyes looked hazy, blocking off any readable emotions.

"I think I need to change up my pre-race ritual. A couple things might not be working for me anymore. But more on that later. Don't want to reveal my secrets." He ended the interview with a lazy smile.

After watching his interview yesterday, I ignored his texts for a whole day. I lasted twenty-four hours before giving in to answering him, the image of him frowning into the camera plaguing my thoughts. Three thousand miles do nothing to ease the pull he has on me.

> **Maya (06/14 1:14 p.m.):** I'm sure you'll place next time. You're one of the best.
> **He Who Shall Not Be Fucked (06/14 1:16 p.m.):** Are you coming to that one? Did you get my earlier messages? I didn't get a response.

I would never peg someone like him to question if I got his

messages. Has he ever sent that to a woman before? The notion makes me take pity on him and answer quicker than usual.

> **Maya (06/14 1:30 p.m.):** I'll be there. Needed a vacation from all the traveling.

I choose to ignore his second message because he crosses lines I'm not ready for yet.

> **He Who Shall Not Be Fucked (06/14 1:43 p.m.):** Good. See you then.

That went easier than I thought. I need to face him, but I need a game plan first, particularly a Sophie-made plan.

CHAPTER EIGHTEEN

Noah

s this what it feels like to be ghosted? I've done it to girls in the past, but I've never been on the receiving end. And to be honest, it totally sucks. *Karma really is a bitch after all.*

I haven't seen Maya since Monaco. She barely answers any of my messages, which makes me second-guess if I kissed her too soon. *Me, second-guessing. What a joke.* Sometimes she seems in to me, but stuff she does makes me uncertain. A foreign sensation to say the least.

I land in Baku two days earlier to get acclimated to the city. That and I want to be around when Santi and his sister arrive because I want to catch Maya when he leaves.

Wednesday goes by without a sign of her during our sponsor meetings and ass-kissing specials. But Maya doesn't come to any of them. I worry she wants to back out of coming to another race because of me.

I give in to my curiosity and ask Santi about her while we walk back to the hospitality suites after our press conference.

"Where's your sister been?"

He turns his head slowly toward me, revealing squinted eyes and a tight jaw. I don't get intimidated by him. His scary face comes off like a puppy dog, not threatening like his dad's.

"Busy. She visited our parents back in Spain. Why?" He glares at me.

"Was curious why she didn't come to the last Prix. Wondered how it would affect your racing." My cocky grin seems to placate him. Back to our usually scheduled programming with one another—me being the cocky asshole and him taking it.

He scoffs. "I did fine. I raced without my sister by my side for years while she was in college. You're the one who struggled this time."

Santi has a fight in him. *Good to know.*

"Yup. You win some, you lose some." I shrug. "Is she coming to this race?" I can't tell if my voice sounds disinterested enough.

"Yeah. She's already here."

I follow Santi to the hospitality suite, disappointed when Maya isn't there.

"Is Maya hanging out in there?"

He stares at me, his head tilting to the side as his lips press together in a tight line. "Nah, she went to hang out with Sophie. Said something about exploring the city for her vlog."

My eyes nearly bug out of my head. They're out alone in a random city they've never visited before where the people speak a different language. What if someone recognizes them?

"They should be more careful. Why do you let them go out by themselves? That's irresponsible."

Santi's gaze hardens. "I can take care of my sister. It's a safe city."

"I think you forget you're worth over twenty million dollars now. Why do you think people are kidnapped for ransom? Hint, it's not always for pretty looks."

His ignorance grates on me.

Santi's jaw ticks. He takes a couple of deep breaths while I stare him down. I piss him off, but he can be a real idiot sometimes.

"Thanks for the advice." He enters his suite and slams the door.

I text Maya to check if she still has a pulse.

> **Maya (06/19 6:58 p.m.):** Thanks for asking. We're all good. Going to dinner and then bed. Good luck at practice tomorrow.

I need to come up with something to do together that doesn't include me shoving my tongue down her throat. Which I still want to do, but we have to do fun stuff too. A plan comes to mind so I enlist my friends to help me. She needs to see what she can have if she gives us a chance.

"Grab the girls and meet me at the Baku kart area."

Liam stares at me like I'm talking to him in another language. Yeah, he speaks German, but he understands English fine.

"Why are we doing this again?" His voice matches the incredulous look on his face.

"Because I want us all to have fun before the race. What's so hard to believe?" I control the urge to roll my eyes.

"Uh yeah. Your usual pre-race fun involves being balls deep inside of a model."

I punch him in the arm. "Fuck you. Don't tell Maya I planned this because then she won't come." My teeth grind together—my new bad habit lately, kind of like stalking Maya's social media accounts. I've become *that* guy. The one checking her profile to the point of addiction, sneaking quick glances at what she does to fill the void of her absence.

Jax and Liam can take credit while I pretend to join because I don't want her to find out I put in this much effort. Her avoiding me for weeks forced me to plan something drastic for her attention.

"All right no need to hit so hard. I'll meet you there." He rubs his arm and pouts.

Liam pulls up to the kart track an hour later. Jax, Maya, and Sophie hop out of the rental car. I didn't invite Santi because I'm not a total dumbass, mainly because he's been paying extra attention to me recently, sneaking random glances whenever his sister gets close.

Maya's mouth gapes open when she sees me standing there.

"We're going karting?" Sophie claps her hands and bounces around, her blonde braids swaying around her while Liam checks her out. He gives me a hard time with Maya when he makes heart eyes at Sophie.

"I haven't done this since I was a kid." Maya looks at the helmet in my hand. She blushes when I pass it to her, our hands grazing against each other.

"You only had an opportunity to ride karts when you stole your brother's. So here's your chance to drive them for real. Don't put any unicorn stickers on them." That totally makes it sound like I planned this. There goes my idea of her not knowing about it. *Real subtle, Noah.*

"Oh, no. But you guys are professionals. How is that even remotely fair?" Sophie crosses her arms over her chest.

Maya rubs her hands together while she shoots Sophie a grin full of mischief.

"Sophie, they're used to fast cars. We've got this."

That gleam in her eye? Definitely should be worried; no doubt she wants to kick our asses.

Turns out Maya does precisely that on the first run. I had no clue she was talented with a kart, and fuck it turns me on. I could blame the fact that I haven't kart-raced in a while, but she's a natural at it. Absolutely wiped the track with us.

My dick twitches at Maya sitting there, gloating in her kart, arms up in the air in triumph. She looks sexy as fuck with her helmet and borrowed race suit. I didn't peg myself for having a racing fetish, but looking at her now makes me rethink the idea, especially when she whips off her helmet to reveal messy hair.

An unknown sensation from the top of my head to the tips of my toes surges through me at planning something she likes. She smiles at Sophie from the mini podium they have meant for kids. I wish she would smile at me like she does with others, beautiful with a hint of trouble. Liam and I grab the champagne bottles I kept hidden in a bag and spray them all over the girls.

"Hello, aren't we the ones who should be spraying champagne?" Maya gets the words out between laughs.

Liam and I pass them new bottles that are the same ones we use on the stage. Went for the full F1 effect today. I pop the cork before letting go, the bottle nearly dropping before Maya grips it with two hands.

Maya proceeds to pour it all over me. The cool liquid runs down my shirt, wet material plastering to my torso. Her eyes heat up at the sight of my abs before they roam over my body. I give her a wicked smile. She hops off the stage, lunging to the side, but my reflexes make me quicker.

I haul her over my shoulder like a fireman's carry. She squirms about, making it difficult for me to hold on to her. My hand smacks her ass playfully to get her to stop.

"Ay! Watch it. That's the no-go zone." She shakes from laughter.

No clue what the no-go zone is, but I'm all for exploring it. She should know by now that I don't follow the rules, preferring to bend them into submission.

"Precious cargo. Everyone, please move out of the way."

Kids and parents part at my request. Maya's giggles turn into a snort, which makes her laugh more, her body vibrating against mine.

"The blood's rushing to my head. I can't think straight."

"Join the club." I refer to a different head than she is. She gets the joke a second too late and her body shakes from more laughter.

"Oh my God, you can't say stuff like that. Like ever." More laughs as I smack her ass again. I love the feel of it beneath my palm, my dick stirring while a smile breaks out on my face.

I carry her to the waiting town car. We all drive back to the hotel, soaking wet from champagne. Maya gives me the biggest grin that reaches her eyes, and damn if my lungs don't burn at my sudden intake of breath.

"Hi, everyone. Maya here with the amazing Noah Slade. He agreed to do an exclusive interview for my vlog." She looks gorgeous with her hair down. Today she wears shorts that show off her golden legs, ones I want wrapped around my waist while I pound into her. I'm so curious to hear the different noises she makes during sex. Is she a screamer? A moaner? I'll volunteer to figure it out.

She smiles at the camera she situated on a rolling cart in the pit garage. We position ourselves next to my race car, the vibrant red calling my name as Maya's ass leans against it. Low beeps from the pit computers sound off in the background.

"You think I'm amazing?" I forget the camera for a second. Like the sad sap I am lately around her, I love hearing anything she has to share, any revelation about her feelings. A fucking breadcrumb would be nice. She taunts me daily despite the way she guards herself, keeping her lips sealed, both literally and figuratively. There are few opportunities for us to be alone. Sophie magically finds us every time we get a moment by ourselves, which makes me want to take drastic measures to spend time with her, including this exclusive interview.

And everyone knows I hate interviews.

She rolls her eyes with minimal effort. "Hush, I wonder if you consume extra calories to feed your ego. Anyway, fans want a backstage exclusive. They're curious to learn more about you. So I copied a famous game called Web's Most Searched Answers."

She passes me a cardboard poster with my name in a Google search bar, along with a bunch of tape-covered questions. I recognize it so I guess I'm famous enough to play it.

"Our first question is…" She expectantly looks at me, making me smile. Her parted lips tempt me to take a risk and kiss her.

I cough to cover up a groan, and then I tear off the tape for the first piece of paper.

"*What is Noah Slade's height?* Well, I'm six foot. Which is considered on the taller end for F1. They make the cars to fit around our bodies specifically. My feet are near the tip of the front wing up against the pedals."

Her hands motion for me to continue. *All right, I get it.*

"*Who is Noah Slade and Santiago Alatorre.*" I pause. "I'm Noah. No surprise there. And Santiago is my partner and Maya's brother." I point at her like an idiot because obviously they know that. "He's a Spanish dude who's loud and rarely beats me at racing. Still needs to work on his overtaking skills and not crashing into me from behind."

Maya sticks her tongue out at me, making me think about her tongue on other places of my body. Not a convenient time for a boner with cameras rolling. I shift against the hood of the car, discreetly adjusting my pants.

"Ha. Ha. Everyone can tune in for your comedy career once you're done with racing."

Fat chance that happens. I chuckle as I rip off the tape to reveal another question.

"*What is Noah Slade's net worth?* I'm not one to brag because that's not polite and I was raised better. But I think last time I checked, about three hundred million. Give or take. Received good advice from my financial advisor about always investing your money. Don't let it sit in the bank gathering dust. So that's what I do to multiply the amount I do have. Not to mention real estate investments."

Maya lets out a low whistle. "I'm impressed. We're talking to a World Champion here who gives free monetary advice."

"You know what they say…the bigger the bank account…" I waggle my brows.

Maya ignores the camera and throws her head back. I love the sound of her laugh; pride surges through me at amusing her. Her exposed neck entices my inconvenient one-track mind.

"*Who is Noah Slade's wife?*"

Wow, she picked hard-hitting questions here.

I continue. "I'm currently on the market. I've never married someone so that's a negative. Is the statement no wife, happy life?" I wink at the camera.

"I think you mean happy wife, happy life." Maya blushes and shakes her head.

I chuckle before I keep going. "*Where does Noah Slade live?* I'm not going to give away my addresses here because I can't have paparazzi and fans at my doors all the time. My limited privacy is the best part of the off-season. But I own an apartment in Monaco, a house in Italy, and a loft in London. Favorite place to live is off the Amalfi coast during F1's winter breaks. Hands down the best food and views."

"Who can resist gelato? I've never been to Italy, but the food is my favorite. I can't wait until the Prix stop in Milan. All right, two more left." She clasps her hands together and looks at me. She crosses her legs again, drawing my attention toward them once more. I lick my bottom lip before continuing.

"*When is Noah Slade retiring?*" I blink at the board. I never think about retiring, choosing instead to focus on the next year.

I'm still young enough to not worry about it. But the question makes me think about what I'll do once I hit my late thirties.

"I bet you anything that Liam and Jax google this yearly. They're probably waiting for my announcement since they're younger. I don't doubt it." Blood rushes to my dick at the sound of her giggle. I need to get out of here before I do something stupid on camera. "Uh. I haven't considered retiring anytime soon. But I imagine if I meet someone special and have kids, I may consider what's best for my family. But for now, I plan on kicking everyone's asses."

Maya looks surprised at my answer. Hell, I am too. When the fuck have I thought about having kids or a wife? But the answer falls from my lips with ease, like I think about the notion occasionally.

"You never know what could happen in the future. But I'm sure you have plenty of time to figure it out. F1 racers don't retire until like forty years old. Basically, you'll be ancient once you leave here. Okay, last one."

Is that even what I want? To keep racing at the risk of not having a life to go back to once it's all done? I don't want to be like my dad, who parties with twenty-somethings on private yachts, cruising around by myself. The thought creeps me out.

"*Best Noah Slade team radio?*" My team radio videos on YouTube are hilarious. "If you look me up on the internet, you can find lots of videos of me cursing at the team and myself. A team radio is how Bandini and I communicate about race stats, car info, and problems. My personal favorite video is the British Grand Prix from 2014. Watch it if you haven't seen it. You'll be entertained. The pit crew forgot to connect my water pump and I was basically a cranky baby without a bottle for an hour."

I glance at Maya. Her eyes look up at me and fill my chest with a warm feeling.

"Thank you so much for joining us, Noah. Those were the most googled questions people wanted answered about Noah so I decided to go straight to the source. This week I'll have exclusive footage from the McCoy team, including interviews with Liam and Jax. Stay tuned. Subscribe if you haven't already. See you next time!" She waves to her camera before shutting it off.

She looks like a natural, both gorgeous and confident. It's cool she's found something she can be passionate about. Especially if it keeps her entertained and coming back to all the races because I don't mind these one-on-one interviews at all.

"You forgot one more question." I don't think as the words leave my mouth. It seems like the perfect chance to have her alone without any interruptions of the blonde-haired, green-eyed variety.

Maya stares up at me, confusion lining her face.

"Will Noah Slade ask Maya Alatorre on a date?" I flinch at my pathetic pick-up line.

Not exactly my best work. I blame it on being out of practice, not the way my heart races in my chest at the fear of her rejecting me.

"A date? You don't date." She messes around with her camera tripod.

My hand engulfs hers to stop her fidgeting. Her body tenses as I rub my thumb across her knuckles, something I noticed she liked during the few times I've done it.

"I want to try. What's one date?"

"Uh, for someone who doesn't ever date…everything." She tugs on her hand, trying to free it, but I don't let it go. Not until I get what I want.

"It's one date, don't be dramatic. I'm not asking for a forever… Are you scared?" I goad her. "We don't need to put labels on anything. Let's have fun."

"Of course I'm not scared. You just want to have *fun*?" Her brows raise and her lips form a tight line.

Maybe she won't be happy with no labels, even though most chicks I get with don't mind. Or maybe *fun* was the wrong word to say because now she looks at me in a way I can't read.

"Then go on a date with me. Tomorrow?" I can't tell if she wants to shut me down.

"My brother can't know. He would lock me up before killing you," she sputters.

All right, she didn't say no. I can work with it.

"What he doesn't know won't kill him. We're only having a good time together." I want to tell her to stop making a big deal of this. *Hasn't she tried no strings attached?* But she agrees, making it a win for me. If there is something I live by, it's how there's no time like the present.

I stride away, throwing a victorious grin over my shoulder.

CHAPTER NINETEEN

MAYA

"**N**o way. I'm not getting on that thing." I cross my two index fingers in front of me in an X. If only my mom could see me making responsible decisions. She'd be proud.

"Live a little." Noah's eyes gleam while mine narrow, not sharing his amused look. He looks eerie with a flickering light above our heads, foreshadowing this bad idea.

A shiny motorbike brings a frown to my face, the steel gray paint polished and sleek, like an alien spaceship. It should come with a warning label.

Hell, Noah should have a walking, talking warning sign.

We wage a battle of wills in the parking garage of the hotel we're both staying at with Bandini. The garage makes the perfect place to meet up for our date since we can avoid the paparazzi and my brother. Just Noah, me, and a dimly lit lot. I don't have my usual chaperones keeping me in check. Much to Sophie's dismay earlier, I declined her invitation to third wheel our date.

Appreciate her loyalty though.

"Come on. It's not scary. I promise."

I roll my eyes. Anyone will say that to get me on the back of a contraption.

He steps toward me, wearing down my defenses. He talks low and slow to me like I'm a scared dog in an alleyway.

I push my lower lip out and cross my arms, not above pouting to get my way. If it works on my parents, then it could work on Noah.

But he doesn't take the bait. I need to work on my delivery because it sucks.

"Don't make me carry you onto it. I've driven motorcycles since I was thirteen. I'm still alive." He waves down his body, bringing my attention to his leather jacket and dark jeans. His outfit screams bad boy in every good kind of way. Instead of making me feel better, he distracts me with his tight-fitting shirt, which accentuates his firm muscles.

How does he make casual look so good?

"Is that supposed to make me feel better? That's illegal! Who in their right mind would let a child on a motorbike?" Did anyone ever watch over him as a kid?

He chuckles, not bothering to address my comment. Instead, he grabs a black helmet from the seat and puts it on my head, adjusting the straps to fit my chin. I'd consider it a lovely gesture if my heart wasn't in my throat at the moment.

I wasn't exactly expecting this when he told me to wear jeans and a comfortable top earlier.

"You're one hard date to please," he grumbles.

I'd rather not have my body splayed across a street like

roadkill.

"Have you even been on a real date? Usually normal people go to a restaurant, have dinner, and end it all with a kiss. Stay within the comfort zone." I paint a picture for him since he seems like a visual kind of guy.

His chest rumbles with laughter. "I've dated before, but I'm far from normal. Why wine and dine you? I'm going to get what I want anyway." He waggles his brows.

Well, excuse me. I can't ignore the pang of jealousy when he mentions other dates. For once, his arrogant attitude wears on me.

Who does he think he is? Sex with me is not a given because I am not one of his bimbos. I don't hand that shit out like Halloween candy.

"That's one of the worst things a first date has ever told me."

Another hand tugs through his hair as he sighs. He may be sharp on the racetrack, but his people skills suck. I withhold the temptation to stick my tongue out at him because it'll encourage him more.

"It gets cold with the wind. Take my jacket." He slides the leather jacket off his back and passes it to me. The moment I put it on, a smell that's distinctly his with a hint of leather surrounds me. It calms me down a teensy bit.

"Please do this for me? It'll be fun, I promise. If you hate it, I'll park the bike and order us an Uber."

His sincerity does me in. I accept my fate and walk up to the spaceship.

It's one date.

I sigh. "All right. Because you asked nicely."

He gives me a wicked grin.

I'm so screwed.

Five minutes later, we speed down one of Baku's seaside streets. The smell of the ocean relaxes me as the city lights blur past us. Lucky for him, I don't suffer from motion sickness because this bike hits maximum speeds. I grip onto Noah's waist for dear life as tires tear across the pavement. My hands accidentally brush up against his abs, and I casually run a finger across them, interested in counting the ridges. He laughs at my failed attempt to be subtle. The rumbling sensation of the motorbike beneath my ass and touching his abs is turning me on.

Did he plan this on purpose? My body presses up against him and my arms wrap around him, leaving no space. Even my legs plaster tightly against his to make sure I don't fall off. If it wasn't risky, I'd wrap them around him as an extra safety precaution. The whole situation comes across as intimate despite my bubbling anxiety.

Everything feels different with only Noah and me. No press, no friends, no distractions. We strip away all the extra stuff getting in the way of us spending alone time together.

He streams music through a pair of speakers, making the whole experience much more enjoyable than I thought. Ocean mist hits my face as we get closer to the beach, and I love every second of it. I won't admit it to his face though because he gets to gloat enough as it is.

Noah eventually pulls the bike into a secluded area by the shore. I hop off, anxious to break our physical connection. My chest tightens at the scene in front of us.

A couple of lanterns outline a picnic area, looking unexpectedly romantic.

"Just fun?" I mumble under my breath, the date not screaming casual to me.

"Relax. Don't make a big deal out of it." He grabs my hand and pulls me toward the colorful blanket.

I settle into one of the cushions on the sand. A picnic basket is open off to the side, along with a bucket with chilled wine. The sound of waves crashing against the shore makes the perfect soundtrack.

A wave of uneasiness threatens to take away my happiness. Noah's lips say casual, but his actions speak differently. People propose in less cute ways. I take a deep breath of the salty ocean air to calm me down, hoping a few inhales can cure my insecurity about Noah's intentions.

"How did you plan all of this?"

"I had a little help." He shoots me a rare shy smile.

"Right. Busy life of an F1 driver." It impresses me how he made an effort to make sure something nice was planned.

"We can pretend for a night that none of that exists. No talk of your brother and no bringing up Baku. You're a girl and I'm a guy on a normal date." He flashes me his usual mischievous smile.

Did I say he looks like trouble already? *Still waiting on the warning label.*

I agree to his terms. We eat together, talking about anything and everything. He tells me about his favorite TV shows and the best cities in America. I say how I've never been there, and he insists I need to go at least once, offering to show me around and take me to the best food places. I tell him about my failed attempts at graduating on time, being held back a year after I figured out I wasn't meant to be a Spanish Elle Woods attending Harvard.

"Let's play a game." Noah hits me with a mischievous grin.

"Seriously?"

"Dead serious. Ever heard of two truths and a lie?"

I roll my eyes with minimal effort. "What are you, eighteen and attending your first college party?"

Noah lets out a rough laugh. "I never went to college. Entertain me?"

I nod because I'd do just about anything with him smiling at me the way he does.

"Whoever loses has to chug straight from the wine bottle for five seconds." His smile reaches his blue eyes as the candlelight flickers across his skin.

"Okay, since this is your bright idea to get me tipsy, you can go first."

He chuckles to himself. "I'm an only child. I spend thirty minutes a day watching the news. And I lost my virginity in the back of a pickup truck."

I cough at his last statement, aware of how this game will go after one round.

"Pickup truck is a lie. You look like a thousand-thread-count kind of guy."

His eyes light up. "Nope. You got it wrong. I hate the news, so I stay away from that shit."

Well, damn. Guess Noah is an American boy after all, getting down and dirty in the bed of a truck. I grab the wine bottle and take a chug, holding up a finger for each second that ticks by.

"Your turn." He winks at me.

"My brother announced his Bandini contract on the same day as my graduation. I've gotten into five fender benders. I crashed my brother's first date."

"Five fender benders? That's excessive for someone young."

I shake my head and point to the bottle sitting next to us. "Nope. I never crashed my brother's first date even though my parents wanted me to. Santi paid me fifty euros to watch a different movie. He got his hookup while I got a new pair of shoes."

"One, how do you still have a license? And two, your brother told everyone about his Bandini deal on your special day? How fucked up," Noah says before taking a chug from the bottle I drank from, his lips wrapped around the same spot mine touched.

I shrug. "I can still drive because the officer felt bad when I cried, begging me to stop. And Santi couldn't help the bad timing."

"Sometimes he can be a real dumbass. He could have waited a day at least."

Guilt runs through me at us talking about Santi this way because I love my brother. Noah doesn't care much for him. Stupid to hope they could get along—for the sake of the team or for me.

"He has the best heart. Truly. I can't get mad at him for more than a day at most. Not even when he stole all my Barbies and shaved their hair off."

"That should have been the first sign of his instability."

A loud laugh escapes my mouth. We play a few more rounds with me losing a couple times while Noah guesses my lies with ease, surprising me how he sees through my bullshit. Wine calms my nerves and takes away my awkwardness. I learn a few things about Noah like how he skipped senior prom because of a race, and how he spent seven different Christmases by himself since his parents were both traveling. A truth I guessed as a lie because who spends the holidays alone?

We move on from our game. I share the success of my vlog, and how for the first time, I feel like I found my place. How I don't worry as much anymore about being successful or comparing myself to Santi's career.

"What's your favorite part of the vlog?" He gives me his full attention, his blue eyes wandering over my face.

"Mm, that's a tough question. It originally started out as a travel vlog, but now everyone loves how I work with F1 and Bandini. Fans seem to be super into it. And they're constantly sending me new ideas of things to do or people to interview."

"I wonder if I'm the best part." His cheeky grin makes me show one of my own.

"I doubt it because people beg for Liam and Jax. Must be their accents."

He scoffs. "It's tough to compete with Jax's British accent. Liam on the other hand… German tends to lack sexiness."

I shake my head from side to side because Liam sounds fine. "There's a reason people like Prince Harry. Or any attractive British guy."

"You find Jax attractive?" His tight smile tells me I didn't say the right thing.

"I mean, people find him attractive. But I went on a double date with him and realized he's not my type." I trip over my own words, wanting to put them out there.

"It wasn't a double date because I was there. That makes it automatically friends hanging out." His eyes glint in the soft lighting.

"Liam's been asking Sophie for a redo, but she keeps saying no."

"We don't want that to happen," his voice rumbles.

When did he get close to me? Our hands are practically touching.

"And why not?" Another breathy sentence from me.

"Because I already called dibs on you." His intense gaze makes me shudder.

"You can't call dibs on people. You sound like a B-list rom-com."

"But I fuck like an A-list porno."

Okay then. Who says romance is dead? My throat tightens as his eyes lower, taking me in. He closes the space between us.

A hand tugs my head toward him. Our lips meet. But unlike our first kiss, this one demands. Noah takes everything from me all at once, his lips brushing against mine, intense and irresistible. This somehow beats our first kiss. We have no one around to stop us, no interruptions to pull us away from each other this time.

One of his hands grips my hair and tugs. The quick bite of pain makes me gasp, giving his tongue access to my mouth. It strokes mine possessively, branding me, not giving me a second to overthink anything. My tongue meets his and strokes back. I want to taste him and make him crave me just as much.

My fingers run through his hair and he groans when I grip the silky strands. I want to pull him in closer, desperate for what he can give me. My body hums with approval as he fucks with my brain and heart at once.

If this was a movie, now would be the moment for cheesy fireworks to go off in the background.

My back hits the blanket and my hands travel across his

chest, checking out the different muscles. He doesn't let up on his own exploration, his hands roaming down my body while our tongues stroke one another. I feel lightheaded from the contact.

I moan when he cups my breasts. My nipples brush against the fabric of my bra, wishing for the barrier to be gone, another obstacle we don't need. My body pushes into his, frantic for more.

His mouth leaves mine. Rough fingers find the hem of my shirt at the same time his lips find my neck. The nipping, licking, and sucking sensations drive me crazy. His mouth does wild things to my body. Aroused doesn't begin to describe the intense burn inside of me as my breasts grow heavy with need and my core throbs.

I rub myself against his hardened length. My jeans feel rough against my thong, temporary friction giving me some relief. Fingers clutch the hard muscles of his back before my nails scratch against the fabric of his shirt.

"You're going to make me embarrass myself if you keep grinding against my cock," he mumbles before returning his attention to my neck. His lips move toward my chest. A new task.

My cheeks heat at his disclosure. But it feels great to make him desire me because this man makes me feel a whole lot of things. The good, the bad, and the absolute dirtiest.

"Don't get shy on me now. Fuck that." His lips meet mine again, this time with a soft and intimate kiss. I find myself unprepared for any of these feelings, Noah overwhelming me. Kissing him feels like so much more.

I regain consciousness and place both of my hands on his chest, pushing him softly. He gets the hint and lifts off me.

"Ah, your brain caught up to you. It was fun while it lasted."

He rubs a thumb against my swollen lips.

"I don't do this type of thing." My hands gesture between the two of us.

"And what is that?" He inches closer again. I hold up a hand, making him pause. His lips distract me and make me want to kiss them again. But I need to get this out before it's too late.

"This. I don't do casual. Random hookups." *Hell no.* Not after kisses that set me on fire and make my brain numb.

He abandons his seductive mood. His grimace makes me second-guess my reasoning, and for a brief moment, I'm afraid about making the wrong decision. I may be irresponsible with other things, but I need to lock my heart up around someone like him. Stay true to my values.

Noah is the type to unwillingly chip off pieces of my armor until I have nothing left. If his kisses make me mindless, I can't imagine what other things with him will do to me. No one told me how much it sucks to be responsible and honest.

"Why not? We can call it quits when the season's over. No harm done."

I seriously doubt that because I can tell from a couple of kisses that's not the case. It hurts to hear him be cavalier about it, but it's not unexpected from someone like him.

His reaction gives me more strength about my decision.

"Uh. I don't think that's true. At least for me. I don't want to catch feelings for someone who isn't looking for a relationship. I'm not *that* type of girl, a no-strings-attached person." I clasp my hands on my lap, preventing any fidgeting. I've only had a handful of exclusive boyfriends in my life.

"Feelings?" His voice gives away his aversion to the idea.

Note to self: he's not a fan of that F word.

"Yes, feelings. People like you leave a trail of broken hearts behind. I don't want to be one of them, another notch in your damaged bedpost."

"I'm not looking for a girlfriend. I have a crazy schedule and racing is my life, so I can't promise you anything but something sexual. And that we'll have the best sex you've ever had in your life. I can tell by our connection."

My exact worry. Looking at him weakens my resolve, but I need to stay strong.

"I'm the type who needs more than a physical relationship with someone. I'm not the booze-and-banging type you usually hang around with. I can't change who I am to be what you want."

"You're really going to deny yourself this?" His reaction shows me how no one denies him. Evidence of his messed-up childhood, the ultimate only-child syndrome shining through. He trails a finger down my neck toward my chest. I gasp at the scorching sensation his finger leaves behind, unhappy how my body becomes aware of his touch instantaneously. It's a shame to deny what my body craves.

"Yes." My panting voice doesn't exude the firmness I need it to. I swat his hands away, ending his spell.

"We can stay friends. Not the benefits kind though, but I'll avoid you less." I nod, convincing myself that this is the right decision. My honesty about avoiding him feels like progress.

"Right." His blank expression fills me with dread. *Am I making the right decision?*

Our dinner went well. Comfortable and easy, something that feels like it can be much more than a casual fling. But people like him don't fall in love. I don't need to open myself up to potential misery with someone from Bandini.

Noah gets up and reaches out for my hand. My skin warms at his touch. *Yup.* I absolutely made the right choice because this is a one-way ticket to heartache. We walk through the sand toward his motorbike. I look back at the picnic area, my heart tightening at the abandoned sight of it. Despite the less than ideal ending, this was one of the best dates I've ever been on and I'll always remember it.

I put on the helmet and his jacket without a fight, a chill running through me at this ending. The smell of him is intoxicating and unfair like it's wrong to breathe in.

Noah stays quiet as he gets on the bike, his mind drifting off to somewhere else, erecting a wall between us. I don't give him a hard time getting on. He starts up the engine, and we take off back toward the hotel. The ride feels shorter as if Noah's desperate to get us back. I don't take it personally.

He drops me off in the parking garage shortly after, pulling the motorbike up to the elevator like a gentleman.

"If it were another life, I'd probably do right by you. I'd take you on dates and try harder. But that's not who I am or how I was raised. I don't know how to be the kind of emotional guy you desire."

My eyes water, clouding my vision. Everything feels final. We've circled one another for three months, and now it's over, gone in the blink of an eye. I respect him for sharing and being honest about who he is.

"Thank you for a great date. It'll be a hard one to top, even with everything." I sneakily inhale one last breath of his jacket before passing it back to him.

"Likewise." His cocky grin doesn't exactly reach his eyes.

"I better get going. Santi will be wondering where I went for so long."

He presses the button. "Yeah, sure." His arms pull me in for a hug while his lips brush softly against mine, giving me a goodbye kiss that should be reserved for lovers—intimate, kind, and packed with unspoken words. My heart perks up before he pulls away.

Elevator doors open, the empty car a welcoming sight. I walk in and turn around.

"Bye, Noah. See you tomorrow."

His intense gaze is the last thing I see before the doors close.

CHAPTER TWENTY

Noah

The first thing I feel when I wake up is the pulsing of my head.

The second thing I feel is a hand crawling up my chest. The third thing I feel is intense regret.

Fuck. Please tell me it's Maya's hand.

I look down at long, red nails. Maya's don't look like these talons scratching at my chest, preferring natural nail colors. These hands are a symbol of my past. Nausea crawls up my throat as I lean my head back down on a pillow.

I comb through the memories of last night, of how I took Maya out on the date I planned. Never thought I could have such a good time with someone while doing absolutely nothing except eating, drinking, and kissing.

The date was my favorite, at least out of my short list.

And the erotic way Maya kisses. *Fuck me.* Kissing her feels like I did it wrong with all the women before her.

But what the fuck happened after? I struggle to remember

what I did once she pulled the stops on me. Images flash of her rejecting me with sadness in her eyes, knowing I can't give her what she needs. The ultimate blow still feels fresh based on the way my chest constricts at the thought.

Memories hit me all at once, flooding my brain with unwanted recollections. Lots of shots. Liam and Jax at a club, groups of women coming onto us at our VIP table. It feels like I went back to a time before I met Maya.

Shit. My crappy decisions proved Maya's point of not being the type of guy she wants to date. Not in the slightest. I sure as fuck wouldn't want to date someone like me.

My back lifts off of the mattress and a blonde girl topples off me.

"You need to go. Now," my voice rasps. Another reminder of my bad decisions, along with my dry mouth and aversion to sunlight.

I don't want to spend another moment with this woman, the look and feel of her all wrong. Her rose scent, mixed in with the smell of sex and booze, chokes me, incomparable to Maya's fresh one. My stomach rolls at the thought of how badly I fucked up.

I head to the bathroom, choosing to brush my teeth first, wanting to cleanse my mouth from the taste of that woman and alcohol. My battered-up face makes me wince. Disgust rolls through me at my sunken eyes and pale, sickly skin.

I take a shower, eager to rid myself of the woman's smell and everything else associated with her and a bad ending to my night. By the time I get out, there's no sign of her, except for the underwear she left on a pillow. My body shudders as I dump her souvenir in the trash.

I pull my phone from the plug, glad I remembered to charge my battery. At least I made one responsible decision because, overall, I'm a fucking idiot.

Are you shitting me? I didn't set my alarm, missing my practice sessions.

Shit. Shit. Shit!

I bolt out of my hotel room, desperate to make it to my qualifier on time.

I've never been so damn irresponsible in my life.

It doesn't shock me when my day goes from bad to the fucking worst. My qualifier starts out as a shitshow. I rush to get my race suit on and chug a gallon of water to make sure I don't pass out behind the wheel under the hot conditions. Sophie's dad looks pissed as fuck about my tardiness, glaring at me as I swallow down a granola bar.

He fails to hide his distaste. "You look like shit. You're not a young kid anymore, staying up late to party. I expect this from anyone but you." His sneer tells me everything. James Mitchell isn't one to fuck around with because he has balls bigger than King Kong. His green eyes stare down at me while he runs an agitated hand across his face. His gray hair remains in place, unlike mine standing up in different directions, the waves untamed from my hands.

"I'm extremely sorry; this will never happen again." No apologies can erase my terrible decisions.

I trip over my feet while rushing to my car. I'm a hot, crappy mess and fuck if it isn't humbling. Embarrassed doesn't begin to describe how I feel. Bandini mechanics look down at me, unsure how to help, as I clamber into my car. Sweat clings to my chest before the engine starts up, a shitty omen for my fuck-tastic day.

The beginning of my qualifier goes okay as my car takes down the first straightaway. That is until I make it past my first turn. Bile creeps up my throat during most of the turns after, the curves of the track not faring well with the alcohol seeping from my pores. I spend all my mental energy on not blowing chunks inside my helmet because I'd never live that down.

My nasty hangover doesn't pair nicely with my car going two hundred miles an hour round and round the track. The qualifier performance is sloppy and unprofessional. The usual hum of the engine fills me with dread, guilt eating away at me as I think about Maya and how she might feel if she heard about my night.

Sweat trickles down my back, soaking the material of my fireproof gear as I careen across the track. Fans watch the worst display of my entire racing career.

I rush out of my car once the qualifier finishes. My body revolts against me as I throw up twice near a patch of grass close to the pit area, the acidic taste making me nauseous all over again. All of this happens while a local camera crew films me. Somehow, I find enough self-control to not flip them off, instead choosing to give a thumbs up to the camera while I hunch over.

My car places fourteenth for the race. Fucking fourteenth. I haven't had such an embarrassing placement since I started out in F1, and I don't know if I'll live this one down.

The only small blessing from today is how I don't have to attend the press conference meant exclusively for the top three racers. I guess sucking comes with benefits.

Since Santi has the pole position, he'll be distracted. I need to find Maya and apologize for everything. Like for taking her out on a date and fucking another girl in the same day. Even if she's disinterested in hooking up with me, it's wrong.

I spot Sophie and Maya talking with Liam and Jax on the main road near all the hospitality suites. A cold feeling creeps its way up my spine at the sight of Jax pulling her in for a hug. It shouldn't upset me but shit it stings to see her wrapping her arms around him and laughing, unaware of how he got a blowjob at the table last night from a random chick.

I don't have a right to feel jealous since I can't give her what she wants. But I can't control it; my fists clench at the sight of them, envy whirling inside of me like toxic air.

Maya's eyes catch mine. The smile she had before slips from her face, and it pisses me off how I've turned her mood sour in two seconds flat.

I stroll up to the guys, keeping it casual even though I barely have it together inside.

"Shit luck today, bro." Liam doesn't look the least bit phased from last night. *Was I the only one who got seriously fucked up?* Come to think of it, he was sober as hell. I don't even think he blinked at any other girls who came onto us. *Shit.*

"Never going out the night before a qualifier again. That was a terrible idea, man." Jax pats my shoulder as he throws me under the bus.

Fuck you very much, Jax.

"You guys look like you had quite the night. Ballsy move before a qualifier." Sophie's narrowed eyes glare into mine.

"Mm, that's why my brother is the best. He puts the team first." Maya's polite smile doesn't reach her flat eyes.

"Yeah, yeah, we get it already. You adore Santiago. At least pretend you want us to do well too." Liam knocks Maya's hat off her head and offers her a shrug. She laughs at him. I want to record the sound for the bad days, like today, because I'm the biggest idiot.

"We better get going. Girls' day and all." Sophie links her arm in Maya's. They head off after saying their goodbyes with Maya ignoring me. It fucking sucks.

"Bro, you got smashed last night. You wouldn't shut up about her." Liam nods his head in the direction Maya left in.

Jax shakes his head. "It was a sad sight until you took that girl home. You even called her Maya once, but she shrugged it off. What was her name? Beatrice?"

Thank you, Jax, for bringing up the last thing I want to think about. I flip him off.

"She was hot. You always get the good ladies." Liam's arms cross against his chest.

"I'm surprised she even went home with him. He kept talking about Maya rejecting him, how she doesn't want a playboy like him." Jax chuckles to himself.

"Okay, guys, I get it. It was a pathetic night. Can we not bring it up anymore? Like ever." My clipped voice matches my declining patience.

"All right. No need to get pissy at us." Liam's last words end that conversation.

I take off in the direction of the Bandini motorhome because I have another round of apologies to get out to Sophie's dad and the pit crew.

Unlike the last time Maya avoided me, we both keep our distance this time. Me because of shame. Her probably because I gross her out, not that I blame her at all.

The rest of Saturday is uneventful, which fills me with relief. I recover from my awful hangover, trying to overhydrate because race-day conditions are hot and alcohol dehydrates like no other. No doubt I'll sweat out three pounds of body weight at least.

On race day, I eavesdrop on Santiago and Maya's conversation, desperate to feel close to her. She keeps her voice low and inaudible. To avoid punching a wall out of frustration, I exit my suite to go to the pit area.

I run through some engine checks and attend a pre-race briefing. Busying myself keeps me from doing something stupid, like finding Maya and giving into her demands while begging for forgiveness. After wrapping up with the top engineers, I head back toward the garage.

I silently curse at Maya sitting next to the computer bay. She wears one of the engineer's headsets so she can listen in on Santi's team radio. A churning feeling of jealousy swirls in the pit of my stomach. Being jealous of her brother...a new low.

A lot of contradictory feelings mix inside of my head. Maya rejects me because she wants more than I can give her, but I don't even know how to try to give her what she wants.

Her vlog camera swings around in full force, filming the busy race-day activities.

I find it difficult to ignore her voice while I discuss the logistics of the car and any last-minute tune-ups. She tours the place and introduces members of the team, a sweet gesture to show off the men and women who are essential to Bandini. Her voice raves about how the crew keeps everything up and running, even introducing them by name, proof of her connection to the team. She has this way of charming people. Unlike me, who has a way of fucking up with people.

I try to hide my shock when she walks up to my car.

"Here we have Slade's team."

I see we are back to last names now.

She does a spin to get everyone in the camera shot. "They're busy doing last-minute checks on his car. He has a big task of catching up to Santiago, Liam, and Jax since he starts in P14 today. It's his worst start since he began racing in F1. Better luck next time."

Thanks, Maya. I take it because I deserve it and more.

I wave at the camera as she pans over my car. Her fruity shampoo hits my senses, instantly bringing me back to the other night. Her lips on mine, the sounds she made when I touched her, when I grinded into her. My dick twitches in my race suit. *Great.*

She moves on to interview one of the head engineers. He subtly checks out Maya's chest in between questions, and it takes everything in me not to push him away.

Concentrate on your car. You're about to go race and you don't have time to worry about her.

I decide to ignore Maya for the rest of the prep. No need for any more distractions, least of all from her since she decided she doesn't want anything casual. She rejected me. Her loss.

I lose the race big time. But I worked my ass off to get out of fourteenth position, and considering where I started, I'm happy with placing eighth. Santi and I even get points for the Constructors.

I head to my suite, not wanting to check out the podium celebrations today despite being glad for Jax and Liam. Santiago, too, I guess. But it was a good day for McCoy, which means a bad one for Bandini.

Maya sits out on the empty balcony of the hospitality area, lying across a couch, cellphone in hand. I like to head up here when I have a bad day, but it looks like she beat me to it.

"Was she worth it?" She baits me, not glancing up from her cellphone screen. My irritability grows with every second she refuses to look at me.

"Who?" I play stupid because I don't want to deal with this shit anymore. We aren't boyfriend and girlfriend.

"The floozie from last night."

My lips twitch up at her word choice. "Oh, her." That gets her to look up at me. I don't like her stormy gaze, the way she comes off indifferent to a situation that bothers the fuck out of her. I'd rather have her mad at me than feel nothing at all.

I meant it when I said I'm a selfish bastard.

"Yup." Her lips pop on the last letter.

"She was a decent lay." I shrug, coming off uncaring, even though my throat feels like I swallowed glass. It feels wrong to lie like this, my words hurting her because I take my anger on myself out on her.

"Mm. Wonder how much alcohol you had to drink to wipe the taste of me from your mouth. Doubt the girl minded, though. Desperation always trumps common sense."

Fuck. She has me there. I'm stunned stupid, unable to get any words out.

"They'll never be as good as what we could have. But this is why people like you never have happily-ever-afters. You're so jaded, you can't see the best things until it's too late."

She gets up, not bothering to give me one last look as she leaves the balcony.

My stomach drops at not being worth a backward glance.

CHAPTER TWENTY-ONE

MAYA

I avoid everything Noah-related for weeks. Anytime I find him in the Bandini suites, I walk the other way. Things sit heavy between us. And not in the "hot and heavy" kind of way, much more like the "my heart hurts whenever I see him" kind of way.

How I feel about him is messy. It doesn't fit nicely into checked boxes or a pros and cons list. I struggle to understand my conflicting emotions, which ends up pissing me off more. Part of me wishes he could commit to trying a real relationship while another part of me thinks he's not even worth the trouble.

He should have waited at least a day before hooking up with someone else. It's basically common courtesy.

How do you fuck another woman right after you go on a date with someone else? It's cold and disgusting. I honestly didn't expect that from him.

Every time I run into Noah, I feign indifference, choosing to ignore the way my heart beats faster around him. Or how my body heats when his eyes roam over me, or the hint of sadness that crosses his face when I ignore him.

I thrust myself into taking my vlog to the next level. Seven hundred thousand subscribers tune in to my vlogs already, and the ads on my videos turn a nice profit. Sponsors reach out to partner with me, something I never thought was possible. The vlog has surpassed everything I'd ever dreamed of. Sophie and I visit different places in every city we travel to, making the most of my time with Bandini while the explorations conveniently keep me away from Noah.

The month-long summer break between the first and second half of the season couldn't have come at a better time. I try to lie to myself and say I don't miss Noah over the vacation. But I do. I check out his social media accounts daily, except he keeps quiet, not posting anything but a couple pictures of the Italian coast. Even gossip accounts have nothing to report on him. He's taken a break from everything. And maybe it's a good thing, seeing as his previous indiscretions finally cycled out of the media.

I spend the vacation with my family, including Santi. Besides the temporary bouts of missing Noah, I have a good time.

Sophie comes to Spain to visit us during the last week of the break. My parents welcome her like a second daughter, sharing how grateful they are for me to have someone to spend time with besides Santi.

Sophie and I come up with the best plan. A talent of hers.

"Repeat the plan back to me. I want to make sure you're convinced." Sophie paints her nails in my bedroom. Tomorrow, we both fly together to the next race because she wants to prep me before seeing Noah at the Belgian Grand Prix.

I jokingly roll my eyes even though I appreciate her friendship and dedication to making sure I keep out of trouble.

"All right. Since I'm now a mature woman who knows better, I'm going to be civil and nice. I don't need to play games with him. We are two adults who can get along for the sake of the team."

Sophie smiles up at the quote she makes me repeat every time I bring up Noah. "And…" She waves her hand expectantly.

"I will not give in."

"In to what exactly? I need to hear you say it."

Ugh, she actually wants me to repeat it.

"I will not fall for his rough yet sweet personality, rock-hard abs, kissable lips, or fuckable body." My new go-to chant.

Her green eyes sparkle. "Atta girl. I'm so proud. Look how quickly you grew in a month. Vacation glow looks good on you." She pinches my cheeks.

"Why does this feel like it's going to be a disaster?"

"Stop your catastrophizing. You're going to give yourself a migraine. What's the goal for the second half of the season? Maybe we need to run through it one more time."

She's so full of it. But I give in because she flashes me two dimples.

"Grow my vlog, find a nice man to go on a couple of dates with, and spend time with my best friend."

Sophie claps her hands like I'm a child saying my first words. The display comes off dramatic and silly, but it fits her.

"Yes, girl. Cheers to that!" We clink our glasses and sip our wine.

The cold liquid soothes my throat. "Where does one find

nice men in F1 anyway? I'm curious."

"Leave that up to me. I'm your fairy godmother but instead of waving a magic wand, I use a magic dildo. Works like a charm. It's guaranteed to land you the best dick you've ever had."

Wine nearly streams out of my nose.

Not sure what I volunteered myself for, but I can't help feeling worried.

CHAPTER TWENTY-TWO

Noah

I regret how I went about everything in Baku, including how my anger got the best of me after the race, making stupid statements to Maya. I messed up big time with her. But I want to fix it and make things right.

I spend a good portion of the break working out kinks in my car and strategizing with the team for the second half of the Championship season.

But I also spend time going to therapy.

Yup. Let that sink in for a second. Me in therapy.

I sit in my psychologist's office, attending one of my two weekly sessions. One session per week wouldn't cut it because I need to work through a ton of shit about my parents, relationships, and my issues with commitment. And I don't have a lot of time before the next race.

The whole process has been a lot to take in. Some days I leave sessions pissed off while other times I leave sad because of how fucked up my parents are and the damage they've caused. Therapy is an emotional struggle that drains me worse than driving one-hundred laps around a Prix track.

"What holds you back from wanting a relationship?" My therapist's brown eyes gaze at me from across the room as he sits casually in his beige chair. I sit on a leather couch, switching between staring up at the ceiling and meeting his gaze.

"I'm not sure. It's kind of a mixture of different things. I've never even tried to have a real girlfriend before."

"Walk me through the combination of reasons." His hands clasp together across his knee. He looks put together with his gray hair combed over and his pressed suit.

"I don't even know what a good relationship looks like. My parents didn't love each other. I was a credit line at Barney's for my mom, an endless tie to my dad's bank account. So I'm not sure what real love even looks or feels like. That's a scary thought in itself." How can I recognize something I have no clue about?

"If you could describe love to me, what would you say?" His questions never let me off easy. No, I consider them shit-stirring instead of open-ended.

"Hmm." I rub the back of my neck. "I think love is about happiness and sacrifice. Compromising instead of arguing. Having someone who is always there for you even when you don't deserve it. Loving someone means you want to spend the rest of your life with them, on the good days and the bad days and everything in between."

He looks proud of what I said, nodding along with me and hanging on each word. A small ounce of pride rushes through me at my thoughtful answer.

"Those are all great ideas of love. And what would be the

reasons holding you back from trying with someone? Let's use Maya as an example since you bring her up during our sessions."

I sit and think about his question for a full minute. He doesn't push me when I stay quiet, instead preferring to wait it out, putting less pressure on me to fill the silence.

"I think I'm afraid." Words leave my lips in a whisper. I don't like admitting fear about anything when I drive cars faster than any other man in the world for fuck's sake.

"Fear is not always a weakness. It's what you do with the fear that shows your true strength. What exactly are you afraid of?" This man and his board of inspirational quotes.

"Not giving it my best and failing. Disappointing her and not being able to be there when she needs me. Breaking her heart and mine in the process. The thought of giving someone power over me…" I look down at my hands. Rough fingertips press together in a fidgeting motion that reminds me of Maya. Ever since Baku, thinking about her makes my chest constrict weirdly like it recognizes how much of a dumbass I am.

"Those are all reasons anyone would be afraid and worried about trying. You're not alone in thinking that. A lot of people share similar reservations when they start a relationship because loving someone makes you vulnerable."

I didn't know that.

"How would you feel if Maya dated another person who is willing to love her like you described earlier?"

I clench my hands. The thought of her dating, kissing, or fucking another guy makes me sick. I don't deserve her, but screw anyone else who tries.

"I wouldn't like it one fucking bit."

"And why is that?" He doesn't flinch at my cursing, further evidence of why I like this man.

"Because I'll be wishing it was me who could do those things with her."

My admission sits with us like a third person. Minutes pass by as I devise a plan, the sound of the clock ticking to the rhythm of my bouncing leg.

"I think I have an idea for what I need to do. But I want to run it by you."

My therapist smiles at me. He helps me build confidence, listening to my ideas while offering insight and opposing viewpoints. I'm fucking done sitting on the sidelines thinking about my mistakes, because I'm the type to be on the front of the grid with a pole-position start.

Time to get my trophy.

CHAPTER TWENTY-THREE

MAYA

"**L**isten, the last date was bad, but this one will be better. I pinky promise. We can ditch together if it goes terrible." Sophie holds my hand before linking our pinkies together, forcing a promise on me before I agree.

I groan. Another date sounds like a terrible idea. "The last one included a guy bringing out photos of his family and ex-wife. He even told me how they got married and divorced, tearing up as the waiter brought out our dessert. I'll never look at tiramisu the same way again."

"Okay, I get it. That wasn't my best work. I'm still fixing the kinks in my magic wand dildo thing. But I picked two good ones this time." Her green eyes fill with hope.

"That sounds so wrong. Who are the new guys?"

Since we both can suffer together, I give in to the plan. I don't want to risk it with another disastrous date because a woman can only take so many photo albums.

"They're two top engineers for McCoy. I met one of them at

a press conference my dad was talking in. They're sweet, I swear. Cross my heart." She drags her index finger in an X motion.

I nod along, agreeing to the plan because of Sophie's good intentions.

"Yay. You won't regret it! They even got us reservations at the nicest restaurant in Milan. Because nothing says a good date like pasta!" She claps her hands and drags us to my hotel room to pick our outfits. For someone who loves sneakers and T-shirts, she sure enjoys getting dressed up.

Here we are on a date the night before a qualifier round, sitting across from two good-looking guys. Sophie shoots me a grin when they look at their menus.

I agreed to this date for her because she's seemed to struggle with Liam ever since they went to Canada. Not that she opens up about it.

The man Sophie set me up with has a head of blonde hair that curls at the ends. He looks kind of cute in a sweet way, and he even has a hint of an accent I can't place. Candlelight dances off his brown eyes as he stares into mine.

"What's it like to be a vlogger for Bandini? At McCoy we always watch them, hoping you'll drop trade secrets." My date, Daniel, smiles wide.

I shake my head. "I'm careful to make sure that doesn't happen. I think they would flag my videos and not allow me to film anymore." I make a zipping motion with my fingers and throw the invisible key over my shoulder.

"Which videos have you seen?" Sophie jumps in, her blonde space buns bobbing.

"We watch a lot of them and they look pretty well done. Do

you edit them yourself?" Her date, John, asks.

"I've learned how to edit better as I continue to make more videos. I'm sure I could upgrade my equipment once it takes off because nice cameras are worth thousands of dollars."

"By taking off, she means more than a million followers. She's close to 800,000 already." Sophie beams like a proud mom.

"How much did you pay Noah to do those videos? Especially the question ones because he never does stuff like that. He even declined *Sports Daily* when they asked for a similar one."

My eyes burn at the memory. Nothing like bringing up Noah to dampen my mood, except my date has no idea about Noah and me, let alone how the industry works.

"I paid him nothing since he volunteered, and I didn't exactly strong-arm him into it. Plus, we don't really pay for things like that in this kind of work. Famous people usually do it if they want to. If not, they say no." I scrunch my nose at Daniel's misunderstanding.

"Doubt anyone could say no to you, not even the great Noah Slade." Daniel's smile doesn't fill me with warmth like Noah's did. I give a weak smile back, not exactly enjoying how he brings up Noah and Bandini.

Sophie gives my knee a squeeze under the table, finding the perfectly painful pressure point. I force the idea of him out of my head. Her new project includes conditioning me into not thinking about Noah anymore, going as far as watching videos on Pavlov's dog.

"Excuse me, I'll be right back. I need to use the restroom." I push my chair out with more force than I'd intended. It knocks into the back of another person's seat, causing the occupant to glare at me.

"I'm so sorry." I speed walk out of there and dart into the dark hallway near the bathrooms.

I pull out my phone to distract myself while keeping track of time. Scrolling through Instagram's feed comforts me.

The screen shuts off.

I breathe in a smell that's distinctly Noah.

Oh God, why does my luck suck so bad lately?

"Date going that terrible?" His hoarse voice grabs my attention, and my heart rate picks up. Calloused fingers lift my chin, making my body respond to him instantaneously like we haven't spent a month apart. Poor lighting in the hall doesn't give me much to look at. I breathe in the smell of him because I'm a glutton for punishment. His textured thumb drags across my lips.

"What are you doing here?" *Did my voice sound husky?* I can't hear it over the blood rushing through my ears.

"I'm out at dinner with friends. It's a popular restaurant."

Okay, so at least he doesn't follow me around. That would be a bit concerning.

Noah's dark silhouette blocks any light, making it difficult to distinguish his features in the dim hall. His lips brush against mine. My lips tingle from the barest touch, a mere caress I feel guilty enjoying. I tilt my neck to the side to evade his lips.

He chuckles. His lips trail down my neck instead, leaving light kisses behind.

"I've missed you." The three words he says feel like everything I want to hear. They make my heart ache because he can't give me what I want, no matter how much I crave it.

"You can't miss what you've never had." If I wasn't currently occupied, I'd clap myself on the back for that one.

"What if I told you I've changed, that the break did us good?" He gets the words out before his lips suck on my neck, what I deem to be my weak spot. Our chemistry has not wavered. It feels as charged as ever; as his lips drag across my skin, my body unconsciously arches into him.

The betrayal.

"Not sure if I believe you. Actions speak louder than words."

Trashy tabloids have kept quiet since the blonde woman in Baku. He may speak the truth, but I don't want to chance it, putting myself out there to get hurt.

"Let me show you. Just give me a real chance."

His lips find mine again. But this time his kiss domineers the situation, just like him, crashing against me and tearing down my walls. His tongue strokes the seam of my lips, seeking entrance.

I keep them sealed off, preventing him from taking the kiss further. He nips at my bottom lip in a silent demand for me to open up to him. His teeth graze and pull, causing me to groan at the feeling.

"Uh. Oh man, I'll come back later."

My head snaps up at the stranger's voice. I bury my face into Noah's button-down shirt, which is a bad idea because the addicting smell of him makes me lightheaded.

I don't move until the stranger's footsteps disappear.

"Hear me out. Let me expla—" his voice croaks.

Nope. Need to get out of this situation ASAP.

"Um. Uh…I have to go." I take off in the direction of my table, leaving a grumbling Noah behind me, not bothering to steal a second glance at him. My brain tells me to run away from

Noah while my body tells me to run toward him.

Sophie's eyes narrow at me when I settle back in my seat, making me feel even worse about what happened.

I ignore her side glances throughout the night because we can have story time later.

My stomach twists in knots as Sophie stares at me from across the room, her sneaker tapping against the carpet. She reads my body language while she sits on the sectional couch in Santi's suite. My eyes gaze around at the plain hotel room in a struggle to find anything interesting to look at. Basically, anything but her face would do.

"What did we say about him?" She won't let me off easy, her voice laced with disappointment.

"Well, I didn't *exactly* fall for his rough yet sweet personality, kissable lips, fuckable body, or rock-hard abs. Honestly, he cornered me in the hallway. I didn't even know he was there. It's not like I chose the restaurant." I may or may not have practiced that line in the bathroom earlier.

"And what, he tripped and his lips fell on yours?" She waves her hands around. *Yup. Definitely ticked off.* My silence doesn't bode well with her because she paces the room, agitated and grumbling about how all her plans fail.

"Don't you dare try to play it off in your pretty head. That's a ridiculous idea. You came back to the table a mess and your lips looked like you sucked his dick in the bathroom. *Did you?* Or did he suck on them like a Hoover vacuum?"

I have no clue how she says the most ridiculous things as seriously as she does, not even cracking a smile.

My chest and face feel fifty shades of pink. I dramatically throw myself face first onto the couch in front of us, grabbing a pillow to drone her out. She means well and all, but it doesn't make it easier.

"I'm sorry. I won't do it again. I learned my lesson." Cushions muffle my voice.

"I sure hope so. Daniel is a nice guy who's hesitant about giving you another chance." She plucks the pillow from my face and stares at me, green eyes glittering under the dim lighting.

"You talked to him about it?" I cringe at my whininess.

She shakes her head. "Not exactly. But I can read these things. Call it intuition."

"Next one will go better. Maybe we shouldn't go somewhere public." I get her hopes up, pretending to agree to another date I have no intention of following through on. No need to lead a poor guy on when my mind is on someone else.

"I don't think it'll happen because we are engaging in stage two of the plan."

Sophie's second phase fills me with uncertainty.

I glance up from my pity corner on the couch. She taps away at her phone, ignoring me.

"I'm bringing in reinforcements." *Tap. Tap. Tap.* Her fingers moving against her phone fills the quiet.

"Should I be worried?"

She shoots me a mischievous smile.

Well, that answers my question.

CHAPTER TWENTY-FOUR

Noah

I try to pinpoint the exact moment my friends started ditching me. Was it after Germany? Or France? I can't exactly place it, but ever since the summer break, I barely hang with Liam and Jax. Every week, they come up with excuses about being busy. By the time we show up in Singapore for the Grand Prix, they're nowhere to be found. Yet again.

The only time I see them is during a press conference after Saturday's qualifier. I ended up driving well and have pole position for tomorrow, securing the best spot at one of the few night races we have. At least things with racing look promising.

Do they not want to hang out with me because I win a lot? The Championship gets competitive after all. Maybe they keep their distance for the brand's sake since teams don't encourage us to hang out and play nice. But when I think back on times in the past, they never got this way, which means it has to be something else.

I hang out all alone in my hotel room, overlooking the city, checking out the view of the famous trees and Marina Bay Sands buildings. Singapore bustles with activity before the race. People flood the sidewalks, looking like ants from my suite's balcony.

Despite all the action, for the first time, I feel lonely.

I'm putting it out there. My therapist would be proud.

I sit on the couch for a few minutes, processing what it feels like to have no one around. My friends rarely respond to my messages. We haven't planned a night out, a strange occurrence for them in the biggest party city on the Prix schedule.

Even Maya avoids me ever since I kissed her in the Milan restaurant two weeks ago. She sticks to Santi's side like a stage-five clinger, playing it smart because I'd never do anything in front of him. But she won't give me a chance to explain myself either. I want to tell her I'm ready to try with her, the whole deal, no more fucking around.

I can't stand how she evades me. So I do what usually calms me and drones out the thoughts in my head. I pull up Maya's vlog on my laptop and click yesterday's upload. My heart drops at her stunning smile, her brown eyes staring into the camera with happiness as she holds a lens to her face.

"Hi, everyone, welcome back. This week we are in Singapore and it's honestly one of the coolest cities we've visited so far during the Championship. I'm here with Sophie, Jax, and Liam."

Now I have my answer about my friends' whereabouts. My teeth clench at the sight of them all smiling into Maya's camera like they didn't ignore my two texts to hang out.

"We're here at the Gardens by the Bay. Viewers asked for a Web's Most Asked Questions with Jax, Britain's favorite playboy. Liam decided to tag along because he has a serious case of

FOMO."

You're not the only one, buddy.

"We decided to do a combination deal here. It's the best of both worlds. I asked viewers what their most pressing questions were about these two clowns. I wrote down the top ones because my Instagram was flooded with options. Ready?"

Sophie grabs the camera and films Liam, Jax, and Maya sitting on a bench with the supertrees in the background. *Fan-fucking-tastic.* A few people walk behind them and wave at the camera.

A burning sensation settles in my gut.

"Some are embarrassing, and others are outright silly, but I can't be biased. I picked whichever ones were asked the most." Maya smiles as she pulls out a paper with a list of questions.

I remember the time I told her she can't be biased. Guess she keeps me in mind someway, making me smile.

My laptop bounces to the rhythm of my knee, nervousness and curiosity coursing through me about where this will go. Most of the questions she asks Liam and Jax are about F1 and the guys' racing careers. Seven minutes pass before Maya asks about personal issues. Can't help feeling like a stalker watching them like this, but she does post it publicly. Screw it.

"Jax or Liam. Or both. The lady subscribers wonder about your relationship status?"

They both high-five each other behind Maya like they're five years old.

"I can answer for myself. I'm single and ready to mingle. Meet me at the Singapore party after the Grand Prix if you're interested in hanging out and getting to know me." Jax rubs a tattooed finger across his chin. Liam grins, not answering the question, that sly little shit.

Maya pretends to gag. "You heard it here first, everyone. I am *not* dating either one of these guys. We're all friends." She nods enthusiastically. Liam stays silent, winking at the camera and tapping his fingers on his thigh.

Do they hang out this much? How did I miss this?

I pull up Liam's Instagram profile. His most recent images are of him and Jax, or the four of them out touring whatever city the Prix is in. Plus, a few hard-to-miss posts of him and Sophie.

When did he clean up his act?

Jax's profile looks similar. He has a picture of him and Maya in a photo booth from a gala event. I recognize the background because I was there too, yet I don't remember seeing Maya there.

Where did they even find the time for all of this shit? But more importantly, could I make time for something besides racing?

I land myself on the Singapore podium. Second place. *Woo-fucking-hoo.*

This time the champagne showers don't feel as fun. The crowd roars but I ignore them, my eyes landing on Maya standing behind a barrier as she cheers Santi on. My eyes stay glued to her for minutes. Her grin falters when she catches me looking at her, but she regains her composure. Jax and I end up spraying champagne on Santi since he impressively won the whole thing. This Prix is a challenge. Humidity is disgustingly high, making it hard for us to race with our heads fully in it. I think I lost at least five pounds after racing today. Not joking, sweat still drips down my back, clinging to my race suit.

Attendants escort us to the press conference after we all have a weight check, an ice bucket bath, and a quick shower. The idea of answering more questions fills me with dread because I'm not in the mood for reporters.

It stuns me to find Maya in her usual corner of the press conference. She gives me a tight smile before Sophie whispers something in her ear, her throat dipping back as she lets out a laugh. Carefree and so damn beautiful. I lick my lips at the sight of her, the hollow part of her neck easily becoming one of my favorite places—to kiss, to touch, to nip.

I'm thankful for the table in front of me because I don't need *that* problem on camera today.

Since press conferences can be boring as fuck, I run through my plan for tonight. I can't skip out on the Singapore after-party Maya mentioned. She glances at me, making my lips tip up into a naughty smile, the first one I've given her in a while.

Her eyes widen.

If only she knew what was coming. I'm done playing games; I'm getting my checkered flag.

I pull out the big guns for this. And by big guns, I mean Sophie because she's the equivalent of a grenade launcher and semi-automatic rifle combined. Without her on my side, the plan is hopeless.

I text her after the press conference to please meet me in my hotel room. She grumbles about it until I text her with praying hands and a promise for chocolate-chip cookies. Girl hasn't changed in all the years I've known her.

"What do you want, Slade?" Her icy glare could make a normal man cry, but instead, I grin. How formal of her to use my last name.

I make myself comfortable on the couch since Sophie refuses to sit. She stands in a power pose, ready to take me on, hands on her hips. An intimidation stance that barely reaches past my head.

"I'm coming to you for help because I really need it. And trust me, I do."

Sophie blows a bubble with her gum before popping it, the sound breaking the tension in the room. She looks like a Barbie version of a mob boss.

"How can I help you? I don't even know what you want." She likes to play dumb, batting her eyelashes at me.

"I think you do." *Let's cut the bullshit.*

"I want to hear you say it. The first step in fixing a problem is admitting you have one in the first place."

Yup. This is why Liam can't help being around her. She gives him a run for his money, all sassy and shit.

I suppress a groan and tug at my hair. "I like Maya."

Her blank gaze gives nothing away. She blinks a couple of times, waiting for me to continue.

"And I messed up. I thought I knew what I wanted. But in reality, I didn't."

"Tell me more." She sits down, her pose looking like my

therapist.

"I took her out on a date. I'm sure you're aware of that." She nods. "And it didn't exactly end well. I told her I could only offer physical stuff. No attachments or frills, and she wanted more."

"No duh. And what do you want now?" Her gaze reminds me of her dad, staring into me like she can sense my sincerity.

I look away from her intense scrutiny. "I think I want more."

"I don't think you should do anything unless you *know* you want more. Maya's the sweetest. She doesn't need someone who isn't willing to go all the way. Like make sacrifices for her."

My fists tighten in front of me. "I can try. I never even wanted this before. But seeing her all the time, from far away, I feel terrible. I struggle to not go up and talk to her, or even kiss her. I want a chance. But I need your help." I glance at Sophie.

She looks at me with a genuine smile and warm eyes, the opposite of how she was when the conversation began. "Share with me what you have planned. I'll see what I can do on my end."

I'm nervous because I don't know if Sophie will hold up her end of the deal. Hell, she concocted half of the plan after she deemed my original one unfit. Once I told her I seriously wanted to date Maya, Sophie became a lot more willing to help, coming up with a few ideas she thinks Maya would like. She nixed my original plan to show up at the Prix after-party, telling me Maya doesn't function well past 12 a.m. Lucky for me, Singapore Prix weekend includes events until the following Monday because they love to party over here.

I sit at an empty table at an exclusive restaurant. Sophie secured a private room that will force Maya to give me her undivided attention for at least an hour, but I hope for more if I buy a good bottle of wine. Because who can resist that? My fingers tap against the table, a nervous tick I picked up from the fidgeter herself.

Finally, after what feels like forever, someone knocks on the door.

"Okay, you guys. This is the strangest dinner plan ever—" Her voice cuts off when her eyes land on me sitting alone.

Her eyes widen while her mouth drops open. She's dressed up in a sexy black cocktail dress with her dark hair flowing around her face in waves, adding to her gorgeousness. I take a deep breath to settle my own nerves.

I stand and walk up to her slowly to prevent her from fleeing.

"What's going on?" Her eyes dart around the room, taking in the two seats, before they land on me.

"Let me explain over dinner." My hand clutches hers as I walk her toward the chair across from mine, hoping she decides to stay. I pull out her seat and usher her into it. A compliant Maya may be my favorite version of her.

"I'm confused. I'm guessing Sophie is in on this plan?" She lets out an adorable soft curse under her breath.

"Correct. Let's order a drink first because we both can use one."

We get situated and order our food right away at Maya's persistence. I take her biting on her lip as a guilty yes that she wants to leave as soon as possible.

I sigh before speaking. "I had two months to get you out of my system. And trust me, I tried."

She flinches at my words.

Fuck, come on. I suck at expressing myself. "Not like that. I mean, I had to sit with my own decisions."

She relaxes in her chair. I take another deep breath, calming my nerves. *Think before you speak.*

"I thought it would get easier with time. But you avoided me, which sucked. I went from seeing you every day, and talking to you and spending time together, to nothing."

"I wasn't trying to ignore you." Her eyes flick across the room.

I give her a pointed look.

"Okay, fine. I was trying to a teensy bit. I told you what I wanted, and you rejected me. I can't expect you to change any more than I expect myself to. It's not fair to either one of us."

"Well, I have changed, and I want to try to give you what you want. Spending all that time alone, I realized I want what you want. To spend time with you before and after races, like going on dates, hanging out at events, being lazy in bed together after mind-blowing sex. Give me all the strings attached." The thought of rejection makes my stomach drop.

Her eyebrows dart up. "How do I know you won't back out the moment you get scared?"

I don't blame her for being skeptical when I haven't exactly proven myself yet. "You don't. And I don't either. But it's what I can give you for now. The real question is are you willing to take it?"

She can back out at any moment. I can tell she thinks hard about it by the way she works her bottom lip between her teeth.

She looks down at her hands. "I guess we can give it a try. What changed your mind?" Something warm spreads through my chest, eating away at the uncertainty and nervousness from before. Her agreement is all I need.

I lift her chin up, craving eye contact. "I mean it when I say I spent a lot of time alone. I reflected on what was stopping me from trying this out with you. Our chemistry is—" her lips capture my attention—"explosive. But I also know there's more. I like being around you, especially when you give me all your attention. I like when you film me without asking because you're afraid of me saying no, even though you can get me to agree to anything. I love the way you laugh almost as much as the way you find your shoes interesting when you get nervous. I really like the special noises you save just for me when I kiss you, or the smiles you give me when no one is looking. I'm serious about trying it all with you. No holding back. I even met with someone to talk about my own issues and reservations, because when I do something, I go all in." *Clearly came down with a severe case of word vomit.*

She looks as surprised as I feel about revealing my secret. And fuck, vulnerability scares me, but I can trust Maya. I *need* to trust her. For once in my life, I don't view leaning on someone else as a negative.

"I'm proud of you. That's a huge step." She grabs my hand and gives it a squeeze. A buzz similar to sticking my finger in an electrical socket courses up my arm.

I nod, not wanting to break the moment by hashing out my parental issues. "I've missed being around you."

"I have too. It's not the easiest thing—avoiding you when all my fans are dying to hear and see more of you." She shoots me a wink. "I had to fill the time with other interviews."

My breath hitches at the easygoing smile on her face, finally getting the grin I've waited weeks for. She fills me with hope. It's a new feeling, wanting someone to believe in me while desiring to prove myself worthy of her.

"We should give the subscribers what they want. I watch your videos." My cheeks heat up at my admission. I chug wine before I continue, needing extra help tonight. "I may be partial, but I think I'm better clickbait than Jax or Liam."

Her giggle fills the room. It's the best thing I've heard all week, even better than winning second place.

And it hits me.

Shit.

CHAPTER TWENTY-FIVE

MAYA

We are doing this. Noah and me.

I never imagined he would come around. Days turned into weeks since the Baku disaster, and he didn't make a move, except for the time in Italy.

Noah hires a car to take us to a party, the lights of the city passing us by. Noah grips my hand on his lap, occasionally giving it a squeeze, checking that I'm still here.

"I don't want my brother to know. At least not yet." I look at him head-on, no shoes stealing my attention this time.

The temperature in the car drops a couple degrees. It may sound dramatic, but I swear it happens.

"Why?" His edgy voice makes me frown.

My eyes plead with his. "It's new. I don't want to distract him from the Championship since you're both teammates and he won't like it. He tends to be overprotective of me."

Noah doesn't talk for a full minute. I shift in my seat, waiting for him to say anything. His frown makes me wish I could take back my words.

"I'm not happy about it because I don't want to treat you like a dirty secret. I'm happy to be with you...but if that's what you want, I'll respect it." He shrugs.

"If it works out, I'll tell him after the Championship, once everything is finalized for him."

His blue eyes stay pinned to mine. "It's going to work out, so we'll tell him when you're ready." His clipped voice has a finality to it.

"Thank you." I move close to him and wrap my arms around his waist, a new gesture that feels right. He gives the top of my head a quick kiss before he returns my hug.

"Now, time for kissing and making up. I hear that's the best part." He mumbles the words into my hair.

My laugh makes his own chest rumble.

I can now confidently say kissing and making up might be my favorite part too.

I've watched extravagant weddings on television, even a few crazy sweet sixteen parties where a kid cries over getting the wrong colored convertible. All those parties one-up each other with new levels of craziness. If I combined every single overdone party known to man, that would sum up what Noah and I walk into for the Singapore celebration. Do all local events look like this—filled with indulgence, celebrities, and glam bordering on obscene? It's a party Gatsby would envy. But I love every second of it, soaking up the activities, including a side stage where people perform.

People say this is one of the best parties of the entire Championship. None of the galas so far hold a candle to it. We stand on the rooftop of the most famous building in the city overlooking the whole island, the supertrees glowing while buildings around us light up.

"Amazing, isn't it? Plus, now I have a date, which makes it ten times better." Noah's hand grips my waist. His sexy smirk makes my heart pick up and my thighs clench. I sigh at the grin he saves especially for me. He wears a navy-blue tux today with black lapels and a crisp white shirt. I love the look on him, especially when my eyes gaze upon the bow tie. He looks dreamy.

He gives me a peck on the lips. My body stills as I search around nervously for my brother.

"I'll keep an eye out for him. Don't worry." His gruff voice vibrates against my chest. Lying to my brother makes me sick with worry, making it difficult to fully enjoy attending the event with Noah.

Darkness cloaks us, giving us the ability to disappear into large crowds of people, becoming one of the many partygoers. We grab drinks at the bar before we search for our friends.

We find them soon after, Noah's fingers tensing before he removes them from my waist. The loss of contact makes me frown. But it's a necessary precaution at the moment, at least for the next two months until the World Championship is over.

We pull up to the table Jax and Liam reserved, bottles of alcohol set up in the center. Sophie sits next to them. I take up a spot next to her while Noah sits on the opposite side with the boys.

"Did it work out between you two?" She yells over the music

into my ear.

I nod my head up and down in confirmation. "I'm surprised you helped pull that plan off. What happened to saying no to fuckable bodies?"

She winks at me. I laugh because it looks way more like a twitch.

"This time it was worth it. I have faith it'll all work out. The magic dildo told me so." Both of her dimples show.

"Hey, I finally found you. Didn't see you earlier." My brother pulls me up for a hug. His words tug at my thin resolve, my lies building a wall around myself.

I play off my discomfort. "You've been busy being a Champion and all. Must be such a hard life. Hopefully your hand hasn't cramped from carrying the trophy around all day."

"If I have to do another interview I'll scream. How do you guys ever get used to this?" He glances at the guys who send him a hello.

"You don't. Eventually press conferences become a running joke. Check some of ours out on YouTube." Liam hands a shot glass to my brother before tipping his own back. He pours alcohol for the rest of us. Sophie and I knock ours back at the same time, my nose scrunching as the alcohol burns my throat.

I try to pace myself throughout the night. *A for effort. F for execution.*

I'm drunk by 12 a.m. Liam and Sophie dance around together. Both look smashed, Sophie stepping all over his toes with her sneakers, but he takes it like a man, chuckling at her drunken display. Pretty much everyone has let go and is having a good time except Noah. My brother left so I get the all-clear to scoot over to his side of the couch.

"Why are you sober?" I try to pout my numb lips.

"I think I'm going to cool it on the alcohol for a while."

Right. He and alcohol have a rough history.

My heart thumps in my chest as he smiles down at me. "You have such a good smile. It's not fair. I want to look that good." My fingers touch his face, grazing the rough stubble beneath them, imagining how it would feel in other places.

His chest shakes from laughing. "You look even better." He brushes my hair out of my eyes like a gentleman. His lips brush up against my temple, pressing sweetly before leaving again.

"Your kisses are the best. Like nothing I've ever had," I whisper-shout.

"Oh, tell me more." He lures me in, wanting to hear my drunk confessions.

I glance around to confirm Santi's gone. *All clear.*

"They turn me on. Like a lot." *Killing the sexy game, I think.*

But he snickers at me instead of answering.

"What's so funny? Why are you laughing at me? I'm busy flirting. Hello." I push at his shoulder to make him stop.

He shoots me a breathtaking smile. My arms cross over my chest, his eyes narrowing as he stares down at my cleavage. I return the favor by checking him out. His messy hair does it for me, along with the bow tie he already undid an hour ago. *Sigh.*

I grin. "Let's blow this popsicle stand."

He throws his head back and lets out a roar of laughter. I like being funny.

"Should I take that as a yes?" I clap my hands together.

"Sure, Maya. Let's go. Meet me outside in five minutes."

Noah gets up from the table and says his goodbyes to the group. He acts like an expert at this incognito stuff to the point that someone could think we'd planned it all before.

I scroll through my phone, a hard job when all I want to do is get up and leave with Noah.

I wait for a total of four minutes before making my grand exit. My brother mopes at my departure after I find him schmoozing with sponsors. His sulking looks vaguely like mine, and I don't like how much I corrupt him.

I check the town car's license plate like Noah told me to. Numbers blur but it looks about right. My body falls into the bench seat dramatically, my dress swooshing around me as material flies everywhere.

The ride back to the hotel is quick with our driver adjusting his rearview mirror in hopes of sneaking a peek at our heavy petting and toe-curling kisses in the back seat. Noah barks at him to cut it out and to keep his eyes on the road. The older man sputters out an apology, the sound of his mirror returning back to normal making me laugh. At least until Noah shuts me up with more kisses.

I struggle to keep my eyes open by the time we pull into the hotel. Alcohol hits me all at once, my body giving up the battle to stay awake. We both get out of the car at the same time since the hotel looks empty.

Noah practically carries me to the elevators. My feet are finding it difficult to keep up with his pace; they're dragging behind me as he holds me up.

I'm a giggling mess, but he joins me like a good sport.

It's all fun and games until he rejects my advances in his room.

"What do you mean, no?" My vision clouds as I take in a blurry Noah, his tux jacket abandoned, and his bow tie lost somewhere in the car ride. He snickers when I stomp my foot for good measure.

"You're drunk. I don't want to risk you not remembering the first time I fuck you. I'm a gentleman, meaning I want to fuck you sober."

"I'll remember. I promise." I lift up two fingers like a Scout's honor. He props up one more to show me how it's really done.

"What do I know, I wasn't a Girl Scout."

Noah laughs as he pulls me toward the bed. It's one of my favorite sounds, gruff and short. He shows me exactly what he can do even if I'm drunk.

CHAPTER TWENTY-SIX

MAYA

I wake up the next morning not being able to breathe. Something heavy lies on my chest, making it difficult for my lungs to expand, not to mention the warmth against my side.

I bolt up and try to piece together what happened. My body relaxes when I find Noah's golden arm wrapped around my stomach. He rolls onto his other side at my jolt, replacing me with a pillow, looking innocent as he hugs it. I smile down at him and enjoy a younger-looking Noah.

My memories come back of how we stayed in his room last night, making out like teenagers.

My phone buzzes on the nightstand with a text from Santi.

> **Santi (09/17 9:13 a.m.):** Where are you?
> You didn't sleep in your bed.

A wave of shame hits me as I type out another lie. My thumb hovers over the send button, unsure about how far my deception will go. But Santi wouldn't understand. At least not during this season, with tensions through the roof between him and Noah. I seal my fate by pressing send.

> **Maya (09/17 9:15 a.m.):** Stayed with Sophie.
> Did you just get to the room?
> **Santi (09/17 9:18 a.m.):** Uh, yeah. I'll text you
> after I take a nap.

A nap at 9 a.m.? He's always preferred to be private about his love life ever since he and his high-school girlfriend broke up after he chose F1 over her. Now my brother keeps his heart locked up like a maximum-security prison.

I squeal when Noah's arms tug me back to bed, ending my conversation with Santi. Warm sheets wrap around my body as Noah pulls me into his chest.

"What are you doing up this early?" I dig how his voice sounds extra gravelly in the morning.

I lay my head on his chest. "Santi texted me to check in. Told him I'm staying with Sophie."

"Mm. When does your flight take off?" His fingers drag through my hair, untangling knotted strands.

"Later today on a red-eye. We're flying straight to the next race."

He pauses his hand movements. "You know what that means?"

Can't say I do. My brain doesn't function in the morning without coffee.

My voice strains. "No. But tell me."

More running of fingers through my hair. "Now that you're

sober enough to consent, I have a few things in mind."

Noah's lips find mine, kissing me senseless. I break away after a few minutes.

"I want to shower first. I feel gross after the club last night." My nose scrunches at the thought of not washing off my makeup. I may or may not look like a racoon, but I need a mirror to confirm.

"What a great idea. Let me help you." Noah hauls me out of bed and toward the bathroom. He places me on my feet before he sets up the shower, turning knobs and checking the temperature.

"It's a tough task. Are you sure you're up for the job?" I bat my lashes.

I don't even know if I'm up for the job. *Are we doing this? Going all the way?*

Noah answers the question for me when he pulls off the big T-shirt I wore to sleep. I don't even question how I ended up in said T-shirt, but I'm going with the flow, not wanting to kill the moment.

"You're so beautiful." He runs a hand through his already messy hair. His eyes roam over my body, taking me in. The way he looks at me makes me feel sexy, invigorated, and brazen.

I find it tough to distinguish steam from tension in the bathroom. It's hot, he's hot, the whole situation is fucking hot. My body feels feverish as he slowly appraises me again. His fingers drag across the slopes of my breasts, my skin pebbling at his touch, while excitement bubbles within me. His hand finds the clasp of my bra and he snaps it off, leaving only my lace panties. The last barrier between us.

My boobs bounce as I move closer to him. I decide he looks entirely overdressed and his boxer briefs need to go. My hand dips below his waistband, brushing against his cock, swiping at the bead of pre-cum on his tip. His body tenses and he groans.

"Let me help you out of these." I pull at the waistband and drag them down his muscular legs. He kicks them off, exposing me to his naked glory.

My oh my, is it a sight indeed. People rave about American football or hockey players or any other type of sport. Ladies don't understand how sexy F1 racers are. I pant at the image of Noah standing before me, all his golden skin visible, muscles tensing at my assessment. *I was right.* He does have rock-hard abs, a fuckable body, and kissable lips. He even has a defined v-cut that I want to run my tongue across. His cock is huge, begging to be touched, licked, and fucked. I'm game for all of the above.

"God. How many hours do you work out in a day?" The question slips past my lips without a filter.

He chuckles to himself, making me glad I got my stupid question out of the way. His body isn't even remotely fair. I shut my eyes and open them back up to make sure I see everything right.

I bite my lip at the sight of him. He pulls me toward him, ending our eye-fucking session.

"How about I show you how much stamina I build up from my workouts. That's the most impressive part." He runs his hand down my spine.

I'm sold.

Our shower remains temporarily forgotten. His lips find mine, his tempo desperate, persistent, and careless. Teeth gnash, bite, and suck. Sensations overwhelm me, making me question if this is too much. I can combust here with a few touches to my center. His tongue strokes mine, invading my mouth and taking me prisoner. *Sign me up for this life sentence.* My heart hammers in my chest, unable to settle down at Noah's relentless kisses. Hands grope his body, testing, touching, wanting, and assessing the ridges of his muscles as I memorize every part of him.

His hands find my underwear. Fingers trail the outside until they dip into my core. I groan as his fingers rub against me, making my body pulse with need.

A snapping sound rings over our labored breaths before loose lace falls at my feet.

"You tore my underwear? I've never had that happen before. I thought that was a thing in movies."

His husky laugh turns me on even more.

"I'm not like any of the guys you've been with before. I may not be your first fuck, but I might as well be." His domineering words ignite every nerve ending in my body.

Noah seals his possessiveness with a kiss. He demands everything from me, leaving no room for objections as he shatters any last bits of insecurity about us.

He lifts me in one easy swoop, my legs instinctively wrapping around his waist as he carries me to the shower. Our lips break contact when he situates us under the waterfall of hot water. Because this is Singapore and the people here are extra as fuck, it pours around both of us from all different directions, like they made this shower with couples in mind. I thank them for their thoughtfulness.

He pushes me against the shower tiles while his mouth finds mine again. Our kisses become lazier, less hurried, as we enjoy the time together. It's the sweetest he's ever kissed me before.

He puts me down and grabs the soap bar. His heavy gaze follows the contours of my body as he runs the soap across my skin, starting with my neck. Suds start to pour down my breasts. He spends extra time there as he brings my nipples to two sharp points. His hand creeps slowly down my stomach, making sure to soap up every part of me. My knees wobble at his caresses. But he takes his job seriously, being extremely thorough, learning every curve and dip of my body.

My breaths come out labored as his hands dip between my legs. His fingers find my center, but he remains focused on his task. I moan as he washes me in my most intimate place and cleans every part of me. He continues to lather me, all the way down to my feet.

A comfortable silence cloaks us; the only sounds in the shower include running water and our heavy breathing. Neither of us want to break the moment with words. I copy his same movements, running my hands across his chest, spreading soapy bubbles. I relish in the feel of him, his muscles straining under my touch. He closes his eyes, enjoying my touch, a moan slipping past his lips. Damn, I feel powerful making him feel just as good.

I commit to my cause, soaping him up wherever my hands go, roaming down his body and the ridges of his stomach. He groans as my small hands wrap around his cock. I pump once, twice, until he places his hand over mine.

"Your hand feels so fucking good, but you don't have to do it if you don't want to. We can wait."

My lips smirk at him. I love how he'd hold off for me but I'm more than ready to go, not needing his chivalry.

I move along, kneeling to wash his legs. My hands return to

his cock after I ditch the soap. My hand wraps around it before I take him in my mouth, the taste of him both salty and clean. His head tilts back against the shower tiles and he lets out a moan as my tongue traces along his shaft. Vibrations from my laugh prompt him to fist my wet hair in his hands and tug. I pull away to look up at him, interested in getting a read on the situation, seeing a disarmed Noah at my mercy.

"Don't stop now. Finish what you started," he growls before tugging on my hair. *All righty then. Don't have to tell me twice.*

I suck him off like it's an Olympic sport. I lick, stroke, and graze my teeth to add a different sensation. He groans, pulling on my hair. His reactions make me feel powerful, seductive, and turned on. My other hand massages his balls, giving them extra attention. Our eyes connect, blue eyes piercing mine as he brands my heart along with my body.

"Where the fuck did you learn to suck cock so good? Shit." He moans as I suck him even deeper than before. His cock grazes the back of my mouth, testing my gag reflex. "Actually, wait. Don't answer me, Maya. Shit, feels fucking amazing."

I'd laugh if I wasn't occupied.

His hands tug at my hair again, the sting turning me on more.

A tingling sensation creeps up my spine. My hand that was massaging his balls moves toward my center. I touch myself, feeling how needy I am. He takes control of my head and allows my other hand to play with my breasts. His hands push my head up and down his thick shaft while I stroke myself in desperation. I insert two fingers, slowly pumping to the rhythm of me sucking his cock.

He looks down at me pleasuring myself. His lazy smile excites me, igniting me from my heart to my clit.

"Holy shit, you're so sexy. Look at you, sucking my cock while getting yourself off. Oh my God. You better be ready because I'm going to come. Now's your chance to back out."

I'm right there with him, my strokes becoming more frantic. No way in hell I'm not tasting him. Warm cum hitting the back of my throat does me in as I swallow everything he offers. He pulls out after finishing, giving me a moment to find relief. I moan as I explode on my own hand. Stars dance behind my eyelids as I come down from my haze, water falling on me while I sit in an unholy prayer pose. No Hail Mary can save me from him. I glance up at him, offering a playful grin in return.

"You're going to be the death of me. I just fucking know it." Noah lifts me off the floor and shuts off the water. He grabs us two fluffy towels, paying special attention to me as he wipes me dry. I wrap the fluffy towel around me like a dress while he wraps my wet hair in another towel. The gesture makes my heart squeeze, aware of how I've never had someone take care of me like this before.

We end up back on the bed, but this time the experience feels different. Noah's movements show no rush to get this show on the road. I sit up as he removes the towel from my head and tosses it over the side of the bed, landing with a thud on the carpet. My eyes bulge at the brush in his hand. I let out a soft moan as he gets behind me and brushes my hair, starting at the bottom, removing knots meticulously.

"This is single-handedly one of the best things a guy has ever done for me." My eyes close, enjoying the feeling of the brush running through my wet hair. I have no shame. Noah brushing my hair turns me on, the sensory experience making my heart swirl with emotions I can't place.

He laughs. "You're setting the bar too low for me."

Noah enjoys the task, giving it his all. Once all the knots are gone, he returns the brush to the bathroom. I turn toward his standing form next to the bed.

"You're gorgeous. A natural beauty." His heated gaze travels down my towel-clad body, taking in my hotel fashion piece. Who knew I could make a towel look sexy?

One moment he stands next to the bed, the next moment he kneels on the floor while his hands pull my legs toward the edge of the bed.

I think I died and went to heaven.

Noah stares at me with intense eyes as he plucks the towel off me, exposing me again to him.

"I've thought about this for months. We're going to enjoy every second of it because I'm in no hurry."

I gasp when his fingers find my core. They part me and his mouth replaces his fingers, making me lift off the bed at the feeling of his tongue brushing against me. One of his hands pushes me back down and holds me there. His mouth is a relentless torture of the best kind, the mind-numbing type. I'm not sure if I could tell you my own name. He knows what to do, making the guys from my past look like amateurs. Let this be the only time I thank all the women before me.

Noah really is a fucking champion. Someone give this man a trophy.

He licks me, marking me, clearly enjoying the sounds that

fall past my lips. Shit, it feels good. His strokes change speed and pressure, lapping at my center, making the most of the whole experience. The rough texture of his tongue makes my core pulse. He adds two fingers that slide easily inside of me, my body aching for his touch as his pumps match his licks. Pressure inside me builds.

"I'm so close. Oh my God, Noah."

His throat rumbles. The sensation of that combined with the unyielding pump of his fingers pushes me over the edge. I combust, my brain soaring away from me. His licks continue as I come down from my high—a lust-induced haze that beats any drug. My brain shuts down, a prickling sensation traveling down my spine all the way to my curled toes.

He gives me a sweet kiss right at my core, making me melt on the spot.

Here lies Maya Alatorre.

"Death by orgasm. Seems like a good way to go." My face heats at my mistake in saying that aloud.

He chuckles. "We're not done yet. Save your eulogy for after the finale." His wicked grin brings a smile to my face and a warmth to my center.

He keeps me in this position as he searches for what I assume is a condom in the nightstand. I frown when he pulls one out, questioning how he knew one would be there in the first place.

He looks down at me, his smile dropping until realization dawns across his face. He sifts through the nightstand, pulling out a box that still has the plastic wrapping. His knees hit the hotel carpet, making us eye-level.

"Brand new pack. I'm serious when I say I haven't been

with anyone. Not since that day." His eyes flit to the side, shame marring his face about Baku.

"I believe you. You said you want to try, that you're all in?" I look into his blue eyes, giving him an out in case he wants to take it.

Noah doesn't blink. "Maya, I'm willing to try. You won't regret it. I swear."

I bring my lips to his, sealing his words with a kiss. He breaks the moment as he stands up, his eyes darkening as he gazes down my body again.

He fists his dick and pumps a few times, pre-cum dripping from the tip, enticing me. I lick my lips at the sight.

"Next time." His thumb rubs the drop before he brings it to my mouth. I suck on the pad of his thumb, tasting his saltiness. His eyes darken as I lick and nibble.

"You're a naughty little thing. I would have never guessed that you like to play dirty."

The quintessential sound of foil ripping fills me with excitement. "You haven't seen anything yet." Yup. Those words came out of my mouth. I blame him because I'm not usually such a mouthy one, but he boosts my confidence.

He smiles while shaking his head. "I'm going to hold you to that."

Noah gives no warning. No sweet words before he grabs my legs and thrusts himself into me, the hotel bed perfectly situated for this position. My eyes water at the amazing feeling of him filling me. His dick is big, and I haven't exactly done this in a while. But he reads my body like he's been doing this to me forever. His fingers find my clit, rubbing it, making my body pulse with pleasure instead of pain. I forget the uncomfortable feeling of him stretching me to my limits.

"You'll get used to it. I promise." He kisses my lips softly. Another kind gesture, his words sinking into me and taking residence in my heart.

He moves inside of me, his previous sweetness abandoned.

"Holy shit." Words breathlessly escape my lips.

"You're fisting my cock so tightly, Maya. It's like a dream. If I had known it would be this good, I don't think I would have held back for this long." His groans fill the room. I grab the sheets above my head, desperate for something to ground me as he pounds into me slowly.

He stares into my eyes as he finds an amazing tempo. Our bodies move together in harmony, our chemistry nothing short of fantastic.

Noah drives it home. He grabs each of my legs and places them over his shoulder blades. The position makes his dick feel like I'm being fucked for the first time. A sweet torment. His pumps speed up as he slides easily in and out of me. Rough hands rove over my breasts, pinching my nipples. I arch my back, unable to regulate my body's responses, his movements becoming eager and uncontrolled.

"Oh. My. God." My voice comes off as nothing more than a hoarse whisper.

He changes his position slightly, making his dick rub against my G-spot. Noah controls the situation. My body quakes as he continues to thrust into me, strategically hitting my spot every time. I throw my head back as my spine curves up toward him.

"You feel fucking amazing. Tell me you're almost there." He doesn't wait for a response. My body says everything my mouth can't with nothing but moans and groans passing my lips. One hand finds my clit while the other grips one of my ass cheeks. He pulls my ass up off the bed, taking advantage of the angle. His roughness adds to his appeal, showing me how eager he is, and fuck it feels good. His desperation is my gain.

"Yes!"

My body vibrates, my release closing in. I can tell by the strain in Noah's face he follows right behind me.

"Noah..." I don't recognize my own voice, the neediness foreign to my ears.

"Fuck yeah, babe, I'm there with you."

Simple words push me over the edge. I explode around him, my moan echoing off the hotel walls. He fucks me like a man possessed, his body straining as he holds me in the position he needs while I lose myself in my climax.

Noah's stunning smile is the last thing I see before my eyes close. His orgasm hits him, his cock twitching inside of me as he rides out his release. Frantic pumps become slower, lazier before his body shudders. He stays inside of me until his cock softens, not wanting to break our connection.

We groan together when he pulls out of me after a few minutes.

"You're so damn perfect, inside and out." Noah brushes loose hair out of my face, running a knuckle across my flushed cheeks.

I smile at him. "You're not too bad yourself."

He gives me a kiss before he takes care of the condom in the bathroom. When he comes back, he drags me back to the head of the bed. We lie there together. I bask in the afterglow of the best sex of my life.

"Fuck, Maya. That was the best sex I've ever had."

I smile into his chest. *Likewise.*

CHAPTER TWENTY-SEVEN

MAYA

Someone knocks on the hotel door, pulling me away from my computer. I open the door to find Noah leaning against the frame. He glides past me and walks into the room, taking up a spot against the gray sectional while I take a seat.

"I want to take you out on a date."

I check the time on my phone. "At ten in the morning?" Staying in the hotel room sounds like a fine idea, unless the date he plans involves brunch and mimosas. I can get behind that.

"Exactly why we better get going." He pulls me off the couch and toward the bedroom to get ready.

I smack his hands away when he tries to help me take off my pajamas. "Hands off or else we'll never make it."

He chuckles to himself.

"Does this date involve breakfast food?" *Please say yes.*

"Nope. But afterwards we can get something to eat." He won't share information. *Suspicious.*

Noah's eyes gleam. I should be concerned because that

look usually leads to hours in the bedroom. Take my word for it because we've bounced around each other's hotel rooms for the past week at all hours of the day.

But I go along with his plan because it's nice of him to set up a date. Noah claims he's changed. Who am I to rain on his parade?

I still can't deny my apprehension about the whole thing. Not the sex part. That part is banging. Okay, I know that pun is bad. I blame all the Instagram captions I have to come up with because being punny is basically a full-time job.

But everything else between Noah and me still remains questionable. It's brand-spanking new with us being in the relationship honeymoon stage. Ask me again once the going gets tough. Like when my lies to my brother about my whereabouts blow up in my face.

Positive energy flows right out of me the moment he pulls up to the location of our first real date. An odd choice for a one on one. I drag my body out of the car and take a step apart from him the moment we get within range of the video cameras in the Bandini pit. We still have to keep up appearances in front of my brother and everyone else that can spill our secret. Only Sophie can be trusted.

"Our date is at the racetrack?"

My eyes assess the crowd in front of us. Not sure why he wants to visit the location for the Malaysian Grand Prix. Should I be worried about future dates if he thinks this is a good spot for our official one as a new couple?

I'll have to take charge of the next one.

Noah rubs his hands together. "Think of this as a trust

exercise. You know how people do trust falls?"

"Uh. Sure?" I nod along. Uncertainty creeps up my spine when he smiles down at me.

"So, I don't want to worry about how you might not trust me yet. I want to make sure you do. Because that's the foundation of relationships." He sounds confident about all of this.

What podcasts does he listen to? I don't know whether I should be concerned or impressed.

"Your smile makes me a little nervous," I blurt out. Nothing good comes from his shit-eating grin, the same look I give my parents when I'm hiding something.

He walks toward Bandini's pit area, a silent command to follow him. I wish I had stayed in the car. Distant sounds of tires squealing across pavement alert my senses.

A group of people rallies around the pit area. Camera crews film people getting inside of neon-colored Bandini cars, perfectly lined, making up the entire rainbow.

I make the mistake of reading the banner above our heads. *Bandini Race Day Experience. Drive like an F1 racer.*

Oh, no.

His hand gives mine a reassuring squeeze before he drops it.

"Please tell me we're doing a press appearance." My voice sounds stronger than I feel.

Hope surges through me at the idea of coming to watch and cheer fans on. Noah can take them for a spin while I stand behind the barriers, a few fist pumps in the air to sell my enthusiasm while he careens down the track.

"We are." He reveals nothing more. My heart rate slows down, confident the date is what I expect. Safety barrier here I come.

He speaks again. "But we're filming from inside that car."

Oh, shit. Please tell me he means I'm going to look inside the car for two seconds. Slap the hands of the nerds who design the cars, take a quick photo, throw a thumbs up. A girl can dream.

My eyes follow his pointing finger. They land directly on a neon green Bandini car with open scissor doors. It looks like a car from the future, estimated at about 500,000 dollars.

"I am not setting a foot behind a steering wheel." *Over my dead body. Hard no.*

"You don't have to worry about that." He fills me with faith before ripping it away. "I'm going to be behind the wheel."

I need to put in a Bandini work order for this man to get a warning sign. Noah all but drags me to the neon green beauty with black leather seats and neon green piping.

A Bandini employee passes me a helmet. I don't put up much of a verbal fight with Noah because people watch us, and I can't be too embarrassing. Press crew follows us, eating up my reluctant display like I drag my feet for the fun of it. My stomach rolls, my face most likely matching the same green shade as our car.

I take deep breaths, trying to relax.

"Here we have Noah Slade taking Maya Alatorre onto the track. Maya, how do you feel about being driven around by one of the best race car drivers out there?" A reporter jams a foam microphone in my face.

"Nauseous?" my voice rasps.

The reporter laughs at me like I mean it as a joke. I shoot Noah a glare, questioning if it's too late to back out. My eyes dart between the car and the pit lane, estimating how quickly I can run before Noah catches up to me.

"It's interesting Maya chose to come out with you instead of her brother today. Any thoughts on this, Noah?"

My palm drags down my face. *Deep breaths.*

"I can't help that she wants to try out the track with me when she's watched her brother drive for years. But there's nothing like taking someone's racetrack virginity."

Pretty sure his response turned me on, and I'm halfway convinced I'm dating the devil in disguise.

He shoots me a wink. "We're going to get going. See you later, guys." He waves at the reporters like the natural he is.

Following his lead, I hop into the passenger's side.

Noah's eyes gleam. "You packed your camera, right?"

I pull the camera out of my purse. He takes it from my hands and sets it up on a conveniently placed camera mount.

"My heart may explode out of my chest. I might not make it through the whole thing."

He chuckles. "You'll be okay, we're only going to go about one hundred and thirty to one hundred and fifty miles per hour. That's not too bad. It's our trust test, remember?"

I no longer feel bad for disgruntled coworkers who have to do trust falls during employee retreats. That has nothing on this cruel version.

I never did find out the recovery rate for having a heart attack at twenty-three. *Regrets.*

"Jesus take the wheel." I do the sign of the cross before putting on my helmet.

"You may have called me God last night, but I'm the only one behind the wheel today." The smug man fucking winks.

His hand finds the stick shift and we propel down the grid area. He laughs as we make it past the first turn, tires screeching against the pavement while he speeds up again.

"Damn, I didn't hear you scream like that last night. Do I need to change my technique?"

"You perv! This is terrifying. *Oh my God.* How do you do this all the time? How is this even legal?" I'd slap his arm if I wasn't plastered to the side of the car.

"I love it. Just relax and enjoy." His voice does nothing to calm me.

"Never tell a woman to relax!" I scream again as we drift on another turn. It's touch and go with my heart, stopping every time Noah turns the car before picking back up again as he races down the road.

"Who can ever be calm at a time like this? If they do, they're certifiable."

Another scream erupts from my mouth. I don't have the chance to feel embarrassed, the loud shrieks pouring out of me with no control.

The engine purrs as Noah's lead foot hits the accelerator. His hand does a bunch of shift changes, which are honestly kind of hot because his muscles strain and tense. I distract myself by staring at him in his element, a smile plastered on his face, beaming at my reactions. My screams stop long enough for me to check out how happy he looks.

He hits me with a megawatt grin. If my body wasn't already in fight-or-flight mode, my heart rate would have sped up.

"Eyes on the road! Hello!" I snap my fingers and point at the pavement in front of us. He chuckles while he turns into another straight section, the car vrooming as he presses on the throttle.

"I could do this track in my sleep. It's an easy one."

"That's great and all but I'd rather live to see tomorrow." I take another deep breath.

He laughs as he checks me out. "Do you trust me yet?"

"I trust that you're secretly a psycho. What kind of first date is this? Haven't you ever seen an episode of *The Bachelor*? This date is not Chris Harrison approved!" I grip onto the side of the car for dear life. Those top handlebar things every car has? Yeah, I learn their true purpose, my knuckles whitening as I hold on with all my might.

Can he quit laughing at me?

"That's not the answer I wanted to hear. I'll have to step it up."

That, friends, is exactly the type of thing no one asks for. It's meme-worthy.

His hands turn nobs on the center console.

"Uh, what are you doing?" My stomach churns as my body bounces up and down, the car revolting against the high speeds Noah pushes it to. The death contraption continues to zoom past empty bleachers. Speakers sound off for the first time the entire trip, the robotic voice sending a chill down my spine.

Traction Control Disabled.

My head whips to face Noah, my helmet bouncing off the window. The movement jars me. Even I know the importance of traction control…it prevents the one thing Noah wants to do.

He shrugs, sealing our fate.

His hands turn the wheel, our car drifting across the road before spinning donuts. Tires squeal against the road. A cloud of smoke swirls around us from rubber burning, floating up into the sky along with my sanity.

"I trust you! I'll never not trust you ever again. You're the best driver ever. You'll always keep me safe. Are you satisfied now?" I half laugh, half scream the words, sounding like someone who belongs in a psychotic thriller movie. There may even be a tear or two leaking from my eyes, but if Noah asks me, I'll deny it.

He stops the donuts and we both end up breaking out in a fit of laughter. His hand grabs mine and brings it up to his lips for a kiss, my previous fear forgotten.

"To answer your question from before, yes I've seen *The Bachelor*. I took notes. This is the first of many for us, so I had to make it unforgettable."

He hits me with a devilish grin before I flash him one of my own.

CHAPTER TWENTY-EIGHT

Noah

There are only two things that can suck the happiness straight out of me.

One is any type of news of someone dying.

And two is my dad.

The second reason sends me a deceitful grin that makes my stomach shrivel up. He stands next to my car in the pit area, his negative energy pulsing around him. Not exactly what I need before a practice session.

Over the years, I've become a pro at avoiding my dad, an easier task since I've never liked being around him when he gets angry. Now that I've outgrown him, he moves on from hitting me to verbal lashings. The time Maya saw him smack me…that was unlike him. He usually keeps calm nowadays, at least physically, choosing to flip out when I perform less than perfect on the track.

"Dad, what are you doing here?" What I really want to say is *Dad, get the fuck out of here. I can't stand you.* But I don't say what I wish to because I prefer professionalism. Unfortunately, my dad funded a lot of my career at the start, his name carrying weight at Bandini. It was his same racing team after all.

"After your poor display at the last couple of races, I wanted to check in."

Sure you did.

But this is my life. Anything below first place might as well be last. The only thing keeping me calm is the sound of race cars zooming by while I breathe in the smell of fresh car wax.

"Right. Hopefully this one will go better." I can win the Japanese Grand Prix since I've done it in the past.

"And here we are getting ready for the next practice session. Santiago, do you have anything to say to your fans?"

For fuck's sake, Maya has the worst timing.

My dad ogles her as she spins around in the garage. *Gross.* She keeps going, asking Santiago questions.

My dad focuses back on me. "She's a news reporter now? What's she doing in the pit area? It's no place for a woman." He still lives in an era where women get married and live the rest of their sad lives in the four walls of their home. *Times have changed, Pops.*

"Nope. Santiago's sister vlogs." *My girlfriend,* I wish to say.

Maya and I haven't talked about titles yet. We only hashed things out two weeks ago in Singapore. But everything about us feels title-worthy because we spend lots of time together whenever Santiago isn't around. In my bed, in hers, in one of the private suites, and secret dates in the cities we visit. My sex drive with Maya rivals that of an eighteen-year-old.

I don't like how my dad looks at her, pissing me off even more.

"Hmm. She shouldn't be filming." His growl of a voice does

nothing to intimidate me.

"They already gave her the go-ahead for it. It's been good publicity and nice for branding since she has a lot of followers." *Shit. Did my voice sound like I am proud of her?*

My dad assesses me, giving me the fucking chills. His perceptiveness makes him cruel because he didn't get where he is today by being stupid.

"I guess it's fine," he says.

Everything about his face screams how it isn't. His eyebrows raise, he rubs his chin, his eyes have an evil spark. A montage of every villain from every movie.

"I better get ready for another practice round. I'll see you later?" I don't want to leave him alone here with Maya, but I have to.

I sneak up next to her before hopping into my car.

"Stay away from my dad. He's a sneaky piece of shit."

Her eyes widen. "Good luck out there!" She gets my message, her retreating form comforting me as I get in the cockpit of my car.

Maya's hand strokes my chest. We decided to stay in tonight and not attend any sponsor events. No loss here. She texts Santi about not feeling well while I tell the guys I have a headache.

"I don't think it's going to end well. I always thought he was a bad guy...but he's not. And now they killed him."

By him, she's referring to Bob on *Stranger Things*. Her tears dampen my shirt.

Wow, she really gets into shows.

"Do you always cry during sad scenes?" I pull her into a hug. It's cute, endearing even. But I don't want her to cry over something not real.

"I have a lot of feelings. Okay?" Her eyes glisten as she looks up at me. I give her a soft kiss on her forehead, her sigh making me smirk.

And the action continues on the TV. Maya snaps her head back, eagerly watching the next part.

I have learned my lesson. When they say, "Netflix and Chill," they mean to pick the most boring show because any other choice means no sex, no hooking up.

I fall into the *Stranger Things* trap. Maya swats my hand away whenever I put a move on her.

"You need to stop sighing every time Steve is on the screen. This crush has gotten out of hand."

My heart surges at the sound of her laugh. A weird feeling I've grown accustomed to whenever I hang around Maya, similar to how my dick gets rock-hard whenever she gets near me.

"I can't help it. That hair, his babysitting skills. Even his personality. Sigh."

How the mighty have fallen, becoming jealous over a TV character. "I can babysit. And my hair is definitely better. Personality? I sure as fuck hope mine's nicer seeing as I'm a real person. And I am older, wiser. I can fucking kick ass with a baseball bat." I flex my arms around her for emphasis.

"What does older and wiser have to do with the appeal?" Her chest shakes against mine.

She's totally teasing me. So I do what any logical man would do in my position. I shut off the TV and show her exactly how more experience comes with age. She stops complaining about the show the moment my lips find her clit.

I creep around, listening in on Santi and Maya's conversation. It's not my fault they're so loud and we share the same walls. Right?

I'm jealous of Santi. There. I put it out there.

Maya spends the whole morning before the race with him, hanging out while I spend the day by myself. She hides who we are from him because she doesn't want to upset him or inconvenience him before the final Prix.

Unfortunately for the Alatorre siblings, I'm not above eavesdropping.

"What are you going to do once the season's over?" Santi's voice carries through the thin walls.

"Mm, I don't know. I've started to fall into my own thing with my vlog. I have over 900,000 followers. That's, like, amazing growth in a YouTube vlog career that started only eight months ago. The travel vlogging is nice, but YouTube F1 videos are what make me trendy and different."

Pride in her voice brings a smile to my face. I watch her videos when I miss her or boredom strikes, or when Santi steals her away because Maya feels too guilty to say no.

We've already traveled with F1 for eight months, with Maya and I dating exclusively for the last four weeks.

"But is that really a job? Following me around?"

What an idiot.

"Uh. I don't follow you around." Maya's voice hesitates, unsure how to handle Santi's obliviousness.

"I don't mean to put you down. But don't you want a nice, stable job? One closer to home with less traveling? I can't have you here forever."

You can't. But I can.

Or at least until Maya doesn't want to be around anymore, *if* she doesn't. We still need to find our footing together.

I think up opinions like I'm part of the conversation.

She lets out a deep sigh loud enough for me to hear. Never a good sign.

"I'm living in the moment. I'm young. I have time to figure my life out. You don't know much about social media, but it's growing—vlogging is a huge industry with good pay by views. And sponsorships."

"That's always your problem though. You may live in the moment, but you gotta grow up sometime. Are videos a career?"

"Wow...*okay*. I don't know what made you so pissed off today, but you're being a crappy brother right now. I'm going to take a walk."

An idea hits me. I open the door to my suite the moment Maya walks past it, hurling her inside.

"What are you—"

My hand covers her mouth before she can get out another word. I bring my index finger up to my lips. Her eyes change from dull to gleaming because I can now change her mood for the positive. *Fan-fucking-tastic.*

I remove my hand from her mouth and lock the door behind her.

I check the time on the clock. We have thirty minutes before I need to check in at the pit.

"Think you can keep quiet?" I whisper. Her brother is a few feet away, and the walls are thinner than a fucking condom.

She bobs her head up and down, eyes lit with excitement.

"Always enthusiastic." I trail a finger from her neck to her chest. My hands find the hem of her Bandini polo and pull it over her head, revealing a white lace bra that makes my dick pulse.

She toys with the zipper of my race suit.

"You look so hot in this. I almost don't want to unzip it." Her words bring a smile to my face.

I shut her up with a kiss because I don't want to risk Santiago hearing us. My tongue explores her mouth, enjoying her exclusive taste, one I find addicting as hell. A magnetic energy flows around us, always pulling me back toward her. Not that I want to stay away. Our tongues dance and tease each other. Our kiss stifles her moan as my hands explore her body, my rough fingers brushing against her smooth skin.

My hands palm her perfect tits. I pull down the soft cups of her bra, revealing her perky breasts and tight, pink nipples. The best fucking sight. I trail wet kisses down her neck, sucking to the point of marking her. Fuck would I like to. But I move along because I don't have enough time.

My dick throbs, rock-hard in my suit and craving her attention.

Her hands get caught up in my hair, tugging me along for encouragement. I'm a man on a mission with a time limit.

"Sh." I rub the rough pad of my thumb against her lips.

Her heavy breathing might give us away. She nods, staring

down at me while I pull one of her taut nipples into my mouth. Her back arches as she pushes herself closer to me. I suck one nipple to a solid point before moving on to the other, my tongue trailing along the divot in her chest.

My other hand finds the button of her jeans. I dip my hand below, finding her slick and ready for me. Talk about the best fucking feeling, to turn her on with minimal effort required.

Her wild eyes and messy hair drive me crazy. Nothing compares to satiating the hunger between us, being able to please her to the point of oblivion.

Maya's hand touches the outline of my dick through the race suit. She palms me, doing soft movements up and down.

"Time to take this off," she says in a husky murmur.

Good girl.

The thrilling sound of the zipper rings through the room. Maybe Maya corrupts me just as much because I never do anything like this before a race.

I pull my arms out of the top part of the suit and finish unzipping to my waistline. The clock tells me we have fifteen minutes left. While I wish I had more time with her, a quickie will do. She tugs my dick out from the tight layers of flame-retardant material.

She gets down on her knees. The sight alone makes my dick pulse, pre-cum leaking from the tip before she grabs onto it. Her tongue darts out to lick the white bead.

My head drops back.

Shit, her mouth feels good.

She traces lazy lines with her tongue across the shaft. It's perfect. She's perfect. All so motherfucking perfect.

She takes me in her mouth, a warm, wet heaven welcoming my cock. Her tongue drags along the underside of my shaft as she pulls her mouth back and forth. She sucks, pumps, and licks me. Sensations make my brain short-circuit.

She pumps me into her mouth with one hand while another grips my ass. I regain enough mental clarity to pull her up, her lips popping as my dick bobs.

"Nope. That's not how this is going to go today."

Her honey-brown eyes narrow. I trail my thumb across her plump lips, loving how she looks after sucking me off. A brief kiss wipes the frown off her face.

I tug down her jeans and thong. She's right there with me, fumbling with taking off her sneakers. The best kind of teamwork.

Red numbers on the clock mock me.

"Now you have to be quiet," I whisper before licking the shell of her ear, her body breaking out in goosebumps.

She likes the quiet game we play, wondering who will mess up first.

I place her hands on the side of the gray couch. The suite is small, not meant for sex. But fuck it, I can make the layout work with a little extra effort.

"Keep your hands there." I grab a condom from my wallet.

Thank God for planning ahead.

I turn back toward Maya. The sight of her perky ass in the air, leaning against the arm of the couch, ready for me. Her tits hang out and her back arches. It's a lot to take in. She bites down on her lip, hitting me with the hungry look in her eyes as she checks out my dick.

I slip the condom on.

"Too bad your suit isn't sex-friendly," her voice rasps.

"My my, do you have a thing for race suits? Should I be concerned? I can lock you away from the other drivers and keep you here for myself."

My hands palm her ass, eliciting a light moan from her. One finger slides down the crease of her ass until I reach her slick folds. I plunge a finger inside, and then another, her wetness surrounding me.

I lean in close to her ear. "Always ready for me. Tell me, do you get this way while watching me race? Does it turn you on?"

She nods her head, the silent admission exciting me.

"It's a dangerous sport. High speeds. Collisions." I leave a path of kisses down her spine.

She turns her head to look at me over her shoulder.

"I'll let you in on a secret though... Fucking you is the equivalent of winning a World Championship. I could never win again and be perfectly fine so long as you're by my side. In my bed. Me inside of you. I like you *a lot.*"

She doesn't have a second to register my words. I have the foresight to cover her mouth with my hand before I thrust into her wet pussy. My teeth grit together as I hold back a groan, her tight body accepting my cock and fisting me like no other. Our connected bodies moving in unison mesmerizes me.

And fuck if that doesn't do something to me, a wave of possessiveness rushing through me as I drag my slick dick out, soaked to the hilt.

She feels tighter in this position, my pants concealed because I don't want Santi to hear me. I let my hand go from her mouth once the shock factor is done.

Maya claws at the fabric on the couch, a gorgeous image of her rattled by me. I ram into her again and savor the feel of her squeezing my dick.

She's heaven. Perfect for me.

My hand grips her ponytail, wrapping it around my arm, thick strands brushing against my skin. I tug, fulfilling a fantasy I've thought about since meeting her.

Her body pulses at the mix of pain and pleasure. Skin warms beneath the touch of my other hand. I squeeze her tit, loving the feel of her pebbled nipple beneath my palm.

I want her to know I'm the only one who can fuck her like this, make her feel like this. I want to ruin her for any man who dares to try to come after me.

I fuck her like she's the last woman on Earth. Because to me, she might as well be.

She does a good job keeping quiet, only letting out a few whimpers here and there. I pull on her hair again in a silent demand to look at me. She blows me away with a view of her brown eyes, hazy from lust, matching flushed cheeks and lips plump from my ravaging. I could come right there at the sight of her.

But I don't.

Because good guys finish last.

My grip becomes more possessive on her hip as I pump unrelentingly into her. I angle myself to hit her G-spot. Her whole body convulses around me, her reaction pulling a smirk from me.

I stroke her special spot and give it all my attention. My dick slides back and forth like never before, her arousal encouraging me as my thrusts become sloppier, less controlled. It feels like magic when she shatters around my cock. Her heavy breathing fills the silent room, her chest heaving up and down as she stares at me with a lazy smile.

Her orgasm gives me the final push. I thrust into her without holding back, balls slapping against her ass as she takes it all. I groan as I find my release. My toes curl at the feeling of her squeezing me, practically pleading for more. The whole thing seems fucking poetic.

My lips kiss her neck as I pull out of her. I dump the condom in the trash and situate my suit, wishing we had more time.

Maya keeps to the same spot, lying over the side of the couch with her eyes closed. Her back moves to the steady rhythm of her breathing. I grab her clothes from the floor, wanting to help her in whatever way, when she finally speaks.

"I think you've ruined me." Her whispered voice rings through the quiet.

Shit. That's the best thing I've heard all day.

CHAPTER TWENTY-NINE

MAYA

I walk into the pit area to wish Santi good luck. Noah fucked my bad mood right out of me, curing me from Santi's negative words.

"Where did you go?" He looks at me with soft eyes and a weak smile.

"I took a walk. I needed a break from our conversation."

Can he tell Noah just fucked me? Post-sex afterglow tends to be a thing.

"You look like you've been crying. I'm sorry if I upset you. I just want to make sure you'll be okay and find what you love to do."

My cheeks heat. Not exactly the crying he's thinking about. His apology makes my heart squeeze, guilt eating up any leftover lust.

"Mm, yeah. I appreciate it. But I am happy, and everything will be fine. I like following everyone and I've made good friends. You don't need to worry about me anymore."

He pulls me in for a hug, our previous conversation abandoned. "You know I love you, right?"

My eyes roll with the least amount of effort because his corny phrase always gets me. I can't hold an argument against him for more than an hour anyway. "You tell me all the time. I love you too. Now go kick some ass. Preferably Slade's."

"Hey! I heard that. You both act like I'm not here." Noah's voice booms over the buzz of the pit crew and machines. My body warms in recognition. I'm so screwed with him, both literally and figuratively.

"You've won three World Championships already. Save some for the little guys." Santi's voice carries over the other noises.

"I'm glad you're not ashamed of being little. That's mature of you. You know what they say—it's not about size but what you do with it that matters." Noah smirks at my brother.

Santi groans while I bark out a laugh.

"You're a piece of shit, Slade." Santi's words don't have the same kick. "Speaking of dicks, what the hell was going on in your room? Changing up your pre-race routine? It's usually silent but your couch kept hitting the wall, in a rhythm I might add." Santi's knowing smile says it all. My throat closes tight, my brain jumping to the worst kind of conclusions. I let out a breath when I find Santi not looking at me.

Noah returns a wicked smile and shrugs. "Sorry about that. I'll be more quiet next time."

If the world could swallow me up whole, now would be the perfect time.

But it doesn't.

"Maybe I need to follow the same ritual. I wonder if that's

how you win so much." My brother, the idiot, smiles at Noah.

If I had a drink, this would be the moment I'd spit the contents out all over my brother. *Oh my God. You definitely don't want to, Santi. Can you shut up already?*

My eyes dart around the garage, avoiding eye contact at all costs with both of them. Santi gives me a quick peck on the head before hopping into his car.

Noah and Santi wish each other good luck before they take off for the grid. I stay behind in the pit area for this race, watching overhead on the TV monitors while Sophie hangs out with her dad. A pit crew member hands me a headset so I can hear what Santi says while he races.

Noah takes off in first place, no surprise there. Cameras switch between overhead shots and racer first-person cameos. Over the past few races, I've caught myself cheering for him as much as I do with Santi.

Noah drives swiftly as he cruises along the pavement. My brother keeps close behind, battling it out for second place with Liam. Noah holds a good distance ahead and avoids any major collisions with other racers. My brother sets a great pace, with Liam behind his rear wing. Aerodynamics of the car make it difficult for Liam to overtake my brother. Air becomes a vortex inside of the track, compromising the speed of any racer who tries to pass the leader.

Santi catches up to Noah, but he's no match for Noah's defensiveness on this track. Noah's turns stay tight, falling right in the middle, making no racer able to surpass him. My heart races as Noah creates a comfortable distance between himself and my brother.

Commentators go crazy as drivers fight for second- and third-place spots. Jax flies by Liam, pulling in close behind my brother. A pit stop will decide who gets out on top between them. Jax overtakes Santi at a narrow turn, causing my brother to spin out before he regains control.

Cars go around and around, lap after lap, rankings switching amongst racers. Jax gains speed on Noah, not compromising a potential first-place win for McCoy. I like Jax's style compared to the boys at Bandini. He makes deliberate moves rivaling Noah's, willing to do anything to get leverage on the first-place racer.

Noah's dad interrupts me, his voice pulling me away from the TV. I withhold my sneer. Noah opened up to me about his dad's anger management issues, telling me all about the unknown side of Nicholas Slade.

He takes up a spot next to me, staring up at the TV like he shares my same emotional investment. A comical display because his intentions become clear once he opens his mouth.

"You both think you're clever, hiding what you're doing."

My body stills but my eyes remain on the TV. Noah and Jax compete for first place. Mechanics buzz as Noah pulls in for his pit stop, distracting me from his dad as the team puts on his new tires. The process finishes in under two seconds. I forget about his dad standing beside me until he fake coughs.

"What do you think Santiago and I are doing exactly?" I withhold an urge to run away.

His laugh makes my skin crawl.

Is it possible to hate someone without knowing much about him? Because what I know is enough. Who the hell hits their child for losing kart races? A man with a small dick and a fragile ego.

"You're fucking my son. It's so obvious from watching you two in the pit area earlier."

My neck heats up, prickling at the dangerous man next to me. My fingers twirl a piece of hair to stop my fidgeting. I avert his gaze, staring up at the TV.

"That's quite a theory. Are you so bored with attending races that you need to come up with stories?" I come off way more confident than I feel.

"You're a smart girl. If you mess around with Noah, and his performance isn't what I expect…"

I keep silent. He wants a fight that I don't need to entertain.

"I'll make sure your brother doesn't have another contract renewal. Not to mention you'll never walk into a Bandini suite again. I don't mess around. I play to win."

I turn my head, taking in his cold stare before returning it with one of my own. His threats don't scare me. No need to give him any semblance of control over me.

"Not sure what you think is happening. I'm sorry you're worried about Noah's performance. But what he does out there is all on him." My voice sounds sickly sweet to my own ears.

He leaves with a smirk on his face, proving to be the asshole Noah described.

"We need to talk." Santi lays himself against the headboard of my bed, occupying the space next to me. Yesterday was a rough day for him after placing fourth in the Prix. He made his rounds to appease fans, but the loss ate away at him and he closed himself off in the hotel suite for the rest of the night. Only room service could push him to leave the four walls of his bedroom.

"About?" my voice croaks. Paranoia riddles my brain, playing tricks on me as I worry if Noah's dad told Santi about my secret relationship. I wouldn't put anything past that vile man.

"We didn't have a chance to talk in private about yesterday. I came off like an asshole and I'm sorry. A lot has been on my mind with Bandini, and I worry about you on top of everything else." His brown eyes pierce mine.

"There isn't anything else to discuss. I get how you want what's best for me." I squirm against the bedspread, unable to find a comfortable position.

"You've been kind of distant and I don't know what's going on. I thought you might want to go back home, but I overstepped."

My chest tightens at his sincerity. "No. That's not it."

"You'd be honest if something was bothering you, right? This world is hard, but I appreciate having you here. It's made the season much better."

Please, stab me one more time in the heart.

"Of course. You're my best friend." A lump in my throat makes swallowing difficult.

"Now that our feelings shit is out of the way, Netflix came out with the new *Stranger Things* season. Let's see it while I have free time."

I end up watching the same season twice because guilt has a funny way of making me do just about anything for my brother.

CHAPTER THIRTY

Noah

I ended up placing runner-up in yesterday's race. Jax put up one hell of a fight for the first-place spot, deserving his Prix win. The hard track and my placement keeps me pleased with my performance.

My dad, on the other hand, is not.

Regrettably, he invited me to dinner, a rare occasion since he never stays after a race, choosing to leave as soon as he can. The whole idea of dinner puts me on high alert. I can count on one hand the total amount of outings we've had together since I joined F1.

To put it short, my father deserves to be fucked right up the ass with a tub of Icy Hot Extra Strength for lube.

He comes off condescending to me and the waiters. My hands curl every time he speaks to someone with a chip the size of a twenty-pound kettlebell on his shoulder. It takes everything in me to not jump over the table and pull him by the shirt, spit in his face and rip him a new asshole to match his personality.

My chest tightens at the thought of acting similarly to him. I want to forget the countless girls, the cockiness, and my attitude. To protect myself, I gave up bits and pieces until I was void of feeling. Deception plays cruel jokes on people. Turns out while I busied myself with putting on a show, I was the person I lied most to. Eventually I believed all the deceits, the excuses I made for my shitty attitude and moodiness, becoming the asshole I was escaping.

My dad's piss-poor attitude drives home all the points I've learned along the way this year. And the worst part? I actually feel bad for my dad. I pity him.

Nicholas Slade has no one, using money and power to get his way, never loving someone else. How can he when the man he adores happens to be his own reflection? To be honest, he doesn't love me. Fuck, he doesn't even *like* me, let alone share any semblance of the four-letter L word. He's a selfish bastard who lives vicariously through me.

But to move forward in life, I have to face these issues from my past. My therapist will be pleased with how I sit silently, taking deep breaths, putting up with his shit.

I put out a lifeline for him. A test of sorts.

"Maya mentioned you chatted at the race together." My voice stays relaxed despite a tingling sensation growing inside of me.

"Mm, yeah. She's a pretty piece of ass. When are you going to drop the bomb on Santiago? It's a smart plan, fucking with his head before the final Prix." His grin leaves a bitter taste in my mouth. How does he sleep at night? Restless, with a soul as black as the darkness that surrounds him.

"She's my girlfriend."

Not officially. But he doesn't need to know.

He tilts his head at me, offering a sinister smile. "If that's what you call your fuck buddies now, all the power to you."

My skin wants to crawl off my body and take up shop somewhere else. I attempt to give him a chance, waging an internal war.

"I'm probably going to marry her one day. I think she's the one." I say the words with confidence.

The idea is a little premature, sure. But I have a good feeling about her. Maya breathes new life into me, not wanting to piece me together but accepting all my jagged parts. Waking up next to her makes my mornings, not because of her phenomenal blowjobs, but for the special smile she gives me when I hit her snooze button five times. I love the way she lies in bed reading books in the middle of the day, unbothered and shooing me away when she hits a good part. She brushes off my gruff attitude with a smile and a kiss because I can be a moody asshole when I don't place first—conditioned because of the shitty man sitting in front of me. Most of all, I like how she makes me want to be a better person. For her, for me, for the whole goddamn world.

My dad gives me a tight smile. "Better hire a lawyer for a prenup then. Women like her are only after one thing, and it's not your shining personality and good looks."

My façade drops. I run out of fucks to give him because he is too far gone to help. I made sure to prepare for this exact moment because I had anticipated the stunt he pulled with Maya. After all, I've watched him for years. I didn't expect him to threaten Santi's contract because I thought he would come after mine.

I let out a long exhale. He looks up at me, his dark eyes glaring at me.

"After spending time with people who care about me, I

realized some things. People who love you spend time with you both on and off the track. They go to events and stay until the end to be around you because they want to. It's not about whether you win or lose. I'm a World Champion and you treat me like a piece of shit on your shoe. Inconvenient and unwanted."

He tries to say something, but I throw up my hand to shut him up. The upscale restaurant he chose allows us the privacy we need for this heart to black fucking heart.

"And you threaten my girlfriend? You actually fucking told her that her brother may lose a contract with Bandini? Like how sad and shitty is your life that you'd do that? I'm done trying with you. You've been a crappy dad my whole life, only caring when it benefits you. In the end, being in my life is more about your image than about being there for me."

I only pay attention to his rapid blinking and lowering my heart rate.

"You can't cut me out when I sponsor your team. I was serious about Santiago's contract renewal. Try me." He hisses like the fucking snake he is.

"Oh, Father. The thing is I have it all handled. Bandini no longer needs your generous donations. I attended almost every sponsor event, meeting, and gala held this year, slowly securing enough sponsorships to outbid yours. You're done with *my* team. Feel free to back another group if you want. Not sure if they need a donor with a crappier attitude than the sewer you crawled out of, but hell, you are a legend after all."

"This isn't over. I'm still a sponsor this year, so I'll do whatever the hell I want."

I throw my cloth napkin on the table. "I don't give a fuck. Do whatever you feel like, but stay the hell out of my way."

No need to sit around and spend another minute with this man, my stomach threatening to rid itself of shame and a sixty-dollar steak.

He doesn't bother with an apology.

I leave my past behind at the table of some fancy-ass restaurant. Fuck him to the farthest galaxy and back because the moon is just too damn close for comfort.

CHAPTER THIRTY-ONE

MAYA

"**T**oday we're here with Santiago since he gets jealous of all the attention I give other racers."

My brother and I sit at a sleek bar top in the Bandini motorhome. I line up two shot glasses next to a bottle of tequila while Santi smiles at the camera situated on an adjacent table.

"Santi admitted he's down about not making it on the podium the other day. So we are going to do an exclusive episode of Tequila Talks because we still haven't learned tequila doesn't fix our problems. I hope this episode goes better than the last one. I'll ask him a series of questions where he has to take a shot whenever he refuses to answer. I end the show after four because he weighs a lot and I can't pick his butt up off the floor. Blame their strict workout regimen and muscle mass."

My brother flexes his bicep at the camera.

"Warning: I didn't come up with these questions. I want to clarify since fans want answers to things I *do not* need to know about my brother." My lips purse at the horny bunch of fans out there—way more than I expect, all tapping away in my inbox about these guys.

I exaggerate a shudder at his mischievous grin and stick my tongue out at him.

"Favorite thing about your sister?" I bat my lashes at him.

"Hmm, who came up with that question?" His brow lifts.

I shrug and fail to answer.

"I love her passion, fearlessness, and carefree personality."

Aw, how sweet.

"Who knew you had such kind thoughts about me? Okay, next question. The worst part about F1?"

"Hands down the fact that I don't sleep in my bed for months at a time. I miss coming home."

Ah, the not-so glam side of traveling the world.

"What you really miss is your gym and bubble baths." I smile at my brother.

"Bath bombs don't feel the same in a hotel bathtub." He pouts.

I suppress a laugh. "Best part of having a teammate?"

"The shared points you get together. Plus, personal tips and recommendations." Santi genuinely smiles at the camera.

"Ugh. I hate this one. Your favorite sex position?"

He winks at the camera and knocks back a shot. *Good answer.*

"Glad that's past us. Next, any special girl in your life?"

He flips his empty shot glass. "Not since high school."

"See girls, boys are sensitive just like us. They get their heart broken once and it's game over."

He chuckles to himself. "See guys, girls are annoying as ever, no matter the age."

Oh, burn. "Moving on—"

"What's going on here?" Noah's voice makes my stomach flip.

"Tequila Talks. Want to join?" My brother has loose lips after one shot.

Sure enough, Noah grabs the extra glass and fills it up. He sits in the seat next to me, ready for questions.

My eyes dart between Noah and Santi. "Wait, he can't join. I don't have questions for him."

"Ask him the same ones." Santi offers me a quizzical look.

"Lovely." My jaw hurts from my teeth grinding.

Noah dares to look smug. *All right, he asked for it.*

"If you could go on a date with any celebrity, who would it be?" I give the camera a warm smile before turning toward the guys.

Noah coughs. I did try to stop him.

"Definity Taylor Hill. That girl is fine," my brother blurts out.

My hands fidget in front of me, anticipating whatever response Noah comes up with.

He mutters a curse before speaking. "Hmm. Adriana Lima?"

If glares could kill, this man would be dead on the spot.

"If anyone from the VS fashion show is listening in, please invite these guys. It'll make their year."

My brother chuckles while Noah keeps quiet, pleasing me.

"Favorite F1 team besides Bandini?"

My brother strokes his chin as Noah takes it away.

"McCoy for me. I like the guys and their work ethic. They're great competition, always pushing us to do our best."

"I like Kulikov. That's a given from our previous history.

There's no bad blood since I left. And the guys hustle."

I move on. "Name five things you look for in your dream girl."

"Attractive, smart, into F1..." Santi pauses. "Oh, family-oriented, and nice."

Noah takes a few seconds to come up with an answer, his intense gaze warming me up inside. I become fascinated with picking at the label of the tequila bottle.

"Beautiful, both inside and out. Funny enough to get my asshole sense of humor. Someone who wants to have a family and likes me for me, rather than for fame. And a girl who will travel around the world with me because this job is constantly on the go."

I think my ovaries explode but it's hard to tell. *Moving on.*

"Best sex story?" *Did the camera catch my cringing?* I'll have to re-watch later while I edit.

My brother takes a breath before talking. "Well, there was this one time—"

My elbow hits him in the ribs. *Hell. No.*

Noah winks at me before knocking back his shot like the Champ he is. *Oh, what a simple wink can do to me.* My lips tip up in a telling smile.

The game keeps going with questions taking a turn away from sex and love interests. *Bless.*

For the first time since Santi started at Bandini, he and Noah get along. It gives me hope that they can be friends after Noah and I come out about our relationship.

But you know what they say about the best-laid plans...

CHAPTER THIRTY-TWO

Noah

Maya tells her brother she wants to sleep over at Sophie's suite tonight. But in reality, we planned an all-nighter together after her Tequila Talks vlog, lying naked in the hotel bed.

"You know I don't want to get with Adriana Lima, right? I needed to say a name."

She sighs. Not exactly the reaction I want.

"Yeah. But you've been with models like her. That's a lot to compete with when I'm nothing like those girls."

My bad decisions rear their ugly heads again. Except this time, I want to banish them forever, no longer proud of my shitty past. Pack them away in a cardboard box along with my bad memories.

"Have you googled me?" I roll on top of her. My hand softly grips her chin, stroking her soft skin.

"*Maybe.* I was curious." Her eyes look up toward the ceiling.

"Google will be the death of me. Don't look at that shit. It's not worth your time or energy when people spin stories to make money." My lips softly peck at her cheeks between words. "You're. The. Most. Lovely. Woman. To. Me."

She giggles at all of the kisses I plant on her face. My lips find hers, my tongue caressing her closed lips, wanting access. I fucking hate when she closes herself off. I slide my hands down her body, wanting her to respond to me. My hands stroke the entrance of her pussy and tease her into giving me what I want.

She moans when I dip a finger inside of her, my dick stirring at her arousal. I deepen the kiss, wanting to show her how I crave and want her. Desire and desperation swirl inside of me. My knee pushes her legs apart and I roll my hard cock against her center. Her groan makes my cock pulse against her smooth skin, her arousal coating my dick as I grind into her. Lust makes my head cloudy, but I need to prove my point.

"I really like you, Maya. I want to spend every day with you, both in here and out there once you let me. Will you be my girlfriend? Officially?"

The way she smiles at me makes my heart skip and my dick ache. She pulls me down for another kiss that speaks volumes because who the hell needs words when their body does the talking?

I struggle to stay awake at the sponsor event, another gala where lots of old men open their big wallets. A dime a dozen around here. With age comes less willingness to attend these events, wanting to ditch the moment I arrive because I have no interest in kissing ass. Not to mention how I can't even have my girlfriend by my side since she hangs out with Santi.

So I do what any horny male would do. I text Maya to meet me in the empty ballroom next door.

She shows up ten minutes later, the darkness of the ballroom cloaking her as she stands near the double-door entrance. Low lighting makes her shape undistinguishable.

"Do you have a public fetish I should be worried about? This is becoming a common occurrence for us." Her voice sounds low and husky.

"Why don't you come over and find out."

She strolls toward me, moving around piles of stacked chairs and empty tables spread throughout the room. My lungs welcome the scent of her shampoo mixed with a light floral perfume. I could get high off the smell of her alone.

She tugs on my bow tie, loosening it.

"I love seeing you in a tux. It's one of my favorite things."

I can wear a tux every day if it makes her happy. "I love seeing you naked. But this will have to do for now." I hiss when I tug up the hem of her lace dress. "You're not wearing underwear? This whole time?"

She replies with a breathy laugh.

I bite down on my lip. "Fuck me. You can't do stuff like that. If I had known…"

She shuts me up by kissing me. Lazy, slow. Tantalizingly sweet—so fitting for her. Her hands run down my chest before they land on my belt. Her hoarse voice whispers in my ear, my spine tingling at her boldness. "We don't need this right now."

Our heavy breathing echoes off the walls, mixed with my

groan as the belt's metal buckle hits the floor. Maya undoes my zipper slowly. My cock stands to attention with pre-cum seeping from the tip. She pulls my dick out of my pants, her thumb brushing against the pearly drop.

I groan. "Shit."

"*Sh*. You're too loud," she says before stepping away and pulling a condom from her purse.

Her preparedness makes me smile. "Thought you'd get lucky tonight?"

"I expected it." Her eyes gleam at me.

"Always dreamed of fucking the sass out of you." I push her up against the wall, done with talking.

My lips find hers while my hands stroke her core, pulling a gasp from her. It doesn't take much work with her, and I love it. Love the way she pushes me for more. To feel, to live, to breathe her in and never let her go. To keep Maya all to myself because fuck the world, they don't deserve her. *Shit. I don't either.* But I can't help my selfishness, the possessiveness I feel around her. A desire to mark her up and leave a trail of bruises from my lips. To bring her over the edge before pulling her back up, shattering around my dick the same way she smashes into my walls.

She puts the condom on me, rolling it along my shaft, making the simplest things look erotic.

I lift her up and her legs wrap around my waist. Maya's thighs clench around me, squeezing me the same way invisible hands grip my heart. But I don't want her to let go. She can take over my whole life with a smile on her face and I'd thank her for it. Her back hits the wall as my lips find hers, smashing, nipping, and tugging at the soft flesh.

I slide into her slowly, wanting to enjoy the sensation of the first thrust. My eyes close when my dick is fully sheathed inside of her. Her breathy sigh pushes me to move after what feels like a full minute of me regulating my breathing.

I pull out to the tip before sliding back in with an unhurried pace.

"Oh God. Noah." Her hands claw at the back of my tux.

My lips move to her neck, finding the spot that drives her crazy. I suck and mark her because I want every fucker to know she drives me wild.

"You're soaked for me. Does it turn you on knowing anyone could walk in on us right now? Find me fucking you against a wall. They might want to watch. Shit, I would."

I squeeze her ass when she tries to lift herself up.

"No," I growl. "I'm in charge."

Thank fuck I work out every damn day and she doesn't weigh much because I don't want to break our connection by moving us to a table. At least not before her first orgasm. Turns out I tend to be selfish everywhere but in the bedroom.

"It's too much." Her strained voice makes my dick pulse inside of her. I get what she means. Our relationship is more than a physical attraction, not limited to a lust-induced fuckathon. I don't fear the emotional tie linking us, instead choosing to embrace it because I'm the only one who fucks her and loves her like this.

Love. One word I didn't understand until Maya.

We intensely gaze into each other's eyes as I slide in and out of her, pulling a few moans from her while she tugs on my hair. Sex has never felt this close for me. Like Maya chips away at my exterior, leaving a piece of herself behind forever.

My lazy tempo continues. I want to brand her, make her mine, drive her as crazy as she makes me. She comes the first time when I brush against her G-spot. I hold her while her body shakes, gripping her ass, and not letting go.

I live for hearing her yell out my name and bringing her pleasure. Obviously, I'm an egotistical bastard, but she likes me anyway, so be it.

I eventually increase my pumping, hitting her in all the right places while I struggle to keep my own orgasm back. She needs to come again because I crave it more than my own. Like chasing a high.

"Yes. Just like that. Fuck, Noah." Her hands run through my hair and tug at the root. I love how she tells me what she enjoys, encouraging me and feeding my self-esteem all at once.

"You're stunning when you come. I don't know if I've seen anything as perfect." I leave a searing kiss on her plump lips.

I carry her to an empty table nearby that looks sturdy enough, needing to adjust my angle. One of my hands finds her clit while the other palms the material over her breasts.

"Do. Not. Stop," she says between my thrusts.

I groan at her request, my dick throbbing inside of her at the desperation in her voice. My pace becomes quicker and messier. A mix of her pants with my deep inhales ring in my ears. Her eyes meet mine, half open and hazy, a masterpiece of lust and love.

And with a few sweet words of encouragement, she explodes around my dick again, milking me. Her nails scratch at the material of my tux. Fuck if that's not sexy.

My dick slides easily in and out of her, her arousal coating me. I increase the pressure and pace. Hurried thrusts match my limited sense of control, becoming more rushed with each push. My heart beats rapidly in my chest. I detonate inside of her with a roar of pleasure, my spine tingling at my release. Lazy pumps until I have nothing left to give.

My body relaxes and I lie on top of her, both of us catching our breath.

"I think you shave off a year of my life every single week," her voice croaks.

"What a year well spent."

Her chest shakes under me, and I smile into her neck.

We both take care of ourselves. I help smooth out her hair while she fixes my bow tie. We're quite the pair, she and I.

"I have one last request." I grab her hand. She glances up at me, her curiosity apparent. "Will you dance with me?"

She nods her head enthusiastically while shooting me a radiant smile.

I pull up the music-streaming app on my phone before placing it down on one of the tables. Thomas Rhett's "Die a Happy Man" croons through the tiny speakers, loud enough for us to hear. My hand grabs hers as I pull her toward an empty area. With one hand on the small of her back and the other wrapped around her hand, I sway us to the music.

This is the best I can get for now since we can't dance together in public yet. The moment feels fitting after the sex we shared, her head lying against my chest as we move around in a small circle. I kiss the top of her head before I spin her around.

She unabashedly throws her head back and lets out a sultry laugh. I make it a goal to make her laugh like that every single day of the rest of my life. She turns me into a sappy motherfucker who can't help it around her, endlessly searching for ways to make her happy and satisfied.

I gather up courage as the song continues because I want to let her know. Because I never want another day to go by without her hearing it.

"I love you." My voice rasps over the music.

Maya always looks beautiful to me. But the moment I admit I love her? She gives me what is hands down the most gorgeous smile I've ever seen, one meant only for me.

I keep saying that. But I'll never forget this one.

"I love you, too." Her voice carries over the sweet melody.

I pull her in close after she says the three words I've wanted to hear for weeks, committing the moment to memory.

CHAPTER THIRTY-THREE

MAYA

Brazil. Home of Noah's beloved Adriana Lima.

I'm joking. No more bitter feelings about that comment since Tequila Talks was a few weeks ago. I'm more mature than that. Plus, Noah loves me. Back in the ballroom, he caught me off guard, looking excited to say those three words. Now he never goes a day without saying them.

Lying to my brother about my current whereabouts fills me with dread. I let him know this morning that I was flying to Brazil earlier than expected with Sophie, telling him we want to explore Rio de Janeiro together before the next Grand Prix. My lie isn't too far off from the truth. See, I am in Rio de Janeiro... but I'm actually here with Noah.

Shocker. I know.

But we have a week off between the last race and the Brazilian Grand Prix. We came to the country early, enjoying the trip he planned. He shows me how he cares, doing sweet things that make me appreciate him even more. Like buying me one of every candy bar when I got my period and sex was off the table. Or how he made sangria when I felt homesick, which led to us getting drunk and playing another round of two truths and a lie.

I carry my camera around while we wander through Brazil's streets, filming private moments of us. Nothing like the hustle and bustle of a big city. Noah shows an interest in my camera, asking people to take photos of us, claiming he wants memories of our first trip together. He hates every camera except my own. I can't imagine being famous, not being able to enjoy fundamental privacy.

We both dress up, currently incognito because avoiding fans has become our new day job. I don't want pictures of us out there on the internet. At least not identifiable ones, so I put myself in charge of the outfits.

"Is the fake mustache really necessary? It's kind of itchy." Noah scratches his face for the fourth time today. I hate to say it, but mustaches don't suit him, especially not the handlebar kind.

"Stop your complaining. I'm the one wearing an Albrecht team shirt. They're like the worst in the whole F1 circuit so I got the short end of the stick."

His throaty laugh makes me chuckle along with him.

Noah taps the brim of my hat. "I told you to wear the wig instead. You refused."

"It's hot outside and wigs get scratchy." I don't even know why I bought that atrocity. It makes me look like a porn star, and not exactly the well-paid kind.

"We'll have to save it for another day."

Noah's heated smile sends a shiver down my spine. He kisses my neck at the bottom of the Christ the Redeemer steps, people pushing past us, grumbling in Portuguese.

"You have lots of kinks. I'm not sure I would've agreed to this relationship if I had known all this beforehand." I step away from him and give him a one-armed shrug. His sexual appetite alone leaves me sore for days because once is never enough with this man.

He smacks my ass while we climb to visit the statue. By the time we reach the top, my lungs ache and my legs wobble.

"You never look this sweaty after sex with me. Am I not working you hard enough?" Noah's smile matches the mischievous shine in his eye.

I shoot him a half-assed glare. "Not all of us like to visit the gym at five in the morning. This is the most I've worked out all year."

He shakes his head at me. "Don't discount all the times I've fucked you. Better than any cardio you'll do at a hotel gym."

"Look at you solving all of my problems." I genuinely smile up at him.

My phone rings, vibrating inside of my leggings' pocket. I may not work out but at least I look the part.

"Let me take this. It's Santi." I walk away before Noah protests. He stays put, checking out the view while I sit on a bench.

"*Hola, hermana.* You forgot to check in earlier." Santi's voice carries through the small speaker.

My hand holding the phone shakes as uneasiness settles in my stomach. "Sorry about that. We got busy." *Not a lie per se.*

"How's the weather over there? Heard a storm may be coming in before the race."

The sun shines down on me, not a cloud in sight. I hang out in the shadow of one of Christ's open arms, which is ironic since I'm lying to my brother.

"Don't worry about that because it's bright and sunny here. You still have a few days before you need to come over anyway."

"How's little miss Sophie doing?"

"Good." I choke on the word. "Hanging out at the famous statue before visiting Sugarloaf Mountain."

I promise once this season is over, I will tell the truth no matter what. Noah tells me how much he wants to date me after the season ends. Hopefully, my relationship with him is worth the nausea I feel every time I lie to my brother.

"Well lucky you're having a good time. Noah stood me up at a sponsor event, which meant I had to spend five hours talking to people by myself. I hated every second of it."

My chest tightens. "Oh, no." *Wow, Maya. Please act less surprised.*

"Yeah, no shit 'oh, no.' He acts tough and entitled, too good to pick up the phone and let me know he wouldn't be saving my ass from dead-end conversations. But whatever, I survived."

The three of us need another tequila bonding session.

"At least you love those types of events. Sucks he didn't show." *Sucks he was in bed with me while you were schmoozing.* I might as well shower in holy water to cleanse myself from my deception.

"Yeah, maybe for the first hour. But I can't even take a piss without someone asking me a question about the season or my teammate."

I laugh at the mental picture Santi paints me. "Well, I better get going."

"Right. Your travel buddy has replaced me."

Santi clenches a fist around my heart without knowing it.

I fight to get the words out. "Never, you're always my number one."

"I better be. Catch you later." He hangs up the phone.

Noah grins at me from across the cobbled platform. I offer a weak smile and a small wave, taking deep breaths to ease the tension building in my head.

I hope all this worry is worth it because unlike Noah, I don't welcome trouble with open arms and a kiss.

"You disappeared three times already tonight. You even abandoned me with Charles Wolfe. Of all people, that's low, Maya." Santi's voice comes out whiny.

I shoot him a sweet smile and shrug my shoulders. He dislikes that sponsor, sharing how the guy gets drunk and has a preference for hugging it out. Brown eyes glare down at me with a hint of amusement.

"I'm sorry. I got distracted." I bring my drink up to my lips because I have to keep my hands busy. If not, my nervousness will give me away.

"You've been more than that lately. I'll have to talk to Sophie because she takes up too much of your time, making me feel needy and jealous."

He fails to notice me choking on my drink.

Way to keep it cool, Maya.

He continues, oblivious to my internal struggle. "It's getting out of hand. Give me my sister back already. We only have two races left and I barely see you anymore. Not even at the press conferences."

"Well, those get boring. I almost fell asleep at one…standing up, I might add." I don't include how Noah had kept me up for hours the night before.

His cold gaze assesses me while he remains silent.

"I'll spend the rest of the night by your side. I'll even help you avoid Charles; I don't think he likes me very much anyway." I link my arm in his, ignoring how my throat feels like I chugged sand.

"You better. He hugged me twice, his sweaty face rubbing against mine. Feel pity for your older brother." Santi winces.

I rub his arm in assurance. "Aw, poor baby. I'm here now and I'll keep an eye out for him."

Not soon after, Noah finds me again. But this time he frowns when his eyes land on Santi next to me. His eyes scream trouble. The delicious kind of trouble, but trouble nonetheless with my brother here. I subtly shake my head from side to side in hopes of discouraging his advances. His lips tip up at the corners.

"Noah, good to see you, man. It feels like you barely hang around these things. You missed Charles today. He hugged me." My brother gives Noah the usual guy hello: hands shaking, backs being clapped.

Guilt eats me alive like a corroded battery in the pit of my stomach. How does Noah keep his face neutral all the time? I need to set up a meeting with Bandini's PR manager because I can use some insider tips.

"Yeah, these events haven't been doing it for me lately. Especially Charles. He's a nice guy, but a bit touchy." He smirks at my brother.

We both know what *has* been doing it for him lately.

Spoiler: it isn't Charles or winning races.

Even though Noah wins most of the races anyway. Commentators think Noah may be the best of our generation and F1 history. Fans obsess over him, attending races with huge posters, some including women's numbers. They line up for hours to get him to sign their stuff. Boobs not included.

My brother and Noah chat while I insert random comments that come off half-assed at best. Noah and his nearness distract me. His tux makes me lightheaded, the look of his roguish smile muddles up my insides. Thankfully Santi doesn't notice anything. I'll tell him soon enough because I can't take the lying anymore.

Soon after, Santi and I call it an early night, wanting to get extra sleep before the qualifiers.

For the first time in a while, I stay with Santi because of his admission about being lonely. He does so much for me, and I lie to him, keeping a secret hidden that he should be aware of.

I don't sleep a wink. Instead, I end up tossing and turning, never finding a comfortable position. Turns out sleep is for the innocent.

"I don't like the way he looks at you," my brother growls before taking another sip of his beer. Noah stares at us across the pit lane, smiling before turning back toward a man he's talking to.

Noah sucks at keeping his cool. He's already talked to us twice at this kid's event, a kart race fundraiser for children with cancer. When Santi and I hopped in two karts, Noah decided to join, claiming he wanted to spend time with his teammate.

Preferably the teammate he spends his nights with.

And damn him for making my heart melt onto the pavement as he played with kids, throwing them in the air and catching them. A total dad move that makes my ovaries happy.

My brother stares at him, dark eyebrows tipped down as his fingers clench around his beer bottle.

He glances over at me. *Crap*. I forgot he said something in the first place.

"He looks at everyone that way. Don't bother getting annoyed." I take a sip of my water, wishing to chug Santi's beer instead.

"No, he doesn't. His eyes stay on you too long. I might tell him something because you're my sister, and he's a manwhore who needs to keep his hands to himself."

My brother is about fifty orgasms too late on his threat.

"You're making excuses because you want to like him, but you both have a dumb rivalry."

Some may call it a stretch, but they bonded over tequila. If that doesn't scream future friends, I don't know what does.

He grumbles under his breath. "Thank God you're not into guys like him."

Should I be afraid of how often my chest constricts around Santi?

"Why?" I whisper.

"Do you really need another reason besides the fact that he fucks everything that walks?"

I fail to hide how my body cringes, but he misses it, too enthralled in glaring at Noah. Santi's words stab at my armor and leave me bleeding.

"Well, people change. I don't want to cast judgments when he's been nice to me this season." I tip my chin up and cross my arms. People can only walk all over your heart if you let them.

Santi lets out a bitter laugh. "This is one of the reasons I love you. You're innocent and trusting of the world and the people in it." His statement makes my heart deflate like a balloon.

"Maybe you need to trust your teammate more instead of looking for everything wrong with him. You can learn something from me." *Woah.* I have no idea where those words came from.

Santi stares at me, unblinking and unmoving. He changes the subject after chugging the rest of his drink. But the air around us remains heavy, a dark cloud looming over me, guilt hitting me like hail.

CHAPTER THIRTY-FOUR

Noah

t takes everything in me to not explode. I grind my teeth and clench my fists as my feet stomp across the pavement, coming face to face with my father.

And look, he brought a film crew.

"Noah, just the man I was looking for. *Sports Daily* wanted to do a special on me, marking the twentieth anniversary of my last World Championship win." His sinister smile makes a chill run down my spine like my nerves know what a slimy piece of crap he is.

My head nods along like I give a shit. Cameras film me, making it impossible to hide my scowl at the unwanted attention, unlike any type of filming Maya does. My dad surprises me by coming back after I chewed him out during our dinner a month ago. He disregards how I told him to stay the hell away from me because he never does anything I ask. *Lucky me*. Looks like I got my listening skills from my dad.

"Excited to compete in the Brazilian Grand Prix tomorrow?"

His bright smile doesn't reach his eyes.

"Sure." My lips remain a tight line, the least bit interested in this chat.

I manage to walk one step away before he pulls me in, his thick arm wrapping around my shoulders and holding me in place.

"Want to tell the cameras how you've been preparing for your racing lately? Fans wonder what makes you tick, what makes a winner stand out from the rest. Interesting strategy of taking a whole week off before the race." His eyes glint in the sunlight. I hate the look on his face, a smug smile meant to intimidate and control me.

"Just the usual, resting and prepping while keeping to my schedule. Don't want to mess with perfection." A weak smile breaks out across my face as I shrug my dad's arm off me.

"You better be careful. Don't want secrets getting out about how you win races." His sly smile makes my stomach roll.

I step away from the bright lights of the camera, putting distance between my jackass of a father and me. First, the issue with Santi's contract, and now he threatens me. A never-ending cycle with us. Me pushing, him punching. A screwed-up relationship that will never be normal, but thank fuck I have new sponsorships and a fresh start.

His game doesn't interest me, and for once, my decisions can affect someone else. I feel like an idiot for telling him about Maya and me because the way he looks at me tells me this thing with us won't be over until he says it is. The ultimate control freak. And worse, he gets off on it.

Fuck me, I really screwed up this time.

CHAPTER THIRTY-FIVE

MAYA

A rainy race day. The worst kind of news for drivers and fans alike.

Roads shine, slick from the downpour, which means tires will have limited traction. Less than ideal conditions pose a threat to drivers. It takes a lot of skill to successfully navigate cars with limited visibility and grip on the road.

The pit crew scurries about with a nervous buzz as they prepare the spare parts needed for the cars. Extra pieces lay outside for any minor crashes, just in case the Bandini boys have a collision.

Santi and Noah discuss game plans with Sophie's dad. I linger, getting in the way of random mechanics who kindly work around me, not asking me to move until I knock over a power drill. They escort me to the computer area where I can wreak less havoc. Sophie sidles up to me.

"My dad bet fifty bucks that Albrecht doesn't make it past thirty laps. Want in?" Her green eyes shine, complementing her tan skin. She rocks French braids, a jean skirt, and another slogan T-shirt.

I chuckle. "Do you ever learn from bets?"

"No. That's why I bet they wouldn't make it past seventy laps." She blows a pink bubble before popping it.

"There are only seventy-one laps."

"Exactly. My dad raised a smart cookie." She taps her temple, sporting a megawatt grin featuring her two dimples.

The drizzling rain let up, allowing drivers to compete, but not enough for the roads to dry on their own. Sophie's dad announces how the race will start in twenty minutes. Noah and Santi meet with engineers near the entrance of the garage, reviewing driving strategies for these conditions, both men in my life working together. Once the crew gives the all-clear, Santi comes to our spot in the computer bay.

"It's going to be fine. You worry too much lately. Just a little sprinkle, like a sun shower." Santi pulls me in for a hug.

Wet ground mocks me. I give the rain a death stare like I can change Mother Nature's mind.

"I wish they didn't make you race in these conditions. It's kind of dangerous. I think of Albrecht crashing every time."

Santi chuckles. "They wouldn't let us race if the risk was that bad. Nothing more than the usual kind, like crashing into barriers with minimal damage."

"They prep for this. Plus, my dad will chat away with them, giving the best possible advice." Sophie flicks a braid over her shoulder.

I give them a tight smile. "Be safe out there. I'll have headphones to hear everything with the Bandini team." I leave out the part where I'll also tune into Noah's radio.

"Atta girl. We'll see you soon." He taps my hat with his car number.

I wave at Noah over Santi's shoulder, wishing I could hug him before he goes out there. Our secret is wearing on me and messing up my sleep cycles. Two races left until I can tell Santi everything, and I'm praying for the best reaction because he gets rattled easily.

Noah offers me a glorious smile before getting into his car.

"Damn girl, I don't know how you ended up with that one. Sex on wheels." Sophie winks at me except it comes off like a twitch.

I let out my first laugh of the day.

Nothing special happens during the beginning of the race. The grid has Liam in P1, with Noah, Jax, and my brother following behind. I don't know how the other teams don't get bored being on the back of the grid. But I guess they live their best lives anyway, happy to compete and do what they love every day. F1 calls them the "best of the rest."

The racers take off, a few cars skidding and sliding across the wet pavement. Thankfully, both the McCoy and Bandini teams make it out of the grid perfectly intact. Our boys drive down a narrow straight with Liam in the lead. Sophie smiles and claps her hands together when Noah fails to overtake him.

Bad news rings through the radio and television. Santi turns rapidly, and with the slick roads, he crashes during a tight turn. His car stalls next to a barrier wall with the left wheel dislodged and rolling away. He retires as a one-lap wonder.

My brother lets out his frustrations on camera. The radio

buzzes with chatter as Sophie's dad calms him down, soothing him like a parent would during a child's tantrum. What a sucky job to work with hot-headed drivers.

"My dad deals with anger like a champ; no wonder he handled my teenage rage so well," Sophie mumbles.

"He puts up with these two all season long so his patience must be endless."

I try to imagine Sophie's teen outbursts, resembling something along the lines of Tinkerbell stomping her foot.

My eyes remain glued on the television. "Santi's going to be pissed for retiring early."

Santi stands next to his car, the camera crew catching him smacking the red metal frame.

The safety car drops my brother off in the garage ten minutes later. I give him a quick hug and some words of encouragement before he heads on up to his suite, claiming he needs a break and meditation. My heart hurts at how defeated he looks, his shoulders hunched over as he disappears.

Sophie nudges me. "That went better than expected, no thrown helmets or dramatic sweeping of tools off a rolling cart."

"Does anyone else comment on your vivid imagination?"

"Duh, Liam—all the time. Says I should write stories and make money off my madness." She nods like she has considered the idea.

Liam and Noah fight for the first-place spot. They each pull off risky moves, trying to get around each other. Anticipation and nerves mix around inside of me. A few times their tires lose traction, but they regain momentum, pulling back onto the track before they stall. Liam's car spins out once as he expertly misses a barrier and gains enough force to keep driving. Another ten laps to go. Noah attempts to overtake Liam at the turn, but the road looks too wet.

My stomach rolls at the live coverage, a helpless witness to the noise of crunching metal and squealing tires, and the gasps from the pit. Sophie's dad yells into his radio, but his words are hard to make out.

Liam's front wing and tire clip the underside of Noah's car. My blood pumps loudly in my ears, making it impossible to hear shit out of the radio. I'm silently sitting on the edge of my seat as time slows down, frame by frame, and the crash happens.

Noah's car flips on its side and proceeds to barrel roll. Once. Twice. Three fucking times. It bounces again before it drags across the road, slamming into the barrier at an estimated one hundred and seventy miles per hour. *Holy shit.* The complete underside of his car is exposed, tires spinning and liquid leaking down the metal.

Tears flood my eyes at Noah's lack of response to any radio calls. Wetness streams down my face. Sophie's dad speaks into the radio, the only voice in the quiet garage.

Smoke billows from Noah's car despite the drizzling rain. It rises, darkening the air above him. More silence from the radio. Orange flames lick at the red paint of the Bandini car, marring it, making it look all wrong.

Noah speaks into the radio.

"Fuck, there's a fire. I'm upside down. Please get me the fuck out of here! Now!" My heart sinks at his heavy breathing, his voice betraying his fear.

Flames engulf the cockpit of the car. Bile builds up in the

back of my throat, my body fighting with everything to keep it down.

Sophie's dad speaks into his microphone. "They're on their way. Keep calm, Noah! We'll get you out of there. Take a few deep breaths. They're bringing the fire extinguishers now."

"Where the fuck is the safety team? The crane? My suit is on fire! There's a shit-ton of smoke coming from the car, making it hard to breathe." His labored breaths garble the radio.

Sophie's dad takes control of the situation and asks if Noah has any injuries. My heart throbs at the panic laced in his voice.

I can't do anything but watch. I am helpless, out of control. The safety team finally shows up with fire extinguishers, white foam pouring over Noah's car, running down the red paint like a cloud. They control the flames in record time, but it still feels like forever. I tune out the commentators on the television. My legs move on their own accord, sitting myself down before my knees buckle.

The crew brings a crane to dislodge Noah's car from the barrier.

I sob at his desperate pleas to be let out, upset about how long it takes. God, it feels like torture. Knowing he feels weak, knowing I can't do anything but sit, watching the safety team do everything. Not being able to help the person I love is ten levels of fucked up.

I take a deep breath when the crane lifts his car. His body crawls out from under the hunk of metal with the help of crew members. An image I'll never get out of my head. He throws his helmet across the grass, the headpiece bouncing around, body shaking as he takes in a lungful of fresh air.

Invisible needles pinch at my heart, watching him get upset on the grass. He lies there vulnerable, no longer his usual tough, competitive, and brave self. Tears run down my face, mimicking the ones on TV. No privacy during a time like this.

My sad tears turn into ones of relief as the safety team checks him out, giving the all-clear. It's sheer luck to walk away from a crash like that unharmed.

Sophie hugs me, her arms squeezing me tight, the smell of coconuts and summer wrapping around me. My nose runs and my vision clouds as the safety team drives Noah away from the crash.

"He'll be okay. The cars are built for these types of things, plus there's all the new safety precautions."

I give Sophie another hug, grateful for her friendship in a time like this. My body freezes at Noah's voice. I push Sophie away and hurl myself into Noah's arms.

His body tenses before his arms wrap around mine, not giving a shit who watches. He breathes in the scent of me, tears springing from my eyes again, hitting me with all types of emotions. I cry into his chest as he holds my shaking body close to him.

"I was terrified. I'm glad you're okay," I mumble into his chest.

"I'll always be okay and come back to you. Those cars are built for a bomb. I love you." He squeezes me as he whispers the words in my ear.

I take another deep breath, Noah's terrible smell invading my lungs. Like a mix of burnt rubber, smoke, and sweat. I try not to gag as I hold on to him.

Once I calm down, I pull away from him and assess for any

injuries. Besides his flushed cheeks, he appears okay. Thank God. His hazy eyes look down at me, shining under the fluorescent lighting.

I let out a long sigh. My spine straightens at the buzzing of pit equipment. After everything today, I need to talk to Santi. With one race left, he deserves the truth because I care about both of my Bandini boys.

We pull away from each other and my eyes fall to the floor.

The slate color looks fascinating.

I toe it with my sneakers while everyone congratulates Noah for making it out safely. His chuckle bounces off the garage walls. Needing a moment to collect myself, I head toward the suites, telling him I need to use the bathroom.

CHAPTER THIRTY-SIX

Noah

Today's crash is single-handily the worst one of my F1 career. Even nastier than Abu Dhabi two years ago. I hope they don't release the radio tapes for my sake because what an embarrassment.

Maya left ten minutes ago, not returning after saying she needed to go to the bathroom. That should have been the first warning sign that something wasn't right. She would've come back after my shitty crash.

A cold feeling trails up my spine as I head up the stairs toward the private suites.

I walk into the hall, confronted with Maya's tear-stained face, an angry Santiago, and my sneering father. Leave it to my dad to have impeccable timing. Calculated, waiting for the perfect moment for my defenses to be down, and I can't do anything to stop him.

I dread looking at Maya. Her eyes hold mine for a second before they shift, looking back at Santi.

"Noah, just the man I was searching for. You must be busy after that little tumble. But I was catching up with Santiago, giving him a few pointers, ways to do better on rainy days."

My fists clench at the sight of my gloating father. I thought I had already hit rock bottom, but man was I wrong. The man who disgusts me leers at me.

"I'd like to speak to Santiago and Maya alone if you don't mind." Because I sure as fuck mind my dad standing here, getting off on all the drama.

Tension cloaks the room. Uncomfortable, unwelcomed, and so fucking wrong on a day like today.

"Actually, I thought we could all chat about the final Championship, mainly because you're coming out about your relationship. How mature of Santiago to be okay with all of this." My dad nods his head at Santiago.

My stomach drops at the surprise etched on Santiago's face. Maya covers her face with her hands, red creeping from her neck to her checks.

"Shut up." I glare at the man who is dead to me. *Finished. Done. For-fucking-ever.*

Santiago's head whips from my face to Maya's and back to mine. His fists ball up as he puts the pieces together. He eats up the distance, pushing me against the wall, his fists gripping my race suit. Up close and personal with his flared nostrils and sharp eyes. I don't put up a fight because I deserve this and more. He presses my body into the wall, my arms remaining flat against my sides.

"You *fucked* my sister?" His words pass through gritted teeth.

I hate how pissed he looks, how his lips curl and his cheeks redden. I hate causing him pain even though I love his sister.

"Look at that, nothing like team bonding." My dad's voice

drips with appreciation.

I don't need to look over Santi's shoulder to know how much my dad enjoys this. Why use Viagra when he has a lifetime supply of drama to satisfy his urges?

"How could you? I bring her along, hoping you're nice to her instead of your usual asshole self, and what? You screw around with her like she's nothing and then get her to lie to me. Is that your kink? Fucking up families because you come from a shitty one?"

Maya groans as she tugs on Santi's shoulder. "Stop, Santi. It's not his fault I lied. I didn't want to tell you, not him. *Let go.*"

Santi doesn't budge. He glares at me, his fingers twitching as he grips my suit, itching to hit me. I recognize the look from my father. But I'm a big boy, I can take it.

"Why only beat you on the track when he can get in your head just as much?" My dad lays it on thick, twisting everything special I have with Maya, selling his dirty story to my teammate.

Santi's fists tighten. I wait for him to take a hit, anything to put me out of my misery. I despise how upset Maya is. Her eyes are red and puffy, her skin a sickly color as she watches us.

"I didn't fuck around with her. I love her. I'll keep loving her through everything, no matter what you or anyone else says, or whatever you try to do to break us up. It's insulting for you to even think I'd be with Maya to fuck around with your racing. She's the end game. I don't hook up with her for a shitty trophy, and sure as fuck not for a Championship win. I want everything with her. Everything after *this.*"

Maya takes a deep inhale, her eyes wide as she looks at me. I smile at her, even though I have a raging Santi pegging me against a wall, a second away from decking me in the face.

"You're a piece of shit. I trusted you. And *you*—" he looks at

Maya for the first time over his shoulder while he holds me—
"I'm disappointed in you." Those four words do Maya in, her eyes
leaking fresh tears.

"Don't take this out on her. *Please*," my voice croaks, "blame
me." I don't mind begging if it saves Maya from her heart
smashing all over the Bandini suite floor.

The most honest moment of my life.

"Seriously, all this drama for a stupid cunt?"

Santi's hands drop me. His reflexes startle me, turning in a
blur of red. The sound of flesh meeting flesh reverberates off the
walls. It all happens in a second. My father clutches his face with
a fired-up Santiago standing over him. In all my years, I've never
hit him, but for once, someone has.

"You're a piece of shit. No one talks about my sister that
way. *Ever*. I don't care who the fuck you were, but I know the sad
excuse of a man you are now, and let me tell you, you don't live
up to the hype."

No words come from my mouth while Maya stares at the
two of us.

Santi's body shudders, his self-control wavering. "Maya, let's
go." He grabs onto her hand like a child.

My heart clenches as fear pumps through my veins, unable
to handle her rejection if she finds this relationship not worth
the trouble, not worth pissing off her brother, not worth a risk
flooded with cons and promises that have yet to be followed
through on.

Except her feet remain cemented to the floor.

"No."

A simple word fills me with hope.

CHAPTER THIRTY-SEVEN

MAYA

No more lies, no more secrets, and sure as hell no more people telling me what to do or how to live my life.

My brother's eyes flare. His mouth opens, but I hold up a finger, needing to talk before I lose courage.

"Santi, I'm sorry for lying to you and keeping my relationship with Noah a secret. I…I love him. And I don't want to hide it anymore, like something shameful because it's nothing close to that. I need to grow up, and you need to let me. Mistakes included. Not that I think this is one, but no matter what happens, I can't live my life worrying about disappointing you, or *Mami y Papi*, or even myself. I love you, but I need to take a chance on my relationship, and you have to accept it."

Words rush out of my mouth, raw and unfiltered like my feelings for Noah. Santi gazes at me in disbelief.

He shocks me. His arms wrap around my body, pulling me in for a hug, as he mumbles into my ear, "I'm so fucking proud of you. But also, I'm pissed as fuck. To find out your secret from this dipshit on the floor, to know my teammate crossed boundaries… definitely not over it. But I want to be happy for you because you deserve everything in the world and more." He lets me go.

His eyes shine under the suite lighting. "Don't ever lie to me again. And you—" he points at Noah—"You better do right by my sister. If you make her cry, I swear I'll make you regret ever being born from your crappy dad." He looks down at Nicholas Slade who has yet to sink back into the pits of hell—from where he came.

My brother walks away. Secrets no longer get in our way, eating me up inside. I let out a shaky breath, my lungs no longer cut off from fresh oxygen.

Noah's dad stands, his usual bravado absent except for malice in his eyes.

Noah takes over, stepping between his dad and me. "You're no longer welcome here with Bandini. If you come around again, I'll have you banned. We're done. Don't call me, don't text me, and for fuck's sake, don't talk to Maya or her family. Go spend your sad existence somewhere else. It's over. *We're over*." Noah's blank face expresses nothing as he looks into his father's eyes. No anger, no love, no sadness. Nothing but emptiness.

He grabs my hand and pulls me away. With no need to look over my shoulder, I turn my back on lies and Noah's past. I glance up at Noah, and for the first time in hours, I smile.

Despite wanting to spend time with Noah after his crash, I need to speak to my brother without an audience. My lies hurt

Santi more than he lets on because he has the softest heart.

I order us carry-out dinner because the way to his heart is through his stomach. When I arrive at our suite, he grabs the bag from my hands without giving me a backward glance. He sits at the large dining table and pops open my takeout box instead of his. His eyes assess the contents before sliding it to the empty seat across from him.

His eyes remain glued to his food as he shovels fried rice into his mouth. I sit and toy with the plastic-wrapped utensils.

"Santi, I'm truly so sorry for hiding the truth from you. I was going to tell you after the Abu Dhabi Prix because I didn't want to upset you. You and Noah have a rough history. But I hated lying to you, and I never want to do it again."

He blinks at me. More shoveling of food and scraping of plastic cutlery against Styrofoam. I deserve his silence and anger.

"I went to Rio early because Noah planned a trip, not because I was with Sophie. I used her as an alibi multiple times and I'm sorry." I don't know what else to say.

He takes a few deep breaths. "We always tell everything to each other. I hate how you lied to me…but I get it. I only want you to be happy, and I'm willing to put it past us." He takes a big gulp of water. "I can accept Noah as your boyfriend under one condition."

I hold my breath, waiting to hear what he says. In usual Santi fashion, he makes me sit with my discomfort, taking a few more bites of his dinner before putting his fork down.

"If you two break up, you still have to come to my races. No bullshit about it being awkward or how Noah broke your heart.

You want to act like a big girl, then you need to deal with the consequences if you have a falling out." He rubs his stubbled chin while he assesses me.

I can agree to those terms. Noah acts confident enough for the two of us about how this relationship will work out.

"Deal."

CHAPTER THIRTY-EIGHT

Noah

The Abu Dhabi gala reeks of extravagance and wealth; crystal chandeliers shine around me as I mingle with sponsors. Everyone wants to talk about the final Grand Prix. About who will come out on top. Whether I will choke or dominate behind the wheel. My head pounds from the barrage of questions, wishing I could escape with Maya because takeout and a movie sound great right now.

Maya busies herself with Sophie, getting drunk on champagne while I schmooze with minimal booze.

I wrap up chatting with a sponsor, eager to spend time with Maya, when Sophie's dad pulls me aside. He wears a suit with his graying hair slicked back, a grimace marring his face. Not exactly the best hello.

"Noah, follow me. I need to show you something." His eyes tell me to not argue.

My brows furrow at his request. I follow him out of the ballroom, curiosity piquing my interest as we walk into another empty room. My lips lift at the memory of Maya and me in this position. Except once my eyes land on the other Alatorre sibling, my smirk turns into a frown. Santi made sure to avoid me at all costs this past week. Nerves make my hands clench as I tamp down the tendency to run a hand through my thick hair.

"All right, you two. I don't like how tense you both have been. Fans notice, the crew comments on it, and I sure as hell don't want to deal with it. Get everything out now. I won't allow any more drama on my team, especially with the final Prix coming up. If I wanted to be waist-deep in shit, I would have worked for McCoy. Santi, I'll allow you one punch. Make it count because everyone knows Noah can be a smug fucker."

My eyes bulge. James is giving Santi an all-access pass to take a shot at me? *What the fuck.*

Santi shares my same surprise, his eyebrows drawn together, making him look like he's thinking too hard. I'd laugh if I didn't want to piss him off more.

"I don't know what to say." His Spanish accent draws out his words.

A tick in his jaw says differently. I should pass Santi my therapist's number, give him some help in the emotional expression department.

"Oh, cut the crap. He slept with your sister behind your back. Now he dates her, even *loves* her—all while competing against you. Of course, you have shit to say. Get it out or hit him. But fix this crap." James taps his shoe against the floor.

Sophie's dad stands tall, not backing down from this challenge, commanding respect from us as our team principal. *Cue the feels.*

"Okay, fine. Noah, it pisses me off how you disrespected me and went behind my back. You have a terrible track record with women, and I don't want my sister to become another number in your long list. Someone to pass the time with until you get bored. Not to mention the fact that she's my *sister*." Santi crosses his arms, his fears and distaste for my past hanging around us like a third teammate.

"I'm sorry for hiding it, but I'm not sorry for doing it in the first place. Don't expect Maya to be either. I want to put it past us, because I love her, and I want to be with her. *Forever*. I can't help my crappy past and decisions, but I can control my future. And she's it."

My confession hangs in the air, willing to admit everything if it stops his moping.

He walks up to me, his clenched fists a warning. *Shit*. His eyes glare at me. I stand there, ready to take a punch, anything for this to be done with.

"I don't need to hit you to feel better. I love my sister too much to mess up your pretty face." He shoves his hand out in front of him, and I take it. His fingers grip mine tightly. I let him pull his man card, not interested in another pissing contest with him. I'll save that for the track.

"I'm proud of you both, settling this like real men. Now get out of my sight. I don't want to hear about any more drama from either of you, so help me God, because I didn't ask for two sons. I deal with my daughter enough." James's voice has a hint of pride in it. We look over at him, catching his grin.

Santi and I walk out together, the tension following us from Brazil no longer a problem.

Santi claps me on the shoulder. "Let's grab a shot? Cheers to the end of the season and to new beginnings?"

"Best idea you've had all year."

CHAPTER THIRTY-NINE

MAYA

"**J**ust so you know, I think I threw up twice in my mouth looking at you two." My brother barrels over after his practice round. The pit crew went on their lunch break, meaning we have a silent garage to ourselves, perfect timing for my filming.

I smile. "Aw, feel free to use the nearest trash can when you need it."

"Quit harassing my girlfriend, Santiago." Noah trails into our conversation. He makes his smug presence known, his palm tapping my ass before sliding into the back pocket of my jeans. Can't say I hate it, now that I reap the benefits of his wicked smiles and dirty words.

My brother groans. "You're the one who just smacked her ass right in front of me. Do you have a death wish?"

Noah grins while my cheeks heat. He lives to get under my brother's skin, despite the number of times I tell him to stop teasing Santi. But at least they both laugh.

"I can't help our burning love for one another," Noah purrs with a dramatic clutching of his heart. *Beautiful asshole.*

Santiago gags. "Did you lose your balls between Brazil and here? Because if so, my chances of winning the Championship just got a whole lot better."

Noah drops his head back and laughs. "I think Maya found my—"

I rush to cover his mouth, standing on the tips of my toes to reach him. "Nope. Absolutely not. Dirty jokes are off the table forever and ever."

Noah licks my hand and winks at me. I pull away, not trusting myself around him because he has a way with words and his tongue.

"Seriously, can't you both make out somewhere in private? Preferably far away from the pit garage where I don't have to see you pushing my sister up against stacks of tires."

Santi scared the shit out of us yesterday. The piles of tires fell like dominos, drawing everyone's attention toward the three of us. My cheeks remained red the whole day after that display.

"We learned our lesson with that one." Noah shakes his head, fighting a grin.

Unlike him, I let out a laugh, unable to rid the mental image of a fuming Santi pummeled by massive tires.

"I'm sorry. We'll be better. That means no more funny business." I give Noah a pointed look.

"Things we do are anything but funny." Noah waggles his brows.

My brother runs an agitated palm down his face. "I hate to say it, but I may prefer broody Noah versus lovey-dovey Noah. That guy kept to himself during race weekends rather than shoving his tongue down my sister's throat at every possible opportunity."

We all know he likes Noah. These two have never been friendlier, with us all eating dinner together each night this week. They even hung out on their own when I went to interview Liam. I came back to the suite to find the two of them playing video games, duking it out with an F1 simulation. I sat between them and spent the night watching TV with the biggest smile on my face.

I situate the two men of my life in chairs facing back to back.

"Okay. Moving along." I click the record button on my camera. "Hi, everyone. Welcome to my last vlog of this F1 season. We're in Abu Dhabi where Santi and Noah just completed their practice round. With only two days left before the final Grand Prix, I wanted to take advantage of Bandini's off-time. Today we are playing the Newlywed Game with our two favorite Bandini boys. The game goes as follows: Noah and Santiago each have two cards. A blue card means Noah, and red means Santi. Every time they both agree on an answer, the team gets a point. After ten months together, let's see how well these two know each other. The goal is to win as a team, so think of your answers carefully. Three strikes and you're both done, proving to the world Jax and Liam are the best teammates." Those two scored thirty points together, surpassing my expectations. I doubt Santi and Noah will make it past ten.

I take up a seat next to the camera, choosing to stay out of the frame.

"Okay, first one. Who has had the least amount of speeding tickets?"

Two red cards go up. Noah and Santiago turn around and smile at getting the answer right.

"American cops pull you over for everything." Noah rolls his eyes.

My brother faces the camera. "Because only an amateur gets caught."

I continue because we will never finish at this rate. "Who has the bigger butt?"

My brother holds up a red card while Noah lifts up a blue card.

"Oh, you both disagreed. One X." I cross out the question.

Noah sighs. "Come on, Santiago. Your ass could never fill out my jeans."

My brother stands up and shows his butt off to the camera. I laugh to myself while Noah gets up to compare, the two of them not coming to a conclusion. Clearly their bonding has reached new levels because they ask my opinion, but I shrug my head. Not touching that debate.

"Who holds their liquor better?"

Two red cards wave in the air.

"Stick to beer. No one wants to see you taking up shop at the nearest pit trash can again."

The three of us laugh. Noah's poor decisions don't hang around us, not after he admitted the truth about his dad to my brother two days ago. My boyfriend, the same man who acted like the whole world could go fuck itself, gave my brother a hug and told him thank you for punching his dad. A freaking thank you. If I didn't already love him, I would have offered my heart at that moment.

"Who is the biggest baby when sick?"

Two red cards go up. Glad my brother sees his man-child

ways because the stomach flu I got the last time taking care of him was nothing short of terrible.

"Who is more stubborn?"

Two opposite colored cards hang in the air.

"Another strike and a prime example of how stubborn you both are."

"You do know it took you like eight months to figure out you liked my sister, right?" My brother flicks his blue card for emphasis.

Noah smirks at the camera. "Not as bad as you taking ten months to realize you wanted me as a friend rather than an enemy."

Oh, shit.

"I didn't need a referee for Liam and Jax's game. Which by the way, you both are going to lose because you can't agree on anything."

"Well, at least we can agree on how we both love you," my brother says with a telling smile.

My chest tightens at the two of them looking at me. I never in a million years would have imagined them getting along like this, willing to put aside their differences to make me happy.

The two of them lose the game after a total of nine points.

Unfortunately, they couldn't decide who cares more about me. *No, I'm just joking.* They couldn't agree on who deserves a World Championship more, with Noah raising a red card while my brother raised a blue one.

Yup, that happened. Jax and Liam may have won the game, but these two won each other over, a seemingly impossible task. And if that doesn't deserve a trophy for the Constructors' Championship, I don't know what does.

CHAPTER FORTY

Noah

My phone rings on the nightstand. And thank God Maya left the suite ten minutes ago because the curse words flying out of my mouth are nothing short of abhorrent.

I don't know what pushes me to answer the phone. Whether because of brewing emotions inside of me or because I have a kink for masochistic tendencies. My finger slides across the glass, my head pounding to the beat of my heart.

"Mother. What can I do for you?"

Why hit her with pleasantries when she has the emotional intelligence of floral wallpaper. If you're trying to make the connection, don't.

"My son."

A classic. Nothing like reminding me of who signed my birth certificate to manipulate me.

"I'm busy and about to leave for my qualifier. What do you need?"

"You can work on your delivery a bit, Noah." Her voice

carries like a melody through the phone. A siren who calls to men with wallets and trust funds, luring them in before ripping their hearts out.

I grunt, unable to produce words.

"Well, I'm spending time with Clarissa and Jennifer in Dubai, and we thought about visiting for the Prix. What do you think about getting us some tickets? Preferably in the VIP section with a better view, not that one near the stands."

Because God forbid, she actually has a view of the finish line. Grandstand VIP sections don't come with complimentary champagne and Instagram street credit.

Every time my mom asks for tickets, I get them. In the whole scheme of things, I never thought to say no because it was easy to do. Easy to give in to my toxic parents. Simple to not put up a fight, not wanting to make waves like my dad despite how sick it made me feel to be used over and over again.

But like I did with my dad, I want to give her one last chance. Being around Maya has made me a forgiving person.

"I can message my assistant. How are you doing?" I hold the phone to my ear, having no interest in asking about any tickets.

She scoffs. "Is it that man who prattles on the phone forever?"

If she means Steven, who likes to ask her about her day, then yes.

"Yup, the same one I've had since I started with Bandini. Can you believe it's been seven years since I began racing with the team?" *Bet you a weekend on my yacht she doesn't catch my mistake.*

"Nope. But with the end of the season means your birthday is coming up. How are you celebrating your twenty-ninth this year?"

I'd say she blacked out for her entire pregnancy except she

couldn't drink. Surprisingly she remembers the month I was born, most likely because my father drops a large sum of money in her bank account as a "thank you for birthing my spawn" gift.

"Actually, I'm turning thirty-one. But numbers blur after so many years." *Insert obligatory eye roll here.*

"Exactly. My mistake." Her laugh sounds similar to nails scratching a chalkboard.

I hate every second of this call, of the battle waging inside of me to not hang up the phone. But I want to show myself why I need to let go. Why I can't fall back into a damaging relationship with my parents because their love is conditional. And if I learned one thing in therapy, besides the fact that crying makes my face puffy as fuck, is how love doesn't come with conditions. No ifs, ands, or buts. It should make you a better person—not because you have to be, but because you want to be. I want to be the fucking best for Maya and myself. Need to love myself and all that jazz.

"Yeah, your mistake. Did you know I met someone while competing this year?"

"That's sweet." She distracts herself with talking to someone else in the background.

That's sweet. Although an upgrade from my father's comments about Maya, she can't say much more than that?

"Clarissa is asking if you could also access some VIP passes for the after-party? We personally like the one with the champagne company, but we aren't against others."

Looks like she can procure more than three words at a time. But like a gumball machine, she only works when you put money in her.

"You know, I don't think this is going to work."

Time to rip off the Band-Aid. Because why the fuck not, with everything else in the Slade family going to shit.

She sighs. "What do you mean?"

"You, me, your ex-lover Nicholas. The whole thing. I can't do this to myself anymore, trying to be a son I thought both of you wanted. Instead, you only contact me when convenient. And shockingly you withheld your one-stop user card for the whole year until now. But in case you didn't know, I got into the worst crash of my career two weeks ago. And how many times did you call on me to check? None. Hell, how many times have you called me this whole season? Besides the one misdial?"

Her silence does nothing but encourage me.

"I appreciate you for giving birth to me, for being whatever you tried to be. But it's over. You should have protected me from *him*. The first time he hit me, you walked away because you didn't want to threaten your allowance. Time and time again, you let me down. So, by all means, let it be my turn. I can't get you tickets. Not now. Not next year. Not ever again. If you have an interest in calling me to get to know me as a person, let me know. If not, have a good life."

I wait, holding the phone to my ear, willing her to say anything. Closure is a funny concept. Everyone talks about how cathartic it feels, but no one describes the pain you experience before. The courage needed to push through tough situations. How much it rips a person up to know they need to let go, not because they want to, but because they have to.

My whole life, I lived chasing an unattainable prize of my parents' love. I sped down racetracks and life, willing it to go faster, but now I want to slow down. Enjoy the moments with people who matter, who want to remember my birthday, or who know five facts about me that can't be googled.

The dial tone greets me.

I clutch my phone, my lungs taking in the fresh air. For once, I have no ill will toward her, only wishing her the best. Everything falls into place. My therapist said I needed to face my past to embrace my future. Looks like I went to hell and back, scoring an angel along the way.

CHAPTER FORTY-ONE

MAYA

"**L**et me get this straight. You invited my parents to the final Grand Prix two days ago? And they said yes?" I struggle to get the words out.

Noah dropped this bomb on me while we watched a movie on our hotel couch. He casually mentioned how my parents boarded a flight last night to come visit us, like we all planned it.

"Yes. Can you believe it? They want to see their two kids after months of being away." His eyes sparkle.

"But why would you do that?"

"Why not?" His lips tip at the corners.

I tilt my head at him. "Don't answer a question with a question."

"Can I answer with a kiss instead?"

Noah pulls me onto his lap, the couch dipping under our combined weight. His lips press against mine, a tingle spreading to my spine as our tongues caress, teasing each other. The charged energy between us never wavers. A constant current, all at the touch of our hands or the press of his lips.

I break the kiss. "Under all that attitude, you sure have the biggest heart."

"*Sh.* Don't let anyone in on our secret."

Noah kisses me stupid, my mind blanking as he shows me how he feels. I love everything about this man. He continues to throw me for a loop and surprises me whenever he can.

His lips move from my lips to my neck before trailing down the V of my polo.

"As much as I want to continue, we have dinner plans with your whole family tonight."

"They are here?" I rush to stand, leaving a lusty Noah behind.

"Better get a move on, dinner's at seven." His dazzling smile reaches his eyes, lines showing at the corners.

I squeal and hug him before hurrying to get ready. Noah keeps to his side of the bathroom, thankfully, because he tends to distract me.

"I still can't believe you flew them out here. Santi thought about it, but my parents said no when he asked. How did you convince them?"

"Are you keen on learning my tactics?" His eyes dance from the bright lights.

I wave a hand in the air. "I became a victim of your skills a long time ago. Why hold back on me now?"

He crosses his arms and leans against the vanity. "I asked them to do it for me."

My face must show the confusion that runs through me.

Noah sighs. "I told them my parents aren't coming, and it would mean a lot to me to have my girlfriend's family here, no matter who wins. Because I would like to get to know them before I whisk you off on a two-week vacation. But most of all, it will make you happy, which in turn makes me happy."

Oh, wow. Okay, I didn't expect that.

I stride toward him and wrap my arms around his neck. Looks like I get to be the distractor today because Noah's sincerity and kindness deserve all the rewards.

We made it to dinner only ten minutes late. I count our delay as a success because if someone had seen my hair after our bathroom romp, they would have called me a lost cause.

Santi scoffs at the role of a fifth wheel, choosing to become the life of the conversation instead of sitting back.

"You know when I gave Maya some rules about our trip, I didn't anticipate Noah being an issue." My brother flips through his menu.

"Isn't the first rule to never underestimate your enemy?" Noah holds back a smile.

"You got me there. I thought you were too much of a jackass for Maya. She tends to go for the nerdier guys."

"That's so not true. Name a nerd I've dated." I cross my arms. Seeing as Noah has slept with enough women to populate a small island, he can sit and handle this conversation. Mainly because I don't believe my brother's words.

"Xavier, for one."

"How was he a nerd?"

"Well, he did like to remodel those computers," my dad

chimes in. *Great, did everyone think Xavier was geeky?*

"He also loved watching *The Twilight Zone* with *Mami*. Talked about how he posted on Reddit boards about it and stuff." Santi hits Noah with a smirk.

I see what he does here.

My mom smiles at the memory. "Such a sweet boy, offering to read the Bible with me."

My brother shoots me a look. *All right, the Bible study group was a bit weird.*

My dad joins in on the fun because why the hell not. "Don't forget about Felipe."

"What was wrong with him? Do you all have *chisme* sessions without me?"

"To be fair, he was gay." My brother hits me with a family secret I had no clue of.

Noah chokes on his wine. "You dated someone without knowing they were gay?"

My eyes narrow at him. "Seeing as this is all news to me, clearly not."

"Sorry. We have to air all two pieces of Maya's dirty laundry in case Noah wants to run in the other direction," Santi says before sipping his wine.

My mom butts in, ending Santi's game. "Noah won't run. He's liked her since Barcelona."

Noah and I look at my mom with wide eyes.

"Oh, don't look at me like that. The way you looked at my daughter is one I recognize in my own husband. You two were just too stubborn to admit it."

My dad grumbles under his breath.

"What's that, *mi amor*?" She smiles at him.

He looks Noah in the eyes. "If he breaks her heart, I'll run him over with the car he loves more than anything."

"*Loved* more than anything." Noah sends me a wide smile that I save for my memories.

CHAPTER FORTY-TWO

MAYA

Noah preps for the final Prix race despite the crash last week, all smiles and jokes as the crew works in the garage. Such a badass. He landed the third position on the grid after a decent qualifying round.

Pit mechanics and engineers act as the backbone of a team, fixing any damage from Noah's previous crash; the car looks brand new with not a dent in sight. Noah thanks the crew as his fingers graze the red hood.

Worst-case scenarios flash through my mind as I hang out with Santi for his last race. I clasp my fingers in front of me, my sneakers rocking back and forth against the concrete floor. Abu Dhabi. The final Grand Prix and home of the infamous crash between Noah and my brother. With a close Championship standing between Bandini and McCoy, it all comes down to this race.

Noah runs an unsteady hand through his hair while he talks to the engineers. Despite me asking him about his nervousness, he feigns indifference. He gives me a quick peck on the lips before he takes off with crew members toward the track.

My brother tugs me in for a good luck hug.

"Try not to crash into my boyfriend this time," I mumble into his chest.

"I was planning on knocking Liam out. Seemed like a safer bet because that guy can't hold a grudge to save his life."

Our bodies shake from laughing. We break apart, and Santi hops into his car, waving at me as the crew pulls him away.

I hang out in pit row, preferring to be close instead of lost somewhere in the crowd. Earlier, Noah reserved Grandstand VIP tickets for my parents so they could experience a Prix like real fans. My heart swelled at the look of appreciation my parents offered him, both of them unaware of how much it means to Noah to have someone rooting for his team. Noah, a man denied of love and affection, craves my family's acceptance more than anything.

Race cars zipping down the track do little to calm me. Noah's car speeds by, a red blur with an engine reverberating off the walls. McCoy cars follow behind, creating a vortex of sound and dirty air.

Noah deserves the World Championship, and honestly, I want him to win, hoping it can help us overcome these worries.

Sorry, Santi. I'm loyal to my boyfriend, too.

A few cars crash throughout the laps. One of the drivers from Albrecht can't catch a break this season, leaving behind a crumpled mess of a car after turn three.

Cars lap around the track. Sports announcers talk about Noah's swift recovery after his tragic loss in Brazil, his racing a testament to his will to win. My heart taps against my chest, unrelenting during the first few laps. No hiccups yet. I take my first steady breaths once Noah makes it through his first ten laps with no issues.

Round and round cars go, careening through the track. Racers complete laps in less than two minutes. The Prix rankings are close, with Bandini seconds away from McCoy, Santi trailing behind Noah with Liam in the lead. Noah's engine roars as he pulls in for a pit stop to get new tires. His last one for this season. He takes off again, spitting himself back out onto the track, eating up any time lost.

Noah completes his forty-fourth lap, only eleven circuits left between him and the winter break. His car hangs behind Liam, putting him in second place. He can't win the World Championship if he keeps the runner-up position.

His car jerks, the movement unfamiliar. Like he hesitates. Noah's reputation for overtaking cars is missing, his usual swagger on the racetrack not coming out.

"Maya, I need you to get over here." Sophie's dad waves me over.

I don't hide my surprise when he hands me the headset that communicates with Noah. He presses the mute button, taking a deep inhale while rubbing his temple. His intense green eyes bore into mine.

"Noah wants to talk to you. The nerves got to him, and he thinks you can calm him down. Help him out. His place in the Championship rests on you working with him. If he doesn't get over this, he may never come back to race because fears like this can ruin a career."

Okay, no pressure. Understatement of the year. But I don't have a second to linger on it. I grab the headphones, situate the microphone, and unmute myself.

"Hi, this is Maya. Do you copy?" I try to imitate team radio videos that Noah and I have watched online.

Noah's chuckle sounds through the headphones. "Hi, this is Noah. I copy."

"Well, I'm going to be shit at this job. But hold on. There's a red car behind you moving pretty fast. There's one car in front of you also going exceptionally fast. About three clicks away."

"You're nailing it. Keep it up. Not sure what three clicks means but…"

I laugh into the mic. Can't wait for sports announcers to listen in and comment on our conversation.

Wanting privacy from the crew, I walk up to the railing that overlooks pit row. A television hanging above offers an overhead view of the track. Cars squeal in the distance. Useless lights blink all over the computer screen, offering me nothing but confusion.

"Hmm, there's an amazing driver with the number twenty-eight on his car. But he won't overtake the driver in front of him. What's going on?"

Noah makes it past another lap. He holds back, not acting aggressive enough to win the whole thing.

"Tell me more about this great driver. I don't know if I see him out here." His voice strains.

My heart dips at the thought of him panicking in the middle of a race. "They say Noah Slade's basically the best. Likes to break records, on the racetrack and in the bedroom. You gotta be careful with him."

He lets out a hoarse laugh.

"This is going to be a terrible team radio video. I'll end up on YouTube, *perdónenme Mami y Papi*. Ignore this."

Noah speeds up after turning. *Good.*

"So anyway, please stop distracting me. And quit the seductive laughs too. Did you know this guy agreed to help the girl grow her vlog? He may be part of the reason she has over a million subscribers now. But I don't think the guy knows he's stuck with her. Stage-five clinger. She's already signed a contract with the team to come to the races next year since they want her to film more behind the scenes action to promote the brand. A whole ordeal."

His voice expresses his surprise. "You didn't tell me. Congrats, Maya. I'm so proud of you; I knew you could do it. Bandini is lucky to have you working on social media."

"*Sh.* This story isn't about me." I laugh at his slip up before continuing. "Pretty crazy. Imagine the girl's surprise that number twenty-eight doesn't want to drive faster. Take more risks. He took a chance on their relationship, and it all panned out. I wonder if he could do the same thing today?" I imagine fans commenting about how cliché I am on our video. *Oh well, I won't be crying myself to sleep. At least not in that way.*

Noah's deep breathing and gear changes ring through the radio. The roar of the engine excites me. His car accelerates, pushing closer to Liam's, closing the gap between McCoy and Bandini.

"Pretty sure the girl told the guy that she doesn't date losers.

But I can't be too sure about that one because I haven't asked her. But you can never put it past these racing fans, all fun and games until the guy doesn't end up on the podium. I think girls have a thing for trophies and race suits—a combo deal."

Noah chuckles into the mic. With only a few laps left to overtake Liam, the Championship is starting to slip from Noah's fingers.

"But that's a lie. Because this girl loves the guy. Like the 'forever and always' type of love. The 'kids playing around outside while the parents have a quickie upstairs' kind of love. Have you heard of that type?"

He stays silent. His rhythmic breathing and the hum of the engine encourage me to continue.

"It's pretty insane. Can you imagine that kind of love? I can because I experience it. The story doesn't end with a happily-ever-after because it starts with it. Because they have the rest of their lives to finish their story. Crazy, huh?"

Noah speeds up at a turn, pushing his car to the limit, sparks flying from his rear wing. He overtakes Liam in one of the last corners.

"Great job, babe! That was an amazing one. I knew you could do it."

"Maya?" his voice rasps.

"Yup?"

"Keep talking. I love hearing your voice."

Happy to oblige.

CHAPTER FORTY-THREE

Noah

lift the American flag in the air. *World. Fucking. Champion.*

I can't thank Maya enough for helping me at the end there. Almost lost my shit behind the wheel, poorly controlled tremors running through my body until she came on the radio. But her voice and words pushed me to the limit and gave me courage.

The crowd wildly jumps around with energy and excitement. I call Maya over from the roped-off VIP section. Security guards let her through, grinning and shaking their heads as she runs up the steps of the stage and launches herself into my arms. The best hello sealed with a kiss. I twirl her around as she giggles, her arms wrapping around my neck while her addicting floral scent invades my nose. Someone passes me the trophy, and I hold it and her in my arms. One of the happiest days of my life.

Our friends shower us with champagne. Maya screams as the cold liquid splashes against us and runs down our bodies. I drop my head back in laughter, guzzling champagne that miraculously makes it into my mouth. Fans scream as I give Maya a mind-numbing kiss that tastes like champagne and happiness.

Amazing how quickly life changes.

I thought winning the World Championship was the best thing, the only goal I had for a long time. Shit, was I wrong. I realize today that the best thing includes winning with your loved ones.

Not my shitty father. But with Maya, my team, and my friends. This is the best feeling ever.

Well, the best for now.

CHAPTER FORTY-FOUR

MAYA

If someone had told me a year ago I'd be standing on the F1 stage, hugging Noah Slade and my brother with each arm, I would have laughed until I cried. My brother stands next to me with the biggest grin on his face after placing third in the entire World Championship. He and Noah shower each other with champagne after winning the Constructors' Championship together. Old rivals hugging like friends.

Funny how life has a way of working itself out. I joined the F1 schedule because I had nothing going for me, a post-graduate with a trail of failed attempts at jobs, stuck living in my brother's shadow whether I wanted to be or not.

I can't help looking over at the man who called dibs on me, the one with wavy dark hair and blue eyes that hypnotize me. A World Champion with a heart of platinum to match the trophy he carries above his head. The same man who says "I love you" instead of "good morning" every day. A self-proclaimed "sappy motherfucker" who begged me to wear his race car number today because he needs to mark me in every single way. A human wrecking ball who came into my life unannounced and smashed through all my expectations, leaving behind rubble, dust, and a fresh start.

But most importantly, Noah Slade, the love of my life.

EPILOGUE

MAYA

Noah and I relax on his balcony, staring out at the Amalfi coast, blue waters glistening under the morning sun. He messes around on his computer while I appreciate the view. I welcome the melodic sound of water splashing against the rugged coast. We hang out in our pajamas, enjoying our coffee— our morning ritual while on break.

A year has passed since Noah won his fourth World Championship. Our team radio from the Abu Dhabi Grand Prix became a viral video on YouTube, fans supporting our relationship immediately. My parents welcomed Noah into our family, taking him in, no longer allowing him to spend time meant for families alone—holidays, birthdays, the works.

F1 still plays a huge part in our lives. I travel around the world with Noah, joining him at every race. My vlog remains popular amongst fans. The Formula Corporation asked me to work with the other phases like F2 and F3, but Noah claims he can't win without his good-luck charm, threatening to hold me hostage if I skip out on his races.

Salty air hits me in the face, rustling my dark waves.

Did I say how much I love Noah's house in Italy? Something straight out of a movie.

I scroll through my phone to check morning updates when I get a strange notification. *Weird.*

I look up into Noah's blue eyes. "Did you click the wrong date for me to upload my next video? I got a notification that it just went live."

"I don't think so. That's strange." He shrugs.

My point exactly. He grabs his laptop and places it on the table. A black screen with an odd title plays in front of us, nothing like the uploaded video I had scheduled.

"That's not it because I picked a different thumbnail. Do you think someone hacked into my account? And what does *More to Come* even mean? I like to be punny. I'd never come up with something like that."

He chuckles. "I'm well aware. Before we report it, let's watch it."

Noah, always a thinker. Exactly why Bandini pays him the big bucks.

The video starts up with a short clip of me at Santi's first Bandini race in Australia. Someone took a video of me giving Noah a death stare. How embarrassing, but appropriate for how I felt about him at the time.

"Oh my God. Who would even upload this? Look at how I'm staring at you. And why were you laughing behind my back?" How interesting, Noah checking me out on day one. *What a player.*

The scene changes before Noah gives me an answer. This time a shot of us at a press conference plays. Noah grins at me while I bob my head, making fun of one of the reporters. He barks out a laugh when I roll my eyes. Liam and Santiago glance at him while reporters look around, wondering what made Noah react the way he did.

How cute of him to look at me like that. I had no idea he checked me out that much, hanging onto whatever dumb thing I'd do next. It makes me feel all warm and fuzzy.

Next scene plays, a clip from the vlog I did with Noah and his car. He sits near the cockpit while I ask him a bunch of questions. My heart warms at the clip, enjoying how he glances at me with an enamored look on his face. *Either that or he looks like he wants to take my clothes off. A true toss-up.* I never looked at the video this closely, not checking for signs of Noah liking me. Noah gives me a beaming smile when I laugh and talk into the camera. He barely pays attention, his eyes remaining on me.

My stomach flutters at the clip. I feel off-balance, being hit with many emotions at once—happiness and nostalgia mixed together.

I have an idea of who created this *More to Come* video. The big guy next to me remains suspiciously quiet, not one peep coming from his seductive lips. But I don't pause the video because questions would ruin the moment.

Another video starts, this time of the podium when Santiago won the Grand Prix in Spain. Noah ignores everything happening on the stage. He gazes off to the side, the camera panning off to find what he smiles at, catching me with my back turned, hugging my parents. The Spanish flag is draped over me as I jump up and down.

My heart beats rapidly, my throat closing up, unable to get any words out. Suppressed happy tears cloud my vision. Noah was always into me, even when I thought he was only interested in hooking up, but his eyes betray the way he feels. It's a sucker punch right in the feels.

Various video clips play, including one of me whistling at Noah as he walks down the runway in Monaco. I embarrassingly yell how I'd like to take his tux off. He winks at me, but I miss it because Sophie distracts me by covering my mouth with her hands. I'd die of embarrassment if Noah didn't squeeze my hand in a silent way of telling me he still finds me cute. Not sure how this video saw the light of day or how Noah got it in the first place. Sneaky man.

Another plays of me dancing up on the podium after the kart race Noah planned. My scream shakes the computer's speakers as Noah sprays me with champagne like a real F1 racer, even making me chug straight from the bottle. Peer pressure is a thing. I dance around on the small step, my arms thrown up in the air. Noah laughs along with me before he winks to the camera. *Ovaries, meet your master.*

His thoughtfulness makes me want to cuddle up to him and never let go. Put a "do not disturb" sign on our front door, sealing us off from the public for an unforeseeable lifetime.

The camera catches him smiling wide as he carries me over his shoulder to the car. Claps for the cameraman because he conducts a perfectly executed zoom of Noah smacking my ass. *A+ filmography.*

Damn Noah and all his cuteness. My throat feels like I swallowed a rock, unable to say much as I watch all of our memories. *Why does he have to be such a sappy yet seductive man?*

Tears escape my eyes. Noah occasionally rubs them away with his thumb, my skin heating up at his touch.

He stays silent. The whole thing almost feels like too much. *Almost* being the keyword since I need to lap up this romantic display and enjoy every second. *Duh.* I'll replay this video a hundred times—to my children, my grandchildren, my next-door neighbor. Everyone in walking distance.

A clip plays of me screaming for dear life while he drives the atrocious green Bandini car. He stares at me and laughs while one hand turns the steering wheel, our car drifting as I grip onto him like a lifeline. *Must have blacked out because I don't remember that.*

A short scene of my Tequila Talks episode plays. Noah answers the question I ask about his dream girl, but he intensely gazes at me while he responds. I stare straight at the tequila bottle and pick at the label instead of meeting his eyes.

I swear my heart has never beat this fast, questioning another cardiac arrest. A swirl of emotions churns inside of me: happiness, excitement, thankfulness. A whole freaking spectrum.

The screen shows a film from a Brazilian fan based on the terrible quality and backdrop. I crack up while walking up the stairs to the Christ statue. Noah trails behind me, alternating between checking out my ass and looking up at the sky like it can answer his prayers. No such luck though because he's stuck with me.

Sappiness leaks out of me, along with my tears. "Die a Happy Man" plays low in the background over the part where Noah twirls me around the air after winning the World Championship. Our smiles mimic each other. A beautiful mess surrounds us, with champagne splashing everywhere and confetti launchers exploding on the stage.

I love this cocky, self-assured, yet equally selfless and loving man. No other can ever replace him. I never thought it was possible to love someone like this. Unyielding passion and endless appreciation. Like he hangs the moon before dancing with me under it. Noah never letting a day go by where he doesn't tell or show me how he loves me. A broken masterpiece no longer defined by his past.

Music cuts out to a black screen. I wipe the tears from my face and look over at Noah.

Except he isn't in his chair anymore.

He looks up at me with the smirk I love, while he's down on one knee, holding a ring box.

THE END

EXTENDED EPILOGUE

Noah

I never imagined getting engaged.

Fuck. Really, I never imagined having a girlfriend, let alone having someone I wanted to spend the rest of my life with. But here I am, about to get married to my rival's sister. I've become domesticated as fuck with weekly family dinners and yacht trips with my future in-laws.

Okay, maybe my version of domesticated is a bit different than others. I never had genuine people to share my wealth with, and now that I've had the chance, I can't go back.

I want to share everything with Maya. Fuck prenups and shit emphasizing the potential for a relationship to fail. If my marriage ends in a divorce, Maya might as well walk away with half my shit anyway. Why the fuck not, seeing as my heart is the most valuable thing she'd take.

Sappy as shit, yet true.

I knock my knuckles against the door of our bedroom.

Our bedroom. The very one we custom made like the rest of our house. The same house we plan on raising our kids in, hopefully with Liam and Sophie living next door. Maya having her best friend a house away would make her happy, which in turn makes me happy.

Sophie opens the door an inch, not giving me much space to see inside. She eyes me skeptically from head to toe. "You're not supposed to be here."

"Why the fuck not?"

"You know the tradition." She moves to close the door, but I'm quicker, obstructing the doorway with my loafer. The same loafer that is about to walk down the aisle.

Did I mention I'm getting married today?

I scoff. "I don't believe in bad luck."

"Oh really? Too bad, so sad because your future wife does." She kicks my shiny loafer with her glittery sneaker. My foot fails to move, making her growl in frustration.

I smirk. "I thought religious people don't believe in luck."

Sophie lets out the biggest sigh of her life. "Noah, go away."

"But I want to be the first to see her."

"You missed your chance since I've seen her first. Now, shoo."

I let out an irritated breath. "Okay, I want to see her before anyone else, minus you. I'll allow the maid of honor exclusive rights to what's mine. Sharing is caring, after all."

Sophie stares me down for a solid thirty seconds. "Fine. Let me ask her. Do not come in here without permission."

I shoot her a wide grin. "Perfect." I remove my shoe so she can close the door.

"Stupid, pushy, entitled men." She frowns at me as she closes the door.

I tap my shoe to the beat of my heart as I wait for Sophie to speak to Maya. Fuck traditions. Everything about my relationship with Maya has been anything but traditional.

I was being honest with Sophie, wanting to see Maya first. It's not due to possessiveness. More so because I have this innate need inside of me to value every moment with her. To see her in private before any fucker gets to watch her walk down the aisle. It's no secret I'm a selfish fuck, but Maya accepts me for all my flaws, so be it.

The door to our bedroom opens. My head shoots up, catching Sophie discreetly stepping out before shutting the door again.

She shakes her head at me. "I don't know what magic voodoo your dick has, but Maya agreed to see you. Don't mess up her hair. Don't mess up her makeup. And for the love of God, don't have sex before your vows. I'll be back up in twenty minutes to take you back where you belong. You know, outside with everyone else." Sophie shakes her finger at me before walking away, the sound of her sneakers echoing down the hall.

I grip the handle with a shaky hand. The idea of a future with Maya makes me edgy with anticipation. The good kind. The best kind. The kind of high I want to chase for the rest of my life with her.

I want to be everything she needs in a partner. I've grown up with terrible examples, and I never want my family to feel the same kind of disappointment I did. To feel unloved and used because of a title and a talent.

I've gone above and beyond with everything in my life, so it's no secret I aspire to be the best husband and father one day. To be the person Maya and my future kids can count on to fight their battles and protect them. To love them unconditionally because I want to, not because I have to.

I take a deep breath and open the door. Maya looks out the window of our new backyard, giving me the chance to stare at her. And fuck do I stare. I stare so damn hard that I'm afraid I'll need glasses by the time I'm done.

The lace material of her white dress clings to her body, emphasizing the curves I love. I'm tempted to tug on her dark, wavy hair falling against her back. She turns, hitting me with what I swear is hands down the most beautiful look she has ever given me. Even better than when she told me she loved me for the first time.

Because this look? It's a silent promise that she'll love me forever.

My eyes roam over her, cataloging every last detail. A sense of happiness I've never felt before hits me, with my eyes clouding and my fingers shaking.

Me. The biggest asshole on this side of Europe, tearing up over my fiancée. I run a hand through my hair. "You look so fucking beautiful."

She drops her head back and laughs, the sound a sweet melody to my ears. I walk up to her, grabbing onto her left hand. I fidget with her engagement ring in a calming gesture to remind myself she is all mine.

For better, for worse.

For richer, for poorer.

In sickness and in health.

With orgasms forever and always.

Okay, the last part is part of our private vows. Santiago would probably pop a vein in his face if I mentioned anything related to his sister and our bedroom. Religious people—all shy and shit.

"You don't look too bad yourself, Mr. Slade." She smiles up at me. Her unoccupied hand goes to fix my bowtie before lingering on my chest. "You couldn't even follow this basic tradition, huh? Why am I not surprised?"

I lift her hand up to my lips and kiss her ring. "I plan on starting new traditions with you."

"Like what?"

"Like this one." I tug her into me, wrapping one hand behind the back of her head as I pull her lips to mine.

I kiss her with every ounce of love I feel toward her. It's an unspoken promise to love her every damn day of the rest of our lives. To be the person she can rely on most in the world, no matter how hard life may get. To offer her endless years of happiness.

The kiss is invigorating, knowing Maya's the only woman I want. Today. Tomorrow. Forever.

I pull away too soon, not wanting to ruin her makeup.

"I like your kind of traditions." Her smile hits me with a warm sensation in my heart.

"Well, I have one more."

She tilts her head at me, her curious eyes making me laugh.

"I have a little gift for the future Mrs. Slade."

Maya's eyebrow raises. "I don't think I'll ever get used to that name."

"You have decades to try." I smile as I grab onto her hand and lead her toward the bed.

"No funny business before the wedding!" She stops.

"You don't want to see my surprise?"

"I've seen everything there is to see of you already. I can promise you that."

I shake my head at her as I tug her toward the bed again. "Close your eyes."

Maya's eyes close on command. I grab onto her waist and hoist her onto the bed, letting her get in a comfortable sitting position.

She attempts to open her eyes.

"Keep them closed or you don't get your surprise."

She lets out a resigned sigh. I kneel on the floor and tug my gift out of my pocket. I lift the hem of her dress up, causing goosebumps across her skin.

I grab her left leg and slide up the custom-made garter I had created for her. Ever since I turned into a sentimental motherfucker, I really go all out. I'm a glutton for punishment, leaving a path of light kisses down her thigh until I reach the garter. She lets out a light sigh as I pull away and stand.

"Okay, all done."

She bends over and checks out her new gift. "Whoa. Explain."

I trace the garter belt. "This is made from the fabric of the Barcelona Grand Prix's checkered flag. That was the moment I was truly screwed with you because I gave up a win to make you smile."

Maya's smile expands. "I knew it!"

"If you tell Santi, I'll deny it. I didn't know it at the time, but I was already a goner for you."

A single tear runs down her cheek as she assesses her gift.

"Shit, you're not supposed to cry." I wipe it away, hoping I didn't mess up her makeup.

"I can't help it. I love you so damn much it hurts." She looks at me with a wobbly smile.

"The good kind of hurt?" I step in between her legs, grasping her chin in my hand.

"The best kind." She runs her hands down the lapels of my tux.

I place a soft kiss on her lips. "I love you so fucking much. Enjoy your last thirty minutes as Maya Alatorre because after that, you're all mine."

She rolls her eyes. "It's only a last name."

I smirk. "No. It's only the beginning of forever."

THANK YOU!

If you enjoyed *Throttled*, please consider leaving a review!
Support from readers like you means so much to me and helps
other readers find books.

Join my Bandini Babes Facebook group for all the grid gossip
about the Bandini and McCoy racers.

SCAN THE CODE TO JOIN THE GROUP

ALSO BY LAUREN ASHER

Collided

The Dirty Air series continues with
Sophie and Liam's story.

Wrecked

Don't miss out on Jax's enemies-to-lovers story.

Redeemed

If you like Santiago, check out his standalone romance.

SCAN THE CODE TO READ THE BOOKS

ACKNOWLEDGEMENTS

Thank you to everyone who read my debut novel. I am grateful for the bloggers and readers who gave my work a chance. You deserve your own champagne shower.

Mr. Smith – I am appreciative of your endless support, including the times you forced me out of my house to eat and socialize. Your patience, help, and positive words pushed me to believe in myself and pursue this dream.

Julie – You welcomed me into the book world with warmth and kindness, and I can't express my gratitude enough. You're a fantastic individual who has been an integral part of this process. Thank you!

To my beta readers – Thanks for giving my F1 world a chance. With your feedback and comments, Throttled became everything it is today. I am forever grateful!

To everyone else who helped me during this process – Thank you from the bottom of my heart! Without you, none of this would be possible.

CPSIA information can be obtained
at www.ICGtesting.com
Printed in the USA
LVHW070837120623
749507LV00005B/246